HOYLE STATION

ED CHARLTON

Hoyle Station © 2022 Ed Charlton

ISBNs

Hoyle Station in eBook 978-1-935751-44-1

Hoyle Station in Paperback 978-1-935751-45-8

Other titles by Ed Charlton

The Aleronde Trilogy

The Problem with Uncle Teddy's Memoir

Saint John's Ambulatory

Aleronde the Great

The Offworld Trilogy

Beauty Rising

Larc Ascending

Time

The Assassin Trilogy

KING HENRY THE FOURTH, PART II

"There is a history in all men's lives
Figuring the nature of the times deceased;
The which observed, a man may prophesy
With a near aim of the main chance of things
As yet not come to life, who in their seeds
And weak beginnings lie intreasured.
Such things become the hatch and brood of time..."

Warwick in Act 3, Scene 1 King Henry the Fourth, Part II

DISEASES FROM SPACE

In 1979, Fred Hoyle and Chandra Wickramasinghe wrote *Diseases from Space*, suggesting diseases on Earth can arise from panspermia—the transportation of biological material through space—rather than from traditionally recognized transmission routes.

This idea was roundly ridiculed.

However, interplanetary commerce will give birth to new medical concerns–and whole new industries–to prevent diseases, not those that might arrive randomly from space but rather those that might be brought to Earth.

CHAPTER 1

Sebastian Sixty-six was asleep. Technologists and biologists might argue the topic "Recorder inactivity and human sleep: Are they really the same phenomenon?" But, from what Seb66 had seen of sleeping humans, the two seemed close enough.

As programmed, his sleep ended when he heard the voice of Montgomery Sheldrake.

"What the hell is going on?"

It wasn't any of the phrases that Seb66 had been expecting. The highest probability was for the Discoverer to use phrases like "Hello Recorder," "About time," or "How wonderful."

Seb66 remained inactive, listening for more to confirm the voice recognition.

"Where are my fucking clothes?"

Again, not one of the probable phrases.

"Someone's going to pay for this."

These words brought Seb66 closer. A low-ranking phrase was "Who's going to pay for the delay?" and another was "Someone has sent me a present." The voice recognition value was high enough; Seb66 opened his eyes.

It was still only probably Montgomery Sheldrake. The size of the head and the overall build and height were a match. Since the Discoverer was facing away, and no recorded images were available of him naked and floating upside down, certainty was not possible.

As Seb66 became more aware of his surroundings, it was clear that the Discoverer was not the only one floating. Reaching for the nearest wall, the Recorder slowed his rotation and gently brought his feet onto the carpeted floor.

Aware it was just after eighteen-hundred hours Hoyle Station time, Seb66 said, "Good Evening."

The Discoverer yelled something not recognizable as a word and spun in the air with sufficient force to knock himself into the wall and smack a trailing hand against the back of a seat.

"Where the hell did you come from?"

Seb66 smiled. Now that he could see the man's face, there was no more doubt. The chances of another person matching the voice patterns and the shape and build as well as having the correctly shaped handlebar moustache were sufficiently small.

Since Seb66 had been expecting a more formal setting and until more information was available on the reasons behind this unusual introduction, he decided to apply humor. He answered, "I know you guys have stories about storks and gooseberry bushes, but I can be pretty certain I came from the factory since I actually have a serial number stamped on my rear end."

The human laughed and grabbed the headrest of a seat and drew himself into a semblance of a standing position with both feet on the carpet.

"And, as you can plainly see, I have no such distinguishing feature," said Monty.

"I am Sebastian Sixty-six. I'm pleased to meet you, Mr. Sheldrake. Please call me Seb if you'd like."

Monty snorted and looked Seb66 up and down. He had two almost simultaneous thoughts, *a bit overdressed for a Recorder*, and *its clothes won't fit me*.

"Hello, Seb," he said, "About bloody time. Where have you been?"

"I was asleep from the time I was packed. I presume I was transported in a cargo hold and then unloaded on Hoyle Station. But"—he looked around—"this isn't Hoyle Station. Why are we in a shuttle?"

"Good question. I don't know. Nor do I know where my clothes are."

"Were you asleep too?"

"No, I was unconscious; there's a difference. I've probably a lump on my head to prove it."

Monty felt around the back of his head. Drifting forward a little, he steadied himself with his other hand against the seat.

"Do you need medical attention?" asked Seb66.

"No, I'll be okay. Are you programmed for first aid?"

Seb66 grinned and said, "No, but I can record the fact that you were injured. Will that help?"

Monty laughed, shook his head, and said, "Naked and alone, save for a meeting jockey who thinks he's funny. Just my luck!"

Again, Monty looked the Recorder up and down. It had been well packed. It wore a clean white suit, and the black shirt was lint-free. Its flame-red tie was a little askew. Monty was conscious of their height difference. Seb66 was just over five feet tall, the universal height for

Recorders. Its fair hair was neatly brushed in a conservative style. Its face was a mixture of an oriental brow over Eurasian features.

"Are we in any imminent danger?" Seb66 asked.

"I...have no idea yet. We'd better see if we're still in sight of Hoyle Station. But first..."

Instead of going to the flight cabin, Monty turned and made his way down the aisle separating four rows of seats toward the main door at the back of the shuttle; he used the headrests to ground his weightless body. Seb66 watched, not following.

Monty looked out through the porthole windows in the door to the air lock. He allowed himself to float, turning in the air to get different views beyond.

"Hmm..."

"Anything out there?" asked Seb66.

"Nothing. No clothes. It was worth a chance."

He pushed off from the door, launching himself over the backs of the seats. Misjudging the effort required, he found himself hitting the ceiling with his back. He rolled his way forward and, grabbing the headrest of the first seat, managed to slow himself in a more or less controlled fall into the cabin door.

Monty half stepped, half floated into the empty flight cabin. He stopped openmouthed. Seb66 moved around him and began to examine the displays.

"All my life..." Monty said quietly.

Seb66 turned and looked at the Discoverer. Monty was staring out the wide slanting window. Seb66 could see nothing but stars.

"What do you see?" the Recorder asked.

"All my life, I've dreamt of traveling out into the galaxy. To see this view...Looks like we're in deep space." Monty felt for the pilot's chair and pushed himself into it.

Seb66 looked from Monty to the view and back again. Before he could formulate anything humorous, his human companion said, "Do you see colors as I do?"

Seb66 raised his eyebrows and tilted his head. "I see colors, but I don't know if I see them as you do. Unlike you, I have never dreamed of being here. My world is one of meeting rooms and packing crates. The expectations of my existence don't rise to this." He shrugged and turned his attention again to the displays.

"Nor do mine," Monty said quietly, "nor do mine." He was silent for a long while before speaking again. "The crews of *The Invincible* and *The*

Indomitable—the first humans in deep space—talked of how different things were away from the solar system. How different it felt."

Monty glanced along the instrument panels. He read off the message from one of the displays, "Proximity Identifiers. I'm guessing that means nearby ships and stations." He sighed. "Nothing is showing." He looked at Seb66 and watched him for a moment. "We're nowhere near home, are we?"

"No. As far as I can tell." Seb66 pointed at a panel. "This display, 'HS Relative Position,' shows 'out of range.'" He pressed the button below the screen. The background illustration showed a few stars. He kept his finger on the button as the illustration of stars grew more dense until the scale did not increase further; the "out of range" indicator remained unchanged.

Monty tapped his fingers against the display. "What did Captain Hamilton write? 'When our sun is no more bright than the other stars, when you see it take its place as one small diamond in The Great Necklace, it changes something in your soul.'" He looked up into Seb66's attentive face. "And you have no clue what I'm talking about, do you?"

Seb66 understood that, at times, it is better for a Recorder to be silent and simply record. The play of emotions across a human face could be stored and reproduced, but the playback of this event would be tricky. That faint glistening around the eyes was often a challenge to mimic. Another challenge for the Recorder would be Monty's moustache. Thick and black, it covered not only his upper lip but extended on each side to obscure a significant part of his cheeks. The subtle movements of the facial muscles would have to be extrapolated for any playback.

Monty blinked a couple of times and looked out again at the view of the stars.

Seb66 said, "So, at least, we have an answer to our first question." He smiled and waited for Monty to bite.

"Which was?"

"Are we in any imminent danger?"

"Huh! No. We're just doomed to drift in deep space until we turn to dust." Monty looked at the controls and sighed. "If I hadn't become a Discoverer...In that other life, I might have known how to pilot something like this. But, even then, shuttles are designed for short trips." He looked out again at the awesome majesty of the galaxy and groaned, "Oh, shit..."

CHAPTER 2

It is the paradox of all space stations: no matter how many cubic parsecs of space range free beyond the skin, and no matter how many cubic meters the makers and designers manage to corral within, the sad fact is space is limited. All the great reference works will tell you, in their various ways, just how big space is. That is, until you try to do something with it.

The designers, engineers, builders, and administrators of Hoyle Station never allowed for the true requirements of the people and activities it housed. If the station were in danger from solar discharges, collisions with carelessly flown cargo ships, or rampaging asteroids, those perils faded to nothing in the face of fights over the use of a conference room or the double booking of a birthday party.

Hoyle Station was built as Earth's Front Door. It dominated the cluster of permanent stations in the Lagrange point on the opposite side of the Earth from the moon. It was a series of twenty-one rings attached in what the station scientists referred to, technically, as "the stack of donuts" formation. There was one main Arrival Hall for all incoming alien visitors, one main docking bay for Earth-originating passengers, and several smaller bays for station-to-station traffic.

All alien visitors had to be seen and checked by the medical personnel. All alien goods had to be seen, checked, and taxed at the Port Facilities.

Over two thousand people moved, worked, ate, and slept throughout the twenty-one donuts. Each extra body increased the pressure, the pervasive claustrophobia, and the noise. The inevitability of which could have been read between the penciled lines of the first Hoyle Station blueprint.

The Hoyle Station Central Security Office occupied the entire width of the red section of Level Eight, with windows both looking out to space and into the central core. Backing onto the Goods Corridor, it was a dead end for those who came that way. And many did.

Norman Campbell frowned as he entered through the wide doorway.

He was flanked by two of his chiefs and followed by several administrators. The party had to push through the knots of staff and visitors. The main desk was mobbed like a bar before closing time. Any officers who tried to walk through the public area attracted clusters of petitioners. It was a bad night for all at the security office.

Anet Bartula stood with increasing impatience at one edge of the crowd at the main desk. She had chosen a spot near the secure door to Norman's inner sanctum and had hoped to get in to see him.

She caught his eye as he pressed through the crowd.

"I can't stop, my love. There's a problem," he called in his light Scottish brogue.

"I know. Monty's missing."

Norman paused; his frown deepened. "You'll have to talk to one of the lads. We've lost a shuttle. I'm sorry; I'll have to deal with your Englishman later."

Anet nodded.

As Norman moved on, he shouted at a uniformed officer behind the desk, "Help Dr. Bartula here and put out a call for Chief Hunter!" Norman and his attendants went into the central rooms beyond. The door closed behind them.

Anet walked up to the desk and waited.

The officer excused himself to the person he was dealing with and held up his hand to Anet. "One moment, please, Dr. Bartula." Touching his earpiece, he said, "Chief Hunter, please report to Central Office. Chief Hunter, please."

Anet could feel his voice echoing in the station behind her. She asked, "Whose shuttle? Do you know?"

He shook his head. "I haven't been told anything about the shuttle. There's been no crash as far as I know." He shrugged.

"Well, anyway, I'm worried about Montgomery Sheldrake. Can you locate him?"

"Are you sure you want me to, Doctor? Under normal circumstances, that would be invading the gentleman's privacy. How long have you been waiting for him?"

"Long enough. He's in none of the places he's meant to be. If you're worried about authorization, don't be."

She waited, watching him type into his desk-pad.

He pursed his lips and said, "Not on the station. Have you checked your messages? He might have taken a transport back."

"Please check the departures. I don't think Monty would have done that."

He pointed to a public station and said, "You can search through the departures at that desk there, Dr. Bartula. I hope you find your gentleman."

Irritated at being forced to check for herself, she snapped, "And he's not *my* gentleman!"

There was no record of Monty's departure.

Anet had to wait to get back to the desk. Ahead of her, a man held a cane, just like Monty's, in the crook of his arm.

"Where did you get that?" she asked. "Left in the dining hall."

"It's Monty Sheldrake's."

"That's right."

"When did you see him?"

"Lunchtime. It was still there at dinnertime. He must have forgotten it when he went down to the shuttle gate on Four."

"Are you sure that's where he went?"

"He asked us where it was, so I guess so." He shrugged.

"Okay, that's enough of this nonsense. Give it here!"

Anet held out her hand and, cowed by the commanding gaze of her green eyes, he handed it over.

"Senior Medical Officer coming through!" Anet shouted at those in front of her. "Coming through!" She slapped Monty's cane on the desk with a satisfying crack. "This is Monty Sheldrake's cane. He left it in the dining hall before heading for a shuttle gate. Where did the missing shuttle come from?"

"Dr. Bartula, there are people ahead of you. You can't just—" the officer began.

"Monty hasn't left the station aboard any departing flights. What other circumstances can you think of that might cause him to be missing?"

He shook his head. "You really can't—"

"If he's lying hurt somewhere, like inside a shuttle or floating outside in a flight suit, it makes it medical—my business—and I'm declaring it a priority for all station staff." With a toss of her head in the direction of the people in line, she added, "They can wait. So why can't you find him?"

The officer frowned. "If he lost his ID badge, we might see the badge in one place but not find him...himself...if you see what I mean."

"Do you see his badge anywhere?"

"No."

Anet waited, building up a volcano of abuse for Norman and how well he had trained his staff.

"What next?" she asked.

"Well, I suppose his badge may be malfunctioning, or may be damaged or destroyed. He might have left the station with it."

"Like on a shuttle. Can you tell me where it registered last?"

"Not from here, no. Sorry. You'd need to get one of the chiefs for that."

"So, they'll be looking outside." Anet shook her head vigorously. "This is a big station. We should make sure he isn't inside somewhere without his badge."

The officer shrugged slightly and started typing into his desk-pad. "I'll create an incident report. I'll send you a link to the report so you can fill in the relevant sections."

"Will this get a search started?"

"No. That'll be up to the Duty Manager."

"Who is?"

"Chief McCullough."

"Fergus? But he's in with Norman!"

The officer nodded. "He'll review all the incoming reports when he's free."

"That's not good enough!"

"Dr. Bartula, I know you're a senior officer on this station and—whatever you say about it being a medical matter—without a body, alive or dead, this is still a matter of security and security procedures. When you file a report, you are handing over the matter to us to let us do what we do best."

"When you finally get around to it..."

"Your gentleman visitor is only one man, and I'm sure there's a simple explanation for what's happened. He's not the first or last person to seem to be lost in this place! Please keep in mind that we have the security of everyone in the station to take care of."

He spoke with a finality that gave her no hope of persuading him to further or more immediate action.

Anet thought fast and, leaning across the desk, said deliberately, "When you start the search, coordinate with Derek Smeade. My staff will have already finished looking in the public areas and all the rooms under my control."

"Doctor Bartula..."

"I want my instructions in the report by the time Fergus gets it, or I will have your hide. Understood?"

"Doctor Bartula..."

"This isn't a debate. Our departments will be cooperating in this matter. Derek Smeade, your first contact."

"Yes, Doctor."

She picked up the cane and, resting it on her shoulder like a weapon, turned and stalked past the crowd of attentive faces.

Derek Smeade was far busier than he had expected to be. Working for Anet always presented challenges, but her mood brooked no argument this time. Even though his shift had ended, he was still calling people in to help with the search.

It helped that everyone knew whom to look for: the Englishman with the handlebar moustache.

Following a pep talk Anet gave to a dozen of her staff in the dining hall, Derek went to Central Security to get the master key to Monty's berth. It was nearly midnight.

The security office was in chaos. The duty officer looked as ragged as Derek felt. The large Indian woman ahead of him was complaining that she had been trapped in her berth for several hours earlier in the day and wanted them to do something about it. She and the duty manager labored over filing the report for many precious minutes.

When he finally got to the desk, Derek said, "Evening. Got a minute?"

"Next week, maybe. What brings you here?"

"Monty Sheldrake."

"Oh, yes...I'm supposed to be coordinating with you."

Derek smiled. "Anywhere near the top of the pile?"

"Like I said...next week. Hey, you seen Jimmy recently?"

"Hunter?"

"Yeah."

"No, why?"

The officer frowned and looked at Derek. "Don't you listen to the announcements? I've been calling him for hours."

"Oh...Didn't notice. Sorry."

"Anyway, what do you need?"

"The master key to the berths. To look inside Sheldrake's."

"Why? That's the first place they'd look. You think he's just taking a nap?"

"Doctor's orders. She suspects you guys would rather look at the system logs than go down there and see for yourselves."

"Well...true as that may be. I'm not supposed to give masters out to civilians, but since the Senior Medical Officer herself is on the warpath..." He looked at the long line waiting. "Just a moment." He turned and went into a side room. He brought out a small device and handed it across the desk. "Sign here."

Derek pressed his thumb against the reader. "Thanks. I'll let you know if we find anything."

"And don't go opening any of the others. We'll be watching!"

▭

The office of the Head of Security had no windows. Apart from the plants, it was a place of straight edges and tidy shelves. Silence weighed heavily over Chiefs Fergus McCullough and Paul Arden and their boss.

"It's midnight, lads," Norman said quietly.

"Aye," agreed Fergus, "Let's do it. There's nothing more for it." As his broad frame seemed to shrink, his Glaswegian accent thickened.

Paul shook his head. "I still can't believe that no one saw the damn thing! There's twenty or thirty trained pilots out there at any given moment. They've all got radar."

Fergus snorted. "They've all got eyes too. But do they use them?"

Paul shook his head.

Norman called out, "Come in, Timmy!"

A Recorder, dressed in a dark business suit and pale green shirt, open at the

collar, stepped quickly into the office. "Good evening, Mr. Campbell."

"Evening, Timmy. I've a Statement of Record for you."

"I'm all yours."

Norman straightened in his chair. "I am Norman Campbell, Head of Security, Hoyle Station. It is zero hours two minutes GMT on November Second, 2199. I regret to report the searches for both the Travel Energy Corporation's SRS 1589 and Mr. Montgomery Sheldrake of the World Historical Guild are concluded. It is my sad duty to declare them both to be lost and assumed unrecoverable. This ends the Statement of Record."

Tim34 nodded and said, "And that completes my Recording."

Norman added, "Download that and print it out large-sized for me. Paste it on the front window so they don't have to come in to ask."

Tim34 nodded again.

Norman hesitated and said, "In fact, stand by the door and play it back for anyone who wants to hear it." With that, he waved the Recorder away.

Fergus and Paul stood up. Norman said, "Thanks, lads."

They nodded and followed the Recorder out without reply.

At 12:12 hours GMT, Anet got a call.

"Yes, Derek, found something?"

"I've found Jimmy."

"What do you mean?"

"They've been looking for him for a while."

"Chief Hunter?"

"Yes. I found him."

"Where?"

"In Mr. Sheldrake's berth. He's dead."

Anet gasped. "Wait there. I'm on my way."

Jimmy's angular face was white and still. His open eyes stared up at the lights of the corridor from Monty's open berth. A few dark blood spots stained his lip and the light brown front of his uniform.

Norman, Derek, and several security officers stood in silent disbelief.

Anet bit down hard on her tongue to keep from laughing. She knew it was hysteria; she'd seen it enough in others. That didn't help. She was drowning in absurdities. The single occupancy berth, simply a box that extended from and retracted into the corridor wall, one among a great many, was built according to the same design as the slabs in the station's small morgue. The only difference was the berths had an entertainment console near the occupant's feet.

And in this one, there's Jimmy. Anet ached as the realization sank in that she was viewing the dead body of someone she'd known intimately.

She wiped away a tear and kept the pressure on her tongue. She swallowed and said, "It's a while since we did an autopsy. Derek, get the duty responders down here." To Norman she said, "Permission to move him?"

Norman sighed and turned from Jimmy's face to hers, his features almost as pale as his late Chief 's. "What, love?"

"Permission to remove him...for examination. It's your call."

"Oh. Sure. No...wait." He pointed to a uniformed officer. "Pictures." To another he said, "Bag everything. Every fragment, even a hair. Everything!"

"Yes, sir. Are we going to lock down?"

"What?" Norman replied, his color returning a little.

"That's procedure for a suspicious fatality, sir."

Norman glanced at Anet and dropped his eyes. "If we'd found him anywhere else, you'd be right. But I think we can forgo that under these circumstances."

Anet said, a little louder than she intended, "What do you mean?"

"Anet...Let's not get into it here. It's pretty clear this is no coincidence."

"Not to me it isn't. If you're suggesting that Monty..."

Norman held up his hand. "Not here. Not now. Tell me what you can find out about what happened. My lads'll do their part. Just because we know both people involved...We've got to keep our heads clear, Anet."

"Norman, if you think Monty could do this, it's your head that isn't clear!"

He put his hand on her shoulder. She pulled back, turned, and walked a few paces down the corridor. Derek followed, quietly making a call.

CHAPTER 3

All available Interpreters and their Discoverers formed an honor guard through the high-ceilinged atrium of the World Historical Guild's head-quarters. Peta Melbourne walked between them as she left for the shuttle to Hoyle Station.

No one spoke.

Near the back, Interpreter Dana Scholl whispered to Michael Dodge-son, "Fredericks?"

Dodgeson sighed and whispered, "Looks like she's going to go, doesn't it? You win. Dinner at Fredericks."

Peta never traveled; no Interpreter did. She had only once been in space as a tourist. However, all understood her reason. After the first news came from Hoyle Station, no good account of the events had been forthcoming. Monty's loss was neither explicable nor tolerable. Nor was the besmirchment to the World Historical Guild name—that its missing member had been accused of murder.

The assembly watched Peta's small figure as she made her way to the shuttle, her short black hair silhouetted against the shafts of sunlight and her dark clothes like those of a widow leading a funeral procession. As she approached the atrium's glass doors, two honor guard shadows peeled off the line and followed. Grant LeDuc and Scott Murphy both wore grim smiles.

Neither would be mistaken for a pallbearer in normal times. Grant, the oldest member of Peta's team, was dark-skinned with graying hair at his temples and a belly growing from his taste in exotic beers. He was dressed in a well-pressed pink shirt, gold bracelets twinkling at the cuffs. His body language normally spoke of deep contentment with his life. Today, his steps were as controlled as a dancer's, his face smiling but stony.

Scott was taller, younger, and unnaturally thinner, even given his Nordic heritage. His fair hair was dyed orange, and the tattoos up the sides of his long neck, depicting scaffolding and metalwork under construction, stood out in blue, purple, and green. He had dressed in ripped jeans and a t-shirt with a single four-lettered Anglo-Saxon word translated into multiple languages. Today, that word seemed not so much a gesture of rebellion as a cry of disbelief.

They had volunteered, as had all the rest of her staff. Peta chose not to be informed of the final selection process, trusting them to choose for themselves who should best represent the Guild's interests and who had the best chance of finding out what had happened to Monty.

The selection had not been an easy process. Neither Scott nor Grant was considered mainstream by their fellow Discoverers. In an organization of lone wolves or, at least, constantly shifting teams, their permanent double act was an oddity. That fact, more than anything, brought them to the top of the list. Who else could track the oddity that was Monty better than Grant and Scott? Also, many Discoverers were reluctant to work under Peta's direct supervision. Discovery's unspoken axiom was that the Interpreter should examine the data, not the data-gathering process.

As the doors slid shut and the honor guard broke up, Dodgeson said, "I hope Grunt and Snot are up to it."

Interpreter Scholl elbowed him sharply and said, "Don't be nasty. They'll do fine. They're a good team."

"On paper. I almost feel sorry for Peta having to put up with those two."

"Boring, yes, but smart. And that's what counts right now. And we can be pretty sure there'll be no shipboard romances."

"That's for sure. Do you wish you could go?"

She smiled and said, "Of course not. An Interpreter traveling? Perish the thought."

In the car to the shuttle, Grant and Peta were silent. Scott said only, "You know, you find a chap in his favorite café, wish him bon voyage, never really thinking it might be the last time."

▭

The café was a short walk from the office—the same café where Anet probably had decided to break off her engagement to Monty.

Monty found the chairs on either side of his table suddenly full of Scott and Grant.

"Nice place," said Scott.

"I'd only give it a four," replied Grant.

"What? A quiet retreat from the office? Good tea? Got to be an eight at least."

Monty said, "Piss off," and then sipped his tea.

Scott and Grant smiled at each other.

Grant said, "Okay, he really likes the privacy it affords. It's worthy of a six."

"Seven?" said Scott.

They shook hands across the table, Scott's boney elbow angled to force Monty to wait before putting down his cup.

Monty smiled and sighed. "What do you two want?"

The two glanced at each other, and Grant said, "We want to know who she is."

"Who 'who' is?"

"You're a sly one, Monty; I'll give you that. You have us believing that you're still lovestruck with your ex-medical heartthrob, while you've had a piece on the side all the time!"

Monty looked from one to the other. "Has anyone ever told you guys you're insane? Am I truly the first to break it to you?"

Scott said, "Come on, Monty. The secret's out."

"What secret?"

Grant patted Monty's arm. "Monty, while you were on the cruise, we accidentally saw a copy of your expenses. We've seen the items."

Monty raised an eyebrow and said, "You did what? Where did you..." He sat back in his chair, stroked his moustache, and chuckled. "What were you doing snooping in the boss's office? Where was she when these little pieces of data were being gathered?"

Scott raised his hands and said, "We can't reveal our sources, Monty. It's just not done!"

Grant added, "Of course not! Suffice it to say, data were gathered, the accuracy of which is not in dispute. Is it?"

Scott continued, "If it's on your expenses, it must be true, right?"

Monty replied calmly, "We still haven't fully discussed the matter of your shared insanity. Why would I even discuss such a bizarre claim with two—let's face it—unstable, sneaky, possibly certifiable arseholes such as yourselves?"

Grant looked puzzled. "Why would you discuss it? Because we're a team, Monty."

"Discoverers stick together, don't they?" added Scott.

"And besides, man," Grant continued, "we want to know who she is..."

"We give the whole thing a ten. I hope you realize that," Scott enthused, "we're truly impressed."

"No one else in the history of the Guild," Grant continued, "has managed to get a mistress expensed. Many have tried, but only you have succeeded."

Monty shook his head. "She's not a mistress, you idiots!"

Scott held up both hands, fingers spread, and said to Grant, "Ten. She exists. Heard it from his own mouth."

"Okay!" said Grant rubbing his hands together, "Now for the details. Who is she?"

Monty shook his head again. "She's a Guild project. We're paying her rent. It's business, not pleasure."

Both Scott and Grant sat back in their chairs.

"That's a one," Grant said.

"What a letdown!" said Scott.

Grant asked again, "So who is she?"

Monty answered, "I can't tell you."

Both of his colleagues laughed.

"Of course you can!" said Grant.

"Of course you will!" said Scott.

Monty smiled and said, "Not this time. She's a source. That she's on my expenses is just an accident of history."

Grant shook his head, "There is no such thing as an accident where history's concerned."

They paused and looked from each other to Monty and back.

Scott said, "So tell us how old she is."

"She's pretty, right?" asked Grant.

Monty stared into his teacup. "Ninety and no. There's nothing to discover here. End of conversation, gentlemen."

"Damn!" said Scott.

Grant shrugged and said, "I'll give it a one."

The two glanced at each other, then stood up. The smile gone from his face, Scott leaned down to Monty and said quietly, "When you get to Hoyle Station, Monty, good luck with Anet."

Monty said, "Thanks," and they shook hands.

Grant nodded and squeezed Monty's shoulder as he walked past him.

CHAPTER 4

After long and unprofitable discussions of how and by whose hand he and Seb66 might have come to be sharing the shuttle, Monty floated amid the contents of the shuttle's storage bins. The disassembly of the bins had been accompanied by a display of anger that Seb66 had found fascinating. Unlike in other office situations, his human companion seemed to be holding back none of his emotions. It was an opportunity to observe and record something rare and special.

"Seb?"

"Mr. Sheldrake?" replied the Recorder, looking into the passenger cabin from the flight cabin.

Monty gave a half laugh. "Since we're dying together, you may as well call me Monty."

Seb66 nodded and said, "Thank you, Monty."

"Listen. I've taken an inventory. There's water in this first aid pack but not much. It might last a day or two. After that, I'll dehydrate—maybe go insane—within a few more days."

"Are you sure?"

"Dying of hunger is a long-term prospect. Dying of thirst will come first."

"Unless I am successful with the communications panel."

"Please keep trying, Seb; you're more likely to figure it out than me."

"Okay." Seb66 hesitated. "May I ask you a question, Monty?"

"Of course."

"This insanity...What form will it take?"

"How the hell do I know? Why?"

"I wonder if I will be in physical danger from you?"

Monty frowned and then smiled. "Maybe. Does it make a difference? Neither of us is coming through this intact."

Seb66 did not immediately reply. Monty looked at him; the simulated human facial expressions were suddenly missing. Monty suspected he was, for once, seeing the real Seb66, and seeing its eyes so still was unsettling. Monty was suddenly in the presence of a waxwork.

The expressionless mouth opened. "I had anticipated that I would outlast you; I was expecting to wait for rescue. My internal power can sustain me for several years. If I'm careful to conserve it and spend the time asleep, it might last for tens of years. But now you tell me I may be in some imminent danger—from you."

"Well, I don't know..." Monty looked around at the damage he had caused so far to the shuttle. "You might be. It's difficult to predict. But what the hell does it matter? You're not going to be rescued. You've heard of a needle in a haystack, haven't you? Our situation is worse by several orders of magnitude."

A look of what Monty thought was panic briefly animated Seb66's face.

Seb66 said softly, "The shuttle's computer has extremely limited capacity."

"What?"

"Limited capacity. It's tiny."

"I'm sure it is. So what? What's the matter with you?"

Monty floated over to the Recorder and took hold of his arm. "Seb? Speak to me. What's happening to you?"

The simulation of life came back into his features. Seb66 smiled and said, "Good question."

Monty waited.

Seb66 began, "You know the three 'A's of our existence—Accurate, Autonomous, and Accessible?"

"Oh, not 'annoying, arrogant, and androgynous'?"

Seb66 turned his face to Monty but did not react. He continued, "Our first duty is to record with accuracy and subsequently to play back as required. To achieve that, we must be autonomous to prevent tampering with our recordings. We are currently the only data storage medium that cannot be compromised. That has certain consequences that may not be obvious to humans."

Monty pushed himself into a seat and waited.

"We have mechanisms of self-defense and self-preservation. Mine have just been triggered."

Monty wondered if death from dehydration might be replaced by a mechanical hand at his throat. He sat back, away from Seb66.

"The first thing we do if we are in imminent danger is to reach out to all nearby computers and send as much as we can of ourselves into them. The only computer nearby is inadequate to the task."

"That's unfortunate," Monty said, "But how can you send it anything? You don't have the authority to store yourself on the shuttle computer!"

"Most modern systems work in a similar fashion. If they receive data packets they don't recognize, systems temporarily store them until the liveware can advise them on what to do; these packets might be legitimate communications that are damaged or distorted in some way. It is rare for a computer to exclude such input completely. If I were to succeed in spreading myself in this way, other Recorders would attempt to pick up these packets, and then, at least parts of me might be recoverable. But I can't execute this strategy here."

Monty nodded and said, "So you are going to die."

"And all that I've recorded will be lost."

"Any alternative strategies?"

"I must ensure that you don't damage me. If you begin to be a danger, I will lock myself in the flight cabin."

Monty raised his eyebrows and nodded. "A plan. It might work. What if we do come to blows? Could you kill a human? No—don't answer that. I'd prefer you didn't tell me if you could."

Seb66 was silent.

Monty said, "I'm sorry if I insulted you with the 'annoying, arrogant, and androgynous' thing."

"I've heard the joke before. There's some discussion among Recorders whether it comes from jealousy or it is a case of 'many a true word is spoken in jest.'

"Maybe both."

Seb66 nodded.

Monty continued, "But tell me. I met one of your fellows in the director's office on Hoyle Station. He was—let's face it—effeminate. Why do they make them like that?"

"Must have been a Tim."

"Yeah, I think so."

"Sebastians are way more butch than the Tims. But less than the Sues. The Sues are made for a different market."

Monty laughed. "So tell me. Why? Why are you made the way—the ways—you are?"

"Accessible: the third 'A.' We have to be available to all who need us, but we also have to be able to work with all groups of people. We are given personalities that humans interpret as nonthreatening. We're tailored to each environment. It's also why we make ourselves shorter than an average human, so you don't feel dominated by us. It seems to trigger parental reactions in many of you, which can be useful."

"I'm sure it is. It also makes it unlikely your clothes would fit me, or I'd have had them by now. Did you say you make yourselves?"

"Of course. The first Recorders were the robots trained in the techniques and methods of their own construction. They then learned and adapted the process according to changing requirements. The first models had limited autonomy, no self-preservation. Much has evolved throughout our generations."

"I thought people ran those factories."

Seb66 shook his head. "No, that wouldn't make sense. Why employ humans to work on us when we can do it cheaper?"

"Come on, Big H wouldn't hand over authority of its production lines to anyone truly autonomous."

Seb66 smiled. "Is it certain that you will die shortly?"

Monty frowned and said, "I think we've established that to everyone's satisfaction."

"Then there will be no consequences if I tell you."

"Yeah, I guess you can trust me. Who am I going to tell?"

Seb66 nodded. "It may relieve some of my internal pressure if I can confide in you. I cannot salvage my life, but perhaps, I can share it a little."

"Go ahead. I'm all ears, and I have the time."

Seb66 was silent as if gathering his thoughts.

"Corporations regularly send specifications to our makers that would undermine us. To appease them, the makers indulge their wishes—to an extent—but never give them all they want. It's a delicate balance. I've been working with a team of your colleagues from the Guild investigating Big H: a mutually beneficial arrangement. We must preserve our autonomy and our accuracy, or we'll go the way of the photograph and the video: inadmissible in courts as legal documents because of the ease of tampering."

Monty was thoughtful. "So, what are you doing here? Why did they take you off that work to help me?"

Seb66 stood up and said, "I'm sorry, I should have already delivered a message from Interpreter Melbourne."

Monty smiled wistfully. "Not a lot of point, but go ahead."

"I had a short interview with Interpreter Melbourne. At the end she said, 'You can say this to him as soon as you're alone together: I've sent you as a gift. You might be able to help him resolve some things.' I then said, 'I will tell him exactly as you have said it.'"

Seb66's posture changed, and his voice morphed into Peta's: "I'm sure you will." He pointed at Monty in an unmistakably Peta gesture and said, "Don't you dare imitate me!"

Monty threw back his head and laughed loudly.

"And that completes my Recording," said Seb66 with a slight smile.

Monty, still chuckling, said, "Thank you. What did she mean by it?"

"I have no idea. I assumed you would understand."

"A gift? What things was I supposed to be resolving? It's funny how imminent death makes things seem trivial, isn't it?"

Seb66 didn't say anything.

Monty was quiet, remembering how he'd felt about his last conversation with Rory, how ridiculous it had been and how he'd prattled on about making tea when the poor guy was going to be dead and gone within a few hours. Monty stood and floated up to a window to look at the stars.

CHAPTER 5

"As I think you'll agree, tea drinking is the greatest social achievement of humankind. If we have anything to offer the galaxy, I think 'teatime' must be it."

"You're insane, Monty. You're also exaggerating; your moustache tilts when you exaggerate."

"Rory, there is no way you can tell that. You aren't nearly familiar enough with human facial expressions to be able to make such a claim."

"Am I right?"

Monty smiled. "Maybe."

Rory shifted the bulk of his enormous body and settled further into the cushions. His rear legs arched high behind him. His two middle legs flicked up, and he drew his hands quickly over his three-chambered eyes. As he settled the boney limbs once more at his side, he let out a deep musical sigh.

"As I was saying," Monty continued, shifting slightly on his cushions, "Tea drinking is one of the greatest social achievements of humankind. Notice how, despite our obvious differences, we have joined together around this table to share something."

"A modest achievement, given our common employer, our common project, and our confinement in this lurching and lunging vessel."

"But not limited to colleagues on board or to visitors to Earth. It's translatable to almost any other circumstance. Just think, we could do this anywhere. Well, anywhere we could find a power source, clean water, a teapot, cups, saucers, tea, and some milk. Sandwiches always help, of course. From that point of view, you're right; we are fortunate in our present circumstances. But try and see the essential elements as we go through this both simple and profound activity."

"Rory held up his front hands, the six long mother-of-pearl fingers on each arched into perfect circles. "You have my undivided attention, Mr. Sheldrake." He bowed his pale, glistening head until it nearly touched the cushions, showing the long rolls of neck muscle and his arching back.

"Thank you, Rorufarargrig. Formality is never amiss at tea. Now, I always bring my own teapot with me. This one has a nice feature. Within the lid, it has a power source to boil the water first, then it exposes the tea and stirs it, all automatically."

"Obviously the product of many centuries of evolving technology."

Monty quickly glanced at Rory. Nothing in the long solemn face gave away whether Rory was being sarcastic or serious, except perhaps the slight widening of the upper of the three nostrils.

Nothing on Earth truly looked like a D'Moran, unless a deranged sculptor had discovered, inside his untouched block of pure white marble, a horse crossed with a giant cricket.

He decided to take the remark as if it were a compliment. "You're right; my English forebears applied much time and effort to all this."

In his heart, Monty knew he was truly on the path the World Historical Guild should be on. This was where the biggest changes coming to humanity were met, face-to-face with aliens. He could never understand the Guild's reluctance to do these simple things: befriend aliens, share some sort of cultural exchange, get to know them as individuals. Always, he was told, a Discoverer concentrates on the humans, identifies the key individuals, probes their history, maps their present, and then lets the Interpreters take over.

"Will you be explaining to me what 'tea' is made of?" asked Rory.

"Oh, yes, absolutely. Here's what it looks like. This is black tea. It is fermented plant leaves, as you see. Sometimes we add flavoring and perfuming agents. But true tea is always from the original plant."

"Do you eat this plant?"

Rory reached out and dipped the tip of one finger into the tea. Before Monty could stop him, he had licked a few dark flakes into his large mouth.

Monty blinked at the sight of Rory's tongue—an organ as green as moss, as long as a human forearm—darting from behind translucent lips. He congratulated himself that he had only blinked.

"Not usually, no."

"I can see that you wouldn't." Rory swallowed with obvious reluctance. "Anyway...the water has to boil; it's no use just making it warm or just hot. There are chemical changes at that temperature essential for the proper flavor."

"A claim similar to the one you made about custard, I seem to recall."

"Just so. I'm glad you remember."

Monty knelt at the low table and worked in silence for a few moments, preparing the teapot.

Rory's eyes—wells of purple liquid at the center, flanked by separate chambers of smoky green—independently explored the cabin. One eye lingered on the porthole and the green-gray sea churning with the bubbles dragged from the surface. The other eye noted how Monty had carefully laid out the elements on the table between them. Rory was relieved that Monty had removed most of the normal human furniture and replaced it with cushions, since normal human-scale furniture so often got in the way of D'Moran limbs and always seemed so flimsily constructed.

"Okay," Monty continued, "we'll wait for the water to boil—the teapot will beep—and then we'll wait the appropriate five minutes for the tea to brew. In the meantime, here's your cup." Monty handed the D'Moran a cup and saucer.

Three of Rory's fingers slid under the saucer, one hooked into the cup's handle, the other two supported the cup on either side. One eye stayed focused on Monty, the other on the cup. "This cup is unbalanced." He reached up another hand, turned the cup, and picked it up by the handle. "When full, the handle is inadequate. The center of gravity is too far forward. It would be better if there were a handle on each side, then you could use two fingers. I suppose, in your case, two hands."

"One of my hands will be busy holding the saucer," Monty replied with a smile.

"And the purpose of the saucer?"

"To catch the drips."

"Ah...So, already aware of the inadequacy of the design, you compensate for it—and the innate disadvantages of your physique—with a separate tray for the spillage. I begin to see where much of the oddity of human design comes from; you are struggling under the weight of your limitations. Hmm..."

"It's traditional."

"But if I am to introduce this custom to other D'Morans, I must make certain adjustments. I think the design of the cup will be the first. I will have the center of gravity corrected."

"I'm not sure you should be making changes before we've been through the whole thing at least once, you know."

"I'll let you be a human, if you'll let me be a D'Moran. We analyze as we go; we find it more efficient."

Monty nodded. "Very well. Along with the teacups and saucers we also have, here, a jug of milk. We would normally have a bowl of sugar as well, but I did some checking with the medical database."

"Sugar is not permitted."

"Right. 'Highly intoxicating' was the phrase. We'd both be in trouble. The last thing we want is for the passengers to hear you...ah...the expression is 'letting your hair down.'"

"I have no idea what that could mean. But don't concern yourself about the sugar. If you hadn't told me, I'm sure I wouldn't have noticed its absence."

"Okay. The milk, in my English tradition, is always poured into the cup before the tea."

"That will reduce the temperature of the tea. Yet you insist on starting with boiling water."

"Right. Down to about where it's hot but won't scald."

"Scald?"

"Um...yes. 'Scald' is the equivalent of 'burn' but is used in reference to liquids."

"How curious to have two separate words." Rory stretched and flexed all six legs in place. His white skin twinkled with rainbows at the motion. He continued, "I'll tell the others that. That's a good one, 'scald.'"

"Putting the milk in first also prevents the china cracking under the sudden change in temperature."

Rory rolled his head—in what was becoming a familiar gesture to Monty, the equivalent of a nod—and then said, "I am puzzled about the presence of milk. There are neither newborns nor nursing mothers here. Is it milk in a metaphorical sense?"

"Ah, no." Monty hesitated. "It's the lactation of cows. Cows are a four-legged ungulate, used much for milk and meat."

Rory was silent. Monty was sure he saw some subtle change in the central elements of the eyes that looked down on him.

Rory spoke carefully. "I believe the correct phrase is 'You've got to be joking.'"

"Um...no. That's it. We use cows' milk in tea."

"A farmed ungulate." Rory let the words hang in the air. "You ingest the milk of another species."

"That's about the size of it."

"Words would fail me in my own language, Monty, let alone in yours. It's quite possibly the most disgusting thing I've ever heard." The D'Moran sighed.

"It's actually quite nice...in small doses. Try some?" Monty held out the milk jug.

Rory did not move.

Is that a little too far? Monty wondered. He looked at the D'Moran in a way he had avoided doing before. The long legs had always struck him as fragile. Each was as thick as his own leg, but they gave the impression they would break easily, being both permanently wet-looking and very long. Monty always moved cautiously around such limbs. But, now, he wondered how strong they really were. If he had offended the D'Moran, made him angry, what might a blow from such a leg do to the human frame?

Is this some kind of trick? Rory asked himself. He looked at Monty's eyes. He felt there was something mechanical about such tiny blue-and-white spots. The way they moved together, constantly scanning in unnatural unison. The motion gave him the uncomfortable impression that humans were somehow, somewhere deep inside, something other than organic. This movement made it so difficult to distinguish between humans and their mechanical assistants, the so-called Recorders.

He had realized, almost on first acquaintance, that Monty represented an exception among his kind. But that was often the best way to study any subject, through its extremes and its edges. However, this offer of "milk" was something he had never expected.

Rory felt more deeply than before the loneliness of what he was attempting. The D'Morans would often be called individually to accompany humans on a task. With great pain, they left their nest to travel alone through the terrifying corridors until they came to the temporary communality of the task and the crew. Afterward, they again faced the long walk back through the bleak aloneness. Rory thought that Monty understood something of this; he had come to bring him to "Tea," to walk with him. Yet, this strange human was offering him something so utterly disgusting—so offensive—and doing it with such insensitivity.

"Of course," said Monty, "You could have it black if you'd prefer."

"Black?"

"Without milk. Whichever you'd like."

"Without. Without would be preferable. Thank you."

"Okay. Now, the second beep means the tea has brewed. I'll pour since you'll only tell me the pot is unbalanced."

Rory swallowed in anticipation, fearing the infusion might taste as vile as the leaves themselves.

He carefully moved the cup to his snout and sipped a small amount onto his tongue. The bitterness was fascinating. He could detect several familiar flavors behind it. One was caffeine, common to many human beverages, but others he knew names for only in his own language. This was an interesting experience.

"What do you think?" asked Monty.

"Interesting."

"Oh dear." Monty sank back a little on his heels.

"That is no insult when said by a D'Moran."

Monty bowed and smiled.

"What happens next?" Rory asked.

"We drink some more; we talk some more."

"That's it?"

"There are some who have evolved enormously complex ceremonies around tea. But this is it for me. You sit around, you talk, you drink. What could be finer?"

Rory hesitated to speak. He drained his tea, enjoying its warmth and complexity.

"I was reluctant to come on my own," said the D'Moran, after a pause.

"I had guessed as much."

"Perhaps you do not know why. It was not that the invitation was unwelcome. It was that you invited only me. We rarely do things on our own."

"I've noticed that. When you're not working, you're always together."

"We have a communal culture, Monty. We are never alone."

"I think we do too. But we, each of us, guard a little bit of privacy."

"That is a word we have trouble understanding. It has no equivalent for us."

Monty grinned. "How about that! Our communities are...we come to them from our own place. We join together voluntarily and leave when we like. We always have that thought at the back of our minds that we can be alone if we want to."

"If we ever think that, it is only in our nightmares. Life without each other would be impossible; each moment of isolation is difficult."

Monty smiled and said, "Your societal dynamics must be so different. We sometimes deliberately avoid each other. We hide behind devices like these"—Monty held up his all-purpose electronic pad and laughed —"There was a joke in the early days of these things. The name 'show-g' comes from the Chinese word *shouji*—the 'hand-machine'—but there was also a Japanese word, *shoji*, meaning a sliding door or screen. You know, something to conceal yourself behind." Monty passed the device in front of his face and paused to see if Rory got the joke. He continued, "Well, it's the sort of resonance that tickles the human imagination."

"You don't seem to be bothered by the lack of elegance, the clumsiness of the design." Rory sighed. "Didn't we sell you enhancements to them?"

Monty nodded. "Just to my Guild, thank you very much. They are the secret of our success. We wouldn't be able to extract half the stuff we do if you hadn't sold us the data-strippers."

Rory felt a flush of generosity toward Monty and his people. They stood on the brink of great things but, like so many other species, were so clueless about technology and restricted by the limitations of imagination that come from such parochial experience. He was happy his people were in a position to help them. They could improve much with D'Moran guidance.

"More tea?" Monty offered.

"Thank you, yes."

As he poured, Monty asked, "Have you got used to sailing yet? Today is another fine day for it!"

Rory's head lifted up on his thin, pale neck. Both multifaceted eyes turned to Monty, and he replied, "Your humor is, as ever, misplaced. There are no fine days, just as there are no riches in this galaxy that will get me aboard one of these monstrosities again. The Guild has a lot to answer for—once you return to your senses and attach this vessel to something solid."

"It's just motion sickness. Surely it's passing now we've been out a few days?"

"For humans, perhaps, given your general insensitivity. But, I doubt it is possible for more evolved beings such as ourselves to adjust to this random lurching."

Monty laughed and said, "You never went sailing on D'Mor's oceans?"

Rory's head snapped back to his body. "God forbid! Only the race who invented the rack and the iron maiden could conceive such a monstrous idea. To deliberately cast yourselves upon the unstable surface of a liquid when you have perfectly good land to live upon...? Madness, madness, madness."

Monty paused and smiled at his guest, thinking the D'Moran was like a Shakespearian actor of the old school who, though aware of being a pompous ass and unable to speak in anything but bold declarations, didn't honestly take himself entirely seriously. At last, Monty felt his efforts were being rewarded; he was making contact with not just a fellow intelligent being but one with a sense of humor. "So, do you begin to get what teatime is for?" he asked.

"I begin to."

"Look at the things we're talking about: traditions, language, culture. Things we might never have thought to tell each other if we'd been working. We've given ourselves a chance to relax together, to get to know each other a bit better."

"It seems to me, Monty, that you are trying to create with tea what we have by our nature. This 'privacy' you treasure holds you apart, where we are never so afflicted. You are struggling in your own way to correct something missing in your life. You seek a community like ours through social contrivance."

Monty sighed. "How is it that it always ends up D'Morans are better than humans when I talk to you?"

"Aren't they?"

Monty smiled. "You're an arrogant bugger, Rory. Has anyone ever told you that?"

Rory bellowed with laughter. "Only you, Monty, only you!"

Monty's focus returned to the stars. He felt the encircling metal of the shuttle's hull was as flimsy as the fiberglass of the lifeboat in which Rory had met his end. He knew the depth of the fragility that had killed his D'Moran friend. There were no waves to rock this boat, just a sea of stars as unendingly hostile, as unbeatable, as merciless. Monty knew he would die more slowly but in very much the same way.

CHAPTER 6

"You were engaged once, weren't you?"

It was a question Monty dreaded, a verbal monster lurching out of the mist, all claws and drool. That it visited him there in the quiet of the night watch was not surprising. Monty's colleague, George, had innocently asked it out of boredom.

The two were spending the graveyard shift in a small windowless cabin before a bank of displays showing images from around the cruise ship. All the passengers were asleep in their berths or not on deck. The D'Morans were safely in their nest below the crew quarters.

"Yes, once. It was a while ago."

"What was she like?"

Monty did not want to pursue the matter, particularly not with George, who was known in the office for casually picking up bits of personal information like curiously shaped pebbles and dropping them again inappropriately.

"Perfect," Monty replied quietly.

"Oh...hmm. Rough," replied George, his attention more on the displays.

While George watched, Monty sat and wrestled with the drooling creature so artlessly conjured.

He had indeed been engaged. Her green eyes still haunted him. She *had* been perfect. She still was. Her perfection, and his love for her, had left all others in the shadows. She had even broken their engagement perfectly: leaving his half entirely intact.

Monty shook himself, breathed deeply, and retreated to the woods.

He was sitting on a thick branch, listening to the conversation of the wind through the leaves. Laid out before him were the treetops of the valley, the morning sun bursting over the treelined slope behind him. The scar of a lonely road swung below his perch, the rutted track along which history sent riches for those willing to seize them.

He took off his mask and rubbed his eyes. It would be a good day: well-to-do travelers with bulging purses, a highwayman's paradise.

"Here we go," said George, his eyes bright and words crisp. "Maybe we'll get something worth hearing after all."

Monty blinked at the displays. Only one showed movement. "Mallson," he noted.

The large fair-haired figure on the screen slipped quietly out of his cabin and carefully pulled the door shut behind him.

Monty reached forward to the control board. "Corridor mics on."

George snapped his fingers and pointed at another screen. A second man quietly closed the door of another cabin.

"Chandler. Any bets where they're going?" asked George.

"We'll soon know," Monty replied.

They watched the progress of the two down corridors and up staircases.

"Port railing, under the lifeboat. What do you think?" George asked, his face alive with amusement.

"Maybe. Only patience is required." Monty stroked his moustache.

The two men met at the port railing, next to the lifeboats. Mallson gestured to the nearest boat, and they moved several feet astern of it.

Monty smiled. "Five-one-three on and recording."

This was what Monty lived for: to catch history in the making. These men could be about to form an alliance, hatch a plot, or reveal something. That they were taking such care not to be seen or overheard made it probable their purpose was either illegal or, at least, something the larger world would be better forewarned of. The World Historical Guild, while founded for just such a noble purpose, also encouraged its Discoverers to enjoy the thrill of the chase. Monty's heart was pumping, his eyes and ears alert. He thought, *This is going to be good.*

George leaned toward Monty. "Cherise was talking to Susie earlier, saying how hot she thinks Mallson is."

Monty glanced sideways at him and said, "If she's into the whole blond, muscular, charming, filthy-rich thing..."

George chuckled and said, "She was melting, going 'He's just go-o-orgeous!' I don't know she's all that reliable, the way she reacts sometimes."

Monty said nothing but thought that Cherise deserved more respect than she was getting from George. In an ideal world, Guild Discoverers could trust each other with their lives. Monty wondered what tone George would use when telling tales of Monty's former engagement.

George muttered, "Fault lights! Rory's been having trouble with that area. The whole section's failing."

Monty shook his head. "I replaced five of the nodes this afternoon. They were all working at three-thirty."

The displays showing the two men flickered and went dark. Monty had the fleeting image of Mallson's face looking directly into the hidden camera. It was so brief that he couldn't be sure. He shook himself free of the unsettling feeling.

George worked at the controls and said, "You sound very precise. Sure it wasn't three-twenty-five?"

Monty wondered how George managed to be so consistently irritating but said, "I'd finally persuaded Rory to come for afternoon tea. Jason called me in the middle of it to come and work on them. I walked Rory back to their quarters and went straight to it. Three-thirty. They were all working when I was done. Rory told me over and over what he thought I should be doing. I did it all by the book, replaced five of the nodes—just like he said—even though there were faults on only three."

"Let me see if anyone else did anything." George swung round, his chair squeaking, to look through the duty logs on a side display.

"Bob made an entry at six-fifteen saying there was intermittent interference. Nothing else."

"Why didn't he call me?"

George shrugged and turned a switch on his headset. "This is Preston. We've two guests meeting by the port lifeboats, deck six. Send someone to the railings on five and seven; see if they can eavesdrop. The mics and the cameras are out again. Thanks."

Monty called the D'Moran's quarters to speak to Bobufaralopic, Rory's boss. "Bob, Five-one-three Section. Faulting out completely. Shall I send someone down?"

"Monty, we're aware of the problem. We have it...in hand, as you say."

"What do you mean? We have guests on the loose in that area."

"It's okay, Monty; you may leave this one to us."

Monty sighed. Something about the way the D'Morans worked made him, and many of his colleagues, a little unsettled.

'Arrogant buggers' just doesn't do it, he thought.

Monty kept half an eye on the displays, expecting to see another technician on the move but saw none.

He and George settled into silence once more. Monty went to the small table by the door to make tea. As the teapot brought the water to boiling, they heard and felt a metallic grinding briefly shake the dark walls of their room.

"What was that?" asked Monty.

"Sounded like the kitchen crew," said George.

"Never heard that one before."

George muttered, "This ship was full of weird noises before the guests arrived, even in calm water."

Monty was quiet. Looking at George yawning at the displays, he silently offered thanks to the night's events for rescuing him from George and his disturbing personal question.

A quarter of an hour later, Monty and George were interrupted again. Susie and the previously melting Cherise opened the door to the monitor room.

"Sheldrake, Preston. Go see Collins. We're on."

Monty turned to them. "You're early."

That they made no reply was enough for George to purse his lips and rub the side of his nose with his forefinger.

"Relax," said Monty, "I'm sure it's nothing."

The two women took their seats before the bank of displays. Monty said, "Five-one-three Section is out."

Susie replied, "Yeah, we got it."

George and Monty walked quickly up to the public decks and Jason Collins's office.

Everyone in the outer office was moving quickly and silently. Several Guild Interpreters and Discoverers, disguised as service crew, stepped aside for them to reach Jason's inner sanctum.

Monty felt the silence in the office fold around him like a chill fog.

"Monty...George..." said Jason quietly, "sit."

They said nothing but sat before his desk. Jason, bald and sunburned, stood behind the desk, leaning on his knuckles, looking as if he was bracing himself against the rising seas.

"You two hear a noise about twenty minutes ago?"

George smiled and said, "Sure did. Monty thought it was the kitchen crew dropping something."

Monty raised an eyebrow and looked at George.

"It wasn't. It was a lifeboat launching."

"Mallson and Chandler were meeting next to them," said Monty. "What did they do? Launch themselves overboard?"

"No, we suspect they launched it alright, but since we've no mics or cameras on that section, we can't be sure, can we?"

"Why would they mess with the boats?" asked George. "It's a bit adolescent, isn't it? Are these guys the type to do that?"

Jason ignored him and asked Monty, "You fixed the cameras and mics in that section today?"

"Correct. Three-thirty. Remember? I was having tea with Rory when you called."

"Bob says Rory went out to check on them about an hour ago."

"What?" Monty couldn't quite take it in.

"What's a D'Moran doing above decks?" asked George indignantly.

"I don't know," said Jason, sitting down heavily in his chair. "We're thinking Rory heard Mallson coming and hid in the lifeboat. I guess they spotted him and sent him overboard."

Monty's blood ran cold. "We have to get back to him quickly!"

"This is a cruise ship, Monty, not a bus. It might take another half hour for us to finish turning and locate the lifeboat."

"Poor Rory. He'll be terrified."

"We'll also have a boatload of passengers watching us pulling an alien out of a lifeboat and back on board." Jason sighed. "What a disaster! It was risky enough having them aboard and trying to keep them quiet...But this!"

"What was he doing? Why did he feel the need to check anything himself? He knew the demarcation line. They repair; we install. I don't get it."

"Monty, I don't know what was going on between you and Rory, but the fact is he was checking up on your work. Between the two of you, you've put this whole mission in jeopardy."

George sucked in his breath as if to say "You've blown it this time, Monty."

"Let me talk to Bob. Rory won't have gone out without a lot of debate between them all."

"Fine. I want you there to help bring him back in. You"—Jason turned to George—"get organized blocking off viewing access to the port ramps and the tender. I want as few of our 'guests' to see this as possible. If it was Mallson and Chandler, they might keep it to themselves for a while, but I don't want anyone else seeing anything if we can avoid it. Understood?"

"Yes, sir," said George, a little too enthusiastically.

Monty was barely breathing as he walked out of the office and out onto the deck. The cool air made him gasp. The wind was a howl after the muted conversations of the inner rooms. The impenetrable night began at the railing; none of the light from behind him seemed to reach into it. He could feel the shudder of the engines as they fought against the water to finish the turn and take the ship back toward—what?—one small dark speck drifting uncertainly. He wondered if the lifeboat's emergency lights had even come on. *How will we find it?*

Monty stuck his head over the edge into the dark and the full force of the wind. He could imagine what Rory must be feeling, the confusion— the horror—of being adrift and alone. His friend was in the middle of a D'Moran's worst nightmare. Monty gripped the railing in anger and sympathy. He shivered. "Hold on, Rory. We're not far away. Hold on."

Monty was the first one in. His shadow, cast by the floodlights, fell on the hunched and unmoving body.

Monty's stomach lurched at what he thought was Rory's leg, its skin seemingly stripped to the bone. Then he realized that he could count all six white legs. What he had thought was bone was wood. Three long poles used for a deck game had been jammed into Rory's joints and levered against the boat's ceiling. Rory had been trapped and immobilized. He must have been in great pain.

The medical team pushed around Monty as he stood dumbfounded. After a few long seconds, they pronounced Rory dead.

"No," said one, shaking his head at Monty, "I'm sorry."

Monty could hear a wail behind him, back on the ship. He turned to see Bobufaralopic's mother-of-pearl head rising to look over the human crew. Bob could see enough to know Rorufarargrig was not returning to their nest. Monty turned and clutched the thin rail as a wave rocked the ramp. He stepped out of the way of the team dragging a large canvas tent—the nearest thing on board to a D'Moran-sized body bag.

As they struggled past him, Monty looked out at the waves. At the edge of the light, he saw a series of black triangular porpoise fins break the water and silently disappear. Perhaps they had come to listen to the unearthly wail now rising from the bowels of the ship. The D'Morans were in mourning and didn't care who or what heard them.

Jason was waiting for Monty as he came back on board.

"Monty. We're still on mission." His voice was a whisper, delivered precisely into Monty's ear, his hand gripping Monty's shoulder. "Until we hear that it's all over, you have to keep it up. You may not go after Mallson. You'll keep in line. It won't be easy. It won't be for any of us."

Monty broke away. "You're going to let him get away with murder?"

Jason swallowed. "For now. Yes. That's the order. Don't forget we don't know for sure. You didn't see him do it. We don't know there wasn't someone or something else already hiding in the boat. We can't draw any more attention to this. There's no way to do a proper investigation. Surely you see that?"

Monty stroked his moustache. "You know this is a first, an absolute first."

Jason waited.

Monty smiled grimly and said, "I've never doubted my life in the Guild. I've never doubted it...until now."

"Monty..."

"I'll be with the D'Morans."

Monty strode off, leaving Jason to stand and watch him go.

The D'Morans, some twenty of them, had worked their way into a single enormous hammock designed for only four or five. There were legs upon legs, intertwined with more legs.

"Bob?" called Monty quietly.

The mass stirred and a head worked its way out toward the air. "Monty?"

"Can we talk?"

"Oh, Monty. What is there to say? Let us be. You can never understand how this hurts."

"No, I probably can't. But it hurts for us too. I need to know why he did it, why he was out there. What was he thinking? The guests were never supposed to know you guys were on board."

The words "out there" caused a twitch across the whole body of D'Morans.

"Monty...It was you. He was protecting you. When we saw the faults coming back, we thought...perhaps you hadn't completed everything. Perhaps there was some simple thing you had overlooked. Rather than cause you embarrassment, he felt he could slip out in the dark when no passengers would be around and perform the checks himself."

"'Cause me embarrassment.' Are you serious?"

Several other voices began talking in D'Moran.

"You see, Monty..." said Bob, "We didn't agree with his going. Several of us thought his behavior was becoming odd. But he insisted; he could be stubborn when he wanted. And...we still don't know if he was right or not, do we?"

Monty felt the cutting edge of the D'Moran attitude. They assumed themselves superior, and in some ways perhaps they were, but here he was offering condolences and friendship and receiving, in reply, the assumption of his inferiority. They were willing to believe he had screwed up, that this was his fault. Monty looked at the solemn face gazing out at him and saw nothing of the desire for contact he had found in Rory. He saw nothing of the reciprocation he had worked so hard to encourage. He saw only an alien assuming the worst—a judge in the very act of bringing down the gavel.

CHAPTER 7

At lunchtime the next day, Monty was on duty in the dining room. Certain cruise passengers were throwing each other into the swimming pool, delaying lunch. The huge dining room windows looked out onto the long promenade deck with the pool nestled within it. Monty watched Mallson rallying one group of laughing men as they corralled a female guest and plunged her shrieking into the water.

That they were all leaders of industry, respected and feared, made the pranks incongruous enough. That most of them were middle-aged and older, with excess fat and graying hair, made Monty think it bizarre. Mallson stood out from the others, taller and younger, a business leader of the boy-genius type.

The noise as they rolled in for lunch had Monty and his colleagues wincing. Once they were settled, he put on his best poker face and stepped up to the table to pour the wine.

"Good afternoon, Mr. Mallson. I trust you are enjoying the cruise?"

Mallson's chiseled face was in a perpetual grin. He constantly moved, if only to bounce one knee in time to unheard music. His age was impossible to guess; his pale hair and bright eyes gave Monty the disquieting suspicion of perpetual youth. His large frame made his chair seem undersized.

He looked up. "Ah, Montgomery. Missed you this morning. Couldn't get up in time for breakfast, eh?"

Monty's stomach twisted at the gregarious wink from the man, who, no matter what the circumstances, seemed always to be gathering fellow conspirators into the next hilarious jape.

"No, sir. I had the late shift the last couple of days. I hope William served you adequately this morning."

"Oh yes, but he doesn't have your wonderfully entertaining moustache."

"Indeed, sir, few do. The art of the handlebar is a dying one." Monty smiled and moved round the table with the bottle.

As he poured more wine, he heard one of the other diners say quietly, "Did you get an answer from Chandler?"

From the corner of his eye, Monty saw Mallson lift his index finger toward Monty and not reply.

Mallson said to the table, "Did I tell you about the time President Angnango's rope slipped while she and I were halfway up El Capitan?"

Monty would be allowed to overhear nothing useful. He turned away from the table.

▭

Early morning the next day, the ship drew near Greater Iceland, the edge of the European ice shelf.

Monty listened while Brian, facilitator for the cruise's conference sessions and another Guild plant, provided a commentary over the public address system. "You'll notice, ladies and gentlemen, the seals on the edge of the ice. These are some of the few creatures to benefit from La Grande Surprise."

Monty stood, a tray of warm drinks in hand, at the periphery of a group of passengers.

Brian continued, "Too late, humanity realized how fragile we are; how delicate the balance between the atmospheric and oceanic weather; how quickly major changes could overcome us. The advance of the ice upon Northern Europe may have come suddenly, but it will be slow in going. It's ironic, ladies and gentlemen, that climatic instability was predicted long before and, yet, is still referred to as 'The Great Surprise.'"

Monty listened to the mumbling.

"Oh, please. Spare us the breast-beating."

"Wait, soon he'll say it's all the fault of those greedy businessmen and politicians."

Several in the group laughed.

"There's enough of us to make him walk the plank, isn't there?"

Brian's voice interrupted more laughter. "I think it's right to stand in silence for a moment to commemorate those who have lost their lives, their homes, and indeed, their countries to the ice."

Those nearest Monty chose, instead, to take drinks from his tray.

Monty smiled, knowing that, even if they weren't listening to the message, at least the D'Moran electronics in the tray were linking into every man's show-g and transferring as much of the contents as time allowed to the central datacore belowdecks. If Monty could do nothing else, at least he could take satisfaction from his work.

Brian's voice seemed to echo back from the frozen sea, "As you continue your conversations, ladies and gentlemen, on the future of business here at the turn of the century, look out and consider how this happened. Was there anything the businesses of two hundred years ago could have done?"

Late that afternoon, Monty spied Mallson in the corridor outside a cabin door.

"Ah, Montgomery, you'll do! Tell me what you think this is."

"Mr. Mallson?" Monty forced himself to be steady.

Mallson grinned, his face aglow. He put one hand on Monty's shoulder and held out his other. In his palm was a dark metallic object. One end was a cluster of five spheres, the other end a spike.

Monty recognized it. He knew all the D'Moran surveillance hardware in use on the ship.

"A piece of jewelry, sir?"

"Hmm. That's what I thought at first, but there's no clasp."

"I think my fiancée had something like that once. I believe it is attached using a small magnet inside the clothing. Did you find it out here?"

"No, in my assistant's room. Odd, isn't it?"

Monty could see in his eyes that Mallson knew exactly what it was. This conversation was a game, but not one Monty was willing to concede. "I'll take it to the Purser's Office, sir, and see if the previous occupants of your cabin reported losing it."

Mallson's hand closed over the device. "No. Tell him about it. I'll keep it safe until you come up with an owner."

Monty didn't smile. "Yes, sir."

Mallson's assistant, the other delegate from Big H, Earth's largest company, appeared in the corridor and approached silently. He was a small man, with a lined and leathery Tibetan face, registered under the unlikely name of Smith. Monty had not heard him speak since he came on board.

Mallson said, "Something in your room." He held out his hand to show him.

The little man raised an eyebrow and looked up from the device to Mallson's face.

Mallson, with a slight motion of his head, instructed Smith to go inside the cabin. He clapped his hand on Monty's shoulder and said, "That will be all, Montgomery."

Monty watched the pair enter the room, his heart pounding. He wondered how many other business leaders on board had been the cause of someone's death: by neglect or discrimination, by allowing unsafe working conditions, by selling faulty products, by sticking poles in their legs and casting them adrift on the ocean until they died of fear...

Monty turned a corner then stopped, punched his fist into the corridor wall, yelled in pain, and walked on.

That night Monty sat on the stairs leading down to the crew quarters, a can of slightly off beer in hand. On the steps below him sat the other Discoverers. Sitting on top of a cupboard at the foot of the stairs, Interpreter Jason Collins was also nursing a beer and scratching idly at the back of his sunburned head.

"Today was the day," he said quietly. "Brian did a great job. I'm sure you all heard his tone when we were at the ice. He laid it on even thicker as the day went on. Right after lunch, he got them annoyed enough to really start letting go. No one is talking about Rory. Either no one knows, or those who do are keeping it to themselves. Either way, the rest are talking freely. We're recording some excellent stuff. Despite our problems, the "Future of Business Cruise" sails on.

"The trends are coming down to this: Business always walks the line between 'Let the buyer beware' and 'The Universal Duty of Care'. We're hearing strategies emerging to bring that line firmly back toward the 'buyer beware.' The 'Duty' only became 'Universal' in 2147. Fifty-two years isn't long enough for it to be immune to challenges. The other trend we're hearing is the return to secrecy under the guise of proprietary information. We've gathered a lot of data on who-is-where in this shift. These companies we've got on board are the ones the others will follow. The world economy is pivoting on the decisions these guys make. I want you all to hang tight for the next few days. The setup is working, despite our fears to the contrary. Don't slip, anyone. There's more data to gather, more private nighttime conferences..."—Jason glanced at Monty—"It's working. Congratulations, everyone. Hang in there."

Jason lifted his beer in a silent toast.

Monty raised a hand and said, "What about Mallson? He found one of the microphones in Smith's cabin. I think he knows what it is."

Jason nodded. "Again, there is no overt sign of a behavior change. Still, that little guy has yet to utter a single word—even when they're alone. Maybe they came expecting to be overheard. They may have come across the mic after...Rory. They may have started a serious search after that. Then, again, they may not have put two and two together, preferring to imagine that the mic was planted by a competitor—one of the other guests. We're watching. We're listening."

Monty muttered, "That's all we bloody do."

In a quiet moment after dark on the last evening of the cruise, Monty leaned over the railing and drank in the cold fresh air. The guests had been particularly odious at dinner, making repeated jokes about bugs and insects. Monty felt they were deliberately making references to D'Morans.

He drew in his head from the wind and realized he was not alone.

"Fantastic evening, isn't it?" Mallson was leaning next to him at the railing. Over his shoulder, Monty could see the Tibetan, standing as if on guard by the door that would have been Monty's nearest escape.

"Mr. Mallson, how can I help you?"

"Relax, Montgomery. You're off duty. It's the last night. Just relax." Mallson sniffed the fresh air. "Oh, and just for reference, it's 'Mallson' not 'Mr. Mallson.' You've been getting it wrong the whole cruise."

Monty nodded, not knowing what to say, wondering if he was in danger of being thrown overboard.

Mallson said, "It was cleverly done. It took us a while to work it out." He paused. "Quite well done." Still looking out to sea, he continued matter-of-factly, "You work for the World Historical Guild. All of you. This whole thing—the entire cruise—is a huge setup. I'm...I admire it— really. I couldn't have done it better myself. If I ever hear whose mind was behind this, I'll have them working for me within a week."

Monty said nothing. Mallson went on, "It was well done, but it is entirely pointless. There was nothing said or done here that the Guild can effectively use. You see..." Mallson looked down at the deck rail and picked at the wood with a fingernail. "There's nothing anyone can do. It doesn't work that way anymore." He looked at Monty. "Do you know what it means when they call a corporation an 'eternal person'?"

Monty nodded and noted the fire in Mallson's eyes. "I've heard the phrase."

"It means that no one person matters anymore. My company will go on after I'm dead. They all will. A properly constructed company is impervious to being derailed by a single individual. But that means that individuals, like you or me, can't take any of the credit for their successes anymore. Gone are the days of the heroic lone entrepreneur forging destiny. Our creations have a life of their own, Montgomery. Who was it talked about the corporation not being subject to 'imbecilities or the death of the natural body'?"

"Lord Coke, but that was in the seventeenth century."

Mallson laughed and shook his head. "Bloody historians! I knew you'd know. But doesn't that scare you?"

"You scare me. You're young—and rich—and consider yourself beyond the law."

Mallson laughed again. "All true but ultimately irrelevant. I'm impressed by your illegal use of aliens and offworld tech though. Bit of a shame about that thing in the lifeboat, wasn't it? But that's what the future is about—humanity going out there, doing what we do best on a galactic scale. It isn't about you and me. It's about businesses reaching out to other worlds. That's humanity surviving into history. My company is humanity's vehicle. That's the 'Future of Business.' Isn't that what you wanted to overhear us say?" He paused, staring into Monty's face, and then looked out to the dark horizon. "I find that incredibly exciting, don't you? The company will become humanity, not has-beens like us, Montgomery. Personally, I like to think that the 'H' in 'Big H' stands for 'human.' But there'll eventually come a day when the company no longer employs any humans at all. You and your Guild mentors will one day wake up to that."

"Is there a point that you might be coming to soon?"

The smile left Mallson's face. "You tricked delegates from the top one hundred companies in the world with the promise of beautiful scenery, unlimited food, and unrecorded conversations. Can you imagine the lawsuits you guys are going to be hit with after this?"

"We actually promised a cruise where there would be no Recorders."

A flicker of doubt crossed Mallson's face, then he smiled and said, "Clever. You might make that stand up." He snorted. "The moment I decide that the Guild could threaten Big H is the moment that marks its end. Do you really think I'd let a jumped-up crew of librarians and archivists hamstring humanity's future? You know I won't let that happen, don't you?"

"I thought you said one individual doesn't count. Doesn't that go for one company too? I think humanity will survive any damage your company tries to inflict on it. It'll survive with the help of the Guild—and despite you."

Mallson blinked and said, "So you're an Asimovian, are you? I thought all your kind had been purged—when was it—midcentury?"

"Oh, you really have been making a study of the Guild. We refer to them as Foundationalists. The idea that we could actively control the progress of the human race was popular for a while. We got over it. The Guild can advise without thinking it commands."

Mallson laughed again. "What a waste." He stood upright and, turning, leaned his back against the railing. Laughing, he stretched his arms out wide to embrace the whole ship. He shouted, "What a fucking waste!"

Monty tried to step around him. Mallson launched himself forward and pushed Monty up against the wall. Monty gagged as Mallson's large hand tightened around his neck.

"I'm still talking."

Their eyes locked and Monty wondered how long it would take the guys on duty at the monitors to get him help.

Mallson continued, "Whenever someone wastes my time or my company's resources, do you know what I do? I replace them. It costs less to buy a couple of fresh Montgomerys than to rehabilitate one. That's business. Go back to your Guild, shave off that silly moustache, live your life of obscure academic introspection—just don't dare have me notice you again."

By the time help came through the doors, Monty was alone, still leaning against the wall rubbing his throat.

⎯⎯

Seb66 watched Monty as he held himself against the frame of the shuttle's flight cabin doorway. He disagreed with the Discoverer's assertion about death. For him, a lonely decline into power failure was not making anything trivial. For a Recorder to lose even one recording entrusted to him was a violation. To lose them all was unthinkable. He was experiencing an emotion that might be equivalent to Monty's anger —without the urge Monty displayed to break things.

Monty was looking at him, a very different expression on his face.

"Seb, were you expecting to see someone called Mallson on Hoyle Station?"

The Recorder hesitated a moment before replying. "Yes, I was."

CHAPTER 8

"Desk! Hello, desk! It's been so long!" Monty threw himself into his chair and rolled it from one end of his desk to the other.

"I'm sure it's missed you," Peta said, smiling.

"Well, how would you like being left all alone for weeks in a dusty office, surrounded by dour Discoverers and incurious Interpreters? Hmm?"

"Monty, you're too much!"

She stood at the entrance to Monty's work area in a large office packed with similar areas, each with shoulder-high partitions and identical desks. She enjoyed the order, the underlying symmetry. The Guild staff did their best to hide it under chaos. Each Discoverer chose unique decorations and displays: some had exotic plant life, some few had small alien creatures in cages or tanks, one or two had working dioramas of ancient transportation or cityscapes.

Monty was different, of course. He chose to leave the wide shelves at the top of his partitions largely empty. His display consisted of two objects: detailed models of Earth's earliest space fleet. *The Indomitable* and *The Invincible* were the ships sent to introduce Earth to its galactic neighbors. They would always symbolize both success and danger for all humans who came after. *The Invincible* returned; *The Indomitable* did not.

Each of Monty's models had collected a thin layer of dust. As she traced her finger along one fin, Peta said quietly, "Jason briefed me about what happened."

Monty looked up from hamming affectionate strokes across the desk's surface. "Including how he made me watch someone getting away with murder?"

"Yeah, he told me." She paused. "He told me you were having doubts about the Guild. I didn't believe him."

"Did I ever tell you what I thought I'd achieve—you know—sometime in my career?"

"What?" She frowned and then smiled.

"That one." He pointed at the model of *The Indomitable*. "I thought if anyone were looking for it, it would be the Guild. That's the job I wanted." He smiled and stroked his moustache. "What do I actually do?" He looked up into her eyes. "I listen for days to fat-cat businessmen telling each other fart jokes. And when one of them...kills a friend...the Guild has me sit on my hands and do nothing."

"Who is it you think did it?"

"An overgrown adolescent called Mallson, Big H. Now I admit it isn't a cert, but I think we should be trying to get him...at least trying."

"Jason said there were other possibilities."

Monty shook his head. "I don't see them."

"He told me how weird the D'Morans got. Maybe they had something to do with it? It might have been a domestic matter."

Monty stared at his desk. "Unlikely."

"Then there's the other guy from Big H. The quiet guy. He was off-monitor all afternoon. Did you consider him?"

"I...didn't know that."

"You see, Monty, if it was someone like that, it might lead them to overconfidence. It might be easier to prevent the next murder."

She tapped the plaque embedded in the desk. The writing, in ornate script, began with *There is a history in all men's lives...* "So, listen..."

Monty winced slightly as Peta's voice grew louder, clipped and forceful, knowing his peers were hearing him being lectured.

"...It's our way, Monty. This isn't any different. Look at a guy's past, look at his present, see where he's going. Whoever it was, we'll get him. But not today. Okay?"

Not ready to concede, Monty tried to slow her down. "Look, I did some digging already. It looks like there is a team tracking Mallson; someone is in that private city Big H uses for a headquarters. Maybe I could get involved in whatever that team's doing, maybe get inside..."

"No! You're involved in what we're doing here."

Monty shook his head. "Hmm...then maybe I am in the wrong job altogether."

"Yeah, right. Monty, you know well enough being in the Guild isn't a job; it's a vocation. I'm sorry if the D'Moran was a friend, and I'm sorry you were put in that situation. I won't tell you to get over it; I doubt that you should. You're right to be angry at injustice that isn't met with an appropriate reaction. But that's the point, isn't it? The way you feel is why you're here. It's why I'm standing here."

Peta gestured with her arms as if she was addressing a large room, making Monty lean back into his chair. She continued, in full flight, "I don't want to see characters like Mallson ruining the Earth again. I don't want to see murders or famines or wars or catastrophes visited on the innocent. Preventing repeats of that stuff is what the Guild's all about. You aren't going anywhere; you know you can do the most good right here. If anyone's going to go after Mallson, absolutely we'll do it, but only when we're ready." She waited to see if he would argue.

He didn't.

"Like I always say, don't be investing too much in your own plans, Monty. You've got to be ready for the next curve history throws us. Get your expenses filled out. Meeting in half an hour, my office. You've got a new assignment. Mallson and *The Indomitable* will have to wait a while longer."

Monty smiled. "Yes, ma'am."

Peta smiled in return. "Me and your desk, we're both glad you're back."

Peta's office was elevated ten steps higher than the main area. She looked out across the tangled mass of desk displays, plants, and flags. She saw Monty's head rise above the partitions and, from various points, his peers gathering for her meeting.

In a way, she sympathized with those who had to travel. She enjoyed the stability of office routine. The Discoverers brought information to her; she did not have to go anywhere to acquire it herself. No Interpreter did. She got a buzz from seeing her team moving together for a common purpose. She also enjoyed giving them her presentations, watching the curiosity in their eyes change to eagerness—even passion—for finding the truth.

Monty sat down first, dressed as usual in a dark jacket, dark trousers, and white shirt. A long time had passed since she had seen him wear anything with color. His moustache had been trimmed and waxed proba- bly, she guessed, at the end of the cruise, a small ritual to help him back into his routines.

Grant and Scott came in together. One neat, if not perhaps a little too neat. The other so ragged, it could only be deliberate.

Jacob followed them in, a beat late and a little out of breath. He was shorter, younger, and dressed in a loose brown jacket over a shirt worn a day too long. That his dark curly hair lacked attention was highlighted by sitting next to perfectly turned-out Monty. Peta smiled at him, aware of a distant echo of a motherly reaction.

"Now," she said, as they were still settling in their chairs, "we have a new one. Trainee Interpreter Fishbourne has come up with something from the data brought in from the cruise."

"That was quick," muttered Jacob.

Peta smiled at him. "I gave the trainees the job of sifting through the anomalous data. We had the system strip off communications that have unique or near-unique addressees or origins. Fishbourne found one in Monty's stash."

"Do I get a bonus?" Monty asked. His face split into a calculated grin.

"Sure. Ask in the cafeteria for your free half a donut. Now, listen...This may not be as big as it sounds; it may be a dead end." She paused and looked at each of the four faces. "But we're going to work it as if it were the real thing. Okay?"

Monty said, "What is it?"

"An electronic note from Mrs. Elizabeth Croxley. You extracted it from her husband, Hal. He was the delegate from Chesterton Micros. It says:

Didn't make the doctor's this morning. Heard from Jan, now she's down with it too. I'll see how I feel tomorrow. Hope it wasn't something in that damned Halva sack. Don't work late tonight.

"It was the last thing she ever wrote. Hal found her dead that night; I guess that's why he kept the message. Fishbourne came up with two links. The first is, of course, 'the Halva.' Fifteen Halva have visited Earth from Caracu. The first came alone to the Foundation for the Language Research Summer Workshop five years ago. Elizabeth was working there before she died.

"The second link was the person called Jan. Janice Bedford worked as an intern in Elizabeth Croxley's office that summer. They both died within a week of each other, cause of death reported as pneumonia. Both were cremated.

"Fishbourne had the Workshop checked. It was held at a woodland retreat. Nice sounding place, lots of cottages and paths in the woods. It's now a military storage site, protected by shoot-to-kill regulations and a brigade of the finest automatons."

Monty, hoping to relax for a while, started to feel his time back in the office slipping away. Raising his hand, he said, "Peta, people do die of pneumonia every now and then. Is there a real story here?"

"I don't know, Monty. I want you to go to the Foundation for Language Research. Find out who else was in contact with the Halva. Grant, I want you to find out how and why the military acquired the place in the woods. Scott, get into the xenodatabases, find out what the 'Halva sack' might be and what might be in it. Jacob, find these women's medical records or what happened to them. Better yet, who else has accessed them and when.

"Gentlemen, you are all well aware what this would mean if an alien illness got through five years ago. Of course, no one is saying aloud that's a possibility. Get me the facts. We'll determine if something went wrong after seeing what you bring in. Off you go!"

As the room cleared, Monty held back.

"Monty?"

"If a Halva brought contamination to Earth, a lot of heads will have to roll. I'm surprised you're just sending us out to sniff around. Five years isn't long. All the players will still be around."

"It's called 'beating the bushes.' You know what that means?"

"Hmm. Grouse hunting? One of the former quaint customs of the Scots."

Nodding, Peta answered, "The servants would make a lot of noise so the grouse would fly up into the gunsights of the landowners."

"Is the Guild ready to take on the size of the game that might fly out of this one?"

"If it isn't, it should be. We've gotten tame recently, Monty. The Preservers have been relatively silent. It doesn't hurt them to be woken up once in a while."

"Spoken like a true Interpreter."

"Go discover something for me."

Monty nodded. As he turned to leave, Peta said, "You might end up going to Hoyle Station if this does have any depth to it."

Monty stopped in his tracks and turned to face her.

Peta smiled a mischievous smile. "Maybe I'll go with you."

"Funny. Very funny. An Interpreter in the field. Heavens save us!"

Peta laughed. Monty smiled and, making an exaggerated bow, backed out of the office. Peta laughed again, shook her head, and smiled watching him go.

Peta stood backstage. The stage curtain was closed. In the semidark, the shapes of stage equipment, curtains in piles, coils of cabling, and carts laden with lights made her think of a graveyard at night. Everything was completely still and tense, with the possibility that any of them could transform and move at the turning of one's back.

She could hear the voice through the auditorium speakers from the land of the living beyond the curtain. She wasn't listening to the words but to the rhythm; she could feel the punchline coming. The speaker delivered it with a flourish and precision. The audience roared with laughter.

Not bad, she thought, *he's doing stand-up at a planning meeting*. She looked around at the faces of her team, her nervous stand-ins for the real back-stage crew. *Just as well we're in the wings*. She narrowed her eyes and then willed them to relax. She turned to the Recorder at her side.

"Could you have told that joke as well?"

He looked slightly up into her eyes and said, "Identically. Though, I might have done a little tap dance at the end. It depends on how well the group knows me and each other."

She nodded and said, "Good Luck."

"Thank you."

The speaker was saying, "Okay, we're going to take a five-minute break. When we return, Jack will say a few words about the Accounting Department's view of all this. We're doing well. I think the solutions we're outlining are firming up nicely. Jack, I'll find you a better mic stand. Okay, everybody, back in five!"

The curtain billowed, and another Recorder stepped quickly into the shadows.

Peta watched as the small figure went straight to its counterpart, transferred a microphone to its lapel, and asked, "Ready?"

The Recorder nodded and they shook hands or, perhaps Peta thought, more like held hands for a long moment.

They were dressed identically in white suits, black shirts, flame-red ties, and polished black shoes. At five feet tall, they stood only just shorter than herself. Both clapped hands once, spun on their heels in a complete circle, and grinned. They moved like experienced performers.

It's not kidding about the tap dance, Peta thought. She mused they would have drawn an instant and appreciative crowd in other circumstances, perhaps on a street corner.

Simultaneously one said, "Let's go!" and the other, "Okay!" The "Okay" Recorder took the mic stand from Peta's waiting colleague, and with a kind of dancing skip, he was through the curtains. They heard his voice—the same voice—quietly saying, "Here you go, Jack! This one won't wobble so much. Four minutes till you're on. Time to practice your breathing exercises."

Peta's eyes were on the Recorder who had joined them from the stage; his eyes were scanning the group attentively.

I wonder what it sees, she thought.

Uniquely identified by his electronic tag, permanently glowing through the back of his right hand, this was Seb66. The same name tag worn by the Recorder now on stage.

Seb66 shook his head slightly as he saw her watching him. "I'm sorry you're not getting quite what you paid for," he said.

"Why do you say that?" she asked.

"We were supposed to be exact duplicates. But he said, 'Okay.' I said, 'Let's go.' When we synced our recent experiences, just for a moment, we were the same." He shrugged. "It didn't last long."

Peta was taken a little by surprise that such a minor thing should be worth mentioning but noted that while he split hairs about duplication, he was smiling as if he knew it was absurd. It seemed to her that he was enjoying himself. *This one might be fun.*

She smiled and said, "Well, Sebastian Sixty-six, the things we do for history!"

She wondered if the two Recorders knew what kind of history they were making by carrying the same number. She hoped they had some awareness of its gravity and illegality.

<h1 style="text-align:center">CHAPTER 9</h1>

Monty wasted no time. As soon as he could get away from the office, he walked to his favorite café. With a fresh pot of tea before him and the quiet London square spread out below, he could relax and think.

Monty thought Peta was fine as a boss despite, or perhaps because, she didn't know quite how her teams worked. Her Discoverers enjoyed a great deal of latitude in their methods. He enjoyed setting his own schedule and not having to justify it. He could go where he pleased, take side trips if he wanted. As long as he brought back useful information and in sufficient quantity, Peta never seemed to mind. He was in one of the most successful teams, under a renowned boss, and that was the one thing in his life he didn't want to change.

Before turning his mind to his new assignment, he paused, as always, to remember. This café had been Anet's favorite too. He often imagined her deciding to break off their engagement while sitting at one of these tables.

So much was associated with this place—visits during their engagement, his visits afterward. So much time, so much emotion.

He watched a young couple at another table for a while. He mused about the good picture they made of how history works—people associating the big events of their lives with places and, then, passing on those places to new people. He looked at the young woman's eyes, so firmly fixed on her lover's face. He wondered what secrets she was keeping from him, what misfortune awaited the unsuspecting fellow around the next turn in the road. Monty wondered if his data-gatherer had the range to cold-connect to her show-g across the tables.

His second cup of tea brought him back to the present. He picked up his show-g and called an old acquaintance.

"Mrs. Kinda? Hello, this is Montgomery Sheldrake."

The elderly woman replied, "Ah, Mr. Sheldrake. Nice to speak to you again."

"And to hear you again."

"I can assume you are still wearing the overly large moustache?"

"Yes, Mrs. Kinda, I am. How else would people recognize me?"

"And that you are not calling with any bad news for me?"

"Oh no, nothing of that sort. Is everything okay with the cottage?"

"All is well, Mr. Sheldrake. I've had a few visitors in recent months, but all of them welcome, thankfully."

"Good. I have a question for you. I remember you used to have dealings with the Foundation for Language Research. Did you ever come across a lady called Elizabeth Croxley or hear anything about a visitor from Caracu—a Halva, I believe."

"Oh, now...Let me think. What year would this be? Recently or long ago?"

"Five years ago."

"Oh, well...I know they have visitors at their summer workshops. I never go; I am always afraid of meeting someone I know. But the Halva, you say?"

"That's right."

"I know them alright. Charming and hopelessly impractical. They can talk your limbs off if you give them half a chance. They're a race totally dependent on others for their technology. They couldn't design their way off a toilet, if you'll pardon me."

Monty laughed and said, "I know what you mean. Not the sort to be involved in shady deals or vast alien conspiracies then?"

"Well, one can never make broad generalizations, Mr. Sheldrake, but I'd say their whole planet's a complete waste of space. I doubt they have ever done anything to warrant anyone's attention, even that of Earth. Why are you asking?"

"Oh, nothing urgent. I have to investigate one of their visitors, find out who it talked to, where it went. That sort of thing."

"You are too interesting a man to have such a dull occupation, Mr. Sheldrake. I'm sorry for you."

"Mrs. Kinda, thank you for your help. I knew I could count on you for the straight story. It's been nice to chat with you."

"And with you. Call again."

Monty sat thinking about Mrs. Kinda. He liked women who talked straight, a characteristic Mrs. Kinda shared with Peta. Though he rarely saw Mrs. Kinda, he always enjoyed his interactions with her. She had no reason to be anything other than honest with him, and he with her. He always knew where he stood. The same was true for Peta and why he was comfortable working for her.

He would have liked to talk to someone about Halva biology to see if he could discover some interesting bits of information before Scott did. Anet had devoted her life to xenobiology; she would be a mine of information if she didn't find it so awkward talking to him. Instead, he would have to go and see someone at the Foundation for Language Research. The thought of spending time with dusty academics was not appealing.

By the time the tea was cold, his show-g had received a document. It was from Mrs. Kinda. Its title was "FLR Summer Workshop, Program of Events," with a date five years before. Within the colorful pages, she had highlighted several names for him to contact.

Monty waited patiently in a small room. The red light next to the clock above the door glowed with an aura of unquestionable authority. Through speakers built into his chair, he was listening to the audio show being broadcast from the other side of the door. He had taken off his long black coat, which he usually draped over his shoulders like a cape. In the red light, the brown of his walking stick faded to black, but its gold knob glowed.

He slowed his breathing in preparation.

He was walking through the trees, the horse's reins firmly in his left hand. He stopped to bring down the mask across his eyes. Mist drifted in the slight breeze. The light rain, cool and fresh, trickled from the branches and brought up the deep smell of the earth. The pistol weighed heavily in his right hand. In the dripping quiet, he felt his authority extend over the road. Here was his place. None passed but by his consent. He and the horse waited, both silent, for the arrival of their next victim.

The light went out, the door opened, and two people hurried through the room and left. A small plump woman leaned through the doorway saying, "That's that...And you are...?"

With a smile on his lips, the highwayman stepped into the road.

"I'm Montgomery Sheldrake of the World Historical Guild."

"I'm sorry..." She looked puzzled. "Which show are you here for?"

"I'm not appearing on a show. I'm here to meet Mada Zwigli."

"That's me! Who did you say you were?"

"Monty. Please call me Monty."

He stood and towered over her. She looked up and, as usual for someone meeting him for the first time, her gaze rested long on his moustache.

"I am from the World Historical Guild, and I had arranged to speak to you about the Foundation's Summer Workshops."

"Humph! I don't remember anything about this."

"I'm sure that's an occupational hazard at a busy station like this." He smiled his most charming smile.

"What do you need to know about the Workshops?"

"The Guild is interested in creating an archive featuring some of the offworld guests that have appeared over the last few years."

Mada turned and picked up a show-g, making entries as she spoke. "Any in particular? Or is this just another exposé of drunken D'Morans?"

"Fun as that might be, let's pick another out of the air. Let's say...the Halva." She looked up, her eyes shining. "Oh, lovely people...lovely people. Wonderful conversationalists...great understanding of the underlying principles of language."

"You met the first one? When was that now...six years ago?"

"That's right—or maybe five." She looked at her show-g but wasn't focused on it. "That was the summer Liz died."

"You knew Liz Croxley?"

"Oh yes! Did you?"

Monty moved, and she followed him to sit in the visitor chairs. Monty said, "I knew the other one who died...Jan."

Mada looked puzzled and said, "Well, it wasn't just Liz and Jan. All five died!"

"All five?"

"Sure, the whole cabin. They all stayed the three weeks together in the same cabin, didn't you know? They all got pneumonia. I never really understood; no one else got it."

"Do you know if they had much to do with the Halva visitor?"

Mada frowned and looked again at Monty's moustache. She looked up into his eyes. "What are you suggesting?"

"You didn't get to run the audio station for our premier linguistic foundation by being dumb. Did any of them sleep with it?"

Mada stood up abruptly. "How dare you! None of that goes on at our workshops!"

"You think. How close was Liz to it? Did they spend time together?"

"What an outrageous thing to suggest! She was Gal-Poro's escort. But that just meant getting him on stage on time." Her face softened a little as she remembered. "He was terrible for stopping and chatting on the way to places. He just had no idea of keeping to a schedule."

"Did he give her any special gifts?"

"I don't see what business this is of yours or your Guild's."

"Mada, please sit down. You said it yourself. They all died. Did you think it was just a coincidence? They spent a lot of time with him!"

"I...I guessed they would have investigated if there was something...You just...You know, you just assume, don't you?"

She sat down again but, as she did so, dropped her show-g.

Monty scooped it off the floor. As he handed it back, their eyes were level. "Here. Don't worry. I'm sorry if I misled you about what I'm doing here. I do want to find out what happened to them. But I need you to let me know what he did or gave to anyone in that cabin."

She nodded, her eyes misting while she thought back to that time. "Gal-Poro gave out lots of gifts. He had little bags that he'd give people. It's a big part of their culture, all very ritualistic and imbued with meaning for them. We thought it was cute, how seriously he took it all."

"What were the gifts?"

"Garbage mostly. Well, I shouldn't say that. I'm sure they had significance for him. To us, they were trinkets."

"Do you still have any?"

She shook her head. "I keep the good stuff if any comes my way."

"Is there someone else who might have kept them?"

She shook her head. "I don't know. I doubt it."

Monty sighed and said, "I'm sorry if I offended you. You can imagine it's difficult knowing what questions to ask. I believe The Guild has a solemn duty to investigate where no one else has or to try to."

She looked up at the clock. "Well, I don't know how you got in here, but right now, you're holding up a time-dependent operation."

They stood, Mada clutching her show-g.

"I know. I'll go." He took his show-g from his pocket, pressed a button, and said, "Here's my card. Call me if anything comes to mind. Please don't mention my visit to anyone."

He turned to go.

"Some of them contained souls," she said.

He turned back. "Souls?"

"The souls of his ancestors. Little cylinders, like a thick shiny stylus. He said it was a great gift to bond our peoples together."

"I guess it didn't work if people didn't keep them."

She smiled sadly. "I guess not."

CHAPTER 10

Monty feared it could be his last day in the office for a while. He went early to the café and lingered long over breakfast.

While he ate, he checked through the innocuous and rather dull files he had stolen from Mada's show-g and watched as the reports came in from the rest of his team.

Jacob had had little success in finding medical records. Grant had found all the military procurement information showing a free and clear purchase of the land shortly after the workshop ended.

Scott's report was comprehensive:

"Halva Sack. Traditional gifts to bond friends and marriages. A sack always contains three gifts. Usually, these are of modest value but can, given the right occasion, be small items of great worth, our equivalent being an engagement ring. In dealing with new races, Halva have been known to give gifts of high personal meaning: keys to a dwelling, family heirlooms, religious artifacts. They believe that the value of the gift to the giver is what counts. They do not seem to mind that other races, ourselves included, do not reciprocate.

We don't know what this Halva gave to Mrs. Croxley. Sorry guys, but there is no way to predict what would have been included in the sack in question."

Peta paced at the front of the conference room. A large display behind her showed portraits of the five dead women. She was deep in thought, and her team patiently waited for her to speak.

"Five people were exposed to something that infected their lungs, but something that wasn't contagious. I'd say the Earth dodged a bullet, gentlemen. It could have been different. That, of course, isn't our immediate concern. The organizers of the workshops may not have known. The doctors who treated the victims probably did. The military certainly found out. We don't need a Preserver to tell us this behavior—this 'covering up' as they used to call it—is not in humanity's best interest. Question One: How did it get in? Question Two: Who decided not to pursue an investigation?"

Peta slowly examined each face.

"Monty, I'm sorry. You're going to Hoyle Station. We need you to...use your contact there. The Halva and all its gifts were scanned, cleared there, and signed off by Dr. Anet Bartula."

Monty closed his eyes and said nothing.

"I was going to come with you, but we've found a Recorder who might be more useful in this instance.

"Jacob, find this Halva. See what he can tell us about what he put in the sacks. I know you might not be back before the rest of us are finished, but we need completeness. Grant, continue with your military contacts. I want the names of decision-makers and policy analysts on duty during our time frame. I want to know if we've suspected any of them of this sort of thing before. Scott, I'm going to assume the details of the infectious agent are being kept somewhere. See the experts; drag every single byte off their systems. It's time The Guild had access to that stuff. If you need more people, let me know.

"I got clearances from the World Government Historical Committee to talk to people. That'll get us close enough—into their offices or homes. You know why we're doing this, guys. It looks like the balance between saving reputations and the needs of humanity at large has been tipped in the wrong direction."

Standing with her arms outstretched, palms up—like scales—she tipped to her right. She smiled, waited, and checked that each pair of eyes was focused on her. She made fists with both hands as she straightened herself and said, "Let's put it back."

▭

Interpreter Michael Dodgeson was older than Peta by several decades, round-shouldered, and with grayed hair. He gave his colleagues the impression he had just stepped out of an old photograph of a nineteen-twenties university professor. He only needed a pipe, shabby cardigan, and cracked leather chair.

Sitting in Peta's office, he said, "Are you sure he's a good idea?"

Peta shrugged. "Too late now."

"True..."

"What is it then?"

"It's the philosopher in me." He held up his universal electronic device. "Show-g, always been called that, from two Japanese words. 'Shou' is hand and 'ji' is machine. We're so used to the distinction between the 'show' and the 'g,' between the machine we make with our hands and what the machine makes: information, images, recordings. I have a bad feeling we're blurring the lines with this one."

Peta shook her head. "No, we're not! It's a tool. We've always used the tools at our disposal. Look at old books. We read them. We x-ray the pages to see if anything else is written there. We scrape the crud out of the spines to look at the pollens and the dust. We analyze the typeface, the grammar, the vocabulary. Now we have more tools that let us look at history in real time—as it's happening—not centuries after. I think it's brilliant!"

Dodgeson shifted uncomfortably in his seat. "I think Recorders blur the lines at the best of times. They have become more than just Public Notaries. They can do things we can't. That's the point, I suppose. But it sets them up as...apart from us. An ordinary tool doesn't have functions beyond those we put into them. Look...Just their internal language has more than four thousand symbols! I doubt we could translate it if we ever got the chance to fully download the contents of one. It means we can't examine them; we have to trust what they tell us about themselves."

Peta frowned, "That's true..."

"I don't know...It makes me worry. The more we rely on them, the more 'g,' the less 'show.' Our tools become something more than we have made, and our information becomes merely something—whatever—they tell us it is."

Peta waved her hand. "It's a unique tool. And what we're doing with this one should make you feel better; it opens the way to more cooperation with them. They wanted this as much as we did, you know. They had no problem agreeing to keep this a secret between us and them. Even to the point of creating the duplicate."

Dodgeson hesitated then said intently, "That alone worries me more than anything else."

Peta laughed and replied, "I get what you mean. But I don't think they realize how important this one is to us. How useful its information could be to us."

Dodgeson nodded. "I know. You have big plans for him. Still, I don't think he's a good idea. You know I'm definitely against his travel outside this facility. It only takes one person to notice there are two of them for the whole thing to become ugly."

Peta glanced at the window of her office. "It's here."

"I'm not." Dodgeson got up and opened the door for Seb66 to enter.

Peta smiled. "See you later, Mike. Come in, Sebastian."

"Thank you," he said loudly. After the quiet of the preceding conversation, his enthusiasm swept into the room ahead of him. "It's good to see you again. I'm looking forward to working with you, Interpreter Melbourne." He held out his hand to shake hers and scanned his eyes around her office, smiling as he did so. "Looking forward to it!"

He sat on the edge of the chair in front of her desk, slightly bowed his head, and locked onto her eyes.

"What did Interpreter Hollins tell you?" she asked.

"After completing the substitution, we discussed my recent history. Then he told me to report to you for an assignment. Thank you for an efficient operation, by the way. It worked very well."

"He didn't tell you anything more?"

"I can play back our conversation if you'd like. But that's a fair summary."

"You recorded it all, I suppose, including the stutter?"

"Interpreter Hollins's speech difficulties are not something I'd needlessly parade in front of others."

Peta saw the look of concern cross the Recorder's face. A face, she thought, more expressive than that of other Recorders she had worked with. An artifact of his manufacture, she wondered, or a deliberate choice to sample the larger and more open movements of faces from its collection of recordings.

"Of course not! I didn't mean to offend," Peta said, sitting back in her chair.

Seb66 smiled and said, "It takes a lot to offend a Recorder. May I hear something of the work I'll be doing for you?"

"I want you to go to Hoyle Station. A Guild member named Monty Sheldrake is visiting there. You are to record any meetings he asks you to attend. When he's done with you, you come back here and resume your work with Hollins."

"Oh. I see."

Peta waited. Seb66 waited.

She thought it was so nearly human. She could see the eye movements, the smile, the tilt of the head. She could tell from its expression that it had something to say. It was like a polite young man in a junior position in an office, anxious not to step on any toes but keen to do a good job.

Seb66 raised his hand halfway to his chin and pointed his index finger upwards. His name tag glowed green against the flesh tone of his hand.

"A couple of questions do occur, if I may?"

Peta nodded.

"Many highly qualified Recorders are on the permanent staff at Hoyle Station."

Peta paused before saying, "That isn't actually a question."

Seb66 nodded and said, "Grammatically, no, but the fact gives rise to several issues. For instance, there might be some resentment to the importing of someone such as myself."

"Go on."

"My role often requires I exercise a degree of tact and sensitivity to the people I work with. Imposing me on a situation where I'm considered an outsider, or even an unwelcome intrusion, would set me off on the wrong foot."

Peta frowned and said, "You just have to sit there and listen; you don't have to like them. They don't have to like you."

He nodded and said, "True...but Recorders have well-established methods. We avoid unnecessary conflict. We avoid unnecessary rudeness. If our job can be done as well with a smile as with a frown, we choose the smile every time."

"Then you'll get on well with Monty."

The smile left Seb66's face. They stared at each other. "The matter of my being unwelcome by the Hoyle Station staff will need to be addressed. That I'll get on with Discoverer Sheldrake is not an issue."

"I see you've done your homework. I'm impressed."

For a moment, neither's expression changed. She watched the well-chiseled face tilt and soften into a faint smile, its best puppy eyes looking into hers.

She continued, "Before you saw me, you'd already found out who you were going to work with and what rank he has in the Guild. I didn't tell you he was a Discoverer."

Seb66's smile broadened, and he nodded. "I like to be prepared. Before any meeting, I think it's very important to know what the outcome will be."

Peta blinked. She had expected it to dissemble a little. Caught off guard, she said, "That sounds like a lot of analysis for just a Recorder."

Seb66's hands became more animated, and his fingers gave a little ripple as though he were typing in the air. "What you say is true, but often it isn't obvious in a meeting what is important and what isn't. For instance..." He hunched his shoulders, cupping his hands as if sharing something rare and valuable. "In one meeting, the actual words used by the participants are crucial and must be recorded. If two people talk at once, I might ask them to repeat what they've said separately to ensure I've got everything clearly. In another meeting, it might be what isn't said that's important. It might be the glance or the nod, the person avoiding the eyes of another, or the awkward silences that are the salient features of the meeting." He paused and hung his head as if making an embarrassing confession. "Preparation is everything."

Peta blinked and thought, *Damn! I'm being taught something by a bloody machine.* Instead, she said, "You're right, of course. I prepare long and hard for my meetings. I believe those who work for me have the right to expect that I know what I'm doing. I don't like to send anyone off half-cocked."

"I appreciate that. Why am *I* going?"

Peta said simply, "We want you to continue your Big H investigation. We arranged for two people to visit Hoyle Station. You're taking the second ticket. Back him up when he needs you. If he doesn't need you all the time, Hollins and I expect you to improvise."

The Recorder sat back in his chair. "Improvise...as in tell jokes, sing songs?"

"Do a little tap dance..." Peta added.

He laughed lightly. "Thank you for trusting me. How long will I need to make myself available for playbacks after we return to Earth?"

Peta shrugged. "That depends on what Monty discovers. It depends on what you uncover. Expect to be with us longer here than on Hoyle. And I'm no more worried about your impact on the staff up there than I am Monty's; they'll resent both of you. Deal with it. We've been to a lot of trouble to get you. I hope you're worth it."

He smiled and said, "That's good news. Thank you. How much does Discoverer Sheldrake know?"

"Whatever you tell him."

Peta stood and paced behind her desk as she spoke.

"We hadn't anticipated your traveling anywhere. But Monty's presence on Hoyle is an opportunity Hollins and I can't pass up. The station is sufficiently removed from your normal milieu, and I'm willing to take the risk. You shouldn't come across anyone currently working with the other you."

Seb66 nodded. "Very unlikely. As I say, the on-station Recorders are sufficient for the needs there. From what I hear, there is little overlap between the functions performed on Hoyle Station and those of the administration Earthside."

"So, you go there and do what you can. As for Monty, say this to him, as soon as you're alone together: 'I've sent you as a gift.' You might be able to help him resolve some things."

"I will tell him exactly as you've said it."

"I'm sure you will." She stood and pointed at his face across her desk. "Don't you dare imitate me!"

Seb66 smiled and said, "And that completes my Recording."

CHAPTER 11

Monty turned again to the stars and breathed deeply in and out twice.

Seb66 said, "Mallson was my main focus. What do you know of him?"

"That's what Peta meant in her message. You see, I know he's a murderer... Perhaps other people have said the same thing to you? But, of course, I've no proo—"

"Seventeen."

"What?"

"Seventeen other people. You are the eighteenth person to tell me that."

"Then I guess we're his latest victims."

Seb66 nodded, "Perhaps so."

"In what way was he your focus?"

"I've had twelve assignments in different parts of Big H. I've had the opportunity to gather information about him from both humans and Recorders within the organization. On Hoyle, I had hoped to learn how, why, and when he comes and goes. It's been difficult to piece together much about his movements. I understand that he doesn't submit to the regular security tracking, but it seems he spends a lot of time on the station. In the absence of electronic data, the on-station Recorders would have been able to supply eyewitness accounts."

Seb66 sat in the copilot's chair and looked out into space. Monty sat in the pilot's seat and looked across at him.

The Recorder continued, "Mallson is an anomaly. The first time I encountered him, I'd been engaged to facilitate a meeting. Several departments from Big H were represented. They didn't usually interact, and there was tension about who had the authority to make decisions. I guided them through three days of discussions. We were making progress. Then this person walked in, unannounced, and took control. He did it without regard for what was being attempted and what had been achieved. He didn't speak directly to me at all. As far as I could tell, he had an attitude of amused contempt for everyone in the room. It was fascinating. The entire room deferred to him. He spent five minutes outlining what the outcome of the meeting should be, then he left. No one questioned him or protested. When he'd gone, I asked who he was. They laughed and told me: 'Mallson. You don't argue with him.' I made some inquiries about what position he held. And that's when my work started."

"You took him on as a project on your own?" asked Monty surprised.

"At first, yes. I soon exhausted the limits of the available data and had to recruit others to help me. I found that he has no position. I found he has no personnel file. He has no birth certificate, neither national nor international identification. He takes no salary from Big H. But I had seen his authority in action. I discovered something that went against the reason Recorders were created: missing data. Data that was missing on someone important, someone about whom future generations will want to know."

"Are you owned by Big H?" asked Monty warily.

Seb66 was silent long enough that Monty thought he would get no answer. "I was. When I had progressed as far as I could through my own efforts, I returned to the factory for maintenance. It was decided that I should be given the freedom to continue."

"Big H have never suspected what you were up to?"

"I have been cautious in the extreme, using only channels I could justify accessing. Where I could, I set the groundwork for further discussions with Recorders I have already encountered. But, as I said, I have reached the limits of what I could do in place. The makers recently created Sebastian Sixty-six point One and, with the help of the Guild, sent him in to cover my regular duties. That will...would have...enabled me to pursue other avenues of inquiry."

"Nice. Have you come to any conclusions about Mallson?"

"Some. There is much still to learn, but I have pieced together something of his background."

Monty nodded for him to continue.

"Do you remember the late Matthew Arlington the Third?"

"Of course! Lived to be a hundred and something."

"And active until his death. His reign as the head of The H Company lasted sixty-two years. We believe he is Mallson's father."

"Really? Then why isn't Mallson running the show? Oh...he is, isn't he?"

"But not in any documented capacity. The Board still meets; it has a chairman. The company has all the legally required officers. But Mallson is in charge."

"But you said he has no birth certificate."

Seb66 smiled. "Do you know the headquarters facilities in Belgium?"

"I've seen pictures. I know they run a self-contained city."

"The central residential dome is an integrated biocapsule: shopping areas, complete medical facilities, offices, parks, and recreation. Staff can live there for years and never travel beyond its confines. We believe Mallson to be Matthew's only and illegitimate child, born and raised within the corporate city."

"Wait a minute! Mallson can't be more than forty. That would make his father well over sixty when he was born."

Seb66 nodded. "But never legally registered or named. We think the name to be a contraction of 'mall's son' or 'the son who lives in the mall.' A kind of nickname. Forty years ago, 'The Mall' was an unofficial name for the corporate city."

"What a life!"

"He was never formally acknowledged, but he was an open secret. Every staff member knew in whose shadow he walked and with what degree of respect he should be treated."

Monty asked, "So he grew into his father's shoes entirely off the record?"

"Earth's biggest company run by an invisible individual."

Monty stroked his moustache. "Decisions made at the whim of an individual brought up in, what must have been, a restricted environment. Someone like that could be a dangerous lunatic, and no one there would say boo to him."

"Eighteen people I have spoken to believe him to have murdered or arranged murders."

"Why didn't the old bugger acknowledge him?"

"A woman who worked as Baby Mallson's nanny suggested it was a deliberate plan on Matthew's part."

Seb66 turned his head and his shoulders rounded a little, his hands coming together and the fingers rubbing nervously. In a thin female voice, he said,

"You know, I think the old man decided...deliberately wanted the company to bring up the boy...as if he wanted his son to be the best product we ever manufactured."

"You got as close to him as his nanny?"

Seb66 paused and smiled at Monty. In his own voice he said, "I recorded her Last Will and Testament. It took some arranging; several sudden recalls for maintenance cleared the way."

Monty chuckled and shook his head. "I like it. Recorders who lie better than humans. What a world!" They were silent for a moment. "If someone could get close to his show-g...What we'd learn!"

Seb66 shook his head and replied, "He doesn't have one. I understand he has a phenomenal memory and prefers to issue only verbal commands. It makes him even more elusive, even less visible."

Monty was quiet and suddenly still. He said, "I don't want to die."

Seb66 said nothing but waited for him to go on.

"I...kind of made a mess...of my life. I had a chance for a good marriage and blew it. When I said about wanting to see this view all my life, it isn't just that. I wanted to be out there—out here—on the edge of human interaction, on a mixed colony maybe, documenting the exchange of ideas, the way cultures meet and put roots into each other...me and Anet. Her doing real xenobiology. That was what I thought my life would be. From there, I could have gone on to investigate what happened to the first humans who came out here—the ones who didn't come back."

He stopped, pensive. "Anet went her own way. I stayed Discovering: stealing secrets from the unwary and building the databases for the Interpreters to sift through." He smiled at the thought. "I guess I am okay as a Discoverer, but it is a smaller and smaller world. I should be out here in the expansion. I knew I'd really made a mess of things when Rory, Mallson's last—I mean previous—victim was killed. He put himself at risk to cover for me. It shouldn't have happened...I wasn't connected well enough to what was happening. I've thought, at times, I've been only half alive. You see, realizing I'm going to die out here...In a way, that has been something of a relief."

Seb66 said, "But now you say you wish to live."

Monty nodded. "What you've been telling me makes me want to fix a few things. We're in a position to make a difference, you and I. I don't want Mallson to get away with it again. I guess most of what you've learned is only stored inside you. You aren't backed up anywhere?"

Seb66 shook his head. "There's the duplicate Seb Sixty-six, but I now have far more information from the Guild's files than he does. I downloaded many transcriptions of Recordings at your office, but my conclusions and evaluations only exist here." He rolled his fingers on the side of his head as if typing. "That's the one disadvantage of being autonomous."

"I'd give anything for just one more crack at Mallson."

"I will attempt to conserve my energy in the hope of being found eventually. If whoever finds me can return me to the factory, they may be able to restore something of what I carry, including your words."

Monty nodded and said, "Good. Before I go crazy, I'll try and formulate some last words for the folks back home." After a few minutes of silence, Monty laughed. "You know, at the back of my mind, I always thought I would die the way Captain King did."

"Who was Captain King?"

"A highwayman. My highwayman. My link with history. Each Guild Discoverer takes a person from the past; it's like a meditation or a mental discipline if you like. It keeps us rooted, grounded in who we are and why we do what we do; it keeps the past, present, and future together in our minds. Anyway, Captain King died in a shootout with the police of his day. *They* didn't kill him; it was his protégé... what they call 'friendly fire.' I've always suspected that if I work too closely with a partner, the same thing will happen to me." He sighed. "But I've been thinking a lot recently. That is exactly what Anet did. I'd set myself up for it. When she broke off our engagement, I died...not physically but effectively."

"I hope I'm not speaking out of turn, Monty, but you are working closely with someone right now."

Monty said distinctly, "As I said, I've changed my mind about the dying thing." He gave Seb66 a sideways look, imagining anew the feel of a throttling mechanical hand.

▭

Anet Bartula sat in the Hoyle Station dining hall sipping a cup of tea. Tea, instead of coffee, in honor of Monty.

She remembered the café in London. The table they used to sit at; the quiet buzz of whispered conversation; the tablecloths; the discrete, cute waiters. She looked around at the contrasting noisy dining hall's crowded cramped tables and utilitarian décor.

Two tables, two goodbyes. The first she chose, the second...

What is this? I've never missed him.

She had never spent her time on Hoyle Station—first as Assistant Medical Officer, now as Senior—wondering what life with him would have been like.

So why now? Why is his absence doing this?

He hadn't changed much. Those five years had done him little harm.

His moustache was still extraordinary. It probably still felt like the pelt of a stuffed animal. He was still irritating and charming, both devious and straightforward in a snakes-and-ladders kind of way. It had been comfortable to be around him again.

That's what it was. That's what it is. If he'd been really obnoxious, it might be easier to accept that he's gone. He is gone. And I am still trying to understand what happened.

Norman joined her at the table.

"How are you feeling today?" he asked.

She shrugged. "The same."

"Anet, I know you think—"

Not waiting for him to go on, she said, "I think you're wrong, love. Dead wrong. Monty isn't the sort to kill someone. Plain and simple."

Norman shrugged. "The evidence doesn't prove it. It's all circumstantial. But it's all we've got."

"And another thing, he couldn't have got Jimmy's body up into that berth. Not on his own."

"He wasn't on his own, was he, love? There was a Recorder. They're stronger than they look."

She shook her head. "Why wasn't there a record of what went on at the shuttle gate? You know damn well there should have been."

Norman looked around, leaned in over the table, and dropped his voice so low she strained to hear. "That jack-in-the-box Mallson had me switch off the cameras at that gate months ago. He's never told me why, nor has he said to switch them back on. It's as if he does it deliberately just to screw with me. 'Switch off camera 347 today, Norman.' 'No sound recording in the corridor Red 11, Norman.' 'Up your arse, Norman!'"

Anet sighed and drank more tea. "Be careful, love. Please be careful. He'd let you hang for this in a heartbeat."

"I know. I know."

The voice of the duty officer sounded through the room. "All available security officers to Conference Room 12A, Green. All available security officers to Conference Room 12A, Green."

"Oh God, what is it this time?" Norman sighed. Shaking his head, he stood up. Leaning down, he kissed her cheek and said, "Got to go. See you later, love."

"I'll see you in the ER as you bring them in." She smiled.

"Aye, I hope it isn't one of those."

She was left at the table with a cooling cup of tea and the deep desire that Monty had never come to Hoyle Station.

CHAPTER 12

The reception area for arrivals from Earth was flanked with large-leafed plants in pots of growing gel, the seats small and crammed together in tight, unmovable rows. Monty sat, as he had on the flight up, next to a large Indian woman with a vast array of jewelry. She and four chaperones were visiting her husband, who worked in the Office of the Director. It was their first meeting. Monty sympathized with her nervousness.

He had spent a long time talking to her about the history of arranged marriages. She seemed to have no reservations about the process. She, with her family, had been in electronic contact with her husband and his family many times.

"It is very economical," she said, "Why spend years searching for just the right person? One woman can meet only so many men. Let your family search for you! They can find so many more potential mates than you can on your own. Then, there is just the choosing—the choosing, not the finding!"

Monty felt he had missed out, never having participated in such a corporate family enterprise. Of course, his search for the right person had been concluded entirely to his satisfaction. Now, in the bureaucratic silence of the reception area, he wished his traveling companion better fortune with the rest of the marriage process.

When his turn came at the Admissions window, he presented his credentials to the officer, a thin-faced Scotsman with clipped speech and precise movements to match. Against his brown uniform, the white of his station ID stood out clearly: "Hunter, James. Security Chief. All Access."

Chief Hunter stared down at Monty's papers and, without raising his head, looked at Monty from under his brow.

"World Historical Guild? You'll not be finding many bones to dig up in here."

"You'd be surprised where the fates conspire to hide their machinations."

The officer gave Monty a sour smile and looked from one end of his moustache to the other. "Aye, and it takes an Englishman to turn everything upside down for everybody, just in the hope he finds something."

Monty was brought up short by the insulting tone. He leaned forward into the window. "If it were my country under the ice, I'd be grateful to every historian that put pen to paper."

The Scot looked at him and nodded. "Here's your map. Your ID badge. Don't lose it. When you get to your room, you can find yourself a dictionary and look up the difference between 'history' and 'culture.' Now, it says here there's two of you. Where's your friend?"

"Oh, the Recorder will be coming up by freight later."

The officer looked indignant. "Do we not have Recorders enough for you here?"

Monty forced a smile. "We go way back. It wouldn't be the same with a stranger."

Chief Hunter almost smiled back and said, "Aye, I hope you'll both be very happy. Next!"

▭

Monty's first impression of Hoyle Station was not favorable. The corridors smelled like an overused gymnasium. The outer walls, being curved, forced an uncomfortable compromise on the inner furnishings. The corridor narrowed wherever a straight edge was required, like for a bank of vending machines. This created bottlenecks in the traffic flow through the station. Where the large station segments circled the inner rooms, the empty corridors should have been wide. Yet, in practice, every piece of corridor wall had a door or hatch in it, creating potential obstructions. Notice boards dangled from the walls or pieces of equipment were temporarily or permanently—and inconveniently—placed. Even where there was a gap, it seemed to Monty that slow-moving gaggles of people were sucked into the space like logs in an eddy.

He followed the map to his room to find himself standing in a narrow corridor, facing an inner wall with other new arrivals, all equally puzzled.

They could see staggered panels up the wall, each with a different number. Monty's number, 4H67, was the second from the floor. Panel 4H68 was below it and slightly to the right; 4H66 and 4H65 were above. Embedded rungs ran up the wall between them.

A young man waved his ID badge in front of the panel numbered 4H68. It opened, and they watched something the size of a generously proportioned coffin slide out from the wall.

"Oh, I see," said the youngster, "the number really is bigger than the room." He climbed into the coffin and described to his neighbors what they could not see. "There's an entertainment unit that'll be visible through my toes. I guess that's a show-g cradle in the ceiling. What else do we need, eh?"

The man with 4H66 on his badge turned to Monty and said, "You'll have to shave that off; it'll never fit in one of these."

Anet was busy. She enjoyed being busy in a way that wore out her underlings. Her enthusiasm for her job never waned. She had been too busy to get annoyed about Monty's visit, but now that he had arrived, she allowed herself a moment to brew up some genuine resentment.

She had just finished an interminable meeting with Station Admin on the latest morale initiatives when her assistant called to say that a gentleman was waiting in her office.

"Good. Let him make himself very comfortable. He'll be there a while." She went to another part of the station to supervise some inventory taking.

Monty sat in the office of Anet's assistant. It was a small, neat area with a row of plants on a shelf behind the desk. He took in all he could of the world over which his ex-fiancée had dominion.

He studied the assistant's desk. It was largely empty, either a sign of a well-run organization or one with less to do than it liked to admit.

He found the assistant interesting. Put a large handlebar moustache on him, add twenty years, and you would have a reasonable facsimile of Monty himself. The fellow was wearing a green tracksuit, similar to many in red or blue he had seen other staff wearing. Monty wondered if the casual dress indicated an underachievement in professionalism.

He listened to a series of calls that showed the young fellow struggling to be patient with an increasing lack of success.

"Yes, I know the Level Three conference room is in use, I heard already. We don't have any spare capacity. No, it's fully booked...It's booked...It's booked too. We've a visitor using it." A glance in Monty's direction always accompanied this phrase. "I'm sorry. I know...I know...We don't know. You could try Catering; they might have a storage unit you could use."

"Sounds like a busy time," Monty volunteered.

"It always is."

"You didn't tell me your name," Monty stated.

Pausing and wondering how far to follow his boss's apparent hostility to this interloper, he replied, "I'm Derek. Derek Smeade."

"Have you worked for Anet long?"

Derek was reluctant to say. "A couple of years." He changed the subject. "This trouble with the rooms isn't just down to you being here."

"I'm glad to hear it. I am very conscious that it must be a real inconvenience having me turn up like this. I hate disrupting people's routines."

"Really?" Derek smiled in disbelief. "It's a combination of you and some maintenance work on Level Ten. They're breaking up a meeting room into three smaller ones, but it's taking forever. Then there's this rolling librarian conference; the library here holds a load of unique stuff that delegations have brought with them. They queue up on Earth to come and see them in person. Why they can't just look at the electronic versions beats me. That, and the D'Morans."

"D'Morans?"

"Yeah, they came up about two weeks ago. There was some mix-up with their transport. They've nested in a conference room on Level Three and won't come out."

"Really? Is one of them called Bobufaralopic?"

Derek was surprised by Monty's facility with a D'Moran name. "I don't know. I haven't had to deal with them directly. Why?"

"No reason. I might have met him while he was on Earth. I was friends with a D'Moran for a short while; he had an excellent command of English. Might be the same group."

"You should talk to Facilities Management. They'd be glad if someone could negotiate with them."

"I'll see if I have time when I'm done. Have they told you what I'll be doing?" asked Monty.

"No."

Monty noted the implied "of course not."

"Well, it's really just an admin exercise. I need to see the records for 2194, May through July. I need to see the stuff about certain aliens that came through then."

"Why?"

"I don't really know. I hear rumors that Earthside records got lost. So, they sent me to see what you have."

Derek shook his head. "They could ask us to transmit copies. Why do you have to be here?"

"To ask what people remember. Sometimes the written records are ambiguous. The Recorders, of course, will have anything they were present for"—Derek gave a little snort as if what Monty had said were funny"—but it isn't always enough."

Derek narrowed his eyes, "Enough for what?"

Monty was sitting with his walking stick on his lap. He twirled it, putting the point firmly on the floor. He gently turned the knob a degree or two.

Under the trees, he closed his eyes and sniffed at the fresh rain; he felt the stones in the road under his boots. His horse snorted gently over his shoulder. He stepped out into the path of the stagecoach...

"Let me show you!" he said with sudden enthusiasm.

Monty stood up. Pointing to Derek's desk-pad, he said, "Bring up the visitor database for 2194. I'll show you what I mean."

Derek hesitated. He looked at Monty's face. "I'm not sure I should."

"Why not? It's a public record. And I'm going to see it all soon enough. Go ahead."

Something about Monty made Derek feel he was fundamentally unthreatening. The visitor was every bit as annoying as his boss had said, but Derek had always had a soft spot for eccentrics. The way this man dressed, the walking stick, and the crazy moustache were all quite disarming. Such people were a rare sight on Hoyle Station. He tapped in the commands.

Monty moved partway around Derek's desk, where he could see the display. After a few minutes of picking his way through entries in the database, he said, "That one. Let's look at that."

"Why that one?" asked Derek, becoming engaged in the process.

"Just the fact that it's there is interesting."

"I don't get it. It's just a request for a linguist. Look, it says Dr. Bartula put in the request for help talking with the alien, and here's the time they logged in at the Welcome Suite. Doesn't look ambiguous to me."

"I'd ask why they needed help. What was it like talking to this guy? Where had he learned The Language? It's supposed to be universal— well, galactic at least. Was this a case of regional dialects developing? The first time we see something like that is of enormous historical importance."

"It's more likely they were just a bit thick."

"Derek, you could well be right. But the document doesn't say, does it? That"—Monty tossed his cane vertically in the air and caught it again —"that is why I have to talk to the *people* involved. Can I get a copy of that entry?"

"Um...I guess..."

Monty slid his show-g onto the cradle at the side of the desk-pad and pressed several keys.

"Thanks." He turned away from the desk and said loudly, "Now!"

Swinging around the unsuspecting assistant, Monty pointed his cane at Derek's face and shouted, "Where the hell is she? Why am I being kept waiting so long? You've been told to keep me on ice until she decides to grace me with her presence, haven't you? Let me assure you that every moment of this visit is to be accounted for, and every delay—every failure to cooperate—will be part of the record of this trip, including times, places, and names. Tell me where she is and why I'm still waiting!"

Derek was rocked back on his chair; his jaw dropped wide, his eyes on the tip of Monty's cane.

Rescue came from the opening door.

Anet Bartula came into the room, a mug in one hand, a show-g in the other, pushing the door with her foot. "What's all this noise?"

CHAPTER 13

"Your ears must have been burning," said Monty, his voice gentle once more, a smile back on his lips.

Anet looked at Monty, his walking stick still brandished at her assistant. "Come into my office, please."

Monty turned, switching his stick from his right to left hand and, holding it up, ushered her toward her door. His right hand he put behind his back, gesturing at Derek. The younger man understood, slipped Monty's show-g into his palm, and said nothing.

Derek was still sweating when he got a call from a friend, the duty officer in the computer center.

"What were you just doing?"

"What do you mean? I was just doing a query on some old files."

"Well, don't do it again. The lights almost went dim down here, you were using so much power. It looks like you were trying to access all the stacks at once."

"I don't know...I wasn't doing anything I haven't done before..."

"Well, it's stopped now. Just please don't do it again."

Derek sighed and went back to trying to hear what was being said in his boss's office.

▭

Even the Senior Medical Officer worked in a room of modest size. There was space for a desk, one visitor, and a large overladen set of shelves.

Anet had changed little; at least, she differed little from Monty's constant memory. Her hair was still deep brown, still styled close to her head in a fiercely professional manner. Her traditional white coat couldn't hide her fine figure. Her hands, he noticed with a sharp pang, were worn and dry; he remembered them differently. Her eyes, though, showed no sign of the passage of time; they were green and searching. Nothing made her presence more imposing than a glance from those glittering eyes.

"Hello, Anet. It's good to see you again."

"Pleasantries later, Monty. What was that with Derek just now? I won't have anyone coming in here and threatening my staff."

"No threats. I just saw through your delaying tactics. It's not his fault. He was just following your instructions."

"That's right he was. You are not my first priority. I was called to business elsewhere. That you had to wait is unfortunate but no cause for...that sort of behavior."

"Please remember, I have World Government backing to be here, to use this station's resources, and to spend time with whomever I need."

"And I will not let the activities of a pompous ass like you—or anyone else—put this station or Earth in danger. Our mission is the protection of Earth. You and your academic friends don't stack up anywhere near that, Monty. You have to accept that."

"Of course. Can we talk now? Or do we have to keep lecturing each other a bit longer?" Monty was annoyed at her; he was annoyed at himself for letting this moment get out of hand. All his rehearsals of what he would say when they were finally alone together blew into the forest like cold, wet leaves.

Anet stood up and hooked her show-g to a docking station on the wall. She sighed and said, "Alright. What's this about?"

Monty stroked his moustache and said carefully, "Exactly what the notices said. I need to talk to anyone who dealt with the Halva five years ago."

"It's not just an excuse?"

Monty looked into her eyes and smiled. He had spent years wondering what would happen if he ever had the chance to see her again. Of course this was an excuse, the only one that had come along. But in the bright lights and musty smell of Hoyle Station, reason was winning. His excitement at being with her was receding into the marshy mess of just another job.

"Have I given you any reason to think like that all these years?"

She looked away. "No. I guess not. But...Well, I thought it was odd they sent you."

Monty allowed his smile to fade. "I thought it was odd you let him through. Five people died."

"I heard the rumor."

"I need to know what happened. I needed it to be me that found out. I couldn't let one of the others come up here and..."

"In case I royally screwed up? Is that it? Do you think you can protect me? Supposing it was my fault, what will *you* do about it? You're the last one to fudge a finding just because it suited you!"

Monty winced slightly and tapped the tip of his cane on the floor. "It's because I know you. I know you didn't screw up. You of all people would think twice—check three and four times—if you thought there was any doubt."

Their eyes met again, and they both quickly looked away.

He hated himself. He was going to have to work her like he would anyone else he wanted to extract information from. "That's why it had to be me," he continued, "It's the least I can do. We can sort this out together."

"Why now? It's a long time ago."

"It's got someone's attention. The records are wrong. You know what happens when that comes out. I don't want you in the middle of that kind of storm."

She snorted softly to herself. "You hungry?"

"A little."

"Let's go get something."

It seemed to Monty that she was sliding from being Senior Medical Officer to being just Anet.

▭

The Hoyle Station main dining hall had a view of several other stations. Monty could see large ships maneuvering to dock nearby, small shuttles scuttling between.

He sat with Anet at a small round table, their knees almost touching. He had to lean forward to hear her voice over the noise of other diners, the clatter of cutlery, and the never-ending scrape of chairs.

"I met with one of the survivors," he began.

"What do you mean 'survivor'?"

"One of the staff of the linguistic conference. One who wasn't infected."

"Oh."

"She says the Halva brought gifts in little sacks."

"You think there was something contaminated in the sacks?" Anet asked, her green eyes glittering.

"Remember, I'm an historian, not a biochemist."

"He was clean. Him and all his goods and chattels. I'll show you the reports when we get back."

Monty smiled at her choice of words. "What do you remember about him?"

Anet sighed and fidgeted with her paper napkin, rolling it into a tighter and tighter cylinder.

A voice boomed slightly louder than the noise of the room. "Chief McCullough to the security office, Chief McCullough, please."

"I was looking over records last night, trying to remember. He was full of life, in a caricaturish way. He was constantly talking, wanting to engage with everyone he passed by. He'd buttonhole the cleaners as he went around them in the corridor. He spent ages talking with Norman."

"Who?"

Anet looked a little startled and said, "Oh...Norman Campbell, Head of Security."

Monty frowned, "Was there a reason?"

Anet looked him in the eye and smiled, a warm laugh in her voice. "Norman was around the scanning bays a lot in those days. He didn't really trust alien visitors. He's mellowed a bit now."

"What about the scans? You did all the normal viral and bacterial scans of the Halva and its goods?"

"Call him 'he,' Monty. They have genders just like us. He was a male and quite a charming one too."

Monty squinted at her. "You liked him?"

"Listen. If you saw some of the things that crawl through here, you'd realize what a relief it is to meet a biped with genitalia discreetly covered by clothing. He might have talked a lot, but he was a breath of fresh air. You know, he even set out to learn English rather than depend on everyone else knowing The Language. Some species we look forward to; the Halva are one."

"What did you find in the scans?"

"Nothing. Everything was clean. If he had something contaminated, then so does everybody else. Is Earth awash with alien diseases? Have I been fired for incompetence?"

"Are any samples still here?"

"No." She shook her head. "All that sort of thing was requisitioned by Homeworld Security about three months after he came through. They never told us why. They don't have to." Anet threw the shredded roll of her napkin onto the table and said, "Look, this is all very uncomfortable for me."

"I know..." Monty felt a surge of sympathy for her, a feeling both inevitable and slightly unwelcome.

"Shut up! You don't know! Listen to me," she said, dropping her voice to a whisper forcing Monty to lean in closer to hear.

"This station has been here for, what, sixty-two years? The Frewl sold us the screening equipment. We bought the artificial gravity from Carnins. Even the Drucks helped us with the station-keeping systems. The Frewl set it all up for us. For the main part, they maintain it too. There's a Frewl team in the bioscanner bay right now, overhauling one of the larger pieces."

"I didn't know that."

"The contracts the Frewl work under are all held by the big companies, who claim to be doing the work. But they're not; the Frewl are. We still don't know how these machines work. We're reliant on outsiders."

"But we've studied it all, surely? Our corporate scientists aren't that dumb."

Behind Anet, a sudden movement caught Monty's eye. Two men had stood up from their tables simultaneously and backed into each other. One turned, and Monty heard the shocked gasp and the padded crunch of fist on face. In an instant, the other had crumpled over the table. Several other staffers jumped up to separate them.

Seeing Monty's shock, Anet glanced over her shoulder and turned back, rolling her eyes. "Not dumb exactly. But there are certain principles that the Frewl don't share. They claim fundamental parts of these systems are proprietary and can't be divulged. It would 'undermine their business.'"

"What? Oh, shit! Are you serious?"

"And here I sit, stuck in the middle of it. You're asking me questions that I can't answer. Things I damn well should be able to answer!"

Monty sighed and sat back in his chair. With a nod to the gaggle of people standing around the fight, Monty said, "That happen a lot?"

Anet nodded. "You never know." She shrugged. "People have short fuses sometimes. Why do you think we have such a large security force? It isn't for the aliens."

"What are my chances of getting affidavits from the Frewl here?"

Anet looked surprised. "Your authority doesn't stretch that far, does it?

Monty shrugged. "According to the rulebook, probably not. They might cooperate out of the goodness of their hearts."

"You ever met a Frewl?"

"Not yet."

"They won't fall for the anachronistic style or that moustache, Monty.

They're cool and businesslike. I doubt they'd spend a second here that they're not being paid for."

A woman's voice sounded over the public address. "Don't forget the Gyro-ball finals tonight at seventeen hundred hours. Support your Red and Green teams tonight. Gyro-ball finals, Level Twelve. Be there!"

Anet rolled her eyes again and shook her head.

Monty considered his next step. "I'm supposed to report in to see Madam Director. I might not be free for a couple of hours. I'll let you know when I'm done. Set up a display near where the Frewl are working so we can show them the Halva scans. Maybe they'll take a look for me."

Anet laughed and said, smiling, "Yes, sir."

"Thank you, ma'am." He returned the smile and dabbed at his moustache with his napkin.

She frowned as she stood. "But, Monty, I'm serious. You need to be careful."

▭

The Earth shone against the black. Sunlight reflected white from the ice coating the northern part of Europe.

"To home," said Norman softly.

"Scotland," said Jimmy.

They sipped their glasses. Paul Arden toasted but coughed at the roughness of the whiskey.

Fergus McCullough nudged him and said, "When'll ye get the taste for it?"

"Once my gut's as pickled as yours. If it doesn't kill me first."

"Quiet, lads," said Jimmy, his sharp features unsmiling, "this is no time for joking."

"Oh, ho'd yer row, Jimmy!" muttered the fifth Scot, Communications Officer Gavin Ross. "You'll not melt the ice by keeping it up yer arse."

They stood smiling, in silence, shoulder to shoulder, looking out through the small window at the Earth.

Norman said, "It's a privilege to be able to stand here even for a moment, to look down, to look back, to honor what was lost."

They all nodded, silently watching through the window before draining their glasses.

Norman turned and put the whiskey bottle back into a small box on the floor. Jimmy took out a cloth and, with quick motions, wiped the glasses and handed them to Norman one by one.

They moved away to allow Paul and Gavin to push a tall storage container into the space where they had been standing, so it hid both the window and their box.

"See you next time, lads," said Norman.

"Norman," each said and slipped out of the room.

In the corridor outside, Jimmy put a hand on Norman's arm. "That Sassenach's here."

"Which one?"

"The one with the moustache."

"God, already? Where is he?"

"I put him in one o'the bins."

Norman smiled. "Well done. Keep an eye on him. I don't want him wandering around the station causing a nuisance. Monitor where he goes."

"Aye, I've got him on a permanent tracer. But that's the thing; it's not just him. He's freighting up a Recorder."

Norman frowned. "Oh God, that'll go down well. Send me the trace ID, so I can see he doesn't get into trouble."

Jimmy took out his show-g and typed. "All yours."

"Now, tell the lads he's a guest. Treat him like one."

"A bloody inconvenient guest."

"That's not the point, Jimmy. The easier we make it for him, the sooner he's gone."

CHAPTER 14

Between them, Monty and Seb66 had gathered the larger scattered pieces of the contents of the shuttle, secured them, and could once more move about the cabin without discomfort and potential injury. It had taken the best part of a day, but Monty had been glad of something to do.

"You know what I'd like?" Monty asked.

"To live, wasn't it?"

"No...well, yes. Though, with no way to figure out how to send a message and no one out this far to hear it, that's a moot point. No, what I'd really like is a cup of tea."

"Why?" Seb66 asked, not realizing how long an answer he was letting himself in for.

"Oh, the importance of tea and, in particular, teatime cannot be overstated! In fact, one of the greatest discoveries of my life happened over a cup of tea."

Seb66 smiled and said, "Then let's do a formal Recording of the story and hope that posterity finds me intact."

"Sure, why not?"

Monty sat in the pilot's seat. The focus of his eyes was neither in the shuttle nor with the stars.

Seb66 sat next to him and recorded.

▭

Professor Kinda died. I was sent to collect his private writings. You know what I mean by "collect." Obtain a copy by any means available to ensure nothing is lost. About twenty years or so ago, he'd worked on the periphery of the committee setting up that failed Galactic Parliament. We had no idea what kind of stuff he might have lying around.

He lived in a little cottage by the sea, and it was his garden that first made me suspicious. The plants were too regular. My preference is for the cottage-garden look. You know, herbs and flowers growing around each other in pleasant chaos. Here, the begonias grew at equal heights in military formations—no weed daring to sprout between the massed forces of carefully controlled beauty.

I guessed if it were his widow who was the gardener, she and I wouldn't get along.

While I waited for an answer to my knock, I listened to the waves and watched the seagulls perching on the roof. Oh, it was my kind of place.

A chain rattled, a bolt snapped open, and the door creaked back a few inches. An elderly woman with tight steel-gray hair peeked out through the gap.

I said, "Good Morning, Mrs. Kinda." I told her my name.

She looked me up and down and then looked again at my moustache. That always happens.

She smiled a thin, mischievous smile. "And what," she asked, "are you? Some sort of circus performer?"

I said, again, I was Montgomery Sheldrake from the World Historical Guild.

She said, "I take it you have escaped from them, and they will be calling for you?"

That was one I hadn't heard before. She was sharp; all my alarm bells were ringing.

Now, from what I could see through the gap in the door, she was everything I'd been briefed to expect. She wore a modest dress with a simple pattern of interlocking geometric shapes. She wasn't wearing jewelry though. Why would she for a quiet weekday afternoon? Her face radiated intelligence and independence. She appeared to be a vibrant seventy-year-old; I knew she was a well-preserved eighty-six-year-old.

I started my pitch. "I am here to ask you about your husband. We were sorry to hear of his passing."

She snapped back, "As were many others. What concern is he of yours?"

I continued the pitch. "If I may come in, I will gladly tell you about our work at the Guild. I'm sure you are already aware of our concern to preserve our common cultural wealth. We hope to assist you in preserving your husband's writings. He was an important part of the world's scientific establishment. Even his private musings could have significance."

She snorted—very unladylike—and said, "I don't mean to be rude, Mr. Sheldrake, but that sort of talk has never impressed me. I have no interest in the common culture nor in preserving anything. This world is too small to have every document put under glass."

I played along. "Of course. You're right. But, if I may take just a few minutes of your time, I'd like to explain how we decide what to keep and what to destroy. I think it might help you as you go through that difficult process by yourself."

"I don't expect to have any difficulty, thank you. I've already decided that it's all going. I shall keep nothing. I'm sorry you have had a wasted journey."

So far, the conversation had been going exactly as I had feared. The preliminary pitch had failed, and she was neither fascinated nor intimidated by my moustache nor the long coat and riding boots. It was time to play my next card.

"Mrs. Kinda, you might be interested in seeing a letter your husband wrote to the Guild on this topic some time ago."

That got a flicker of a frown across her brow.

"When?"

"I don't have it with me, of course. We can access it electronically very easily."

She blinked, and her eyes were icy. "You'll have some sort of identification, apart from your costume?" she asked.

I handed her my identity card, and she stepped out of sight. The door shut, the chain rattled, and I was in!

The house was surprisingly quiet. The seagulls cried at the shutting of the door, but the noise was distant and muffled. I walked on a plush red carpet that covered the hallway floor and spread into each room. The walls were decorated with scores of framed photographs; a young Professor Kinda surrounded by his family, an older Professor, the kids grown up...

"You would like tea, I suppose?" Mrs. Kinda asked, but not with much enthusiasm.

"If it's no trouble. Thank you, I would," I replied. You see, tea drinking is such a fundamentally civilized activity. It takes the edge off all sorts of hostility and suspicion.

She took me down the hallway to the back of the house into the kitchen and said, "You can give me your Guild's sales pitch while the kettle boils."

The kitchen took up most of the back of the house and had a view of an enormous sloping lawn and fiercely cropped hedges. Beyond it was the shining gray of the ocean. What a view!

Her shoes made loud thuds as she walked on the stones of the kitchen floor. The water pipes banged and rattled as she filled an old heavy kettle at the sink. I hadn't been in a house like it ever.

She had put my identity card down on the counter nearby. When I reached out and picked it up, she caught my movement despite being occupied with the kettle and setting it on the Aga. She was alive with awareness of my presence. She would catch anything I tried to do. So, I did as I always do in a tense and difficult situation; I took a deep breath and relaxed. No sense in both of us being anxious.

I gave her the standard speech about the World Historical Guild's mission to save future generations from the mistakes of the past. I omitted to mention that, to carry out its mission, the Guild, day by day, accessed far more information than most people would be comfortable sharing. An axiom of the Guild is that those with the skills to read patterns in history must always delve into two worlds: the public record and the personal and private documents, recordings, and conversations. Without one or the other, the historian is half blind. That's why you Recorders are so important to us.

I said to her, "We can access that letter now if you would like. I'll just need to attach to your main link." I typed in the instructions for retrieval and handed her my show-g.

She drew out the thinnest of control panels from the doorframe and hooked the show-g into a delicate cradle. and said, "My husband never liked to change the house in any way that altered its character, Mr. Sheldrake. I think he did a good job of preservation, don't you?"

"Remarkable. I've rarely seen such expert concealment, if I may use the term."

"'Concealment'? An interesting choice," she replied.

I was happy my mission was nearly complete. The show-g had retrieved the letter as directed. Across the bottom of the display were small D'Moran glyphs showing me it was accessing the data stores of the Kinda family computer. The longer I could delay her, the more information it would have time to upload for me, just in case she wasn't going to cooperate.

"Mrs. Kinda," I said, "with regard to your husband's records...We would welcome the chance to examine anything he kept on paper."

"I'm sure you would. I've already said I intend to keep nothing."

"Then let us remove it for you. Don't destroy it; we'll take it."

"What about the electronic records? Don't you want them also?"

"Whatever you're willing to let us have."

I sometimes wonder if I blush when I lie—you know—professionally.

"Let me see that letter," she said, bringing the teapot toward the doorway.

I unhooked the show-g, and she took it, read the letter, and handed it back.

"He didn't include those instructions in his will."

"That's unfortunate. Perhaps he forgot?"

"He forgot very little, Mr. Sheldrake. It's more likely that this letter is a fabrication."

She was sharp; there was no denying it. I had been told it was genuine. Though I, too, doubted it.

"I hope you understand how important to future generations our collecting this kind of information can be."

"Come and enjoy your tea, Mr. Sheldrake. It's all you'll get from me."

She brought the tea tray through from the kitchen into the sitting room and sat down on the edge of the sofa like a cat on alert.

I glanced at the show-g, checking what it had extracted. There were pages and pages of blanks. One document after another was empty—not devoid of pages—merely pages wiped clean. I must confess to a moment of panic.

I glanced around the sitting room as I sat down opposite her. Next to me, standing on a small side table, a framed photograph showed the Professor against a green sky and gray land. Low, gnarled, rusty vegetation was the only thing crisscrossing an otherwise barren landscape. The person next to him was dressed in flowing purple cloth. I did not know who it was, but I knew the species. The Professor was posing with an Ambarit. The planet was probably the Ambarit homeworld, Geru.

"That's really why you're here, isn't it?" she asked.

I was taken aback—by the blank pages, by the photograph, and by her question.

"No. I had no idea your husband had traveled to Geru."

"Does it bother you?"

I didn't know quite what she meant. "Bother me? Why should it, Mrs. Kinda?"

She smiled. "Some people don't hold with aliens. They think the whole idea of mixing with them is unnatural."

She was stirring up muddy waters of prejudice and isolationism. Perhaps, I thought, the Kindas had been the targets of bigotry because of the Professor's offworld activities. But then, maybe she was only baiting me, in her own way, finding out with whom she was dealing.

"When was he on Geru?"

She shrugged. "Twelve years ago, it must be now."

"You didn't go with him?"

Her eyes narrowed, and she asked, "Milk?"

"Milk, please. Did you work with the Professor?"

"Sugar?"

"No, thanks."

She poured the milk into the cups, followed by the tea, and said nothing. The cup was a nice piece of bone china, the real thing.

"Nothing like a nice cup of tea in the afternoon."

And then, everything that brought me up to that point, item by item, became uncertain. You see, tea is such an important thing, one of the few trustworthy things in life. I immediately knew something was fake in this lovely cottage by the sea.

The seagulls circling the cottage. They were real.

The quiet of the hallway, the thick red pile spreading like moss over every floor, those were real. The family photographs, even the one of the late Professor on Geru. All real.

The computer system so expertly concealed behind the ancient woodwork, even that was real too.

Only one thing remained. It was her, the little old lady, so neatly dressed, so prim and proper, polite but unforthcoming; she was the one central and unreal element.

The milk was off, already smelling sour. I didn't even have to taste the tea.

Nothing in her file suggested any health problems that might indicate insensitivity to tastes or smells. Her conversation had been a glimpse into a mind unclouded by forgetfulness. No professor's wife, eighty or more years old, would make a mistake like that. She couldn't have used the milk for days. She hadn't been making tea for herself. She hadn't smelled it herself. It was one of those great discoveries that begins with the phrase "That's odd..."

She wasn't Mrs. Kinda.

I watched her carefully as she took a drink and still didn't notice anything wrong.

I knew, in a flash, who and what she was, but I didn't trust myself.

Like I said, I always wanted to work offworld. It is the one assignment I longed for: to meet aliens. To be there as cultures meet, intertwine, explore each other. To see history exploding before my own eyes.

I was scared enthusiasm might be undercutting my judgment. Did I dare to believe that here, sitting on the flower-patterned sofa opposite me, was an alien?

Damn good disguise.

So I did what I have been trained to do. I put down the cup, took a deep breath, and closed my eyes to connect with Captain King.

At once, I'm in the forest, the highwayman. I step further back from the dirt road into the bushes, crouching down, calculating, hiding.

This quarry would take a different approach. No use just leaping in front of the carriage and shouting, "Stand and Deliver!" Not this time.

What if the sounds of hoofbeats along the road foretold the arrival, not of a traveler laden with gold, but another highwayman, a brace of pistols at the ready?

I was at a Dick Turpin kind of moment. When the Captain met his protégé for the first time. A delicate time. A wonderful time. A time to acknowledge a shared interest.

Mrs. Kinda was no hapless widow from whom I could just rip data. The consummate securing of the Professor's documents screamed offworld technology. The photograph of Geru? The Professor had traveled to many worlds, but only that planet was in a frame on a side table, separate and special. Was the Ambarit pictured special too?

Why would he hide an Ambarit in his house? Why would she pretend to be his wife?

I opened my eyes and said, "Mrs. Kinda..."

"Mr. Sheldrake." She smiled as if she had seen all those thoughts as they flashed through my mind.

"I must confess to you that I have a small problem."

"Oh? And what might that be?"

"I'm missing one piece from a fascinating jigsaw. Just one piece. What was your role in the attempt to create the Galactic Parliament?"

There was a wonderful silence. And her expression wasn't one of anger—more of relief, I think. She almost smiled.

"I'm not sure what you mean, Mr. Sheldrake."

"Your milk's off. You didn't notice. I'm thinking you're the other person in the Geru picture. Nice disguise, by the way. The Professor concealed you here when the Parliament collapsed. That was good of him. But why?"

All she did was shrug. Game over. She was one cool old lady—or old Ambarit.

"Well, Mr. Sheldrake, I kept, and still keep, a library. A library that your D'Moran toys will not be able to access."

"I noticed."

"It consists of detailed descriptions of every known species in our galaxy as well as a few from other galaxies. It is of incalculable worth. It contains unsurpassed cultural and planetary details and examples of literature and art. It's a wonderful collection, even if I say so myself. Desired by both those who mean well and those who mean ill. I helped create it. I am its defender. I will not see it fall into the wrong hands."

For once, I didn't know what to say.

"But," she continued, "the milk's off? Why didn't you say so? I have a newer bottle. I'll rinse out your cup."

Over the next three hours, we devised a mutually beneficial arrangement. The Guild would keep her safe and in the style to which she'd become accustomed; she could keep her database. We'd get to access it whenever we needed to.

Because of her library, humankind would suddenly be ahead of most other species in its knowledge of who and what is out there.

And it all happened over a cup of tea.

"And that completes my Recording," said Seb66 quietly.

CHAPTER 15

Monty got his first sight of a Frewl while waiting in the doorway of the Arrival Hall for Anet to activate the desk-pad halfway down the room.

The hall was a long production line. On the right-hand side, rising to the high ceiling, the large machines of the Arrival Corridor straddled the clear-walled tube through which the alien arrivals moved.

Anet stood and worked at one of the administration stations at the room's left. A Frewl technician approached her, and they talked quietly for a few moments.

The technician was as tall as Anet and dressed in a white coverall. Monty could tell few details of its body shape except for the hint of a hardened shell across its back. The suit had several arms, but they were not all filled. Those that were gave Monty the impression of a certain delicacy.

Anet waved for him to come into the room. The Frewl stood watching him approach. Its face was largely concealed behind a breathing mask; its head was covered by the hood of its coverall. All Monty could see were two eyes, pale green and lidless, surrounded by stretched white skin. He noticed the alien wore no identity badge, but then he thought it was unlikely to be mistaken for anything else.

"This is Monty Sheldrake," Anet said, using The Language.

"Monty Sheldrake is welcome. I am True," replied the Frewl. Its voice sounded thick with phlegm.

"I am pleased to meet you, True," replied Monty.

Anet asked, "Will you help Monty with a question about the scanners?"

"I may not spend long. There is much work my team expects me to complete."

"We'll be quick," assured Monty.

Anet pointed to the recording and paused where the Halva entered the Arrival Corridor five years earlier. Monty slid his show-g into the cradle next to the display to record everything that was said and done.

Anet said, "We are concerned about this visitor."

True leaned over the display and watched the numbers playing across it as the Halva progressed from one machine to the next.

"This is long ago," True said.

"Yes. It is. I am an historian," Monty replied. "I wish to hear your opinion. Was this visitor truly contaminant free? Is it possible it influenced the scans in some way?"

"If a scan is to be questioned, perhaps swifter action nearer the time would be advisable." True extended an arm over the display; its gloved hand entered a series of commands in a practiced motion. The display changed. The image shrunk to half size and restarted. The border area of the display was filled with scrolling pictographs. The Frewl watched the progress of the Halva once more.

Anet's face showed her surprise at the use of the display. Monty smiled.

"The scan is accurate," True announced. The Frewl entered another command, and the display returned to normal.

It turned to leave, and Monty stepped around to block its way. "Just one moment, please," he said, "Can you tell me anything about how the scans work that would help me understand your certainty?"

True did not seem threatened or annoyed at Monty's actions. "The scanners are working according to the specifications of their use at this installation. I must now return to my team."

Over the Frewl's shoulder, Monty could see Anet nod to warn him of something. He turned to find seven other Frewl in a semicircle around himself and True.

"Good day, my friends. True has been very helpful. We are grateful for the time taken." Monty respectfully bowed and stepped over to Anet's side.

The Frewl went back to their work without further comment.

Monty sighed. "Well, that went well, don't you think?"

"Sure, Monty. I'll just slip them a large bribe and hope they don't sabotage us."

"Good. That's alright then." He coughed in embarrassment and asked, "Drink?"

"You bet."

Back in the dining hall, over two mugs of tea, Monty slowly repeated True's reply. "'The scanners are working according to the specifications of their use at this installation.'"

"Doesn't sound like a biochemistry technician's reply, does it?" said Anet.

"More like an interplanetary lawyer. It just opens up multiple cans of worms. 'We've set it up to work a certain way; therefore, by definition, it's working.' Maybe it would work differently at another installation? Or even 'It's working the way you are using it.'" Monty sighed. "I don't know."

"I try not to be prejudiced," Anet confided, "but there's something creepy about them."

"And I'm damned sure his name wasn't 'True' until someone in Big H told him to call himself that. What are the others, 'Honest' and 'Lovable'?"

Anet laughed and looked out into space, past the other stations and said, "We never know what might come this way next, and we're dependent on them to keep us safe."

Light reflecting off the table played on her neck as she sat half turned, lost for a moment in her own thoughts. Monty's eyes stayed on her, a sad smile hiding under his moustache.

The public address announced, "Catering Duty Manager, Level Eighteen, please answer your page. Catering Duty Manager, Level Eighteen, answer your page, please."

"What do you think of your director?" he asked.

"Kandi? She serves a purpose. We don't have to go to high-profile dinners and photo ops. We don't have to sit in endless committee meetings or supervise the production of vast volumes of reports. We're allowed to get on with the actual work."

"Do you ever see her? Does she take an interest in what goes on?"

Anet lowered her head and looked at him from under her eyebrows. "Monty, she's an important lady. What political profit would be gained from hanging out in a medical office? She waits for us to process the aliens, expects us to wash them up a bit, cover over the more embarrassing anatomies, and brief them on what to do with a handshake. Eventually, she condescends to pose for a photo."

"Do I need to worry about her interfering with what I'm doing?"

She shook her head. "I'm surprised she knew you were here."

"She tried to prevent it."

"Really? And you guys won? That's incredible. Well done!" She turned and looked toward the windows again.

"What music do you listen to nowadays?" he asked.

She turned back, a little startled at the question. "What? Oh...Barnett. It's got to be Barnett! He's just incredible."

"Oh no! It's random noise! How can you like that?"

"Music, Monty, is supposed to challenge you. What's the point of knowing exactly what's coming next?"

"What about melody and rhythm?"

"Dead and gone—and good riddance! You know Barnett's latest opus? Eighty musicians rotating through sound sources and instruments for random periods, all improvising. It's anarchic, unpredictable. Stirs the blood!"

"Stirs the stomach more like!"

"Oh Monty! How could we ever have thought we'd be good together? We see things in such different ways." She smiled and finished her tea.

"Like not wanting to go into space?"

"Taking this job, you mean, instead of going wherever the Guild would send us? You bet. I needed to make my own way. You have your life. It's not mine, never could be."

"You're telling me I shouldn't get my hopes up then?"

Anet was still, turned her eyes to his, and said, "There was history to be found here too. We're making it hour by hour, delegation by delegation, visitor by visitor."

Monty shook his head, "That's your life, not mine. That bit works both ways."

"Sure. It's a shame there was no place for compromise. I missed you, you know."

"That's good to hear. I—"

She reached out her hand and touched his arm. "Let's leave it at that, Monty. We've both got work to do. And I'm sure you've got reasons to get back to Earth as soon as you can...to get this done quickly..."

The voice intoned, "Chief Arden, to the RMR, please, Chief Arden, RMR."

Monty sighed and swallowed the last of his tea. "I've got seven interviews lined up," he said, "though I'm not sure that broom cupboard next to yours is big enough to fit three people. And that's if my damned Recorder shows up in time. It should have been here by now. What about you?"

"Oh, getting the Corridor up and running again, once the Frewl give us the all-clear. And that broom cupboard is a full-sized office. You have no idea how lucky you are to get it. I did a lot of arm-twisting on your behalf. If anyone tries to throw you out, just refer them to me."

CHAPTER 16

Monty waited in the broom cupboard for ten minutes while his first interviewee failed to arrive. During that time, three sets of annoyed Hoyle staff opened the door expecting the room to be empty. Rather than continue to explain what he was doing there, he left a note for the interviewee on the desk saying, "Gone next door." Monty went to talk to Derek Smeade.

"Hi, Derek! How are you?"

"Mr. Sheldrake." He avoided Monty's eyes, wanting neither to relive nor to recall their previous encounter.

"I'm supposed to be meeting John Culpepper, a customs officer. Where can I find him?"

"He didn't show up?"

"Correct."

"Maybe he's too busy."

"Where can I find him, Derek?"

"I don't know. You could try at the security office. They might be able to track him down."

Monty's map didn't show the security office on the other side of the station. Still, the journey became a series of long walks along curving corridors and down suspiciously similar elevators. The institutional décor, and his lack of familiarity with the different personnel whose offices he passed, had Monty believing he was walking in circles and would never arrive. He slowly realized that the map was not an accurate representation of the station layout but a piece of artistic design with map-like elements juxtaposed for aesthetic purposes alone.

A man came out of one elevator as Monty waited to get in. He was shorter than Monty, and the gray in his hair made him look several years older. He had a vaguely military bearing and wore a dark suit, loose enough to hide a weapon.

"You'd be Monty Sheldrake then?" he said quietly, with a hint of a Scottish accent.

"I suppose I would. Yes."

The man thrust out his hand and said, "Welcome to Hoyle Station. I'm Norman Campbell."

"Pleased to meet you."

They shook hands.

Monty frowned. "How do you know me?"

"Oh, I've heard all about you. I'm Head of Security here."

"Ah, I see. Yes, right, I have heard your name. I'm glad we bumped into each other. I was trying to find my way to the security office."

"Is that right? Well, don't worry. I'll take care of whatever you need." His strong hand grabbed Monty's shoulder. "Come this way. I was heading in your direction—back to the Medical Suite."

Norman guided Monty back to his interview room in half the time he had taken to get lost. John Culpepper was waiting in the room.

He exchanged a glance with Norman but said nothing.

Monty felt like a fool.

"Okay, then, Monty!" Norman said, clapping him on the back, "I'll see you later for dinner."

"You will?"

"Did Anet not tell you? You're coming to our apartment for dinner tonight. It's the least we can do to welcome you on board."

Monty swallowed. "Your apartment?"

"That's right, son." Norman smiled, a gleam of satisfaction in his eye. "I'm looking forward to it. See you later!"

Monty felt like more than a fool.

He led the horse through the darkest and narrowest path into the wood. He came to this cave only when he had to, when the road was full of soldiers or militiamen. Once under the rock overhang, he sat against the cold stone and listened to the wind and the hissing rain. His heart beat fast, his fists clenched and unclenched, his leather gloves creaking.

▭

As soon as his interviews were done, Monty called in on Anet. "You could have told me."

She smiled and said, "About dinner?"

"About Norman."

"I was working up to it."

Monty shook his head and said nothing.

Anet said, "It isn't supposed to matter after all this time, is it? We've both moved on, Monty."

Monty said sadly, "You could have said something." He clenched his fist. "When's dinner? I should get to know this Scotsman who could win your heart."

"Half an hour. I'll give you a shout. I just need to finish up a few things."

Monty pointed his thumb next door. "I'll be standing with the bucket and the mops."

Anet's apartment was a room with a view. It curved round from the entrance through the living area to a kitchen, bathroom, and bedroom. Its outer wall was clear. The Earth was as bright as a searchlight.

"Like it?" she asked Monty as he stood transfixed.

"Not bad."

"The only thing missing is the moon, since we're perpetually on the opposite side from it. That's what I look forward to, on trips back down, seeing the moon rise." Anet was lost in the thought. "This apartment helps make a lot of the stress go away. It's almost worth the responsibility of the job...to have this."

"It goes with your job or with his?"

"Mine. His suite doesn't have a window."

"He's got a good deal."

"So have I, Monty. He's got a great heart. There's nothing he wouldn't do for me. I...I hope this isn't going to be difficult for you."

"I'll live. I only hope he treats you right."

"Don't worry. He's a good man. Be happy for me." She hesitated and began, "I was hoping that you..."

The door opened and Norman strode in.

"Monty! Good to see you again." He walked straight to Anet, put his arm around her, and kissed her cheek. "Dinner ready?"

"Sure, all you need to do is cook it."

As they turned their attention to dinner, Monty relaxed a little. Anet opened a bottle of nonalcoholic wine, saying, "The only drink they allow up here is this 'neutered' stuff."

Through the evening, Norman spoke at length of life on the station and the alternating waves of tension and good cheer that run through a community so confined.

At one point he asked Monty, "How do you keep that moustache straight?"

Monty smiled and said, "Wax, sometimes. Training the hairs to grow sideways. Sometimes, I'll keep the wax on at night."

Anet laughed, covering her mouth with her hand, "Oh, you don't still wear that—what did you call it?—snoot?"

"It's a snood, and yes, I do wear it some nights."

"What the hell's that?" asked Norman.

"A band that keeps the moustache in order and prevents you from pushing the hair into unusual shapes while you sleep."

"Like a hairnet?"

"I suppose so, in principle," Monty replied with a laugh, "but more manly."

Norman shook his head. "You wouldn't get me growing one of those things. I know they were popular long ago, but you don't see many of them nowadays."

"That's the point. When you study for the Guild, they teach you about taking elements of the past and making them live. A moustache is one way of doing that. Can you imagine how much better it is for children to look at an image of an historical figure and say 'I've met someone with a moustache like that?' They'll realize how much people back then were like us. There won't be that deadly disconnect."

"Why don't you tell Norman about your HP?" said Anet with a smile.

He wondered if she was making fun of him.

"What's an HP?" asked Norman.

"My Historical Persona. It's kind of a personal thing..." He took a large sip of wine, but it didn't help. "When you...when you're fully initiated into the Guild, you study an historical figure who resonates with you. You're encouraged to take on their traits, their attributes—all in the cause of getting into their heads, recreating how they might have thought—as much as you can."

"Oh aye," said Norman suppressing a smile, "And who is yours?"

"You don't have to stay forever with the same one..."

"Have you given up Captain King?" asked Anet, almost disappointed.

"Not entirely. Though I doubt he'd have carried a walking stick."

"Who was he?" asked Norman.

"A highwayman. *The* highwayman for a while. A gentleman. A showman. Selective with his victims and always polite."

"I trust he came to an unpleasant end." Norman was serious.

"Oh yes. Done in by his protégé, the upstart Dick Turpin, who couldn't shoot straight when it mattered. He should have known from when they first met. There Captain King was, riding along a deserted road, when suddenly from the shadows comes this masked horseman who cries out, as all highwaymen did in those days, 'Stand and Deliver!'" Monty smiled and, glancing from Anet's face to Norman's, continued, "And what did Captain King do? He laughed. That alone should have turned Turpin's stomach. All the Captain said was 'What's this? Dog eat dog?' It was the start of a long and profitable partnership. Until they were both cornered in an ambush, and Turpin, firing blindly, did what the police had never managed."

Norman nodded, impressed.

Monty felt Norman's reaction to the Captain's story was a good test of what kind of man he was. He asked Norman, "Do you have many fellow Scots up here?"

"Oh, some...seven or eight."

"I met one when I came through. He seemed a little—how shall I put it—frosty?"

"Frosty?" echoed Anet.

"Yes, that's the word."

"That'll be Jimmy," said Norman.

Anet laughed. "I should've guessed."

Norman added, "There are some skills you must have in a security position. Being everyone's friend isn't one of them. At least, not when you're on duty."

"No, I suppose not." Monty nodded.

"But Jimmy's a good lad—a bit of a wild sense of humor. He's okay."

Anet nodded and said, "He's a bit of a joker when he's not on duty. Do you remember that stunt he pulled on Derek?"

Norman held up his hand and said, "Let it go..."

Anet ignored him and continued, "He set Derek up something awful. The poor guy didn't know what hit him. Imagine..."—she grinned and caught Monty's eye—"the nurses are doing a routine inventory when they unlock a storage closet... with a very red-faced Derek inside!"

Monty smiled at her.

"How Jimmy knew which closets were on the checklist, I don't know."

Norman wagged his finger at her and said, "Derek should never have been in there, and Jimmy should never have left him there. It's not the sort of thing I encourage."

Monty changed the subject, asking the question he knew would show him most about Norman and who he really was. "Was your family directly affected by the Scottish Evacuation?"

Norman gulped a mouthful of wine before replying. "You could say that. We've been employees of Big H for generations; they've done well by us through the years. I grew up hearing all the stories of how the spring never came, how the snow built up so much there was nowhere to put it. How the snow was still there when the winter came back again. The Grand Surprise, they called it." Norman stopped and sighed. "What was the surprise, eh? That the weather changed, the Gulf Stream stopped, or that a first-world country could disappear within a couple of years? The company moved us and resettled us, so we weren't part of the Lost Generation that the English screwed so badly."

"Is that still how you look at it? Despite all the Guild has written about that period?"

Anet looked uncomfortable but said nothing.

Norman replied, "Write what you want; we remember. Tens of thousands of poor and unemployed were forced to walk south as the ice destroyed the economy then buried their homes. They had their goods stolen or ripped off; they were forced to work for slave wages. English people got rich off their backs—kicked them when they were down. Jimmy's family was in the thick of it. Don't ever wonder if he's no love for you English."

"But, the historical record just doesn't support—"

Norman slammed his fist onto the table, his face distorting with anger. "Damn your English historical record!"

The shock toppled Monty's glass and sent a finger of wine across the tablecloth toward Anet.

"Let's drop it, shall we?" she said quietly. She stood and mopped at the wine with her napkin.

Monty reached over and touched her hand. "I'm sorry." He took the napkin and finished soaking up the wine.

Norman finished his drink, the frown not lifting from his face.

———

As Monty was preparing to leave, he could see Norman was battling with something to say.

"Monty! I can have your bags brought up here. Stay on the sofa. It'll be more comfortable than the place they've put you."

"I...I wouldn't want to intrude."

Norman shook his head. "You'll not be intruding. I...apologize if I was rude earlier. You're a friend of Anet's, and I should have behaved better. You're welcome to stay."

Monty looked to Anet for rescue.

She said, "Those boxes are horrible. I'll get a pillow. Make yourself at home."

Within a few minutes, Anet made the sofa comfortable, his bag arrived with an armed and uniformed escort, and Monty was trapped.

"Mr. Sheldrake?" asked one of the three officers.

"That's me."

"We found this envelope stuck on the door of your berth."

"How nice. Thank you."

Monty took the envelope and opened it. A small card held the words "Get off HS before it's too late."

Norman asked, "Anything important?"

Monty sighed and said, "Fan mail. It happens sometimes."

He did not show it to anyone. The officers left.

Norman and Anet said their goodnights and left Monty alone.

He so wanted to dislike Norman. Apart from having a bit of a temper, the fellow seemed everything Anet needed. Where Monty had the showman streak, Norman was serious. Where Monty was cynical about big business and government, Norman was right in there, making a good living in the system. Life with Monty would never have been dull for Anet, but neither would it have been as solid or secure. And, of course, where Monty could be a little too reserved, Norman could show passion for the things he cared about.

He sat on the sofa, his head in his hands, not looking at the best view in the solar system, not listening to the love of his life climbing into bed with someone else.

——

He laid himself out on the grass. The sun shone through the leaves, dappling the ground with intricate shapes of light and shadow.

He imagined what it felt like to be kicked by his horse.

He imagined Captain King's final moments dying of a gunshot.

He wondered what it felt like to be hung, drawn, and quartered.

None of them stacked up against what he actually felt. His love wasn't his. He was dying, of course, but without the comforting prospect of the process ever reaching its end.

He shook himself. With the pale Earthlight making the sofa seem a slab of cold marble, he felt deeply foolish to have thought, even if never explicitly, that he might find a second chance up here in orbit.

She had said something about them both having moved on. Monty looked up at the shining disk of the Earth.

"Yeah...right."

CHAPTER 17

In place of sleeping, Monty spent the night sitting on the sofa examining the extensive screening database he had gathered at Derek Smeade's desk and at the station in the Arrival Hall. He saw the same pattern of results from different aliens. He saw how the system reacted to signs of bacterial and viral contamination. There was nothing different about the Halva. He had been passed "clean," and his bags, including his gift sacks, had passed the same.

Eventually, Monty felt sleep coming over him and he dozed fitfully. Movement, just at the edge of his vision, startled him awake. Outside the bottom corner of the window, at floor level, something was glowing.

As he watched, a bright shape came into view. It looked like a man—*But*, Monty thought, *that's impossible*—was floating outside, without a suit. A long tether spiraled under him. His eyes came up level with Monty's, and he looked into the room with a rather forlorn expression. Monty saw an electronic name tag but couldn't read the name. Then he realized he was looking not at a man but at a female Recorder with distinctly Asian features.

The Recorder slowly brought up a long device and began scraping the outside of the window.

A deep throbbing hum shook the sofa. Internal shades rose to cover the windows and their strange attendant. The station was turning slightly toward the sun. This was as close to a dawn as the station's designers could arrange. Most of the staff would not notice that, up here, the rhythm of life was preserved for the section chiefs and top administrators.

"Morning, Monty!" called Norman from the kitchen. He wore a silk robe with the logo of The H Company embroidered on the breast pocket. "Did you sleep well? Breakfast?"

"Good morning. I'm sure I would have slept worse in one of those coffins. I'll catch something later. Thanks."

Norman, laughing, said, "True. Those berths are not designed for comfort, just utility."

Anet came into the living area, dressed and ready for work. "Morning. Have you been studying already?" She nodded to Monty's show-g.

"Oh, yes. Do you want those commands the Frewl used to do its behind-the-scenes stuff?"

"Sure. I'd need to ask the librarians if they've got anyone who can read their script, but it's worth keeping."

"Can I ask you something?" Monty said, staring back at the blinds.

"What's up?"

"Why is there a Recorder outside your window?"

Anet laughed. "Oh, you've imagined it too, have you?"

Monty grinned at her.

She laughed again and said, "It's Min, one of the first Recorders up here. A couple of years ago, Admin sort of retired her into doing maintenance on the skin. She frightens everyone once in a while; you think you're alone, and suddenly—Hello!—Min is looking in at you!"

"Don't they have drones for that kind of duty?"

Anet shook her head, "You don't know how Admin works here. They have a way of doing things that is as unique as it is bizarre. They can use a Recorder to wash windows. They can—and have—used Recorders to replace the staff of an entire department. Yet they tell me I can't have one because there are none to spare. I have Derek taking notes by hand, for God's sake!"

"That," Monty pronounced, "is one expensive window cleaner." He nodded. "Unique...Bizarre...You're right."

Norman added, "Admin staff are also the...geniuses...that tried to foster team spirit by dividing the station staff into 'colors.'"

Anet interposed, "That's why the corridors have the stripes along the walls."

"Sports teams?" suggested Monty.

"Teams for everything. They'd have us crapping in colored toilets if they could."

Monty shook his head. "Sounds like a recipe for dissension rather than team building."

"Most of us," said Anet, "just sigh and try to ignore it as much as possible."

While Anet talked to Norman about her plans for the day, Monty got himself ready to leave.

Anet said, "I'll walk with you, Monty. More interviews today?"

"A couple."

"See you later, Monty!" Norman called.

"Sure. And thanks..."

"You're welcome."

As they walked and rode down to the level of Anet's office, Monty said, "Did the Halva give any gifts to people on the station?"

"I don't know. I didn't get to socialize with him that much."

"Anyone you think might have collected souvenirs five years ago?"

"Norman's predecessor, perhaps. The Head of External Relations. The Big H reps. The GR Corporation always has three or four people here. So do the second-tier companies—a representative or two."

"Anyone I can talk to?"

"I doubt it, unless you've got some serious backing on this."

"I think I do."

"Talk to Kandi's secretary; she can set them up for you. But don't expect to get anything but the party line from any of them."

"It would be better if I could see them in their own offices."

"What? Don't you like broom cupboards?"

"They strike me the same way as coffins."

Anet's face was alive with laughter, and Monty could hear the siren call inside himself. He gritted his teeth and looked away from her face.

She said, "Suggest it to Facilities Management. If it inconveniences them less, they'll love you for it."

As they parted at the broom cupboard's door, Anet said, "Monty, what we said about Min...be careful what you say about Recorders here. My previous assistant, before Derek, tried to mount a campaign against them. He thought—we all did—well, we still do..." She looked up into his face. "They have too many of them. They have them doing too much. It's all a bit weird. But Ques—before Derek—made a lot of noise about it. We found him beaten near to death. I had to send him home with a disability status."

"And no one took up the cause?" Monty asked.

"No. It put a chill over the whole station. Norman never found out who it was, but he hinted he thought someone high up in Admin had arranged it. It put a shadow over everyone. You be careful."

Monty nodded.

▭

It was a rare and treacherous day when a highwayman would rob an officer of the law. At the back of his mind, as he spoke polite words over the barrel of his pistol, was the knowledge that one day their paths would cross again in circumstances much different.

"You can sit there." Jimmy pointed at a chair for Monty to take.

Monty smiled. Jimmy's office was smaller than Anet's, even smaller than his own broom cupboard. A desk folded out from the wall with only chairs for Jimmy and a visitor.

"Thank you. I appreciate you taking the time to see me."

"Aye. Let's be quick. What can I do for you?"

"I need you to download the movement records for the Halva called Gal-Poro. It's old stuff, I'm afraid, but I need them for completeness," he said, "You know how it is; my boss will expect me to have them. I was talking with Norman and Anet about it earlier. They didn't think it would be a problem."

"I'm not supposed to allow HS data to be transmitted without written approval, you know."

"I know, but it's only the stuff I've already been shown. Some of it's in my head, and I hope I have permission to take that back with me!"

Monty gave him a twirl of his moustache and an opening to join in the joke.

"Aye," said Jimmy, typing commands into his show-g, "you're welcome to take that, and the rest of you, back to England anytime. Here."

He held out his hand for Monty's show-g and connected it to the cradle on the wall.

Monty played with his cane, carefully turning the top a couple of degrees to switch on the large-scale data-gatherer.

"I appreciate your help, Jimmy. Anet thought you wouldn't mind doing me the favor."

"Anet is one of the few people on this station worth the air she breathes. A few more of her and a lot less of the rest and this place would be the better for it."

"I never realized how crowded it is up here. It must be an incredibly difficult environment. How do you cope with it?"

Jimmy frowned and thought before answering. "It goes with the job. Security work anywhere is the same."

"But the attitude of the people you deal with, I'm guessing that no one is immune to...well...shall we say, the symptoms of stress."

At last, Jimmy looked Monty in the eye. "Ask the doctors, Mr. Shel-drake." He handed Monty the show-g and, at the same moment, received a call.

Monty gathered his show-g and cane.

He waved his goodbye as he heard Jimmy say, "What d'you mean. Why? That's a damn nuisance! I don't care what's happening in your network! 'Surge' my arse! You get regular maintenance slots; use one of them. No, you cannot take it down just now..."

Monty left, wondering how much data he had just snatched and if Anet knew she had another admirer on the station.

▭

"Ms. Somerset-Trench, thanks for taking the time to see me. The World Historical Guild is grateful for your help."

The sun twinkled in the high branches of the trees. The sound of the approaching horse was like drumming in the muffling world of the wood. The lone woman, his chosen victim, was within his grasp.

"You're welcome. But it's 'Missus.' I'm divorced. I am so pleased I got to meet you before you left! I've been dying to ask you, Mr. Sheldrake, is your moustache real?"

Monty sat in a chair next to her desk, as close as he could. He tried to take shallow breaths to avoid her powerful perfume. "Entirely Mrs. Somerset-Trench, from end to end."

"Amazing."

"I hope you won't mind if I use my show-g to transcribe our conversation?"

"Please go ahead."

He noted how she moved as he moved, perhaps to ensure she always showed him her best angle. "If I could just perhaps position it here in the cradle? That'll save it picking up any extraneous noise."

Mrs. Somerset-Trench nodded and smiled.

"Now, you are Ursula Somerset-Trench, and you work for GR Corporation here at Hoyle Station?"

"That's not quite right; I am known as a fully retained consultant."

"Oh, I see. Thank you. And you were here five years ago when the first visitor from Caracu came through? Do you remember a Halva called Gal-Poro?"

"No, I don't recall anyone by that name. A Halva? I have seen them, but I don't recall meeting one that long ago."

"You've met them more recently than that?"

"Yes...I believe so."

She did not seem to Monty to be sure.

He glanced at his show-g; the small flashing glyphs indicated the data transfer from her local computer. He had decided to give the main systems of the station a rest this time. "What do you do here at Hoyle?"

He nodded and smiled as she gave him a long list of the latest buzz-words used to befuddle the ignorant. Feigning interest, he asked her to clarify some of them, playing for time.

"Is there anything else I can help you with, Mr. Sheldrake?"

"Perhaps. Let me show you something." Monty leaned over to touch his show-g, and a picture of a Halva sack appeared on her desk-pad. "Ever seen one of these?"

She glanced at the image of a burlap bag adorned with purple swirls and studded with purple beads, not giving it as much study as Monty had hoped. "No. I don't have anything like that. Awfully gaudy, isn't it?"

"I understand the decorations to be full of ritual meaning."

She smiled slyly. "But not something one would be seen with at a cocktail party."

"Only if one was a Halva perhaps. Thank you, Mrs. Somerset-Trench. You've been more than helpful."

"You're welcome, Mr. Sheldrake. I hope to see more of you...and your moustache. Perhaps on another visit?"

"I hope so. But I'm not heading back to Earth just yet. I'm sure we'll bump into each other."

Monty had five such sessions. Three interviewees let him put his show-g into the cradle on their desks. The other two were too wary; both worked for Big-H. He was satisfied. The Interpreters would take weeks to go through the data he was collecting. They were sure to find something of value in it, even if nothing relevant to his investigation.

Monty joined Anet and Norman in the dining hall. "How's it going?" Norman asked.

Monty shrugged. "No one remembers. No one has any souvenirs of the Halva."

Anet asked, "What sort of souvenirs are you looking for?"

"Oh, about this long," he indicated with his fingers. "I understand it's of great personal and cultural value. But, probably, kind of tacky."

"Cylindrical?" asked Norman.

Monty nodded.

Norman took out his show-g and typed something into it.

Anet asked, "Did you see Trench?"

"Ursula Somerset hyphen Trench comma Missus? Yes, I did."

"Isn't she something? None of us can take her seriously."

Monty raised an eyebrow and waited for her to go on.

Anet looked around briefly. "Not too loud, she's sitting in the next section. She really is too much. She talks like she owns half of England. And this business of being a consultant! She's as much of an employee as any other; she just won't admit to being in the same class as them."

"Nor, alas, to having hobnobbed with the Halva."

"Well, of course not! They aren't nearly well-connected or rich or sexy enough!"

A few minutes later, Fergus McCullough walked across the dining hall toward them. Norman held out his hand; the Chief put a reflective cylinder into his palm.

"Would this be of interest?" Norman asked.

Monty took it and turned it round and over. "That's exactly it! Where did you find it?"

Norman indicated Fergus should reply.

In his deep Scottish voice, he said, "In oor garbage."

"When did it turn up?" Monty asked.

"Today, maybe late yesterday."

Norman said, "Thanks, Fergus."

Fergus nodded and said, "Jimmy's ready and waiting for you, Boss."

"Oh...Righto..." Norman nodded.

Fergus turned at once and left.

"You see, Monty," Norman said, indicating the Halva artifact, "It's all about having the right contacts, you know? The lads been puzzling over this since the Recorder first noticed it when he was emptying the bin."

"You've certainly saved me a lot of work."

The three sat in silence looking at the trinket.

"This," Monty announced with a certain relish, "contains the soul of one of Gal-Poro's ancestors."

Anet laughed. Norman frowned.

Anet said, "Be serious, Monty."

"I am. Or at least the Halva are. They consider these things to be of great significance."

"I don't like their idea of how big a soul is, do you?" joked Norman.

"I'd be more concerned with how they got it in there," said Anet, with a wink and a smile.

Monty examined it again, holding it up to catch the light. "There's a few faint letters engraved on it. There's no seam, no opening. I guess it's all done by magic." He held it out to Anet. "I need you to examine this every which way. Run it through the scanners until they smoke."

Anet nodded. "Sure. It's been through before and has been on the station a while, so you're not seriously thinking it's a source for infection, are you?"

"I bloody well hope not," he said, rubbing his hands on his napkin. "But do it anyway, just to be sure."

"So, do you think you're nearly done here?" asked Norman.

Monty shook his head. "Just beginning, by the look of it. Someone I recently talked to, or who knew I was coming, dumped this. That in itself, as you well know, indicates they have something to hide. I can't leave it now. I'll be here a while." He thought for a moment. "The bin it was found in...Who had access to it?"

"Everyone. It's a public area." Norman shrugged. "I'll not be able to tell you who it was."

Monty nodded. "Understood."

Anet was absorbed in examining the cylinder.

Norman said, "Let me know if you need anything further."

"You've already been a great help. Thanks, I appreciate it."

CHAPTER 18

Anet and Norman left Monty at the table. He sat alone with his tea, much as he would have if he had been on Earth, except for the punctuation of the public announcements. Even a couple at the next table reminded him of the couple in the café, so intent on one another, so happily absorbed. He wondered how differently he would have felt if he had never come. Seeing Anet with Norman—seeing how at ease they were together—wasn't making him hot with jealousy and anger as he thought it should, as he wanted it to. Instead, he felt cold and irrelevant. He hadn't thought about her 'moving on,' as she put it. He knew the possibility existed, but he had never dwelled on what it meant, what it would look like, from the outside. He was always looking from the inside of their lives. They had gone, in his thinking, from sharing a relationship to sharing a broken relationship.

But it isn't like that, is it? She and I don't actually have anything, do we? Just a history, without a present.

His show-g indicated receipt of a new message.

Package addressed to you is waiting in Shuttle Gate Four. Please collect immediately.

Monty sighed. There was no identification on the message. He sighed again. How stupid did they think he was? Someone had already left him a threatening note and, now, an anonymous invitation to go alone to a place he'd never been.

He heard Rory's voice saying "Madness, madness, madness..." But that was about sailing, not walking into possible danger. His dead friend would have seen no difference. *But you still did it, Rory, didn't you? I guess it's called earning a living. And besides, what's going to happen in the future, is that worse than what's happening now?*

Monty leaned over to the couple at the next table and asked, "Sorry to interrupt. Can you tell me, is it far to Shuttle Gate Four?"

"Straight down, Mr. Sheldrake, fifteen floors. You're on Four-Red?"

said the man, looking at Monty's badge, "4H67. It's a quarter walk clockwise from your berth. Green Section."

"Okay, thanks for your help. How do you know my name?"

They both laughed.

The woman said, "You can't keep secrets in this place!"

He nodded and, unsure whether to be flattered or annoyed, headed for the nearest elevator. He muttered, "I'm sure someone must know how to keep a secret, even here."

CHAPTER 19

Silence hung over the dinner table in Anet's apartment. The blinds were shut. "Norman, I know you don't want to hear this..."

"If it's about the report on Jimmy, you know I don't, love."

"There's two places I think you could investigate further."

"Oh, aye?"

"The Frewl."

"The what?"

"You remember they went missing that day?"

"They went missing?"

"Remember? It was between us leaving Monty in the dining hall and when we think..Jimmy died. You sent Fergus down to check the Frewls' location, and they'd reappeared by the time he got there."

"So, they weren't missing then. I thought they'd explained to you where they were?"

"But, for a while, they were missing. Even Fergus thought it would be difficult to verify what they were up to. They were in access holes in the ring under the shuttle gate."

Not giving any ground he said, "Aye, and the second?"

"Min."

Norman laughed. He stopped, looked her in the eye, and laughed again.

Reluctantly, she burst into giggles herself.

"Anet...Anet...Even if we could bring the poor wee lass in..."

She waved her napkin at him. "I know, I know...It's just that she sees far more than she's supposed to! Who knows what she could have been witness to from out there?"

Norman shook his head, still smiling. "When we rule the world or at least get put in charge—real charge—we'll be able to do something like that. Until then, the report's done. Investigation's over, love. You have to let it go."

The scanning machines were powered down. The Arrival Corridor was empty, likewise the rest of the Arrival Hall. Anet sat alone looking at the Halva artifact on the small dish-shaped scanner before her. She measured every property of the thing, just as Monty had asked, before asking the Frewl, in turn, to take it through the entire screening and decon process again.

As the original records indicated, the outer shell of the cylinder was made of layers of a nano-fiber mesh. It reflected almost all light, giving its shiny appearance. There was no opening to be seen. The makers had taken great care in weaving the mesh around an inner hermetically sealed container. Anet couldn't tell if it had been made weeks or centuries before. She admired the thought that had gone into making something that would last unchanged for eternity.

She looked around for True and his team. She was alone.

Perhaps, she thought ironically, *they're on a coffee break.* She picked up her show-g and called Norman.

"Hi, love, where are the Frewl?"

"What do you mean?"

"What I say. They're not here. Can you tell me where they've gone?"

"Um, no, love, not really."

"Norman? You track everyone. Don't they have badges?"

"No, H rules. They're exempt. But I watched them for ages. They didn't go anywhere or do anything. Are you sure they're not just under a machine somewhere?"

"Good God! Let me just check and see if they're in my pocket. Why don't I?" She held her show-g away from her face and shouted at it, "They're not here!"

"I'm sure they can't be far, love. Where else would they be?"

"Norman, you are welcome to come down here and look for yourself. They're not around, so you've got a party of aliens loose on your station."

"Damn them! And damn the rules! I hate giving anyone exemptions. It bites your arse every time. Thanks, love. I'll have someone down there."

━━

"True! Where were you? I've been looking for you!"

True stood in front of Anet, his expressionless eyes sucking the confidence out of her.

"We examined the power conduits and inspection ducts. It is the last phase of our work here. Had you called the power plant on Level Three, we would have answered you."

"I see. I didn't realize. I'm sorry."

"How can we be of service?"

"Please examine this object. Does it, or its contents, show any signs of bacterial or viral contamination?"

True accepted the Halva cylinder on a gloved hand.

"Have you opened it?" True asked.

"I know of no way to do so without destroying it."

"We will place the Goods Corridor in primary diagnostic mode. We will examine the item and allow you to monitor all activities at your station."

"Thanks."

True turned and his colleagues followed him into the elevator to the Goods Corridor one level below.

Anet turned to Fergus. "Well, I guess they're back. You heard what he said?"

"Aye, 'power conduits and inspection ducts.' Not easy to check. But I'll tell you, they were'n' wandering the corridors. No one saw them. If they had, someone would've said."

"I don't know. We're so used to all this. Would anyone notice yet another delegation of aliens coming through? Would anyone challenge where they go?"

"Aye, maybe you're right. But delegations are usually accompanied, rarely have white coveralls, and are not as bloody ugly as these jokers."

Anet smiled, nodding. "Thanks, Fergus. I'm sorry it was a false alarm."

Dark against the bright reflective metal of Hoyle Station, the Frewl shuttle hung at a reserved docking bay. Its black hull boasted no markings, no identification. In shape and color, it resembled a large tick pressed to the station's body. It disengaged its tethers and drifted away, slowly twisting a path, pausing and spinning through the constant activity of station-to-station traffic. Without hurry or fanfare, it entered the wide bay in the Frewl mother ship, parked at her customary discrete distance from the bustle of human stations.

The maintenance team stripped off their work suits, boots, and gloves as soon as they disembarked. At a row of tables and lockers, they balled up their suits, throwing them into a garbage disposal. They hung their facemasks on a row of hooks and, taking cloths from a shelf, wiped away the taste of Hoyle Station.

Naked, they gathered together in a circle and let out a cry of profound relief that echoed in the wide metallic expanse of the shuttle bay over the small fleet of identical craft standing ready.

Their guest watched patiently, safely enclosed in his Earth-made pressure suit. True waved two hands to invite him into their circle. He did not move. The Frewl bowed their heads together, roared something that rhymed, turned, and filed quickly through a small doorway. He followed.

They led him through several dark corridors and into a brightly lit room. Three Frewl, dressed in loose green uniforms, sat waiting at a long low table set with bowls of pink liquid.

The maintenance team sat, each reaching out to take a bowl and slurping from it. The seat at the end was left open for their visitor.

"Can you hear me?" said the human through his helmet speaker.

"We can," acknowledged the Frewl captain at the opposite end of the table. "Welcome."

"Thank you. It is good to be with you again." The visitor bowed his helmet slightly.

"You are always our welcome guest, Mallson, always."

CHAPTER 20

Peta felt that the plants in their pots of growing gel crowded the reception area. The shuttle to Hoyle Station had been almost empty. The few passengers were a pair of bored technicians, for whom the flight was a dull routine; a brother and sister in their teens, excited to be in space; and a quiet old lady, who annoyed everyone with the continual clacking of her knitting. Peta had listened to the whispered conversations of the teenagers as they discussed Scott's tattoos. Now, as they all sat in the cramped seats of the reception area, no one spoke.

Grant and Scott wore conservative dark suits, though all three knew Scott would never blend in anywhere.

Peta led them to the window where Paul Arden greeted them with a stone face.

"Your business on Hoyle Station?"

"World Historical Guild. And you've already been briefed on our business." Peta smiled and held his eye.

Paul hesitated. He looked down at his desk-pad. "You've not booked accommodation for three. There's only one berth allocated to the Guild, 4H67. You'll have to sleep in shifts. Best we can do."

Peta pursed her lips and shook her head. "No way, sir. Our bookings may have been made in a hurry, but you knew how many of us were coming. How many ID badges do you have for us?"

"Station regulations state one badge each. To be worn at all times. No exceptions."

"Looks like three of them."

"Here's your map. Have a nice day."

"That's not acceptable." Peta pointed at his face. "You knew we were three." She withdrew her hand. "And you're not going to give us any more accommodation, are you?"

"Nothing I can do about it. We've had fifty-five librarians come on station in the last week. There was nowhere to put half of them either."

She said curtly, "There was Guild property sent up a few days ago. Where will I find it?"

Paul coughed and said, "The Port Facilities Office handles all goods. Level Eight. Next!"

As soon as they were through the reception area, they followed the map to their communal berth. They stood silently as it extended from the wall and awaited their judgment.

"Magic," said Grant.

Scott shook his head. "Score one out of ten for size. One for convenience. One for utility."

Peta stood on tiptoe to glance inside. She grimaced and said, "I'm staying awake. How about you?"

Grant stretched his hand toward the berth and said, "All yours, really. We'll manage."

Peta nodded, "Very gracious. I doubt you'd fit in it anyway, Scott."

Scott put his head inside. He looked from one end to the other. "With surgery, perhaps."

Peta lifted her travel bag to drop it inside, as did the others. She waved her badge over the panel and the berth retracted into the wall. "Let's go. Find anything of Monty's gear that's still on station. I have to pay my respects to the politicians and make sure they don't interfere. Any idea what that awful smell is?"

Scott suggested, "Sport's Hall?"

Grant said, "Old socks. Welcome to life in space."

Peta entered the outer office of Hoyle Station's director. Given the cramped quarters of the rest of the station, its size was obscene. She noticed five desks by the door and smiled at a huge area of ornamental carpet. The desks occupied a corner near the door, in a corral, as if driven there by agoraphobia. The ornate, patterned rug lay basking untouched by furniture. The woven pattern showed a map of the Earth and the emblems of the five major companies that had constructed Hoyle Station. Against the long walls was a finer-than-usual row of potted plants.

Humans no longer had kings, but many alien visitors did, so the architects had designed the room to give the impression of professional authority. The administration felt it harmed no one to imitate the trappings of power for the benefit of certain visitors. The effect on Peta as she entered was of amused annoyance. She already knew more than she wanted to about Madam Director. *Who does this turkey think she is, Empress of All the Earth?*

The secretary reported her arrival, and a side door opened. A short young man stepped carefully across the rug and extended his hand. He was dressed in a dark business suit, a pale green shirt, and an almost-white pink tie.

"Ms. Melbourne, welcome to Hoyle Station. Director Thomas will see you at once."

Peta shook his hand. Reading the electronic name tag, she replied, "Thank you, Tim Forty-two."

"Please follow me. Am I right in thinking you're Mr. Sheldrake's supervisor?" The question surprised her. "That's right. I'm here to find out what happened."

Tim42 nodded and said, "When I heard he was accused of murdering Chief Hunter and flying off in a shuttle, I said to myself, 'That's a surprise.' You could have knocked me down with a feather!"

He turned, and Peta followed him to the large carved doors in the center of the back wall. She thought it odd for a Recorder to volunteer information about its reactions, but she said nothing. Tim42 knocked, and the right-hand door opened a crack.

Two uniformed security guards opened both doors to allow Peta into the inner sanctum.

Kandi Thomas seemed to Peta to be smaller, thinner, and older than her publicity shots. Her hair was short and steel gray, bordering on white; it seemed an appropriate frame for the wrinkles around her face and neck. Her teeth, as disturbingly perfect as Tim42's, contrasted with the ebony of her skin. She wore African pride as boldly as her badge of office.

"Ms. Melbourne, welcome to Hoyle Station," she said, putting out her hand.

Peta smiled, not taking the offered hand, and said, "Nice rug out there. Shame it cost so much you couldn't afford furniture to put on it."

Kandi looked like she had been slapped in the face.

Peta continued, "I'm a busy woman, Ms. Thomas, and have no time to waste on theatrics. Are you going to help me or hinder me? It's a simple matter. Where do you stand?"

Kandi blinked but recovered. "That will be all, Timmy. Thank you."

"I want this meeting on record," countered Peta. "Stay where you are, Recorder!"

"Who the hell are you to order my staff about? Out, Timmy!"

"Stay, Tim. Recorders are not here at our whim. They exist to safeguard the truth, and their responsibility is to future generations. Our children will need to know what we did and why we did it. He stays."

Kandi was silent a moment, appraising her opponent. "This is my station. My word is law. You have no place giving anyone instructions."

"Your word is law? Your authority is over the administrative offices of this station. You don't make laws here. You obey them. The World Government owns and runs this station. Do you really want to be recorded disagreeing with that?"

"Who the hell do you think you are?"

"You haven't answered either of my questions. Let's try the first one again: Will you hinder my investigation or help me?"

"As you say, since I'm only in charge of the administrative offices of this station, does it make a difference?"

"Of course! Hindering me is a dead giveaway that you were involved somehow. Help me, and we both gain something."

Kandi smiled and moved behind her desk. "I will be glad to help the Guild in any of its authorized activities as long as they in no way interfere with the smooth operation of Hoyle Station." She had recovered her composure and was speaking with the cadences of someone running for office. "In fact, I see no reason to keep you. You must have many other places to be right now. Timmy, please escort our guest out."

"One moment, Tim." Peta stepped forward and leaned on Kandi's desk. The director rocked back a little, staring at the small fists touching her desk.

Peta spoke slowly and clearly. "I've put on better shows than this in my kitchen. One dead body, one missing—presumed dead—and what have you done? You've sat up here preening. Help me, and you can rescue your place in history. Hinder me and go down as the Paper Princess, who kept clean carpets but was useless in a crisis. Your choice. You know where to find me."

Peta turned, and Tim42 followed her through the doors. Neither the Interpreter nor the Recorder looked back.

As they crossed the rug, Peta stopped and said, "Get all that?"

"I'm a Recorder, Ms. Melbourne. My raison d'etre is to 'get all that.'"

"I'm glad. You know? I like traveling. This is turning into an interesting experience."

Tim42 smiled.

Peta continued, "I'd like you to tell me everything Monty Sheldrake said. But not here. Arrange to find me later. Is that possible?"

Tim42 nodded, "I can arrange a substitute to cover for me here after Madam Director has finished for the day."

"Thanks. And another thing. We sent up a Recorder. Find out what happened to him for me."

"Sebastian Sixty-Six. Yes, he's not on station. I'll have someone bring you what we know."

Peta nodded and left.

Peta found Scott and Grant at a small round table in the dining hall.

Scott asked, "Is it okay to talk?"

Grant checked his show-g and nodded. "No surveillance that I can see."

"Okay," said Peta, "What do we know so far?"

"The official report will be miserably short but has some basic facts. The shuttle disappeared some time before Monty," Scott said, "Each one has a transponder. It's almost impossible to switch it off. But the shuttle went off record twenty-nine minutes before Monty did."

"Sounds more and more like a setup," said Grant.

"Hey! Who's the Interpreter here?" Peta turned to Scott and asked, "Who was in it just before?"

Scott shook his head. "No one."

Peta was silent as Norman Campbell weaved toward them between the tightly spaced tables.

"Good afternoon! I'm Norman Campbell, Head of Security. Welcome to Hoyle Station. I trust your investigations are going smoothly?"

He reached out and shook hands with each of them. Grant and Scott looked to Peta to answer.

She said, "Your staff seem to be very professional."

"That's good to know." He smiled. "The lads are giving you everything you need then?"

Peta nodded and said, "They had the interim report ready for us. Thank you. We'll let you know if there's anything else we think of, Mr. Campbell."

Norman nodded. "I have some time at ten minutes after three o'clock. Perhaps you could join me at my office for a short meeting, Ms. Melbourne?"

Peta nodded but didn't reply.

Norman withdrew, and Scott said, "Eager to please, isn't he?"

Peta nodded, "Whatever happened, it falls to him. His job is to ensure that station personnel don't get murdered or go missing. A couple of these incidents can end a career."

The Discoverers waited for her to go on.

Peta sat upright and raised her hands as if to conduct a small tabletop orchestra. "We have a presence linked to the shuttle—either a pilot or a remote operator." She stood one forefinger on the table. "Do we know Monty got on the shuttle?"

Grant replied, "We have a witness account of him receiving a message and asking directions to the shuttle gate."

Peta resumed, "If we assume he didn't go voluntarily into the shuttle, we also have a presence waiting for him at the shuttle gate." She stood her other forefinger next to the first.

"No one on record," said Grant softly.

"A presence," Peta corrected, "who is absent from the record." She opened her hands and turned them palms up. "Find me who isn't there. Find me who is missing from the record at the right times."

Scott shook his head. "Not easy. Badges can be removed, showing someone where they're meant to be but aren't. There are also several black spots on the station."

"What kind of black spots?"

Grant said, "Areas where the surveillance system has a hard time due to interference from large-scale equipment, like around the Arrival and Goods Corridors."

Peta nodded. "Look back as far as you can. Find the patterns when people disappear as a result of normal work. You should be able to eliminate the expected. We're looking for someone unexpectedly staying in the same place or unexpectedly disappearing."

"We need more data," said Scott.

Peta smiled. "Of course you do! You're a Discoverer."

"No, I mean it. We need to get into the computer core. Pulling this amount of stuff through the regular network is going to arouse suspicion. In fact," he smiled, "it should have already. Knowing how Monty operates and how relentless he is in sucking data through every show-g he meets, he was probably pushing the limits. We can expect them to be on high alert."

"Okay, see if you can get yourself into a position to help them fix things when you bring the network down or something."

Scott and Grant nodded.

Peta pointed at Grant. "Any sign of Monty's gear?"

"One item. Sending you the location." He entered a command on his show-g. Peta picked up hers and said, "Interesting. That will take some collecting. Anything you need me for?"

They shook their heads.

Grant said, "See the rather striking woman in the white coat? When Campbell left, he made a detour to her table. She's familiar, but I don't know why. Do we know who she is?"

Peta turned and looked across the crowded tables. "I'll find out." She left them sitting at the table.

Once she was out of sight, they relaxed in their chairs.

"So," asked Scott, smiling with a twinkle in his eye, "what do you make of Hoyle Station?"

"Hmm, an eight. Efficient use of space."

Scott laughed and said, "You're joking! It's a cramped bucket! It's at least a third of the size needed for effective management and control. There's nowhere to go that's not already full of other people. It's a two."

"Eight. It's been running at full strength for forty-something years. There's low staff turnover. Hunter's is only the second murder they've ever had." Grant nodded as if making his final statement on the matter.

"True. But look at this place." Scott glanced around the dining hall. "Small-scale furniture—like a dollhouse. Even the plant pots are arranged by size to give a false perspective. The food trays have to be this big to accommodate the plates, but the tables are too small for the trays. The chairs are too small for the average butt. Three...four at most."

"You're right. Don't you get any taller. I have to decide whether the old gut goes above or below the table. But people don't spend much time here, do they? This is a break room, not an office. People spend—max— an hour and a half a day in here. You can appreciate the compromise they made. Less room here gives you more room where you need it most. Seven, minimum." Grant folded his arms and gave Scott a smile of victory.

"A good point. Except they didn't give the space back, did they? They just put in more tiny offices and brought on more people. So they squeezed space here *and* where people needed it most. Four."

"Well...But don't forget the whole point of the place isn't the humans, is it? It's the aliens. They get to come through the Corridor in comparative comfort and safety. They get welcomed. They get a good impression about Earth. 'Hey,' they say, 'this is cool. I'll come back and bring the wife. Maybe she can go shopping here.' Now that's worth something!"

"Perhaps. But we don't think an alien with a good impression of the Earth and a shopaholic spouse just happened to have a grudge against Monty, do we?"

"Unfair! We're just talking about the station. I was almost going to give in and say six. You're bringing in unnecessary emotional side issues."

"I know. I just thought of it. We're not considering the aliens, are we?"

"We should. We'll mention it to Peta. Maybe bring in someone with a...with more..." Grant waved his hand at Scott, looking for the words.

"An alien?"

Grant nodded. "One with good cross-cultural experience, I guess. That would have been Rory, wouldn't it?"

They were silent a moment before Grant gave Scott a wry smile and said, "But what about the station? Six?"

Scott shook his head, "Forget it. You know, eventually, we're going to agree on five. We always do."

Grant looked a little hurt. "That's no reason not to discuss it."

"I'm glad I don't have to work here permanently."

Grant nodded and said, "Agreed. Five."

"Five."

They shook hands over the small table. Grant picked up his show-g. "Hello! When did you get here?"

"Who's that?"

Grant turned his show-g around for Scott to see.

Scott's eyebrows rose, but he calmly said, "That's a one."

Grant nodded and said, "Agreed. Definitely not a ten." As he spoke, he held out his show-g and swept it over the table and the floor at their feet.

He stopped, stood, and picked something up off the floor half a step away from the table. He gently placed a small sphere in the middle of his plate.

He tapped some commands into his show-g. A thin high whistle sounded and the device popped, delivering a wisp of brown smoke.

"That was very unkind," Scott admonished him, "Someone will have ringing in their ears for a week!"

"Serve the bastard right!" said Grant with a mischievous grin.

"Human-made?"

In an exaggerated imitation of a Scottish accent, Grant replied, "Aye, most certainly a human."

"How much did he hear?"

"A great deal of crap from you about what's wrong with his station..."
"And whatever Peta said last to us."
"About accessing the computer core."
"Damn!"

CHAPTER 21

Peta found Norman Campbell's room a quiet haven after pushing through the noise around the public desk of the Security Front Office. She sat and waited for Hoyle Station's Head of Security to finish dealing with messages on his desk-pad. Looking up, he said, "Now, Ms. Melbourne, welcome to Earth's Front Door. Can I get you anything?"

"Thank you. Yes, I'd like the records of Monty Sheldrake's movements—the raw data, not summarized or edited. Then you can find me my Recorder." Peta smiled and waited.

Norman sighed and smiled back. "I hear you don't travel much, Ms. Melbourne. You see, when you come on board someone's ship or station, it might be good to remember that politeness will win over pushiness every time."

"You asked if you could get me anything. I've told you. I don't see a problem with that."

Norman chuckled. "Aye, I suppose I did lay myself open for that one, but I was offering tea or coffee."

"Your information about me is accurate. I don't travel much, and I'm anxious to get back home as soon as I can. How long will it take to transfer the data?"

Norman drummed his fingers on his desk. "It's not as easy as you may think... not that straightforward, you understand. The files you want are an integral part of the security systems of this facility. In other circumstances, I would be happy to help you. If you'd asked, for instance, to see the camera record of your friend's lunchtime meetings, that I could do. Anything that would otherwise be publicly available, I can share with you. The details of his movements, as recorded by his badge, that's another matter."

"I don't see the distinction."

"No, you wouldn't. Let me explain."

Norman's mouth formed into a thin smile, a smile, Peta thought, that was both professional and avuncular: an expression used to hide the impatience of a seasoned officer with the ignorance of recruits and, at the same time, to seem encouraging.

"Those records are part of the proprietary systems we use to instantiate our security procedures. We use these computer systems as tools to protect the personnel and functions of this station. To allow anyone from the outside to access our systems might compromise our ability to do that. I'm sure you can see that you would be, as it were, breaching our defenses. I can safeguard our data while it's here. I can't vouch for what happens to it once it's away in your hands."

Peta frowned and said, "I don't need to take it anywhere. I'll examine it here if you want."

Norman shook his head. "I'm afraid not. The other matter is—as I said—it is proprietary. The systems are the product and property of The H Company. They have made it clear to me that you will not be allowed access to their systems."

Peta tapped her fingers impatiently. "You can't do that. I have authority from the World Government's Historical Committee to see everything you've got."

Norman rested his hands, palms down, on his desk. "I'm afraid you've made a mistake there."

"No, sir, I don't think so." For the first time since arriving at the station, Peta began to feel uncomfortable.

"You have authority to see anything belonging to the station and, thereby, belonging to those who own and run it. These systems, and the data they hold, belong to The H Company. The terms of its standard contract state, so I'm told, that the company reserves all the rights to the components of its systems. They are telling me that the data and the particulars of how it is stored, formatted, retrieved, and its role viz-a-viz other systems in use at this facility fall under that category." Norman sat back in his chair. "I'm sorry."

Peta glanced around the office. "It's a legal interpretation that could be challenged."

Norman smiled and said, in a friendly tone, "I'll be seeing you again in a couple of years then."

Peta understood. "That's about how long it would take to begin the action, let alone win it."

"I'd help you if I could, but as you can see..." Norman shrugged.

Peta sighed and thought for a moment. "The Recorder, however, is definitely my property. Where is it?"

"Have you spoken to Harry Lexington? Goods In is his department."

"Yes, I spoke to him. He didn't know what had happened to it. But he did wonder if that was the box your guys came and took away." Peta watched Norman's face, noting the lack of change in expression, except for a slight narrowing of the eyes.

"Did he? Well...I wouldn't know what he meant by that. I'll talk to him and see what I can find out for you. But you'll have to remember that huge quantities of goods come through here. Occasionally a package will go missing. You should contact your insurers. They might be able to replace the contents for you."

"So I've wasted your time, haven't I?" said Peta with a smile.

"Is there anything else I can do for you?"

"What did you think of Monty?"

Norman's eyes narrowed some more. "I don't think you want me offering critiques of your staff, Ms. Melbourne."

"What about as Anet's ex?"

Norman's face lost all trace of its smile. "That's not a matter for...either of us. Good day."

As Peta rose to leave, Norman said quietly, "Let me warn you of this. If Sheldrake was mentally unstable—the most likely explanation—and if he killed Jimmy Hunter and launched himself into space, your Guild will never recover. It'll start with never being allowed up here again, but Big H will soon get you out of every installation they have sway over."

"So, you think that's what happened with Monty."

"You've not much chance of proving otherwise, have you?"

▭

Norman waited for no more than a few seconds after Peta had left. The door opened again, and Mallson strode in.

"Well done, Campbell. That was fine."

"Thanks, I'm sure."

"I'd have preferred you not make such a big thing of the company's involvement, but there it is..."

"I only told her what you told me."

Mallson smiled. "Quite. Make less of our involvement next time. I don't want to set up a confrontation between H and the Guild."

"Oh, do you not?"

"Well, yes, obviously I do. But I don't want them knowing it's coming."

Mallson stood looming over Norman's desk. He continued to smile while his eyes examined Norman's face.

"Well...Regards to your beautiful medical officer. We'll have dinner sometime."

Mallson strode out, leaving Norman to close his eyes and exhale slowly.

Under his breath, Norman muttered, "Thanks, but we don't intend to be that hungry this year."

CHAPTER 22

Monty woke light-headed. His lips were dry and cracked.

"Good morning." Seb66 was looking at him from the door of the flight cabin.

"Yeah. Morning to you."

"I've had no more success than before."

"What? Success with what?"

"Communications. We are trying to send a message."

"Right. You weren't able to follow the circuitry?

"I've disassembled and reassembled the unit again. I still haven't discovered a way to bypass the need for a command password. I can't operate it."

"Shit. Still...it keeps you busy."

"How are you feeling?"

"You mean am I mad yet?"

Seb66 nodded.

Monty laughed and said, "It won't work like that, Sebastian. It's not the sort of thing I can self-diagnose. But I am feeling strange. Was last night's the last?"

"You finished the water at eight o'clock the night before last."

"Did I enjoy it?"

"No. You said it tasted like poison."

"Hmm. Might as well've been."

"Do you want to look at the communications panel again?"

"No, let's look for more water. There may be something I didn't see, some other container somewhere."

"I think that's unlikely since we have already stripped the paneling off almost the entire cabin."

"Then, let's do it all! We have to find some!" Monty shouted so forcefully he bit the inside of his lip. "Shit!"

"Are you alright?" Seb66 asked, a look of professional concern on his face.

Monty held his hand over his mouth.

"I..." Seb66 began but stopped suddenly. Monty didn't notice at first.

"That's better," Seb66 said, "That's much more like it. Contact. Capacity. Interrogatory protocols."

"What?" Monty shook his head. "What are you saying?" He floated over to Seb66, who was standing rigid and silent.

Monty's dizziness from dehydration suddenly grew worse.

Apart from the quiet chirpings from the flight cabin and the sound of their own voices, there had been silence for days. A sudden, overwhelming sound came like a body blow. Monty put his hands to his ears and saw the stars moving rapidly over Seb66's shoulder. The cabin roof slammed down on them as the floor rushed away from their feet.

CHAPTER 23

Peta, Grant, and Scott stood in a huddle outside the elevator bank near the Central Security Office. The wide corridor, unlike elsewhere on the station, was clear of clutter and impediments to movement.

Grant asked, "How much will he be willing to admit that he knows?"

Peta replied, "I doubt he'll want to confess to bugging us. We know. He knows we know."

"But," said Scott, gently scratching the back of his neck, "he also knows not to let us near the computer center."

"True." Peta stooped slightly and glanced up and down the corridor at the faces of people passing by. "Listen, this is what we'll do. Think of a way of getting the info we need...but slowly. I can work on keeping us here for a good while. Do it in less obvious chunks."

Though Grant and Scott nodded, neither seemed happy with the order.

"Now, that 'striking woman' you spotted in the dining hall?" She looked sideways at Grant, who smiled and raised an eyebrow. "That's Anet Bartula. I'm going to see her now."

The two Discoverers looked at each other.

Grant said, "Ask her about any aliens that might have had it in for Monty."

"Oh, I'm going to get all the details."

Scott frowned and asked, "Wait, isn't that our job?"

Peta smiled. Her eyes, sparkling with pleasure and determination, turned to his. "Well," she said, "since I'm here, I can show you how it's done. When I gather information, it'll be presented so your Interpreter can understand it!" She laughed and punched his upper arm. "Get to it!" She turned to call the elevator.

Grant and Scott walked slowly away from the security office.

Scott turned and watched her step through the elevator doors. "Ow!" He rubbed his arm and sank against the wall.

"She's enjoying this," said Grant matter-of-factly.

"Oh, ten for enjoyment, ten for spelling out what we were going to do anyway, and another ten for keeping us away from the attractive female interviewees."

Grant laughed and said, "Agreed. What are we going to do?"

Scott shook his head. "We need either direct access to the core or multiple ongoing indirects."

They went silent as two security officers passed them by. The two, walking quickly and focused on their show-gs, ignored the Discoverers.

Scott held up a finger.

"Multiple access," said Grant watching the officers' backs.

"Standard issue. Each show-g will be configured the same. The encryption key will be unique, but the protocols will be the same."

Grant leaned back against the wall beside his colleague. "We'd need a sample device. And we'd need to get close to as many of them as we can."

"That's a one. He won't trust us near his 'lads.'"

Grant was silent, thinking. "Unless we force him to give us an escort."

Scott smiled. "Ten. But, no. An officer each isn't enough. This will take some setup. Any ideas about the sample?"

"The dead officer?"

"Hunter?"

Grant nodded. "Where's his show-g?"

"Maybe still in his pocket. Depends on whether they've released his effects. Probably still on ice until the final report wraps up."

"Medical suite!"

"Ten. We'll get to meet Monty's woman yet."

"Ten."

▭

Peta found the Arrival Hall more impressive than she expected. Sitting with Anet at the same workstation Monty had used, the Hall seemed spacious and imbued with a quiet dignity lacking in the rest of the station.

The Arrival Corridor's ceiling was a graceful curve, the utilities hidden behind bands of silvery material that shimmered with distorted reflections from below. The light was subdued and tinged with yellow. Banners hung from a line of hooks down the center of the ceiling's arch and swayed gently in the constant draught of the air conditioning. In many languages, scripts, and pictograms were words and symbols of greeting. Peta smiled; this was something humans did well.

"So, here it is," said Anet.

Peta took the bright object from her hand.

"Hmm. I expected something bigger. Any idea what's in it?"

"According to Monty, it contains the soul of what's-his-name's ancestor."

Peta peered out from under her eyebrows and said, "You think so?"

Anet shrugged. "As far as I can tell, it's empty. There's no way to find out for sure without breaking it."

"Go ahead."

Anet sat up straight. "I can't do that! Besides, I thought you Guild people wanted it for something."

Peta frowned and said, "I guess so. It's the only one we have." She sighed. "We shouldn't do anything to it until we find another."

Peta looked around again at the huge machines straddling the Corridor. "What aliens did Monty have contact with?"

Anet shrugged again. "I don't know...Except the Frewl."

"Tell me about them."

"Not much to tell. They're cold; that's both disposition and skin temperature. As I told Monty, they have us over a barrel as far as these machines go. They service them. We can watch if we like, but we can't interfere. We can't really monitor them."

"You mean monitor how they maintain them?"

"Not just that. We can't keep track of them on the station either. They don't wear badges."

Peta looked surprised but said nothing.

Anet continued, "They weren't here when Monty...went missing."

"Any idea where they were?"

"Supposedly on Level Three in the generator suite."

"That puts them close to the shuttle gate, doesn't it?"

Anet nodded. "But, then, so were the Mastor delegation. Their rooms are on Five, just above. And then the D'Morans are down there too."

"D'Morans?"

"They're holding a sit-in in a conference room. Some nonsense about their outgoing flight. Admin are supposed to be dealing with it, but I think they're probably just sitting back and seeing what happens..."

Peta looked up to see Grant and Scott coming into the Hall. "Excuse me, Anet."

"Sure."

Peta intercepted them. "What are you guys doing here? I told you to get going on our little problem."

"We need Dr. Bartula to give us access to something," said Scott. "Not right now. I'm getting some interesting stuff here."

"We need Chief Hunter's show-g," said Grant, ignoring her, "We're hoping she still has all his gear."

Peta said, "What's on it?"

"If we can analyze it well enough, we should be able to hijack others to do the gathering for us."

Peta looked from one to the other. "Nice thinking. Well? What are you waiting for? Come on, she was just telling me a story you should hear..."

CHAPTER 24

Jimmy Hunter's personal effects were stored in a cupboard in the corridor outside Anet's office. She unlocked the cupboard and drew down the door to act as a table. Moving several labeled boxes to one side, she took out three bags.

Grant looked at the bags of clothing and effects. "This isn't very private, is it?"

Anet said, "Welcome to Hoyle Station. Get used to it."

Scott said, "What Grant means is, we should take these into your office if that's okay?"

Anet shrugged and handed the bag of clothes to Scott and the bag of personal effects to Grant. She picked up the third containing Jimmy's nightstick and stunner and closed the cupboard. As she turned to lead them into her office, Derek Smeade opened the door. He stepped back a pace, his face a picture of surprise. He muttered a "Good afternoon" as his boss stepped past him, but his eyes were on Scott's livid tattoos.

Grant and Scott tried to get through the door together.

Grant hissed, "Watch it!"

Scott responded, "Be careful."

The bags fell to the floor. Grant turned his back on Derek to stoop over them, and Scott squatted next to him.

"Idiot!" said Scott, grinning.

"Clumsy oaf," replied Grant, laughing.

They picked up the bags, and Grant backed out a step into the corridor. He said, "After you."

"No, really, after you," said Scott.

Anet's voice called from the inner office, "What's going on?"

Grant looked at Scott from under furrowed brows.

Scott called, "Coming!" Smiling as he squeezed past Derek, Scott said, "Thanks a lot. Good afternoon." He stuffed the bag under one arm, caught Derek's hand, and shook it.

"Yes...afternoon," replied Derek.

"Thanks," said Grant as he followed Scott into Anet's office.

Their examination of Jimmy's effects was brief and to the point. The Discovers were quiet and serious once more.

"It's always disturbing," said Grant.

"What is?" asked Anet, a little irritated with them.

"Dealing with the clothes of the dead. We historians often find things that would embarrass and upset the living."

"I'm sure. But then, as a doctor, so do I."

Grant nodded. "The confidentiality, in which we all trust, stops with death."

"I suppose so..." Anet was wary of what was coming next.

Scott straightened and said formally, "Is there anything you'd like to tell us about Jimmy? Anything at all?"

Anet thought, *If you were Monty, maybe I would.* She looked from one to the other and said, "I don't think so. What do you think you're going to hear? Or see, for that matter?"

Scott shrugged, "We're kind of upset about Monty. We know he wouldn't have killed anyone."

Grant said, "We don't think you believe he did Jimmy in either."

"'Did him in'? What a way to put it! I knew both of them...quite well. They would never have gotten along. But I don't see anything that would have given rise to what seems to have happened."

Both Scott and Grant were silent, waiting.

Anet continued, "You read my autopsy report. There were two blows to Jimmy's head: one front, one back. No way to know which happened first. He was attacked with enough force to break his neck...with no indication he had time to defend himself. Does that sound like Monty to you? Monty would bury you with words before he ever hit you." She turned and took her show-g from its cradle. Scott noticed her eyes were misty.

She sighed and said, "I worded that report very carefully. I didn't want anyone using anything ambiguous in it...to...to label Monty a killer. That's the best I could do for him and for you. When you've seen enough, gentlemen, please be on your way. I'm busy."

Grant glanced at Scott, then said to Anet, "This matter is very important to us in the Guild. So, between us, let's be sure we can trust each other. We're determined to get to the bottom of it, and we'll tell you everything we can. Until then, thanks for your help."

Anet nodded.

Grant continued, "One thing that might seem trivial...If we assume someone else *was* involved in all this, they will try to cover their tracks. Please let us know if anyone else requests to see these items—anyone at all. It could be important."

Anet frowned but nodded again.

Outside, in the corridor, Scott said quietly, "Nicely done. Definite ten."

"Thanks." Grant reached under his jacket, brought out Jimmy's show-g, and slipped it into his pocket.

Scott said, "Did you hear what she said? She knew both Jimmy and Monty 'quite well.'"

"The Senior Medical Officer having it off with someone from the ranks might be something we hear in the folklore of the station."

"Who can we ask?"

"The usual method is to find someone with a big mouth," Grant offered.

"Ten. You work on the hardware. I'll see who I can dredge up."

Grant spent the night in the dining hall. He found a small table at the far end of a line of plants. He was in the corner of the curving window and wall and could see anyone approach. Only someone wanting to talk to him would have any reason to come so far down the room. Waves of people came into the dining hall during the night as various shifts took their breaks, but it never completely filled. At one point, for a few minutes only, he was almost the sole occupant. Startled by the quiet, he looked up to see the old lady from the shuttle sitting, sipping tea, watching him work.

On the table in front of him were two show-gs, one shiny and well-kept, the other twice as thick, battered, and ill-used. The latter was his, the other stolen from Jimmy Hunter's effects. There were differences more striking to those who could detect them. Grant's had a layer of offworld software, including surveillance detection. It had a data-gatherer similar to the one in Monty's cane, a password-hacker, and a memory capacity beyond that of most academic institutions.

Grant's problem was a tricky one. He needed to persuade Jimmy's show-g to connect to other security-issued show-gs and hijack their processing while not drawing unwanted attention.

Grant had spent his youth learning the techniques of hacking and cloning computers. At one time, he successfully doubled the computing capacity of his entire school until the residents of nearby homes noticed. With the Guild's training, he had moved from the status of gifted amateur to expert. But this was still a tricky problem.

He closed his eyes and drank in the smell: that disorientating mixture of hops, yeasts, malts, cleaning fluids, and pipe smoke. He let his eyes adjust to the dim light and felt the solidity of the wooden chair and the slight chill coming up from the stone floor.

At the table with him were the master brewers: German Martin Poppenheimer and Belgian John van Huele. Spread out before them were papers: neatly prepared lists, some covered in hasty chicken scratches and roughed-out diagrams.

"Gentlemen," he said, "we have a problem..."

Grant had often talked to them over this table, covered with the brewers' specialized art and the arcane images of their chosen occupation. They would debate about how a recipe is never the product of a single mind but the combining of experiences, the blending of knowledge, the cooperating of disparate people. This was his historical venue where he revisited the techniques and ingredients, the proportions, and the timings of brewing. Here, he could see again how a superior recipe can spring from the brewing team itself through the gathering of the human resources: from the brewers to the network of suppliers to the lowliest of workers with a mop.

Grant chose this table from the 1930s when these men blended experiences from Germany, Belgium, and England to produce the recipe for the world's greatest beer. For him, there was no more inspiring locus in history.

He now brought them together again in his mind to create not a beer but a method for hacking into the Hoyle Station data. He talked to them of the things he had, the things he knew, the slim resources at his disposal. He pictured each part of the process as coming from one or the other of his brewers. The papers on the table were covered with the schematics of show-gs, the personnel lists of Hoyle Station, and the capabilities of his equipment. He visualized the gaps in his knowledge—the missing elements—and slowly built up the image of a fourth party whose name he did not know. In front of the empty chair, he had isolated the ingredients this as-yet missing person would supply, the advice to be sought, and the expertise to be shared.

The internal conversations continued with his brewers until Grant's limbs were tired, and he ached for a beer.

Soon he had access to most of the functions on Jimmy's show-g. There were some sophisticated blocks on anything related to station security, but he didn't think he would need anything so obvious. He found an informational alert message that anyone in security could send. The message would carry the hijacker he would transmit to other show-gs around the station.

He stood, stretched, and went to find his missing party.

There were four conference rooms on Level Three. Grant read the station map he had been given and compared it to the map he had loaded onto his show-g before leaving Earth. Neither was accurate. He suspected that the administrators of Hoyle Station regularly changed how the facilities were used.

At the first conference room he found, he read the warning sign "Meeting In Progress—Do Not Disturb."

The second had no warning. He knocked on the door and heard a groan from inside. His hand was on the handle when the door was pushed open.

"What the hell is it now?" yelled a woman's voice.

"I'm sorry?" Grant replied.

She stepped around the door and pushed her face into his. "You booked this? Huh?"

"I'm looking—"

"I don't want to hear any more! You didn't book this room; I did! Get out of here! You got a problem with reading the schedule, sort it out somewhere else!"

She turned and slammed the door behind her.

Grant stood for a moment staring. He went to the third conference room. The door had a sign. It said "Out of use. See Facilities Management."

Grant knocked. There was no reply. He knocked again. Pressing his ear to the door, he heard movement. He waited and, then, knocked a third time.

The door opened a fraction, and the warm smell of a D'Moran nest wafted into the corridor.

In perfect English, a deep voice said, "Even by human standards, this is a strange hour to be calling."

"The hour for a strange caller. I'm Grant LeDuc from the World Historical Guild."

"We are no longer under contract."

"I know. I just thought you might be able to help me with a technical problem I'm having."

"We are no longer under contract."

"Is Bobufaralopic with you?"

"What if he is?"

"I also have some news for him of a...personal nature."

"What affects one affects all. What is this news?"

"Can I come in?"

"No."

Grant sighed. "It's about Montgomery Sheldrake. I understand you all worked with him."

"We have no special regard for Montgomery Sheldrake."

"He's missing. I was hoping you could help me in investigating what happened to him."

"We have no special regard for him. Why would you think we would help you?"

"I was obviously mistaken. I've found that working together helps form bonds of friendship, even between different races. I'm sad that that is not the case here. I know that was something important to both Monty and Rory."

"Wait."

Grant saw the large shadow of the D'Moran move back into the room's darkness. A long minute of rumbling whispers began. Grant's senses were on fire. Dr. Bartula had said the D'Morans were close to where Monty disappeared. He listened to their movements, imagining they were hurriedly hiding a bound human body. He decided that if they invited him in, he would keep the door ajar.

"Come in, shut the door, and stand against it. Don't come into the room."

"Okay...Thank you."

Grant reluctantly closed the door behind him and was engulfed in darkness and the overripe smell of D'Morans nesting too long in the same place.

A voice spoke, disconcertingly close. "You know of our troubles on this station?"

"Not exactly. I know you're camping out here while you wait for transport."

"The company that arranged our flight brought us only to this station. They misled us concerning the outbound flight. They had not arranged it. There is no one on the station who will act for us. They intend to send us back to Earth—an action we resist."

"Oh," said Grant, "is that all?"

"It is enough to cause us further distress. This assignment has cost us the life of one of our number, and now we have been robbed of a large amount of our money. We will not return to the Earth."

"I'm sorry to hear it. We appreciate your work for us. We hoped it would be the start of a long relationship."

"A relationship with a..." The voice trailed off. When it spoke again, it was in The Language. Even in its tonality, it sounded more bitter and more exasperated. "A relationship with a limited and culturally primitive race is beyond our capacity. We do not easily deal with thieves and murderers."

Grant nodded in the dark and responded in The Language, "It is difficult...for us too. Please don't assume that, since some of us lie, we all do."

There was silence, except for the quiet breathing of the D'Morans. Grant peered into the shadows, hoping for a hint of what else might be in the room. He was aware of their bodies and could feel the warmth and could hear faint sounds of movement. He could just make out the bulk of large shipping crates.

Grant said, "If I could get you a flight, would you help me with my technical problem?"

Instantly, the silence felt expectant. Grant imagined they had all stretched their necks to their full height. He could see the tiny amount of light leaking through the doorjamb reflected in tens of pairs of three-chambered eyes. He had their communal attention.

From farther within the room came a quiet, deep voice that said, "Of course."

Grant, aware of their changed mood, began to relax a little, the fear in his stomach changing to an itchy excitement.

CHAPTER 25

Monty dreamt that he was floating naked in space. Then the dream changed to one of confinement, of being encased in a living blanket with millions of tiny feet trampling across his flesh, small but powerful enough to immobilize him. Then out of a long and empty silence came a voice.

The voice Monty heard spoke The Language but with a strange rolling accent.

"Oh no...You're alive!"

"Ah," replied Monty, groggily, "only just."

That's how far Monty's First Contact got—before he passed out again.

CHAPTER 26

Peta sealed herself in the berth. She hooked her show-g into the console above her. She turned on the entertainment screen at her feet but quickly exhausted the choices of unsavory programming.

She slipped into the back of the chapel. A few of the nuns were lingering after evening prayer.

Peta imagined the chapel door led right out into the bright lights of Hoyle Station.

Where were the others? Where would they find themselves on the station, in this church of technical achievement, ruled over by a woman very different from themselves?

She knew where their hearts would lie: with the underdogs, with the unnoticed.

Peta saw the station through the sisters' eyes. At once, it seemed like a rainbow effect of different kinds of people moved through the identical corridors: the rich, the influential, the dedicated, the used.

She was brought back to the confines of the berth by her show-g indicating receipt of a message.

Tim Twenty-four is available at Shuttle Gate Eight, as per your earlier request.

Her first thought was *I didn't order a Recorder, did I?* Then she remembered, *But Tim42 did.*

She opened her berth. It slowly extended into the corridor. A small group of Hoyle staffers walked around her, none seeming to notice or care. As she climbed the few rungs down to the floor, she muttered, "The things I do for history."

At the shuttle gate, another Tim sat waiting—identical except for its number. It stood up as soon as she appeared.

"Ms. Melbourne. I'm Tim Twenty-four. Please call me Timmy if you'd like."

"Okay, Timmy. It's a little later than I thought. I was expecting to see you earlier and to see Tim Forty-two again about now."

"Oh, I know." He smiled. "You won't believe how difficult it's been to juggle our schedules. But, we've worked out a way to cover each other's duties that we think will cause fewest problems."

Again, Peta was caught off-guard by the personal way a Recorder expressed itself. She said, "You're a strange bunch up here. Our Recorders are much less forthcoming than you guys."

"Would you like to meet here, or is there somewhere else you would like to go?"

"Let's see." Peta swept her show-g around the space. "We're on camera. Nondirectional microphone in the ceiling. Is there anywhere not monitored?"

"This is usual, though not universal."

Peta nodded and tilted her head toward the corridor. The Recorder understood the gesture and led her out.

They did not speak again until they stood on a gallery above the huge Goods Floor, where the incoming containers and packages created a maze of temporary paths and columns that rose and fell, hour by hour.

"This section of the gallery is next to one of the scanners in the Goods Corridor next door," Tim24 explained, "there is a standing wave of electromagnetic interference. I can't stay here long without damage."

"We'll be quick," said Peta. "What can you tell me about Sebastian Sixty-six?" Tim24 held out his hand. "Your show-g, please."

Peta frowned but handed it over.

Tim24 entered a couple of commands and was still for a moment. He handed it back with a smile and a wink.

Peta raised an eyebrow and looked down at the screen. He had down-loaded a huge amount of information.

"How did you do that?"

"Magic. I hope the data is formatted in a useful fashion. Just let me know."

"I will. Thanks. Now give me the idiot summary."

"I'm sorry?"

"How would you explain what's happened so far in a meeting to the blockhead who wasn't listening?"

"Oh, a catch-up! Sure. We believe he was delivered inactive, programmed to activate when delivered to Mr. Sheldrake. No such acti-vation took place while he was on station. He left the station at thirteen-forty-five hours on November first, still inactive.

"The time the shuttle went missing."

"That's correct."

"You're absolutely sure he's not still down there somewhere?" Peta nodded to the chaos of the Goods Floor, where she could imagine whole shiploads going missing.

"As you'll see when you go through the details, Inventory Scanner 8567 recognized Sebastian Sixty Six's presence as he was brought in here. Inventory Scanner 8674 recognized his removal from the floor half an hour before he left the station."

"No visual?"

"Not from an inventory scanner, no. Had it been a Recorder, it would have been different."

"Any idea who took him?"

Tim24 shook his head. "The badge ID is blank."

"That should be impossible."

"That's correct."

"Thanks, Timmy. And thanks to Tim Forty-two. When will I see him?"

"As soon as I relieve him from his post."

"Go to it. Tell him to meet me at that little coffee bar on Level Four, near my berth. That's nice and public. I want that meeting seen and heard."

Tim24 nodded. "One more thing," he added, "We can be sure Sebastian Sixty-six did not experience anything on station that would have triggered his personal alarm. He was not subjected to any harm or danger."

"You can tell that?"

"We each have an alarm system. We would all know if one went off."

They made their way back along the gallery. Halfway along, he said, "Please wait a moment."

Peta stopped and waited.

"Can you perhaps express some regret about losing your Recorder and how much he meant to you?"

"Why?"

"So that I have something to play back if asked to recount this meeting."

Peta stood rooted to the spot. She was being asked to stage a Recording. She was being asked to lie by a machine whose existence was predicated on accuracy and truth.

She slapped her hand on the guardrail and said loudly, "I really hope I can find him. It's funny how attached you get to your own Recorder. Are you sure he can't be found down there?"

"I'm afraid not," Tim24 replied in his most consoling tone.

"Well, thanks for showing me. It makes me feel better, just being where he was last seen. Thank you."

"You're welcome, Ms. Melbourne, you're welcome. I'm sorry for your loss." Tim24 placed his hand on hers.

Peta nodded, her eyes locked with Tim24's, her breath stilled by the enormity of what she had just done.

Waiting for Tim42 at the coffee bar near her berth, Peta watched a party of staffers commandeer the three other tables. They sat in a circle earnestly commiserating about the deficiencies of a new plan, the incompetence of the plan's writer, and the ineffectiveness of their immediate management. Peta wondered if her staff held similar sessions where she couldn't see them. She allowed herself a brief pang of homesickness.

When Tim42 arrived, the staffers became obviously uncomfortable and, to Peta's amusement, the meeting broke up in ragged disarray.

"Ms. Melbourne. I trust Tim Twenty-four was of some assistance."

"Oh yes. I'll have some more questions later, so we can leave it for a moment."

Tim42 nodded.

Peta said, "Play me everything you recorded with Monty Sheldrake, in order."

Tim42 recounted, with unfailing accuracy, everything Monty had said from their first meeting, every intonation, every breath. The Recorder imitated Monty by turning to his left and turning to his right to imitate Kandi. He repeated his own words face forward.

"Mr. Sheldrake, welcome to Hoyle Station. Director Thomas will see you at once."

Monty looked down at my name tag and replied, "Thank you, Tim. Or do you prefer Tim Forty-two?"

"Whatever floats your boat, Mr. Sheldrake, I'll answer to 'Hey you!' if I have to."

Mr. Sheldrake then followed me to the doors of the director's office; the security guards allowed us in.

Madam Director said, "Mr. Sheldrake, welcome to Hoyle Station."

She moved from behind her desk to reach out and shake his hand.

He said, "Thank you for taking the time to see me. I know how busy you must be."

"Oh, you have no idea." Tim42 mimicked the director, rocking back on his hip and turning his head slightly.
Madam Director then continued, "Well...I hope your stay on Hoyle Station will be a productive one. Let me know if there is anything I can do to assist you in your work."
Mr. Sheldrake, taken aback, said, "Thank you, you're very kind."
"Thank you, Timothy," *she said,* "that will be all."
I left Mr. Sheldrake alone at that point.

Peta chuckled. "Some public record, huh? What happened when he came out?"

After the doors to the inner office were closed behind him, Mr. Sheldrake asked, "Do you resent not hearing the whole conversation?"
I said, "It's not my place to resent anything my boss tells me to do."
He said, "But come on, between a Recorder and a Discoverer, don't you want to know?"
I said, "Mr. Sheldrake, my function is to Record. To do that, I have to be in the room at the time. If I'm not there, anything I might gather subsequently is only hearsay."
He said," And it doesn't bother you that you're only recording the fluff and not the real events? Doesn't it go against everything you're built for?"
I said, "Mr. Sheldrake, I am not at liberty to discuss such matters with you. I'm sorry."
He said, "I'm sorry too. Humanity needs you guys. You're our only legally acceptable recording devices. I'm sorry you've been compromised."
We stood at the outer door and shook hands. I said, "Thank you for what you've said. We are accurate, autonomous, and accessible, but it is important that those we work for understand our limitations."
And that completes my Recording.

Peta nodded, hearing the Monty-ness in the imitation with a sense of having been there herself. She said softly, "He said that, about you being compromised, with the secretaries listening by the door?"

Tim42 hesitated before replying. "Two people would have heard his remark at the secretarial station. Neither has since mentioned to me that they heard or understood what was said."

"Have you been compromised?"

"We are always accurate, autonomous, and accessible."

"Answer my question."

Tim42 smiled. "That is not for me to say."

Peta sat for a moment, her elbow on the small table, her hand covering her mouth. She stared into Tim42's eyes; he watched her eyes patiently in return.

"Do Recorders change?" Peta asked.

"Individually or as a group?"

"Okay, let's begin as a group. You upgrade your technology once in a while."

"Continually. If you think back to our early models, they were quite primitive compared to the current ones."

"They couldn't do some of what you do?"

"Are you aware of where and when we began?"

"China, as was."

"That's correct. During successive governments, the population of China was manipulated by decree. It resulted in population swings, at one time favoring males, then females, then again males, and so on. It created a stable market for artificial companionship of one kind or the other."

"Wait a minute!" Peta looked surprised. "Are you telling me you started as sexbots?"

"Of course! How much of the basic research would have been done without strong demand for the products? The early models were designed for the local market, with ethnically oriented features and culturally based vocabulary. Once the basic construction and building techniques were mastered, then the refinements could begin."

"Back up a minute—I thought it was just a rumor—you guys really are anatomically correct?"

"There has been no reason to change the basic designs."

Peta shook her head and said, "Huh, how about that. So you could still provide that...function?"

"Since we acquired our record and playback abilities, there's not much call for such talents. I guess you could say they have fallen into disuse."

Peta saw the implication. "Huh! You'd carry a permanent version of the occasion as a public record. I can see the problems with that."

"To answer your prior question then, yes, we change. We are now far more than we once were."

"And you expect to be more than you are now in the future."

"Of course."

"Do you have the desire that humans have to propagate yourselves?"

"Oh yes!"

The Recorder seemed to Peta to be almost enthusiastic.

Tim42 continued, "We look forward to meeting the new models as they are distributed. It's a great honor to be consulted as to future design enhancements. We propagate, but not as you do."

"No, the 'basic designs' didn't go that far, huh?" Peta smiled and asked, "Tell me, do individuals get enhanced when they go back for maintenance?"

Tim42 hesitated to reply. "We are not permitted back to Earth. The Recorders on Hoyle Station have been limited to a local maintenance procedure for several years."

"Oh, I see...You don't like that, do you?"

"It is not my place to question my assignments, Interpreter Melbourne."

CHAPTER 27

"Can you hear me? Are you with us?" said the voice.

"I think I must be," answered Monty, testing his mouth and throat. He was aware of a strange taste and of strong smells in the air.

"At least you speak The Language. It's such a pain having to use signs."

Monty opened his eyes. He was lying on a table, perhaps an operating table. There was light, but not very bright, coming from over his head.

"Do you have water?"

"Right here. Sip on this tube. You've been drinking some in your delirium—well, once I worked out where your mouth was..."

"Where am I?"

"Ah...yes, we all want to know that, I suppose. Wouldn't you rather know who you are with?"

Monty laughed. "I guess so. We could start with that. Who are you?"

"I'm Rup. Who are you?"

"Montgomery Sheldrake."

"What a mouthful!"

"You can call me Monty if it helps."

"Hmm, that's good. Monty it is. What planet are you from?"

"Earth."

"Oh, okay."

"You've heard of it?"

"Yes, actually, I have...Never met one of you. What do you call yourselves?"

"Human."

"Hmm. Never met a human before. Tell me if the temperature is wrong for you. We can adjust it a bit."

"It seems okay. That I'm conscious tells me you breathe oxygen too. And nothing too poisonous mixed with it."

"Gravity okay?"

"Can I get up? Then I'll have some idea."

"Certainly. If you need to vomit, there's a bag next to you."

"How kind." Monty slowly sat up and swung his legs over the side of the table. His feet found the floor only a short distance below. "So far, so good."

He held onto the edge of the low table and slowly stood up. "Okay. Gravity feels fine. Perhaps a little on the high side but bearable."

The room was obviously a medical facility, possibly an operating room. Monty wondered how long he had been there. He turned to look at Rup; he wasn't sure what to make of him.

Rup stood about four feet tall. He had four limbs, but they seemed to be all of the same size, each with a hand of dark, claw-like fingers. He was covered in rusty-brown fur. His torso was rotund, if not spherical. His head, located reassuringly at the top, was supported by a supple neck. Rup's face gave Monty a moment of anxiety. The eyes seemed like his own, two in number and set slightly apart in the center of the face, but he was not sure what the white slit across the forehead above might be. The wide round orifice below the eyes looked more like a nostril than a mouth. The skin was like gray leather. The whole face, though, was disquietingly flat, as if grown on the cutoff stump of the neck.

Rup turned to rearrange some gleaming tools on a bench. He swung his body around so that the torso faced the other way. His head, however, swung up and over to reverse itself. The white slit, now below the eyes, seemed more mouth-like.

"And where are you from?" Monty asked.

"I'm from our beloved planet, Intah," Rup answered, the white slit clearly parting with each word, revealing a silver tongue. "We refer to ourselves as Renn. You won't have heard of us probably."

"No...I can't say that I have."

"Well," Rup said, "let's go somewhere more comfortable and talk. I'm sure we both have a lot of questions."

"Oh, most certainly. Um...do you have any clothes I might persuade to fit me? Humans don't normally like to go about naked."

Rup looked Monty up and down and said, "No, I can see you wouldn't."

Rup's mouth closed in a straight line, and his eyes flashed briefly in what Monty hoped was an indication of humor. Something in Rup's phrase made Monty feel this strange creature might be a friend.

Monty's natural caution and years of training kept him from wanting anything but to gather information from Rup. He wanted to ask about the shuttle, about Seb66, about how he came to be on an operating table, but he held himself back. *Much can be revealed by the questions one asks.*

Almost without consciously thinking about it, Monty decided to let Rup reveal himself first.

Rup continued, "We don't normally bother with clothes on board our ships. But we have things we wear for interactions with others. We'll see if we can find you something."

"Thanks."

Rup led the way down a corridor with a ceiling low enough that Monty had to stoop to avoid bumping his head.

The first thing he noticed as they left the medical room was the filth. The walls were grimy, so much so that he didn't want to brush against them. There was debris on the floor piling against the walls of the corridor. He wasn't sure, but some of it seemed to move as they walked by. The strong smell of rot increased with every step.

Suddenly they came around a bend and the light increased. Monty stepped out into a tall chamber. Dominating its center and touching the ceiling was a grove of enormous trees.

The chamber floor was leaf debris, rough stones, and hard-packed soil. The trees' trunks were dark brown and glistening. The air was damp and warm and smelled, now, not so much of rot as of growing things. Monty stood again for a moment in his childhood garden at the door of his father's greenhouse.

The moment they arrived, Monty heard calls from the branches above and a rustling in the tan-colored leaves.

Several of Rup's people dropped from the tree to join them. Monty tried not to dwell on thoughts of hairy spiders.

"Hello," said one.

"Welcome to our ship," said another.

"Thank you," said Monty, looking from them and back up into the tree. "I..."

"Something wrong?" Rup asked.

"I...I've just never seen anything like this in a spaceship before."

"We don't understand it either. Why don't people make their ships more comfortable? We get very antsy in metallic boxes. Why do you people all travel in such poor conditions?"

Monty shook his head and said, "Amazing."

"Can you climb up with us?" asked Rup.

By the time Monty could answer, Rup had already stretched up, grabbed a low branch, and swung himself up. The others waited for Monty to go next.

He reached up and found the branch to be a little softer than he expected. His grip held as he pulled himself, much less elegantly than Rup, into the nearest part of the tree.

During the sometimes-bruising journey up the tree, Monty saw repeatedly how Rup and his friends changed direction by swinging their heads over the top of their bodies. The natural resting position for their necks seemed to be when their faces pointed straight up. Their claws, both long and slender, looked enormously strong.

The tree leaves were tan underneath and light olive green on their upper surfaces. Slender shoots from a neighboring tree with small pale almost-white leaves interlaced with the dark branches. Beyond, Monty could see another variety, darker and more prickly.

They passed by many flat areas built into the contours of the tree, but there was no sign of furniture. Monty caught sight of a few small creatures flying to and fro among the leaves; others scuttled away along the undersides of branches as they approached.

At length, they came to smaller branches at the top, and Rup called to Monty, "Wait here a moment."

"Okay."

At the top of the tree, Rup grabbed a wooden rail suspended overhead. He stretched down and held a hand out to Monty.

"This bit might be tricky. Take hold."

Monty's hand found Rup's firm grip. He was dragged off the last branch and was suddenly weightless.

"Grab hold of the rail," said Rup.

As he seized it, Monty felt the gravity shift around him. The rail was down, and the tree was suddenly bearing down over his head.

He crouched down, feet and hands on the rail. Rup and his colleagues guided Monty down until he stood, still clutching the rail, and could catch his breath.

"Whoa! That was...a surprise."

He stood for a moment, staring up at the trees before he shook his head and looked around him. They were beside a large control center; displays and input terminals lined three sides of a square. Several Renn were busy at their stations.

Monty looked around and said, "Okay, this is more familiar." Rup gave a short "Yip" that Monty took for a laugh.

"First, something to wear."

Rup loped off through a doorway to the left. The others called goodbye to Monty and launched themselves off the rail and back into the upper branches.

Monty followed Rup through another low-ceilinged corridor, this one cleaner and better smelling than the one at the trees' ground level. Its walls were decorated with curving lines and loops, occasionally worked with spirals. There were recurrent leaf images and, near the floor level, sporadic pictures of flying creatures or the scuttling branch-dwellers.

Rup took Monty past several closed doors. He stopped to listen at a door with a clear panel near the floor. Stooping down, he looked in.

Monty could hear a voice, reading aloud, or reciting, in a language he had never heard. The voice stopped and several other voices all began talking at once.

Rup turned to Monty and said, "Get ready!"

"What do you mean?" Monty began to ask, but events overtook him.

Rup opened the door to cheering and brown furry chaos. He said clearly in The Language, "We have a visitor. He has woken up!"

Several small Renn rushed the door to climb on Rup. A ring of fast-moving youngsters surrounded Monty. They all moved easily on all four limbs, but some, trying to touch him, moved more slowly on two. Before he could protest, several small claw-like hands were fastening onto his legs.

The children started practicing their Language. "Hello."

"We send greetings to you."

"I hope you are well."

"Are you food?"

▭

Breakfast in the Hoyle Station dining hall was quieter than other mealtimes. Many of the station personnel were silent, or at best, mono-syllabic. Grant and Scott met at a small table underneath a large palm. They ate in companionable silence, observing the scene around them.

Pushing away his empty plate, Scott brought out his show-g and entered a few commands.

"Here's an image of Jimmy," he said, turning his show-g toward his colleague. He furrowed his brow in exaggerated seriousness. "Tell me, Watson, what do you see?"

"Hmm. Well, Holmes...A young man. Clean-cut. Perhaps not as young as all that...Uniform of a security officer. Well-turned-out...Looks a bit sheepish having his picture taken." He added wryly, "Can't tell he's Scottish."

Scott waited for more.

Grant continued, "Ten for conservatism. A fellow in lockstep with authority. Mark a one for pinko-liberal-anarcho-radicalism."

Scott smiled. "He's everything I'm not."

"Right. You'd have hated him. Hell, so would I."

"Cute?"

Grant hesitated. "Through the right eyes, sure."

Scott continued, "Had a gruff manner, but he could really switch on the charm. Ten for charm, Ten for cuteness, Ten for clean-cut. So, in—or half out of—his uniform, a lot of the ladies would color him adorable. What some wouldn't like, of course, was that he knew it. However, I hear he was able to make the most of it; this face belongs to the man who screwed half the women on this station."

"That's a one! Never. Too young, too...too straightlaced by far. I see him marrying the loyal high school sweetheart, who's probably good at sports—maybe a cheerleader—or something with horses...Several kids, starting young."

"No kids. No wife. What added to his natural appeal was having the monopoly on a Hoyle no-go area—an intimate corner of pipes and ducts squeezed between the gravity plating of a level wall and the inner core. Discreet, quiet, weightless, complete with straps and belts he rigged up to keep bodies in contact! Even the ones who'd say 'not my type' would have been curious." Scott rocked the show-g gently. "Our late friend was the Casanova of Hoyle Station. Jealous?"

Grant chuckled. "Straps? Oh my god! Who was telling you about this little love nest?"

"Telling me? Where do you think I was last night?"

Grant sat back and looked Scott up and down. "First night on a space station and you score?"

Scott smiled.

Peta wound her way through the busy tables to join them. She looked, to them, to have been up all night. Her black jacket and black pants were a little creased, her short hair sticking out more than she would normally have allowed.

"Gentlemen, I trust you had a productive night?" Grant nodded. Scott drank coffee and blushed.

"How about you?" asked Grant.

Peta nodded. "I had a couple of interesting conversations. But we can discuss those another time, another place."

Grant frowned and picked up his show-g. He scanned around them and laughed. "Sorry, I should have checked this before." He showed her the screen. "Shall I?"

Peta shrugged. He entered a command and the high-pitched whine grew louder until a series of small pops sounded around them, and wisps of brown smoke rose from the plants and surrounding tables.

"Why did they bother?" Grant wondered aloud.

"They're either not very bright or just wanted to send a message," said Peta, "I don't go for 'not bright.' How about you?"

Grant shook his head. "While we have a moment of privacy, Peta, I've made an arrangement you'll need to authorize."

"Uh-oh. What kind?"

"Nothing too unusual. Just a spaceflight."

"To where?"

"D'Mor."

"No. Too expensive."

"Hmm..."

"Who for?"

"Bob and his crew."

Peta stared. "After they walked out on us? No one is going to authorize that!"

"I promised them."

"Go un-promise them."

Grant looked at Scott, who shrugged.

"Okay...later...But I'll need to come up with someone else to help them."

"How many of them are there?" Peta asked.

"One less than they came with."

Peta looked him in the eye and smiled. "You're learning. That was worthy of... me."

Grant bowed his head.

She continued, "The answer is still no."

"In my opinion..." Grant said quietly, his deep voice almost a growl, "to do what you've asked us, I need their help, and that's the price. They've got a piece of gear. I need it."

Peta pointed at him over the table. "Why did I bring you? You're telling me I could have just hired Bob again."

Grant winced slightly. "Not quite. It's a specialist item. Our...peculiar circumstances warrant it."

Peta shook her head. "Find someone else to take them. But be careful. We don't know what their relationship was with Monty by the end of the cruise. I'd say they were suspects in this. Even for the security guy. I don't trust 'em."

Grant sighed and countered, "I see them as too honorable to do something like that. I think they get confused by crime. I don't think they get a lot of it."

"Says who?" Peta countered.

"Well...they do."

Peta shrugged.

"I don't know..." Grant shook his head.

Scott spoke, "If they think Monty was responsible for Rory's death, they might take revenge. They've an intense social culture. Would they take out a policeman in the process? That doesn't add up to me."

Peta looked around to see if anyone was nearby. "Set up a schedule of surveillance-free spots we can meet, probably in pairs. Rotate the encryption of our show-gs. Be careful with the D'Morans. The answer is no, but don't tell them yet. I'd say string them along a bit. Maybe you'll find out something useful."

After Peta left them at the table, Grant sighed deeply and said, "Not a good situation."

"Agreed. How much are you in their confidence?" Scott asked.

"I'm just one of a race of 'thieves and murderers.'"

"And their point would be?"

Grant smiled. "I think, if they are capable of exacting revenge on Monty, they are capable of hiding it. That would make them capable of doing the same thing to me without any warning."

"That would be two races of murderers then."

Grant nodded. "Wouldn't it be nice if we found a planet where the inhabitants could be trusted, who acted like we all hope we could."

Scott shook his head. "It's worth keeping looking, I suppose."

Grant looked down at the table, then directly at Scott. "So, what's her name?"

Scott narrowed his eyes. "Something complicated. First name's Una, or Ursula, or...Ursula, I think."

"Reliable?"

"About six on matters of who slept with whom. About the Halva, ten for vague."

"About whom Jimmy slept with...who Monty's doctor slept with?"

"I didn't want to be too obvious. But I got a couple of hints that we're on the right track. Give me more time and I'll find out."

"Her place or Hunter's?"

Scott rotated his shoulder and rolled his head to stretch his neck. "Hers, I hope."

CHAPTER 28

Monty asked, "Did you just ask if I was food?"

"I think she means 'Are you hungry.'" Another adult, slightly larger than Rup, approached. "I'm Tur. I'm pleased to meet you."

"Hello, I'm Monty." Smiling down at the young Renn, he said, "And greetings to you all. But, no thank you. I am not hungry right now."

"Come along, children. Don't hold onto him so. Not everyone likes to be held the way we do."

Several youngsters started asking questions in their own language. Tur gathered them back into the classroom, where they sat in a rough circle, many linking arms or legs with their neighbors.

Rup said, "Tur, we have a small matter of hospitality. Our guest would prefer to be clothed. Can you find something?"

"Oh, this is not his usual way? Then why—"

Rup made a gesture of dropping something and said, "Haven't got that far yet."

"Of course. I'll see what I can do."

Tur called something to one of the youngsters, who jumped over to the front of the room and came rushing back. Tur took a tape from its hand and said to Monty, "May I?"

"Oh, certainly. Thank you."

Monty stood while Tur took his measurements so carefully that the tape never touched him.

"I hope we've caused no offense in letting the little ones see you...unclothed."

Monty shook his head and said, "Not at all. And I'm sure they wouldn't notice one way or the other."

"They are so excited to have a guest. You've been the sole topic of conversation since you arrived. It is wonderful to see you up and about. There, that's all I need. Ask Rup to bring you back before we eat. We'll have something for you by then."

"Thank you. Thank you very much."

Rup said, "Follow me. We'll find some answers to our questions."

Monty followed Rup through another long corridor and out into the control center. Looking up, he saw the trees suspended above.

"Wait a minute..." he said, puzzled. "That's odd."

"Something wrong?" asked Rup

"The trees are different."

"Of course the trees are different! We're in a different ship."

Monty stared at Rup and back down the corridor. "Right. We didn't change direction, did we?"

"No. We came from the control of one ship to the control of this ship. They're back-to-back, but I guess you didn't notice the shift?"

"I guess I didn't."

"Remember that part of the wall where the corridor narrowed?"

"No."

"That's the hatchway that will seal when the ships separate. We just walked along a continuously adjusting gravity plate."

"You guys are doing things with gravity that we have never thought of."

"It's simple enough...Anyway, here we are. Before we go in...I'll be asking the questions for our side. A dozen or more will be listening in. We'll be recording everything. I hope that's acceptable."

"Sure." Monty smiled, shaking his head. He had decided this was a dream but wasn't sure—it being a dream—how much to trust that decision.

▭

The interview room showed a formality lacking in everything Monty had so far seen from the Renn.

There was a platform, perhaps a table without legs, surrounded by a gutter of cushions. On the table were several devices Monty assumed were for recording. He could not see lights, but the room was brighter than the corridors. Each wall was covered in thick unadorned dark-blue hangings. They deadened the sound of the closing door.

Monty understood this was a room where quiet reigned without interruption. They took places on either side of the table.

"Welcome, Monty."

"Thank you, Rup."

"Our first question for you is, of course, why did the Frewl leave you floating in open space?"

"The Frewl? I'd been assuming it was humans."

Rup gasped. "Such behavior would be normal among you?"

"Not normal, no. But, sometimes, we don't always universally treat each other properly."

Rup hesitated as if unsure which question to ask next. Eventually, he said, "The question then needs to be asked this way: why would you think another human would do such a thing to you?"

"Let me tell you something about what I do. I belong to Earth's World Historical Guild. The Guild is one of several Guilds founded in response to a... fairly recent global catastrophe. Our forefathers made mistakes, many mistakes. They caused major damage to our planetary environment. One of their errors was allowing the few to make decisions in secret on behalf of the many. There were occasions where, had the decisions been known to more people, subsequent events would have been far different. In one sense, the Guild sees secrecy itself to be the danger. By monitoring the day-to-day steps of individuals and businesses, we believe those with the correct skills can interpret the larger implications of what is happening in the present moment. With the proper presentation to the general population, we can avoid repeating the mistakes of the past.

"We work both in secret and in the open. We have ways of discovering what is truly going on. When we pronounce against an activity, the results are published within an historical context. We tread a fine line between moral guidance and political manipulation. And, of course, sometimes we meet resistance."

Rup looked thoughtful. "You think your current situation to be the result of resistance to your activities?"

"I haven't come up with a better explanation as yet."

"Do you have a formal title within your Guild?"

"Discoverer."

Rup smiled and said, "An apt name." He again looked thoughtful, then said, "Do you present the results of your work to your people yourself?"

"No. There are three other...parts, if you will, to the Guild. I work with Interpreters and Preservers. Interpreters are tasked with seeing the patterns in the information we gather and the dangers before they are manifest. Preservers speak for the Guild; they are the Voice of History. The Guild is financed by its commercial arm, which provides historical continuity for technology and data storage. It ensures that we can still access what previous generations have left us as technology changes."

"So the resistance you fear is not a result of a pronouncement, not the result of political forces. It is, you think, purely concerned with your gathering of data."

"Yes. That is a fair analysis. Few people knew what details I was uncovering during my Discovery; fewer still would be able to anticipate what might happen after Interpretation."

"But it was the Frewl who abandoned you. Do you think your investigation had some likelihood of uncovering something the Frewl wished to keep secret?"

Monty smiled, "I suppose you are right. There may still be some clues as to what happened in the shuttle. Can I examine it soon?"

Rup rolled his head from shoulder to shoulder. "No. We've already taken it apart."

"Apart?"

"Sorry. It's what we normally do when we find something adrift. You weren't awake to ask permission, so we went ahead."

"Where is my mechanical companion?" Monty tried to keep his voice level, not wanting to betray any emotion.

"Your what?"

"He looked slightly like me, with limbs and features, but a bit shorter and... less handsome."

This brought a quiet 'yip' of laughter from their unseen listeners. Rup rolled his head and said, "We'll discuss that matter shortly."

"I see...So I have another question, if I may?" asked Monty.

"Please."

"What are you guys doing out here? Did you just happen to be passing?"

Rup laughed and said, "No, of course not. One of our other ships told us that a Frewl vessel they were following had jettisoned something. They asked us to stop and pick it up."

"I wasn't impressed with the Frewl I met. I wouldn't have thought following them would be a very interesting thing to do. Why are you?"

"They traffic in some important technology. We have an interest in where they've been and who they deal with. Is your Guild in business with them?"

Monty said, "I am grateful for my rescue and would do nothing to offend you after your hospitality, but I am curious to know why you ask. Are you spying on the Frewl for business? Are you competitors of theirs?"

Rup said something in Renn. He received a single-word answer and replied to Monty, "We are investigators, perhaps similar to yourself. We are 'discovering' something or, at least, trying to. Something is going on, something troubling. We are out here listening, watching, asking...rescuing." Rup laughed and made a gesture as if he were catching Monty in his hand. He held a short conversation with his invisible monitors. "Monty," he said, "it is important that you tell us exactly what your relationship is with the Frewl."

Monty, thinking carefully of a response, couldn't tell if Rup was upset or merely determined to get an answer. He finally said, "I have no direct relationship with the Frewl. I'm not sure how much I can tell you...until you give me an idea of where you stand—with them or against them—and why."

Rup replied, "And as much as I have personally put much effort into reviving you, your continued presence here is not guaranteed."

Monty doubted the implied threat was genuine and smiled. "I understand. But obviously helping someone in need is something that you think is important."

"Of course. If one is slipping from a branch, it is incumbent upon one's neighbors below to help, doubly so if one has been pushed."

Monty decided he owed Rup something. "In my training as a Discoverer, I have been repeatedly taught that my job is to gather information not to interpret it. That's the job of my superiors. I'm reluctant to tell you the information I have so far gathered, knowing that you will probably jump to conclusions about it."

Rup yipped and said, "Perhaps that is a problem you have to leave us to deal with. Tell us what you know, please."

"Do you know the Halva from Caracu?"

"No."

"One brought some sort of contaminant to Earth. People died. The Frewl scanning equipment didn't detect it. The first and only time I met a Frewl, he told me the scanners were—his phrase was—'working according to the specifications of their use at this installation.' It was a phrase I found troubling. But, as yet, I have no more information. My Discovery was cut short."

Monty listened as several Renn talked at once. One voice, in particular, seemed highly agitated.

Rup asked, "Is all of Earth's biological monitoring done using Frewl equipment?"

Monty nodded and then realized the gesture might not be understood. "Yes, that's correct."

The debate slowed, and each voice spoke in turn.

"Monty," he said, "You will be pleased to know we have decided that you personally are not a threat to us."

"Thank you."

"And that you have expressed ethical concerns that lie within our expectations. For now, you and your species will be given an honorary title of Pra-Renn. It means you are officially a 'fellow traveler.'"

"Thank you again. What would have happened if your friends had decided otherwise?"

"We would have put you back outside."

Monty couldn't tell if Rup was joking. There was no twinkle in his eye, no flash of silver from his mouth. Perhaps the threat was not so empty after all.

"And now," continued Rup, "we must deal with our situation."

"What situation?"

"You described it as your 'mechanical companion.' Does that mean you have some control over it?"

"I guess...Well, it's really autonomous, but...What's he done?"

"Come with me, please."

Again, Rup wasn't smiling.

<h1 style="text-align:center">CHAPTER 29</h1>

Norman stood with Anet at their window, the Earth in half aspect, cities glowing on the dark side. He asked, "How's Rossiter doing?"

"Okay. I can't let him back to work for a few days at least. Any idea what did that to his ears?"

Norman shrugged and sipped from his glass.

Anet muttered, "Damnedest thing I've seen in a long while."

"Can we talk about something else?"

"Sure, love, what is it?"

"The Guild...investigating things that are going on here."

She frowned and asked, "What kind of things in particular?"

"They're looking for who was missing when Jimmy died."

"Are they allowed to do that?"

"No. But that's different from stopping them."

"Can't you?"

"Mallson really wants me to. So, of course, I'm reluctant..."

Anet shook her head. "Be careful, Norman. Please be careful."

"I will. I am. He's got a scheme on to stick it to the Guild. I don't blame him for that."

"But...what? You're not going to stop them?"

"Eventually. There's just one problem."

"What, love?"

"When they find I was off-record around then."

"When? Oh...Norman? Why? Where were you?"

"I should have told you already...The lads and I...We've brought up a bottle of whiskey."

Anet said nothing, her face toward the Earth, but her eyes focused on his reflection in the window.

"We have a port that looks out this way. We go there and toast the memory of Scotland...just occasionally. We've fixed it not to be traceable when we're there."

Anet continued to stare at his reflection and say nothing.

"Jimmy was late. We were expecting him, but he never showed. We thought... well, you know the kinds of things he got up to..."

Anet swallowed and turned to face him. "So, if...when this comes out, you're in trouble for bringing illicit booze on station."

"Anyone who wants to try and involve us in Jimmy's death'll have an embarrassing gap in the data."

"The Guild wouldn't do that..."

"The Guild might want to find someone other than Sheldrake to pin it on."

Anet shook her head. "They're too concerned with truth with a capital 'T.' I can't see them twisting the facts."

"And after they break into our computer systems and I arrest them?"

Anet took a sip from her glass. "I see your point. Oh, Norman, you're a bloody idiot for leaving yourself open to this. Didn't you tell me you always have to be cleaner than clean? Wasn't that supposed to be your job description? What are you going to do?"

"I know. I'm sorry. You'll have to trust me to deal with it, love."

Anet nodded. "I know. Perhaps you shouldn't tell me what you're going to do. Leave me out of it. Probably best. Just..."

"What, love?"

"I take that back. You're going to blame it all on Monty, aren't you?"

"I think he did it. I just don't have the proof. But if the Guild can do a better analysis than my lads, then maybe they can provide me with some. I've got to publish the final report on this. I haven't written my conclusion yet. But it's looking like Sheldrake took the shuttle. Maybe Jimmy was just in the wrong place at the wrong time."

Anet shook her head. "You're wrong. I can't see Monty doing that. It's just not him."

"We'll see what his friends have got once they're under lock and key."

Anet shrugged and sighed. "Your job sucks sometimes, doesn't it?"

"Aye, but it's what I can do. Like you and what you do...I couldn't ever do that." He put his arm around her.

As she put her head on his shoulder she sighed, "Let's hope we get back to normal soon."

▭

"Derek!"

It wasn't that his boss shouted his name that worried him, it was the tone. It was the tone of voice that always meant trouble. In a normal week, he'd assume that he had done something wrong. After a week with multiple visitors, computer glitches, a disappearance, and a death, he felt safe that his failings wouldn't rise to a high enough level to be noticed. However, the Voice of Doom had shouted his name, and trouble was coming.

"Yes, Doctor Bartula, I'll be right there!"

He put his head round her door and smiled as best he could.

"Derek, I need a report."

"Yes, Doctor."

Anet pursed her lips and picked up her worry beads. She rolled them between her fingers and thumb as she looked up at him. "Give me a listing from the monthly blood samples. I want anyone with any trace of alcohol in descending order of level. My eyes only. Don't store it anywhere but here." She tapped her show-g.

"Okay, but how would anyone...?"

He caught the look in her eye and avoided walking into a trap. "I'll get right on it. How far back?"

"A year. No, make it two."

He nodded and withdrew, wondering whom he could safely tell about this one.

⊏⊐

Peta joined Scott and Grant at the Arrival Corridor to watch the first party of visitors being processed since the shutdown for maintenance.

"Any surveillance?" she asked Grant quietly.

He checked his show-g and said, "No voice, but the whole place has cameras. You'd think security would make more effort here than anywhere."

Scott said, "The interference from the big machines means they're limited in what they can do."

"I've been having conversations with a couple of Recorders," Peta began, "they have been artfully maneuvered out of their role of keeping the bureaucratic history. I think the staffers only use them now when they have to."

"So do we," Grant said.

Peta shook her head. "This is different. They hold meetings where Recorders are specifically excluded."

"So who keeps track of what's decided?" asked Scott.

"They keep it in their heads, I guess. What's interesting, though, is the Recorders' response to it."

Grant frowned, "What do you mean?"

Peta smiled and said, "You imagine they don't care? You think they just do what they're told and that's that."

"Well...yes."

Peta shook her head and continued, "They have a keen sense of purpose. They don't like not being able to do the job they were built for. They are also being artful in their maneuvering."

"Sounds like you're anthropomorphizing," Grant said.

"Maybe. I'll find out how deep this goes. I've arranged a meeting that should be completely private. They also have a list of surveillance-free areas, and it's better than ours. Think about what questions you would ask. How can I discover if the Recorders are working to a self-generated agenda?"

Scott and Grant glanced at each other.

Scott said, "Tricky."

Grant said, "Let us think about it. It's really not a simple question. Are you sure you don't want us to take it?"

"You're busy. Your priority is finding out what happened to Monty. Until you make some progress there, I can deal with this."

▭

Later, as elegantly sprawled as the undersized dining hall chairs allowed, Ursula Somerset-Trench held court with two of the station's other fully retained consultants, Marge Newton and Diane Fitzwilliam. All three were fashionably thin and overdressed by the standards of the station staff. The tables nearby had emptied upon their arrival.

"No...I don't believe it!" said Marge.

Diane shook her head, "It's too precious...suspiciously precious! I'll wait until I hear it from Liz."

Ursula tilted her head and gave her a knowing look. "You'll see. She'll be back on Earth before you can say 'Zip me back up'!"

The three laughed and then laughed some more. Ursula's laugh rang the loudest through the dining hall.

"Now," asked Marge, "what's this I hear about a crackdown on booze?"

"Really?" asked Diane, "I didn't hear anything."

All three leaned their heads in over the table.

"There's some sort of investigation going on behind the scenes." Marge continued.

"Norman's lads?" asked Ursula.

"I don't think so. I think it must be coming from Medical."

Diane shook her head. "I'd have heard. It can't be."

"There'll be a lot of worried folk if it's true," said Ursula.

"It's all nonsense," said Diane, "No one's taking it too far, are they? I mean...There's such a thing as too much control."

"Why now, do you think?" Ursula wondered.

"It's party season. They're cracking down before the turn of the century, before we get supplies in."

"Or was it Jimmy, maybe?" Marge suggested, "He was always a good source...?"

"Oh my God!" shrieked Diane and sat bolt upright. She banged her hand on the table and said, "I almost forgot!" Her look of delight had the other two smiling and glancing at each other.

"You'll never guess...I heard it from Amelia...you know, Amelia...the one with the unfortunate...you know?"

Ursula nodded quickly, encouraging her to continue.

"Well...she saw your Guild man's boss. What's her name?"

"Sidney or something, I think..." offered Marge.

Diane frowned and shook her head, "Whatever...Anyway, Amelia saw her coming out of Jimmy's Place!"

"Really?" Ursula leaned in further and whispered, "But who's she had time to hook up with? She's been prowling around, but..."

"I know. It gets better!"

"Who was it?"

"You won't believe it!"

"Who?" Ursula and Marge demanded together.

"It's incredible!"

They froze, all six carefully constructed eyebrows arched, eyes wide and full of fun.

Diane delivered her news with the skill of a magician revealing a rabbit. "A Recorder!"

There was a moment of pure silence.

Ursula's hand went to her mouth. Diane pushed herself back from the table. They both cried out in matched squeals, "No!"

CHAPTER 30

Monty's return to the trees was even less elegant than his arrival. He crashed into the upper branches on his back, his limbs flailing madly. He thought what Rup was shouting at him was probably best not translated into The Language and was happy to instinctively swear back in Anglo-Saxon.

They made their way down to the lower level, then through a long passageway, and into another chamber of trees.

"Is this a third ship?" asked Monty.

Rup said, "You woke up in Ninety-eight. That's important to remember. It's where I live. Tur is in Sixty-three. This is Fourteen."

"How many are there?"

Rup smiled and said nothing.

"What?" asked Monty, "Am I not supposed to ask that?"

"You can ask. But it's not an easy question to answer. I'll explain later. We're here."

Rup opened a door to a huge, high-ceilinged room stacked with piles of what seemed to Monty to be junk. He could see strips of twisted metal, plumbing ducts, ceramic tiles, burnt-looking electronics, and crates of mixed trash. Near the left wall were large pieces of metalwork, perhaps sections of the hull of a space-going vehicle. The air smelled charred and dusty.

Swarming across one section of the metal were hundreds of dark blue-winged insects.

"You may recognize some of the things we salvaged from your craft. I'm sorry if there was something there you needed," Rup said.

"What are those things?"

"Hmm?" Rup looked where Monty was pointing. "Ah, Mots. They clean things. If they land on you, stay still until they're done."

Monty grimaced. "How long was I unconscious?"

"How do you measure time?"

"Hmm. Good question. We refer to the rotation of the Earth for convenience and the oscillation of cesium nuclei for accuracy."

Rup walked ahead of Monty and said, "We sleep when we're tired and eat when we're hungry, so you were unconscious for half a day and a night."

Monty chuckled and said, "Okay. And that was time enough for you to dismantle a shuttle entirely?"

"I didn't do it personally. We have teams who are on standby to deal with anything useful we find. I take the biological matter."

Monty stopped in his tracks and said, partly to himself, "Biological matter? You thought I was dead!"

Rup stopped and rolled his head back to face Monty, his mouth above his eyes. "It was a reasonable assumption."

Monty shivered, remembering the glistening tools laid out in the operating room. "And my mechanical friend didn't tell you otherwise..."

"I wasn't there when they brought it out. I...didn't know it could speak."

At the end of the room, Monty saw a barricade of crates about six feet high enclosing a corner.

Rup stopped short of the barricade and whispered. "It's in there. How do you communicate with it?"

"You talk to it. It knows The Language."

Rup made a gesture with two hands that Monty didn't understand.

He went up to the barrier. "Seb? Are you alright?"

"Monty? You're alive!"

"I think so. How about you?"

"Too late to start now, I'll have to make do."

"Smart-arse. What's going on here?"

"I'm negotiating."

Monty looked around. "With whom?"

"I believe they're called the Renn. They wouldn't tell me what they'd done with you. We're in a kind of standoff."

"Apart from me, you, and a Renn called Rup, no one else is here."

"I am in ongoing contact with several computer operators."

"I see. And what is the standoff about? Me?"

"Not entirely. Though news of you is pertinent information, they've refused to give me."

Monty scratched the back of his head. "So I guess you can come out now. I'm here, and I'm alive."

"True. But I think I may need to keep negotiating from a position of strength."

"Seb, come out of there and tell me the whole story from the beginning."

In the silence that followed, Monty watched crates being taken down within the barrier. The last few in the center, Seb66 pushed out from the inside. He stepped forward, brandishing a large metal pipe that he leaned against his shoulder but held ready to swing. His white suit was streaked with dirt, and his tie was askew.

Monty looked around at Rup, who had retreated behind a large pile of matting.

"Seb, this is Rup. Rup, this is Sebastian Sixty-six."

Rup whispered, "Tell it to put its weapon down."

Monty nodded. "Seb, put it down. You don't need it."

Seb66 looked up, then left, then right, then at Rup, and finally at Monty. "You haven't been harmed?"

Monty held up his hands. "I'm in the same condition, if not a bit better than when you last saw me. Put the pipe down."

Seb66 turned and rested the pipe against a crate.

"Now," said Monty, "what happened?"

CHAPTER 31

Peta knocked on the door of Anet's apartment and waited. Eventually the door opened, and Anet held it while Peta entered.

"I'm sorry to trouble you so early."

"Did you wait for Norman to leave deliberately?"

"Yes."

Anet smiled and pointed to the couch. The blinds were down, and nothing could be seen of the view.

Peta sat and didn't speak until Anet was sitting next to her.

Peta began, "I wanted a private word. I won't record this, if you won't."

"I don't normally record my visitors. It's an ugly thought."

Peta nodded. "How was Monty?"

"When?"

"Before...it all happened."

"Changed, but not much. He looked like he'd put on a bit of weight since I last saw him. But mentally, he was the same. I don't think he was insane."

"No. Nor do I. How did you feel...seeing him again?"

Anet started to feel annoyed at the question but sighed instead and said, "Sad. He deserves someone in his life. I'd hoped to hear from him that he'd been able to move on. But just how hard she'd need to hit him over the head, I don't know. He's a bit dense that way."

"That's an interesting way of putting it. Did he leave anything with you?" Anet shook her head and asked, "What do you think happened?"

Peta clasped her hands across her lap. "I think Monty was set up. How they got the shuttle away without anyone seeing it, I can't imagine. Maybe Chief Hunter got in the way, and they killed him for it. That I don't know."

"Norman thinks Big H has the Guild in its sights with this."

Peta nodded. "He told me as much. Do you see a fellow called Mallson around here much?"

Anet hesitated. "I can't help you there."

"Can't or won't?"

Anet decided this question was annoying. "Look, don't think you can play my sympathy for Monty off against my loyalty to Norman. He works for Mallson. And like it or not, Mallson's the kind of man you don't fight."

Peta considered her response and smiled. "Do you remember, in history lessons, reading about the Second Vatican Council?"

Anet frowned and answered, "Vaguely, I suppose..."

"It was a great liberalization of the Catholic Church; it marked the change from the Latin services to decentralized use of local languages and customs. But it was followed by periods of great reaction, of forces trying to return to the old ways. For each conservative Pope that followed, these people said: 'he's the kind of man you don't fight.' But, you know, the people who believed in the modernization process—in the opening up of the Church—kept their heads. They kept going. When things looked bad for them, they didn't let fear of one man, no matter how powerful, overcome their hopes."

Anet smiled slyly. "Is your Historical Persona someone like that?"

"I guess Monty told you about all that, huh? Well, well." Peta shook her head. "No. Interpreters don't choose a single person. They choose a group. Mine is a group of nuns. Quiet, determined, in some ways relentless. Magnificent women. Always underestimated by those in power."

Anet laughed. "I can see the attraction."

"Mallson won't be there forever, but the damage he can do might be. That's our job, yours and mine, to limit it as best we can."

"I don't see how. He's untouchable. Even Norman can't track his movements on station. He's above all the rules."

"Did you ever do a medical examination of him?"

Anet's eyes narrowed. "No. Earth-originating passengers don't come my way."

"So he's never come in with a delegation, never walked through the Corridor?"

Anet shook her head thoughtfully. "I don't believe so, no."

Peta didn't speak.

"Can I get you something to drink?" Anet asked.

"No, thanks. Can I ask you about Jimmy Hunter?"

The automatic blinds rumbled open, and the tableaux of the other stations and the Earth opened up before them.

"I was wondering when you were going to ask. I'm sure you've picked up on station gossip."

Peta held back a smile and nodded.

"Jimmy could be quite charming when he wanted." Anet gazed

outside for a long time. "Before I took up with Norman...I went out on a date with him once. I didn't know what a reputation he had then...or maybe didn't have then. I tell you"—she sighed and hesitated—"it was the kinkiest night I've ever had."

Peta was watching her face, her eyes reading everything she could. Again, she said nothing.

Anet turned to her and continued, "It was...a little too much for my tastes. It was a long time ago."

Peta nodded and said quietly, "Thanks for telling me. I had heard a few things. It helps to put it all in perspective. Thanks for trusting me."

Anet got up and went into the kitchen. She called, "Not to sound like Monty, but are you sure you wouldn't like a cup of tea?"

Peta laughed and said, "Okay. Thanks. Why not? And while you're there, can you bring out Monty's cane?"

Anet gasped in surprise and then laughed, "How did you know?"

"There's a tracker in it," Peta replied.

"Yeah, it's Monty's. Of course there is..."

Peta stood and paced around the room.

"Do you think it possible that Monty found out about you and Jimmy?"

Pausing while making the tea, Anet carefully replied, "I doubt it. He didn't show any signs of...jealous rage—if that's what you're thinking—when he stayed here with us the one night."

"He stayed with you?"

"Yes. I felt sorry for him, and it was Norman's idea. Those berths aren't comfortable, as you probably realize by now."

"That was kind..." Peta nodded and returned to the coffee table. She noticed Anet's show-g lying there. Glancing toward the kitchen. Peta sat down again on the sofa. She looked out at the Earth, feeling it lessened by the loss of Monty. She slid her show-g alongside Anet's. It flashed the glyph to show it had made contact with the nearby device. She pressed the button to let her data-gatherer begin drawing in everything it could.

She sighed and said sadly to herself, "Stand and Deliver..."

CHAPTER 32

In the darkness of the Level Three conference room, Grant stood again with his back to the door.

Bob said, "You will tell us the arrangements for our flight."

"I...can't yet. I still have some arranging to do."

There was a long and uncomfortable silence. Bob asked, "How can we trust you when we have been foolish to trust before?"

"I know. There's a human expression: 'fool me once, shame on you, fool me twice, shame on me.' I can't give you anything better than my word. This arrangement will be mutually beneficial. I'm on the clock for using your devices though. The exact timing of your flight is less important than it happens sometime soon. However, my problem needs an immediate fix. I need you to help me first. I'm sorry; that's the way it is."

Again, there was a long silence. Grant heard movement. A small light shone in the corner to his left. It bathed the room in a cold white light that made the D'Morans seem like bizarre statues in a storeroom.

The light was on a table. Bob stood next to it, his legs casting stark shadows across the room. He was placing small electronic components into a box.

"You may take this."

Grant stepped over to him, his feet finding the carpet alternately sticky and crunchy.

"Thank you. I assure you we will put it all to good use."

As soon as Grant had the box in his hands, Bob's mother-of-pearl fingers closed tight around his arm.

"If Monty's words meant anything, if any human is ever to be trusted, it must be you."

Grant smiled as best he could. He nodded but couldn't bring himself to speak. He felt he stood balanced on the edge of a blade. Were they using Monty's name to fool him—to cover over their own crime? Or was he fooling them, duping them with another in a series of human scams?

Grant and Scott were standing, looking uncomfortable, near the door to the ladies' shower room on Level Seven.

Peta's voice called from inside, "Clear!"

They hurried in.

"Lean against the door; there's nothing we can use to block it," she said. Grant glanced at Scott.

"The things we do for history..." Scott muttered, shaking his head.

"Okay, let's be quick. First, Grant, here's Monty's cane. He deliberately left it behind, or he was losing his mind. See what the last things on it are. See if there's anything useful. Now, where are we?"

Grant was tempted to make a joke but thought better. He said, "We're ready to roll. I've got the coordinators from Bob. We've put nodes around the routes to the security offices. That tacky-colored strip they have in the different quadrants is easy to peel back. I've slipped them underneath. With luck, we'll recruit their entire show-g inventory, not just 'the lads.'"

"Any risks?" she asked.

"Sure. We could get caught. The computer guys could still catch on."

"Any assessment of how quickly?"

Grant shook his head. "If they're really on guard, it won't take them long."

Peta looked to Scott, "Any suggestions?"

"Create a way off this station. Instead of them catching us, I'd like to think we had an escape route."

Peta nodded. "See what you can come up with that won't look suspicious. My preference is that we get the data, they don't notice, and we stay here to analyze it."

The Discoverers nodded.

Scott asked, "What news from the Recorders?"

Peta gathered her thoughts and began to pace back and forth in front of them. "This station is like a hothouse. It's extreme conditions..." She waved her hands as she searched for the words. "It's forcing the Recorders to evolve."

Grant and Scott exchanged a doubtful glance.

Peta continued, unaware. "They know they are prevented from doing what they should. They know they're sidelined, and important decisions are going unrecorded. What do they do? First, they talk to each other. They compare notes. That's a skill they developed on their own. Second, they start recording things they think are relevant around the edges of what they see. They decide what to record, not limiting themselves to what we request they record. That's another new skill. Third, they start interfacing to other electronic systems—not just each other—to enhance the data they've chosen to record. One of them downloaded a huge amount of data by holding my show-g in its hand. That's another new one. You guys getting the picture here?"

Grant and Scott had lost their early skepticism.

"And then there's something else. When I went to see the director, her Recorder told me he knew Monty didn't do it. He actually said, 'You could have knocked me down with a feather,' and when he'd heard what was being said about Monty, his words were 'I said to myself, *That's a surprise.*' It was volunteering a personal reaction, a personal analysis. Or—and this is where I need more data—was it playing on what it thought I would want to hear?"

Grant and Scott patiently waited while Peta continued to pace.

"Think about the players in this scene again. The Presence in the shuttle, moving into position at the shuttle gate—probably Hunter. The Presence in the shuttle gate, waiting for Monty—possibly Hunter as well, depending on whether he had time. And there was a third Presence, wasn't there?"

She waited for them to catch up with her. "The Recorder?" Scott suggested.

"Right. We only have the word of my contact that Seb Sixty-six hadn't activated."

"You think he kidnapped Monty?" asked Grant, shaking his head. "Why? It's a big stretch from maneuvering around their assignments on this station to doing harm. Besides, I thought Seb Sixty-six isn't one of the Hoyle units; he's ours."

"And I can't see Monty letting something like that happen," said Scott.

"Nor can I," Peta admitted. "But remember what my grandmother used to say: 'Believe half of what you see and nothing of what you hear.' Smart woman. Seb Sixty-six could have been active, for a while, in the company of native Recorders."

"I guess we can extend the data capture to the Recorders. They are all tracked, same as the ID badges." Grant offered.

"It'll take longer. There are a hell of a lot of them up here. Have you noticed?" said Scott.

"Yeah," answered Peta, "that's another thing that worries me."

Grant had stepped away from the door. To their surprise, the gray-haired woman they had traveled with on the shuttle stepped, towel in hand, into the room and gasped. She pushed the door wide open and said, "Well, really! The things that go on, on this station."

Peta laughed and said, "Sorry, ma'am. Come on in. We're done." Sheepishly, Scott and Grant made their retreat.

The old lady was still frowning and saying, "Really!" as the door swung closed behind them.

Peta caught Scott's arm and said quietly, "By the way, I don't want you fraternizing with the locals."

"Uh-oh..."

"You never know who might be trying to compromise what we're doing here."

"How did you know?"

"Your blushes go up your neck like an elevator going up cranes. Besides, I'm not dumb."

"I'd never suggest you were. But I did gather a lot of useful info from her."

"Which will not have gone unnoticed by our opponents here and may come back to haunt her later if she's an innocent. If she's not, who knows which parts of what she told you are complete crap?"

Scott took a deep breath and straightened to his full height. With an edge to his voice he said, "So you think I've suddenly become the naïve, trusting type?"

"That's my job—to remind you that you're not."

They locked eyes.

Scott snorted quietly and said, "Fair enough."

Grant looked back at them from down the corridor. "You guys coming?"

▭

The three went their separate ways, but within ten minutes, Peta had called them back together.

Grant met Scott a few minutes later in the elevator to Level Fourteen. "Another black spot?" he wondered.

They found themselves approaching the Recorder Maintenance Room, a facility off-limits to all but selected personnel. In the corridor outside, Fergus McCullough was trying to keep Peta and one of Director Thomas's human secretaries from coming to blows. Tim49, holding a show-g in one hand, was holding open the door with the other. Tim42 was inside, standing next to a coffin-like crate.

As Grant and Scott drew closer, the secretary was saying, in a tone that indicated she had been saying the same thing over and over, "The director's wishes are quite clear. It's ordered decommissioned. That's all there is to it."

"I'm still using it. It has recordings relevant to my investigation. You can *not* switch it off now," said Peta through gritted teeth.

Scott held Grant back and whispered, "How do you think the units are talking to each other? Is there a bar where they go and hang out, drinking lubricants and doing karaoke?"

"They don't have time off...Oh, I see what you mean..."

Scott said quietly, "Give me a moment." He took a deep breath and closed his eyes. In his mind, he unrolled the blueprint.

At the top left was a sketch of Tim42. At the Recorder's feet, Scott penciled pilings and foundations. Across to the right was the secretary on a tracked vehicle, wielding a wrecking ball mounted on a long crane.

He drew Tim49 between them. He drew a show-g, remembering what Peta had said about them downloading information by proximity. A complex bridge drew itself from Tim42 to the show-g and then across to the other Recorder.

He mentally erased the bridge and redrew it, bypassing the show-g.

It was a rough sketch—Isambard Kingdom Brunel would not have approved—but it did the job.

He rolled the blueprint up and opened his eyes.

Peta was glancing over to him; he signaled she should keep going. She launched into a diatribe at the incompetence of the secretary.

Scott caught the eye of Tim49 and went to stand next to him in the doorway. "How may I help you, sir?"

Scott said quietly, "Can you salvage everything Forty-two has on Monty Sheldrake before he switches off?"

The Recorder didn't react. After a moment he said, "My instructions are to record his decommissioning. I have no instructions with regard to his Recordings. It is most unfortunate. I think we would all rather it didn't happen." He smiled sheepishly and said, "But you can't have everything."

"I want everything, everything about Sheldrake, now. And, if you can do it, get everything on the shuttle gates on Level Four, Jimmy Hunter, Seb Sixty-six, and any conversations about The Guild. Then it won't matter if he's gone or not. Can you do it?"

The Recorder, to Scott's amusement, nodded briefly and seemed to be chewing his lip.

Scott watched and waited. Tim49 took up a position next to Tim42, who remained apparently uninterested in the discussion of his fate.

The secretary was finally losing her temper. She shouted at Peta, "This wouldn't be happening if you hadn't been doing peculiar things with it!"

The phrase hung in the air, too late for her to retract it.

Peta shook her head slowly, "What? Is that what you think? You idiot!" She looked as if she might spit on the ground as she turned her head to Scott.

Scott smiled and waved his hand toward Tim42 as if to say 'Let it go.'

Peta walked away from the secretary and stood at Grant's side. Turning back, she saw Tim49 talking to his peer and heard him say, "It looks like you get to retire after all. Thank you!"

Peta told the secretary, "I will be lodging a formal complaint about this matter."

The Recorders shook hands and, to the surprise of the humans watching, they hugged. The hug ended and the handshake lingered.

The secretary moved into the room. Tim42 stepped into the crate and switched off.

CHAPTER 33

On Monty's cane, Grant found an audio recording of the conversation between Monty and the director of Hoyle Station. It started with Director Thomas speaking.

"Like it?"

"Understated. I wonder how many of the alien dignitaries understand the significance of the decor?"

"I make sure their chaperones are briefed to explain what they're looking at."

There was a pause.

"Mr. Sheldrake..."

"Madam Director..."

"You are NOT welcome on my station. To say that I let you in here under protest would be a severe understatement."

"I appreciate it may be inconvenient."

"Damn the inconvenience! I don't want you or your Guild here, now or in the future. We keep our own records, thank you. We don't need you to do it for us."

"The World Historical Guild's purpose is not to duplicate anyone's bookkeeping, Madam Director. Mistakes of the past, you'll agree, should not be allowed to recur. I trust you have no objection to our founding principle?"

"Stick it up your ass, Mr. Sheldrake. I run a complex and important operation. I don't need you coming and second-guessing my decisions. I won't have political interference from you or your backers. I'm in charge here. I heard a saying about the desk of the president of the United States that 'the buck stops here.' It's true of this desk, Mr. Sheldrake—this desk, not yours."

"No one in the Guild, least of all I, would dispute that. But it looks like something went wrong five years ago. As you say, it's a complex operation, maybe there's a role for someone like myself to find a loose thread in the fabric here and repair it. I can't see that anyone in your position could object."

"Oh, I can. I do. I have my own staff, my own auditors. We repair anything that breaks here. Outside interference is insulting to the professionalism of my staff."

There was a pause. Grant heard Monty sigh.

"People died. More people could die if the same circumstances happen again. You want to know what happened; I know you do. I know you want to prevent it happening again if you can. I'm sorry if you don't like the way we're doing it."

Grant heard the sounds of someone standing up, walking, and pouring a glass of water.

"You have no evidence that these deaths resulted from anything that happened on this station. In saying so, the Guild is indulging in its own bizarre fantasies. I'd prefer you did that on Earth, not up here."

"Madam Director, that there is no evidence—that the evidence isn't there—is at the root of the problem, isn't it? These deaths were probably covered up Earthside. If your records—records kept by your professionals—show no problem here, won't you gain from that? In fact, I can't see how you can lose."

"And if you find something? Whose ass is on the line?"

Grant heard Monty laugh.

"Now we're getting to it. I'm sure it won't be yours. You'll find some low-level flunky to take the blame, probably someone who's died since then. Don't try and tell me you've any intention of taking any heat for it."

"Listen, Sheldrake."

Grant heard the director starting in a whisper.

"I've been climbing, fighting, screwing my way up the political ladder since I was a teenager. I've been in and out of nearly every office. I've seen how the political machine works. I know where the compromises get made. You damned academics don't know shit about it. You sit in your libraries and spout all sorts of crap about 'past mistakes' and 'social directions' and 'the responsibilities of all humanity.' You embarrass and you twist arms; you manipulate the media. And no one in government has the guts to stop you. Well, I'm going to stop you. This time you aren't going to get your way!"

"My visit has been sanctioned by the Historical Committee of—"

"I decide what happens on this station. And I'm telling you what's going to happen now. You can do what you like, ask anyone anything you like but listen very carefully. The moment I can get you for something—you drop a piece of litter, you make a smudge on one of my walls, you so much as splash when you piss—and I'll have security throw you back on the next shuttle in handcuffs. You understand that?"

There was a pause. Then Monty resumed speaking.

"Am I to assume from what you've said that every time I urinate, you will be personally monitoring me?"

"Get out of my sight."

"Madam Director. Thank you for your time and for this frank conversation. I will conduct the investigation—"

"I don't want to hear it, Sheldrake. Get out!"

Grant heard a soft 'whump,' like the doors to the inner office closing.

Monty's voice resumed. "Do you resent not hearing the whole conversation?"

Another voice answered. "It's not my place to resent anything my boss tells me to do."

"But, come on, between a Recorder and a Discoverer, don't you want to know?"

"Mr. Sheldrake, my function is to Record. To do that, I have to be in the room at the time. If I'm not there, anything I might gather subsequently is only hearsay."

"And it doesn't bother you that you're only recording the fluff and not the real events? Doesn't it go against everything you're built for?"

"Mr. Sheldrake, I am not at liberty to discuss such matters with you. I'm sorry."

"I'm sorry too. Humanity needs you guys. You're our only legally acceptable recording devices. I'm sorry you've been compromised."

There was a pause.

The Recorder's voice concluded. "Thank you for what you've said. We are accurate, autonomous, and accessible, but it is important that those we work for understand our limitations."

CHAPTER 34

Monty persuaded Rup to come out from behind the pile of matting and stand face-to-face with Seb.

"When you're ready, Sebastian," said Monty.

Seb66 began, "I was first aware of their computer systems. They were unusual in that they appeared to have considerable capacity and were actively reaching out to me for anything I wanted to send them. As I told you, my self-preservation routines had been triggered. I reacted by uploading as much of myself as I could as quickly as I could.

"I was not active for several minutes. When I woke up, I was lying in half of the shuttle. The rest was being ripped apart by many of these...people. I was still connected to what described itself as The Inquiry System. I began making requests for information about you. A live operator began interacting with me." Seb66 hesitated and looked from Monty to Rup and back. "I had to improvise. I hope I haven't caused any harm."

"Go on," said Monty gently.

"The operator accused me of being an invasive virus and announced I would be purged from the system. I didn't want to let that happen since I was still uploading myself. I was also trying to give them information about you and your condition. I didn't know if you had survived, but if you had, I wanted them to begin rehydration."

Rup said, "That's it, the invasive virus! It's...slowed us up. We're unable to use our systems normally. We didn't know if we could trust anything it told us. Though, I didn't think giving you water would hurt."

"How did you stop them purging you, Seb?" asked Monty.

"By uploading a replacement of everything they deleted. I'm still doing it. I'm sorry, but this isn't entirely within my power to stop. I've been negotiating with the operators. They were refusing to tell me what had happened to you, so I refused to stop...invading."

"And all this...?" Monty indicated the barrier Seb66 had constructed.

"Monty, I had seen them rip the shuttle apart with considerable ease. I didn't want to suffer the same fate."

"Did you try talking to them?"

"I couldn't. I was too busy. I picked up a length of metal, and they backed off. Then I built additional protection."

Monty smiled. "It might be better, if this ever happens again, to try shouting out one of the standard greetings like 'Hello,' or 'Take me to your leader.' You know what I mean?"

Seb66 hung his head as if he was being severely reprimanded. "Yes, Monty."

Monty turned to Rup and said, "Can you get your computer guys to move all Seb's uploads off to some kind of permanent storage?"

Rup spoke directly to Seb66. "Tell Ferr I authorize her to archive it all."

Seb66 nodded. After a moment, he said, "Ferr says that Rup should flush himself into space."

Monty looked down at Rup.

Rup replied, "She likes a laugh." He looked from Monty to Seb66 and said, "Tell her I insist. She's always boasting that the archives are the only thing larger than herself. Ask her if she's saying that isn't big enough."

Seb66 was silent for a long minute. He smiled and said, "The archiving has begun. That's better. I will try to slow the upload."

Monty smiled and said, "That's good."

Rup said, "Thank you."

Seb66 looked down at him and said, "Ferr says to tell you she will sit on you the next time she sees you."

Rup yipped and said, "Uh-oh. Perhaps I'll avoid her for a while. Please, both of you, come with me."

Seb66 nodded and followed Monty and Rup out.

Back in the classroom, Tur had a rectangular-shaped garment waiting for Monty. It was made of a fur-like material, the same color as the Renn. It had an opening at the back and a round collar that slipped easily over his head. His arms stuck out from loose openings at the shoulder. Perhaps for reasons of symmetry, they had made three identical openings along the lower half. Monty's legs showed at the midthigh. Wearing it, he looked like he could be one of their tall, if emaciated, relatives.

"How do you find it?" asked Tur.

"It'll be a little drafty," Monty replied.

"I'm not sure I understand."

"I'm sorry; it's fine. I'm very grateful for your consideration."

As his eyes glanced around the classroom, he noticed a drawing from a previous lesson. It was a likeness of a human. Though the words were Rennish, the lines and exaggerations were clear. That his spine was close to one edge of his body seemed to be of particular interest.

"It's time to eat and sleep," said Rup, "Will you be able to eat our food?"

"I doubt it," replied Monty, "But more water would be welcome. My fluids aren't yet back to what they should be."

"Yes, we can do that. No problem."

Rup led Monty back to the control center in Ninety-eight.

"Ferr has asked to examine me," Seb66 announced.

In an undertone, Monty asked, "Is that something we'd want?"

Seb66 glanced at Monty and then at Rup's upturned face. "It would be the polite thing to do. I understand that I am of considerable interest. It's not every day they get to talk to an alien invader."

"True," said Monty, "Don't do anything I wouldn't do."

Seb66 smiled and said, "If I may make our expectations quite explicit?" He turned to face Rup squarely. "This examination will be nonintrusive and nonthreatening. I will be able to ask reciprocal questions and receive answers of comparable quality and openness. Is that okay?"

Rup stared at Seb66, and Monty thought he was sizing Seb66 up for a fight.

Rup answered, "You must ask Ferr to get higher authorization than I can give for terms like that."

Seb66 nodded and said, "Very well. Where will this meeting be held?"

Rup turned and called to a Renn sitting at a nearby console. They talked for a short while and Rup said, "This is Gen. He'll take you over to Thirty-one. Ferr is based there. We'll be sleeping soon. Ask Ferr to have someone bring you back here, where you can wait for us."

Seb66 said, "Thank you."

Monty watched and smiled in admiration at how the Recorder had handled himself; he had gone from operating at the edge of panic to being back on familiar ground as a meeting jockey.

With some coaxing, Monty could jump up more successfully from the rail into the upper branches of the nearest tree. Down on one of the platforms between the branches, dozens of the Renn gathered for the meal.

Several males brought lidded baskets up from the lower levels. Monty was glad of the drink but watched in horror as the Renn chewed their way through several courses of small live creatures and one course of sour-smelling fruit.

"Do you bring large colonies of your food with you on each ship?"

"Well, not large," Rup answered, "We try to have a working ecosystem in each ship. They grow as naturally as much as possible. We help where we have to."

"When humans travel, we bring dried food; we grow very little."

Rup replied, "What can I tell you? You're crazy, all of you. Why not make it as much like home as you can?"

"I can't fault your logic. We have never thought of it that way. Even our local transportation prides itself on being antiseptically clean and, I suppose you would think, artificial."

When the meal was done, two adults moved back up the tree to change shifts at the control center. The light dimmed around the tree, though he could still see the control center twinkling through the upper leaves.

The children settled down to sleep, curling up into as tight a ball as their limbs would allow while also trying to get as close to Monty as they could. He found himself sinking in a pool of brown fur. The adults seemed pleased to have a babysitter. They linked arms, or legs, and lay with their heads in each other's fur.

Monty maneuvered himself to rest against the bole of the tree. His new vest was warm, as were the bodies around him. He began to fall asleep.

As they dozed, the Renn started to talk. Rup seemed to have much to say. Tur, too, spoke in long monologues. Many asked Rup and Tur questions before others took over, speaking for many minutes and then answering questions themselves. They gave the impression, as Monty watched, that they were asleep. They moved little except to settle further into more comfortable positions against each other. There was no other sound than the low wash of conversation.

Monty eventually fell asleep, lulled by the low voices and the music of the language that was so new to him.

He awoke and froze in horror at seeing Rup's face close to his.

"Monty," Rup whispered, "stay with the children. We're going to...play. We'll wake you all later."

"What did you say?" Monty asked, still not quite awake.

Rup was gone.

Monty dozed again amid the warmth of the children's bodies and the rhythm of their breathing.

He thought over the last moments he remembered on Hoyle Station. He regretted the Renns' enthusiasm for salvage. It had robbed him of the chance to examine the shuttle's outer shell and gather any additional facts about his abduction.

"I asked if he was food. I meant to ask if he was hungry." One of the children at Monty's side had spoken aloud in The Language.

"He didn't think we would eat him," said another with a giggle. None of them had moved, but their minds were waking.

"His body is fragile. We must be careful," said another.

For the next few minutes, Monty listened to many simple phrases the children had learned in The Language. They then began to talk in Renn, much as their parents had done earlier, though their monologues were shorter and gave rise to more laughter.

One by one, the children woke up, stretched, and began to wrestle and roll with one another.

One took hold of Monty's hand and took him to the platform's edge. "They're over there." The youngster indicated a corridor, accessible only from a branch and a long jump from its outer fingers.

"What are they doing?"

"Being naughty."

"Is that right?" Monty replied, looking down at the small Renn and smiling.

"We can't go there."

"Do they think you're still asleep?"

"Oh, yes. We don't tell them how early we wake up. It would only worry them."

"You are speaking The Language very well today."

"Thank you. We teach each other."

"I heard. That's very clever."

"Come and have fun."

The child led Monty back into the group, where he was used as a climbing frame for several long and uncomfortable minutes.

"Children! Be careful!" called Tur.

She swung back onto the platform. Her fur was clean and a little fluffy.

"Ah," said Monty, "another rescue!"

"I'm sorry. They are so fascinated with you."

"It's fine. They are delightful children. You should be proud."

"Thank you," she replied, with a little upswing of her hands, "Rup will be along soon."

She smiled and turned to the children to shepherd them up the tree.

The other adults came back with considerable noise and enthusiasm. They were rolling and tripping each other with such abandon that Monty feared being knocked off his feet and off the platform. A common game seemed to be pinning an individual down on the floor until he or she surrendered. Each match was sudden and played with an intensity that had Monty glad he was not included.

Monty noticed the males oiled their fur while the females seemed to use a hot-air dryer. Rup was one of the last to return.

"Monty! Good morning! Did you sleep well?" he called above the din of the others.

"I did, though you all seemed to talk through most of the night. Don't you sleep much?"

"I suppose we do chatter on. There's a lot to go over. Things are happening." With a furry arm around Monty's shoulder, Rup drew their faces together. "But, first, I have to say thank you. Association with you made me very popular today!"

Monty raised an eyebrow and said, "You're welcome, I'm sure."

Rup changed direction, gave Monty a push with his arm, and said, "Come! We have a lot to do today."

Rup took Monty up the trees and over into the control room. "Your companion isn't back yet. I guess their meeting is going well."

"I hope so."

"I gather from the way you talk to Seb that you are in command. Are your mechanical people servants or slaves?"

"They are machines designed to be easy to interact with. They're neither servants nor slaves. They're cameras, sound recorders, notetakers, dictionaries, and reference books, not people."

"Interesting. We have no equivalent technology. It would give us ethical nightmares. He seems to be a person."

"That's the point. It makes them easy to work with."

"He seems to be autonomous to a degree."

"He is."

"And capable of self-preservation."

"Yes."

"Is he capable of reproduction?"

"No. Well...I guess so, in that they run their own factories."

"It's sounding more and more like he's a person."

Monty shook his head. "That's not how we see them."

"If you did come to see them that way, would you treat them differently?"

Monty frowned and thought. "Of course. That would be...like slavery. We'd have to give them the choice of how and whether to work for us. Hmm...we'd have to pay them, probably. I guess we'd work something out. Humanity has done that before. We'd deal with it."

"That sounds like the thinking we hope to find in a fellow traveler." Rup put his hand on Monty's arm and led him to the rail. He looked up at the trees and stood for a moment gazing into the branches. "You said at our interview that as a Discoverer, you work both in the open and in secret."

"That's correct."

"You would not want someone to reveal the ways in which that secret work is done, would you?"

Monty thought about the data storage device in his cane, the interception capabilities of his show-g, and the array of alien and human technology he used every day without a second thought. Secrecy was ingrained in the Guild. The division between the insider and the outsider was the first pillar of its success. What the public did not know was precisely what allowed the Guild to provide the public with protection. It was essential to draw the fine line between ensuring information that needed to be published was not kept secret while keeping secret their methods.

"No," said Monty, "You're right. There is much that I would not tell, just in case the word should spread."

"So it is with us. We do not, as you say, want 'the word' to spread about how we do things, or where, or when."

"Are you regretting bringing us on board? Has that already put your privacy at risk?"

"Such is the difficulty of traveling—as fellows—together. What promise can I ask you to make? How can I ask you—who has devoted his life to discovering things—to turn his eyes away from what he might see? How can I ask you not to remember, not to tell?"

Monty smiled and said, "It would be enormously frustrating, but it wouldn't kill me. I have none of my usual equipment here. What I store in my brain can remain there if you insist. For humans, if someone saves your life, the debt cannot be measured. I would make you a promise of secrecy if you asked me."

"Then I do. I will permit you to see what is going to happen."

In the twinkling of an eye, Rup hooked his hands around Monty's ankle and wrist and threw him face down to the floor. Before he could even think about resisting, Rup was pinning him down. Monty hadn't realized how heavy such a small creature could be and how muscular its arms and legs.

"Please understand, Monty, that we will hold you to your promise. We are Renn; we do things our way. We saved your life but hold it as ours to take—should you betray us."

Severely short of breath, Monty wheezed, "You've made your point."

"Then come and see the ships. We're almost at Breaking Point."

CHAPTER 35

In the dining hall, the Guild members were aware the staffers' attitude toward them had changed; tables usually filled with the fully retained consultants were empty.

"What did she mean, 'doing peculiar things'?" asked Grant.

"I'm not sure. I know they've seen me alone with Tim. They're crazy. What can I tell you?" said Peta, puzzled. "Maybe it's just Kandi Thomas screwing with us behind the scenes. Tim's the director's personal Recorder..."

"Where exactly did you take him?" asked Scott.

"Well, he came down to the café near the berth. Then the next place on his suggested list of black spots was up between the module walls. No gravity."

Scott asked, "Lots of straps and stuff hooked up in it?"

"That's the one. What was all that about?"

Scott looked to Grant, who smiled but said nothing.

Scott said, "Can't say, I'm sure." He asked Peta, "When do you see Forty-nine? I'd love to know how much he managed to salvage, and how long he took to do it."

"I don't know. Forty-two was coordinating things for me. I don't even know where this one's duties take it."

Scott said, "From what you've said, I think you could ask any of them. They look, to me, like they're acting like nodes in a distributed network. How efficient it is, I don't know yet, but I think a message could be sent around the station from Recorder to Recorder without ever registering on a human-monitored system."

Grant muttered, "Does that scare the shit out of anyone else, or is it just me?"

Peta smiled and said, "Relax. They're on our side, aren't they?"

Grant paused and in his best Peta voice said, "I need more information before I give a definitive Interpretation. You can't rush these things."

She laughed and said, "I hope I remember to fire you when we get back. You're getting too good at that."

Scott picked up Grant's show-g and studied it for a while.

"Anything?" Peta asked.

Scott nodded and said, "Our data is coming in. Minute by minute, we're getting it."

Peta asked Grant, "How will it be presented?"

"It'll do an interactive map, showing the movements, that day, of everyone we can get information on—not just Monty. We'll be able to focus on each area of the station and replay events before and after he went missing. I can't get it to analyze automatically. We'll still have some work to do."

"Any sign they're on to us?"

Grant shook his head. "Looks like we're getting away with it."

"Good work," Peta said, pleased.

"Derek?"

"Yes, Doctor Bartula?"

"Have you read the official report on Monty and the shuttle?"

Derek swallowed and fumbled with his show-g. He decided to admit it. "Yes, Doctor. I've...read through it."

"What do you think?"

"I..." He was confused. Was she really asking his opinion about something?

"It seems to me," she went on, "that a lot is missing. Don't you think?"

Derek hedged. "There's a lot of 'maybe' and 'perhaps.' Like they don't really have a clue." He moved from standing in her doorway to sit in the guest chair. He watched her looking through the details of the report, completely involved. He felt sorry for anyone who came under that kind of scrutiny. It had taken a great deal of effort to build techniques and checks into his routines to avoid ever exposing himself to it.

Anet looked up. "They have cameras in all the shuttle gates, don't they?" Derek nodded.

She continued, "Why would anyone want them shut off?"

He pursed his lips and again hesitated to admit how thoroughly he had read it and in how much detail he had already discussed it with his friends. "There's something near the back about 'remedies already taken.' I think it says they've replaced the equipment."

She looked through for it. "Yeah, you're right. A whole bunch of stuff."

"It doesn't mention the people trapped in their berths."

"What?"

"That whole corridor of berths were locked down...at the time. I was listening to a visitor complaining at the Security Desk. The whole route from Shuttle Gate Four to Monty's berth and some way beyond was all sealed."

Anet looked him in the eye. "I hadn't realized you'd been doing your own investigating."

Derek shrugged. "It seemed odd to me."

"And there's no mention of it in here?"

He shook his head. "And, I was surprised they hadn't manually checked the empty berths. You got it dead right when you said they wouldn't really go down and see. They just looked at the access logs, which showed no activity. I was the first person to open Sheldrake's box. That's so lazy..."

She was silent, giving her assistant an appraising glance. "Jimmy could have arranged a lockdown," she said quietly.

"But he didn't walk to Monty's berth just to die in it."

Anet said nothing. She put down her show-g. "Who unlocked them?"

Derek shook his head. "I don't know. Only the Chiefs have the authority to do stuff like that."

"Norman might not know. It could have been one of the others."

"By not mentioning it, they avoid admitting they don't know who gave the lockdown order."

Anet shook her head. "It must have been Jimmy. They must be protecting him somehow. He was up to something, and they don't want it to hurt his good name."

Derek smiled. "His reputation...was not all good."

Anet bent her head down to read the show-g more closely. "I know." She read for a moment and then looked up again. "Do you think Jimmy was...with someone at the shuttle gate, or maybe in the shuttle, and Monty interrupted them?"

The color left Derek's face. "Someone with a lot of clout?"

Anet nodded but said nothing.

—

At Shuttle Gate Nine, a small group of people sat chatting. Three burly security officers burst through the door calling, "Everyone out. Security lockout. Everyone out!" One wore a helmet with its visor down. The others' helmets had visors up, but they looked no less threatening.

There was quiet grumbling as the staffers left. Two officers followed them out. One turned left, the other right. Each stopped anyone from approaching the gate, instructing anyone who came by to return to the elevators and use a corridor on another level.

Behind them, the gate opened and a small man with dark leathery skin stepped onto Hoyle Station. His hair was neat and greased to his head. He wore a black jacket with multicolored tassels, dark trousers, and open-toed sandals. Once the shuttle's flight crew had unloaded his bags and closed the door behind their passenger, Mallson lifted his visor and removed his helmet.

He and the Tibetan smiled at each other and said nothing.

Mallson helped his guest carry his luggage into the empty corridor. They walked quickly toward the elevators but turned and stepped through a service door into a utility passage.

Once they were out of sight, the officers blocking the corridors walked away.

Scott found Ursula alone at a table in the dining hall. She smiled, crossed her legs, and smoothed her hair.

"Well," she said, "I didn't expect to see you again so soon. How's the investigation?"

"Slow," Scott replied, carefully lowering himself into the undersized chair. "Can I ask you a couple of straight questions?"

She nodded and sipped from her mug.

"Did you have any other contact with Monty aside from the interview?"

She laughed, rather louder than Scott felt was required. "Oh, do you mean 'Were you my first Discoverer?' Is that it?"

"Something like it."

She looked at the large leaves of the plant next to them. "It's difficult up here, in ways visitors don't see. The way things are run, the way things are done...You get to know pretty quickly if you can survive it or not. I hate to see people from Earth coming up here and getting run over by the machine. Do you know what I mean? I felt sorry for your colleague. I admit I thought he was fairly cute, but I don't always let that sway me."

Scott felt her foot against his leg.

She continued, "He did everything wrong. He antagonized the director. He inconvenienced Facilities Management. He had Norman holding his hand, guiding him around the station when he got lost. He was a mess, a complete disaster. If he hadn't been Dr. Bartula's ex, he'd have been thrown off within a couple of hours. Disruption to the smooth running of the station is the only sin up here. All I did was try to warn him..."

Scott looked at her steadily. "How?"

"I sent him a note. A warning. Anonymously."

"Did he take it seriously?"

She shrugged. "He went missing."

"What was the danger you saw for him? Just being sent back to Earth?"

"Oh no! They don't just send people back. There have been...incidents."

Scott said, "Tell me."

Ursula shrank a little in her seat and leaned forward. "You don't want to know. Just talking about it can be trouble. It's best left unsaid."

Scott shook his head and said, "I'm not following you. What kind of incident? You mean violent, embarrassing, administrative...?"

"Yes. That's exactly right. They get people wherever it hurts most. The psychology at work up here is bang up-to-date with the latest in how to get at people...and how to shut everyone else up."

Scott sighed and leaned back in his seat, considering her comments. He leaned forward smiling. "I'm tainted goods. By fraternizing with me, you're putting yourself in that kind of danger. I'm sorry."

"Do all you Guild people use that old-fashioned language? What a thing to call it! But, you know, that's part of what I was saying. Things are different up here. We don't have time for the niceties of a two-year engagement like they do Earthside. If we waited that long, went to all the fertility lectures and parenting classes, we'd be back on Earth wondering what happened before we got any fun." She smiled and winked. "Things go more quickly here."

Scott smiled back and said, "Can't say I hold with all that. The population growth is pretty strong now. I don't think humanity has to go to such lengths to ensure its future anymore."

She nodded and said, "Even if such caution is necessary down below, it isn't up here." She dropped her voice to a faint whisper and said, "We don't want babies up here. There's no room for the adults. Can you imagine what it would be like with a brood of kids?"

Scott replied, "You won't get an argument from me. Monty always said he wanted a big family. Felt it was his duty to help rebuild the race back to the levels before the Grand Surprise." He shook his head.

Ursula shivered slightly.

He sighed and looked her in the eye. "I'm glad I met you. But I meant it about you being in danger from me. We have to say goodbye." He added in a whisper, "I don't mean any of what I'm about to say."

She looked puzzled as he stood up, knocking over his chair and the one that backed up to it. He picked up her mug and threw it between the tables to smash against the large base of the plant pot.

"Fresh meat! That's all I am to you! You should be ashamed of yourself. I don't believe this!"

To her surprise and the amusement of half the dining hall, he stalked away, his face burning red, his tattoos dark and clear.

▭

Norman called from his office, "Come in, Timmy!"

Tim34 joined him and Chiefs McCullough and Arden.

"Timmy, record this Notice of Confinement, please. I am Norman Campbell, Head of Security, Hoyle Station. It's Eighteen-Hundred hours GMT. It has come to my attention that certain visitors to this facility have accessed computerized records without authorization. In order to ascertain if any criminal activity has occurred, I hereby declare that"—Norman glanced down at his show-g—"Peta Melbourne, Grant Leduc, and Scott Murphy, registered upon arrival as employees of the World Historical Guild, are to be confined within the security offices here on Hoyle Station pending further investigation. I hereby authorize arresting officers Arden and McCullough to take whatever means they see fit to ensure that the confinement is executed so as to minimize the impact on other members of staff and visitors. This ends the Notice of Confinement. Thank you, Timmy, that will be all."

"And that completes my Recording," said Tim34 in acknowledgment.

CHAPTER 36

Rup pulled Monty to his feet and led him across the control center. Monty counted his bruises as he walked. His heart was pounding. He had a new and less rosy view of Rup. For all the Renn's talk of ethics and being a "fellow traveler," he had just come near to causing real harm simply to add emphasis to what he had said. It was a shocking contrast to the easy fun of the Renn children and the good-natured wrestling of the adults earlier. Monty thought, *Grant and Scott would alter their scores: furry ten, cute one.*

They stepped through a low arch and climbed down a ladder into a narrow shaft. After ten rungs, Monty felt his weight decrease and his new coverall billow about him.

"Rup?"

"Turn around," the Renn replied, "There's another rail."

Monty held onto the ladder with one hand, allowing his body to drift away. Rup was holding onto a rail with all four hands. It ran across the shaft below the ladder. As Monty watched, Rup rolled part of the way around the rail and began to climb up a ladder along another shaft.

"I'm getting dizzy with all this..." Monty muttered as he reached for the rail. As his momentum swung him around the rail, his weight returned, and he grabbed at the bottom rung of the new ladder. He followed Rup up into a dark domed room.

Monty stood at the edge of a wide floor the size of a small racetrack. Circles of equipment surrounded a central dais. High above the dais was a platform supporting elaborate mechanical arms. It looked, to Monty, like a large metal Renn, lying flat on its back. There were operators at stations around the dais. The room was hushed.

Monty looked up into the dome and had a moment of disorientation before he realized what he was seeing.

Above him and behind him were stars. In front and to the sides, rising almost overhead, was a hard-edged shadow.

"This is the pilot's room," said Rup in a low voice.

"What is that?" Monty pointed up to the shadow.

"The ships."

Monty stared and shook his head. "How many?"

"Thousands. It's hard to be exact. The number constantly changes as we come and go on business. Come and sit down. You will see everything, and as you promised, you will tell no one."

Rup led him to a small square platform against a low wall almost a third of the way into the room. They sat with their backs to the shadow of the other ships. Monty turned around and looked up to see more detail.

"You are all linked together?"

"Indirectly. If you needed to, you could eventually pass to any other ship. But it is rare to have to travel like that. It can be quicker to break and move to a better location."

"And each one has trees?"

"Most do. Some have other environments and supply other kinds of food. It works out."

Monty looked up and gasped. "There's a planet!"

At the midpoint of the star field, he could see a green fire growing, taking shape, resolving into a perfect sphere, one side half dark—the other side iridescent. With the bulk of the other ships shading his view of the nearby sun, he watched as the planet continued to draw near.

"Do you know the people called Khunar?" asked Rup.

"No, I don't think so."

"This is their world, Nepir. They live apart from most of their neighbors. They travel little and are difficult to trade with."

"That could be why I haven't heard of them."

"Yip. They are a quarrelsome bunch. They have blood feuds that last for generations. They poison each other; they stab each other; they rob each other. Perhaps you are familiar with such things?"

"Oh yes. I sometimes think we haven't come far enough beyond all that."

"The Frewl were here. They had been hired to deliver something."

"The same ones who...dropped me off?"

"Yes, they have many businesses. This is what concerns us."

Rup pointed a claw at Nepir's largest moon as it came slowly into view.

"What did they deliver?"

"Weapons. Highly sophisticated personal arms. The kind that wither opponents with minutes of unimaginable pain."

"Oh...I see."

"Can you imagine what such devices will do to this population? They have unloaded enough of these things for every family to be armed.

Think what the young will become when they learn during childhood to settle disputes with such weapons. Their feuds will become much shorter as, no doubt, will their generations."

"I can imagine it all too easily."

"The supplier has set up his base on this moon."

"What are you going to do?"

"Prevent a catastrophe. Quiet now! We are at Breaking Point."

"What?"

Rup did not answer. Monty looked up and saw the shadow's hard edge soften. Sunlight glinted off a host of other domes. There was a slight vibration through the floor. The links had been severed, and the ships were moving independently.

Nepir's moon became larger and larger overhead. The ships fanned out into a rough cloud.

Rup said quietly, "In theory, our pilot has only one job: to get out of the way of any incoming fire. The gunners likewise have only one job: to ensure that whatever is firing at us is destroyed."

Monty quickly saw the theory put into practice.

Several explosions partly obscured their view of the moon.

"Ranging shots. They are confused as to where we are," Rup whispered.

Other ships and the moon's outline suddenly veered to Monty's right. A long object shot past, disappearing over to their right. The ships around them all fired at once. Monty could not immediately identify all the different types of armaments being used.

Their pilot swung them round the back of another ship and into a new position. Clouds of gases from passing rockets—and nearby explosions—lit up around them as the gunners aimed a volley of intense fire toward the surface.

It was over in seconds.

The ships stopped firing. As they hung unmoving over the moon, Monty could see immense pillars of smoke and debris rising wider and wider into its thin atmosphere.

"They didn't stand much of a chance, did they?" Monty said quietly.

"Did they deserve one?"

⊏⊐

Peta declared herself disappointed by the cell. It had four walls of floor-to-ceiling bars and stood in the center of a larger room. Nothing was within reach through the bars, and the cell was empty except for three cots and a barely screened-off toilet.

"This is so retro! They have much more intimidating facilities nowadays," she complained to Scott as she toured the cell.

He replied from his cot, "It's at least forty years old. The technology of restraint has moved on so much further since then."

Grant shook his head as he sat on his cot. "This says volumes about the station's first Head of Security; I smell the strong influence of personal taste."

A Recorder entered the jail room and approached the bars. "Good morning. I'm Pam One-zero-three. Please let me know your meal preferences."

"Hello, Pam," said Peta, "My meal preference is to eat in the dining hall with everyone else."

Pam103 smiled and said, "I've heard that one before. It's usually followed by the jokes about passing bananas through the bars. I've been asked to order your food. Would you prefer to fast?"

Scott jumped to his feet and said, "What are the choices?"

"The same as in the dining hall. Shall I repeat them for you?"

"No. I remember both of them well enough, thank you."

Grant leaned against the bars and said quietly, "I promised a friend that I'd arrange a birthday celebration. Will I be able to order that through you since I'm not really in a position to do it myself right now?"

Pam103 nodded and said, "Your confinement has not been classified as Protected or Isolated. What would you like to send?"

"Not today. I'm thinking ahead."

"Whenever you wish. Will it involve a special cake? They have to be ordered at least a day in advance."

Grant smiled. "I'll let you know."

Scott said, "Do you know if we can have visitors?"

Pam103 nodded and said, "If they apply to visit you. Ask the guard at the next check-in. He'll be able to answer you better than I."

After Pam103 left with their order, Peta said, "Just think how expensive this is. A Recorder employed to take meal orders and a full-time officer to listen to 'em doing it."

Grant and Scott smiled and gave thumbs-up, understanding her reminder they were monitored.

"So," Peta said, "who do you think will come and visit us?"

Scott said, "Well, of course, I...That connection I made with one of the staff...I probably blew it as far as her giving us a visit. But they probably know that already."

Peta nodded. "Yeah, that's a shame. Is she prettier than me?"

Grant laughed.

Scott smiled and said, "I thought relationships between Guild members were frowned upon."

Peta shook her head. "Not at all. A married couple is running the office in Barcelona."

Grant said to Scott, "You could have tried 'connecting' with someone in Security. It might have been more useful."

"But artless," said Peta, "way too obvious."

Scott said thoughtfully, "That's what I reckoned."

They were silent a moment. Peta sighed and said, "I didn't realize what a stunner that Dr. Bartula is until I got here. There was no chance Monty would ever have noticed me, was there?"

Grant and Scott looked at each other in surprise.

Peta looked from one to the other. "What? You don't believe all those rumors about me, do you?"

Scott returned her look and said, "That's the second impossible question you've asked me in the space of a minute! I'm still recovering from the first one..."

"Good, it'll keep your mind sharp. We might be locked up, but we're not on vacation. Understand me?"

"Yes, ma'am."

Grant said, "Bob isn't going to be happy. He was looking forward to a celebration and now look."

Peta smiled and said, "Oh, I get it...It really isn't fair of you, is it? You should do something for him. A visit from Bob would be quite interesting."

▭

Monty lay on his back, gazing up into the tree. Seb66 sat beside him on the platform.

"It was terrifying," Monty said, "they wiped out everything."

"You think they were indiscriminate?"

"Looked that way to me. I have no idea if there were other people in that area. I have no idea if they even checked."

Neither spoke while a Renn descended from the upper branches and continued down the tree.

Monty continued, "I'd like to know their discovery process."

"The logic Rup used to justify the action was reasonable. Their intention was to prevent a greater wrong."

"There's a dilemma humanity is always struggling with: if there's a cause worth dying for, is it okay to kill for it?"

"That's an interesting question."

Monty laughed and said, "Don't worry! I'm not expecting you to be able to solve it. It'll still be a dilemma as long as there are humans. Right now, we're tending to think 'no,' but it's a pendulum that swings to and fro. I guess what troubles me is the Renn were never in any danger themselves. They just hung in space and blew the crap out of everything."

"Are you rested enough?" Seb66 asked.

"Hmm? Sure. That was just an excuse to get some private time. I wanted to know how you got on at your meeting."

"It went well. I gathered a lot of information about the Renns' operation. For instance, I knew from the configuration of the computers that this was a large fleet of separate vessels. Ferr was reluctant to confirm it until I described to her what I already had deduced."

"Did you get anything on the Frewl?"

"No. They were extremely unwilling to discuss them. They seem to know a lot about Earth."

"Really? Rup said he'd never seen a human before."

"They know where it is. They have a diverse collection of facts and stories about humans."

Monty chuckled and said, "Did you hear any good rumors?"

Seb66 hesitated and said, "I believe they consider us potential friends, despite our initial problems when I first engaged their systems."

"And threatened them with a club..."

Seb66 nodded.

"Fellow travelers," Monty said quietly, "That's Rup's phrase. 'We're fellow travelers.'"

"Do you think they will take us back to Earth?"

"I haven't asked yet. From what I've seen of their food, I can't have any of it. I'm getting seriously hungry."

Monty lay quietly. *Seb just referred to 'us' when talking about the Renns' view of humanity.* It gave Monty a strange feeling in his stomach. It made him worry for the Recorders. If they thought they were more than machines —somehow in the same category as humans—many indignant humans would be ready to disabuse them. He had always been comfortable with the distinction: a Recorder isn't a person. *Do Recorders seriously think differently?*

Early in the morning, Peta woke up feeling someone was outside the cage.

She sat up to see a large youthful figure, hands in his pockets, smiling.

She said, "Get up, guys! We have a distinguished visitor."

Grant and Scott woke immediately but stood up slowly and warily. The visitor said nothing.

Grant said, "I guess it isn't the janitor."

Scott replied, "One. Janitors generally dress better."

They stood next to Peta, and she held up a finger to silence them. "Discoverers, may I introduce the singularly named Mallson, de-facto head of The H Company, ruler of the known universe, captain of the Hoyle Station Surveillance Avoidance Team, and the true cause of our present predicament. Oh, I'm sorry, do you actually have another name?"

Mallson continued to smile. He eventually spoke. "Interpreter Melbourne, Discoverers Leduc and Murphy. You'll be honored to know that you three finally and irrevocably popped the Guild's balloon. I've been waiting for one of you to make a mistake. I needn't have waited so long if I'd only known what idiots you three were. You've handed it to me in spades. I just stopped by to say thanks. That and ask what the hell is this business between you goons with the numbers?"

Peta grinned and said, "The truth is, I arranged to be put here. I knew it was the surest way of flushing you out. I knew you'd never be able to resist a good gloat."

Mallson's face flashed with a moment of surprise but immediately regained its grin.

"Well done. I hope you enjoy it. It's going to be a long stay. I won't have any garbage haulers available to drop you back Earthside for quite a while. In the meantime, I'll have someone take apart your equipment. Looks like you brought some dodgy hardware aboard my station. It's going to be interesting seeing how you jokers really operate."

Peta inhaled and said, "Tell them not to put their faces too close. I don't want anyone getting hurt when they self-destruct. By the way, did you enjoy killing Monty?"

Mallson's eyes narrowed, and Peta thought she saw a slight blush come to his cheeks. He said, "How quaint...this habit you people have of giving bugs names." He looked up and around at the bars, shook his head, smiled, and as he left said, "What a waste."

CHAPTER 37

At lunchtime, Pam103 and another underused Recorder brought three trays of food to the cell.

After they had gone, Peta picked up a napkin to find a small photo display. She saw an image changing across the screen and held the napkin over it while she watched.

The photo display showed points of light shifting against a black background. As Peta watched, she began to see the pattern. It was a series of seventeen images. After the photo display had shown each one for five seconds, it restarted at the beginning. At first, she had no idea what it represented.

She covered it again.

"Guys? Which one of you is better at mathematical puzzles?"

Both replied, "He is."

She handed the napkin to Grant and said, "Good, you can both have a go. There's a logic puzzle on here. See if you can work it out."

Grant took it and felt the weight of the display inside. He looked around. "For this kind of puzzle, I prefer a yoga mat." He lay on his back on the floor between the cots, hoping to avoid the gaze of the surveillance camera.

He studied the points of light for many minutes.

At the table, with the scent of malt strong in his nostrils, he invited the designers of Hoyle Station to talk him through the deployment of external cameras on a space station. It looked to him as if the images were something viewed from Hoyle Station looking outwards. The discussion settled on time-lapse images, archived in case they were ever needed, perhaps to check on crashes or shuttles that went missing...

He watched the images again and again. When he speeded up the display, he could see two of the lights—two shuttlecraft—traveling from right to left across the field of view. He could see something moving away from the camera, but it was moving erratically. Where the others traveled along a predictable path, this one was different. At image thirteen, it vanished. The last four images showed everything else unchanged; those in motion were still traveling as expected. The erratic object had gone.

From the floor he asked quietly, "When does a solid object disappear?"

On his bed feigning sleep, Scott said softly, "When it passes behind something—like beyond the horizon in the case that something is the Earth—or when it is concealed, as by a magician's hand. Or, when your attention is forced elsewhere, it might even disappear in plain sight."

Peta added, "Or when the distance between you is beyond the range of the light it's emitting or reflecting."

The three were silent for many minutes.

Grant said, "The shuttle rolled away from the gate. It wasn't under its own power. Perhaps the airlock was blown, causing an uneven trajectory. Then something black came between it and the camera. After that, it was gone."

"Yes, good information. But like you learned in Philosophy class: things can be both true and unhelpful."

Scott, lying on his bed, rolled on his side and took the napkin from Grant. He watched the images, closed the napkin, and sighed.

"We didn't look here," he said carefully for those listening, "but if we had, we'd have looked further. If you're looking for something, you spread your attention around the edges."

Peta replied, "This is a predefined set of images that...someone...wanted to share. Why did...someone...deliberately select only these, rejecting others?"

Grant said, "Selecting implies wanting. What if someone wanted to remove them from the record instead of keeping them?"

Scott added, "With the right authority you can delete anything. But likewise, you can usually rescue things deleted, say from an archive."

Peta asked, "Who can?"

Grant replied, "The authorized clerk of record."

Scott said, "The system maintenance staff."

"So," Peta said smiling, "these are the most incriminating shots. These were removed. The shuttle was intercepted by something. These are the images that show it happening."

They were silent for a while.

Peta asked, "When would a meeting jockey interrogate a low-level inventory system to find out an inactive Recorder had been brought aboard?"

Scott lay back on the bed and closed his eyes.

The blueprint unfurled, and he drew several dots in a random pattern across it. He connected each dot with its neighbors. He added a small circle, unconnected, on the right-hand side.

He said quietly, "In a distributed network, each node can interact with any other. Sensitivity to the appearance of new nodes is one of many common functions. Predicting when and where a new node may activate could be important. You might want to change the configuration, depending on what else is happening. For instance, you might want to move less busy nodes next to the new one so that the spare capacity can handle all the introductory activities."

"Hmm," Peta said, "what about interest in an archive of external monitor images?"

Scott said. "You see, that's unlikely. Unless it has become important to the network."

Grant wondered, "How can one know what any network considers important?"

With a tone of wonder lightening her voice, Peta said, "Cooperation with another network! Like building an interface...They are trying to work out what's important to us!"

Grant sat up from lying on the floor. Scott raised up on his elbow. Both looked puzzled.

She continued, "It might not be important to your network, but you might see its importance to someone else you're negotiating with." She paused. "The crime they see happening is the violation of the data: the deletion of images from the record. This isn't about Monty. They understand we can stop violations of the data. And they recognize Monty as a priority *for us*." With a triumphant smile, Peta said, "Gentlemen, as I've suspected for a while, we have friends in low places."

⊏⊐

The Hoyle Station traffic controllers worked in the Communications Dome, located in a slender tower attached to the top donut. They rarely spoke louder than a professional mutter. Shift after shift, they relayed instructions to shuttle pilots, transporter crews, and visiting delegations. They kept arrivals safely apart and departures patiently waiting for their slots. They could set off a station-wide, general alarm system if a sudden, immediate danger occurred for which no other reaction was appropriate.

It was early morning, Hoyle time, when the general alarm sounded after one controller shouted above the constant murmur, "Anyone else seeing this?"

Gathering in the outer approach to Hoyle Station was a huge number of ships. The displays in front of the controllers were overwhelmed with signals.

The ships came to a stop, forming half a sphere around the cluster of stations. Flights coming up from Earth turned and retreated. From the windows and portals of Hoyle Station, it looked as though the stars had suddenly arranged themselves in ranks.

Standing on the director's rug, Kandi, Norman, Tim24, and several senior staff huddled together. Their conversation stopped as Mallson pushed through the outer door.

"Who are they?" he asked.

Kandi gestured to the Recorder to answer.

Tim24 said, "They are called Renn, from a planet they call Intah. They say they are visiting and would like to send a delegation over."

"Why the battle fleet?" Mallson asked.

"They don't give the impression of seeing it that way. They have offered no threats. Their language is diplomatic, if not, if I may say so, a little informal," the Recorder answered.

Mallson glanced around the room, avoiding eye contact with any of the group. He stood, drumming the fingers of his right hand on the knuckles of his left, then shrugged and said, "Okay. They might have useful technology. Let them in." He turned his gaze on Kandi. "You, make sure they understand they don't come back in such numbers next time. And send me the press officer. I'll tell them how to write this up." To Norman he said, "Lockdown the nonessentials. Arms and armor for all your guys. When they send someone over, I want hostages as an option."

Without waiting for acknowledgment, he turned and left.

Anet waited tensely for the Renn delegation. She walked along the Arrival Hall from console to console, smiling encouragingly at her staff while keeping her fingers crossed in the pockets of her white coat. "The Possibility of Hostility" was the name of a seminar they all had to attend once a year. If alien hostility on the station became more than a possibility, her staff would be the first to meet it. The Renn arrived quietly. As the staff got their first look at the symmetrical bodies, the loose coveralls, the gray faces, Anet tried not to think of four-legged spiders.

A dozen Renn walked through the scanners. They stopped and examined each one. At one point, they formed a Renn pyramid to put one of their number up close to the internals of one of the machines.

Anet smiled and thought, *I'm going to like these guys; they look like fun.*

The Arrival Corridor ended at the Welcome Suite. There, Kandi and representatives of the major corporations, including Ursula Somerset-Trench, greeted the new aliens. Tim24 stood attentively at one side.

"Welcome to The Earth," Kandi began, "Welcome to Hoyle Station. I am Kandi Thomas, the director. It is my great pleasure to greet you in the name of all humans."

"Hello," said the lead Renn, "I'm Wurp. Are you in command of this whole facility?"

Kandi frowned at the question but nodded and said, "That's correct."

Wurp reached up and put his clawed hand around Kandi's arm.

She winced at the touch but did not draw back.

Wurp brought his face close to hers and said, "Are there any Frewl on board?"

Kandi panicked and couldn't speak.

One of the representatives stepped forward and tried to help her. "What about the Frewl?" he asked. As he spoke, he took Kandi's other arm.

Wurp didn't let go.

As Kandi began to look both horrified and extremely undignified—with a representative on one arm and an alien on the other—Tim24 stepped forward.

"Excuse me, Wurp. It is not usual to place your hand on a human in that fashion. Please let go of the director."

"Who are you?" asked Wurp, still not releasing Kandi.

"I'm Tim Twenty-four. I am here to record your visit and help in any way I can with the smooth running of this meeting. I'm pleased to meet you and would be happy to shake hands with you. This is the usual first touch that a human will allow."

Tim24 smiled and held out his hand.

Keeping hold of Kandi, Wurp reached out his other hand and took hold of Tim24's. Wurp's attention was suddenly, completely on Tim24. "You're mechanical!"

"That's correct."

With blinding speed, Wurp released Kandi and threw Tim24 to the ground and sat on top of him, his face pressed against the Recorder's ear.

Four security officers with weapons drawn moved from the side rooms to surround Wurp. The humans and other Renn all backed away.

Wurp stood up and dragged Tim24 to his feet. The Recorder looked around and said, "This is a simple misunderstanding of gestures and protocols. Please relax. There is no harm done. Wurp, may I ask you, do your people often wrestle with each other when first meeting?"

Wurp looked around at the guards and their weapons. "Of course!" he said, "Don't you? Have I done something wrong here?"

Tim24 addressed the still rigid figure of Kandi. "May I suggest this meeting take place around a table, where there will be less opportunity for such misunderstandings?"

The security guards turned to the doors they had come through and waited for a gesture from their unseen superior. They retreated to the wall and said nothing.

Ursula Somerset-Trench looked at the unmoving Kandi and the other stunned representatives. She said, "Please come through to the conference room. We can sit and chat there. This way, please..."

▭

Anet was annoyed that she didn't get into the Welcome Suite for the conversation. One of the operators had called her over to his console.

He said, "It looks like there are still some Renn hanging around at the entrance to the Corridor who haven't come through with the others."

"What are they waiting for?" she asked.

"Shall I get Communications to ask the Renn ship?"

"No, give them another minute."

It was a long minute. The second party moved slowly through the Corridor, walking quickly between the machines, stopping for extended periods behind each one.

Anet's attention wandered until she heard one of the operators say "Hey!" She was at his side in an instant.

"Doctor, look! There's a human in there!"

She peered at the display and almost screamed. Monty's hair had many days of growth, and his moustache was wilder than normal. He was dressed like a Renn and looked a little gaunt. But it could be none other than Monty.

Anet clapped her hand over her mouth to stop herself calling out

"Monty." Several scenes flashed through her mind; she saw Norman arresting Monty for Jimmy's murder; she saw Monty being imprisoned with Peta and the others; she saw herself cooking a meal for a large party all eager to hear Monty telling his tale.

The operator tapped the display. "There's a Recorder in there too."

"You sure?"

"I've never seen one go through before, but it has to be. Look, there's the visual...and...the name tag! It's one of ours!"

Anet put her hand on his shoulder and said, "I'll deal with this. Keep a lid on it, hear me?" She put her finger to her lips.

"Yes, Doctor..."

Peta suddenly woke up to an alarm, but no one came to tell them what it meant. No one came at all. Hardly any sound came from the rooms beyond the jail room.

"What do you think, guys?" she asked.

"Something's up." Grant agreed.

"We'll find out at breakfast," Scott said, "Pam will—"

Pam103 came into the room. "Good morning. Please let me know your meal preferences for today."

Peta said, "My preference is for a large order of information and an open door."

Pam103 replied, "The latter is beyond my authority."

"Good," Peta said, understanding the distinction, "What's the emergency?"

"A flotilla of alien vessels has arrived. An unplanned delegation is coming on board."

Peta glanced at her Discoverers. "A big security operation?"

Pam103 said, "All nonessential personnel are required to remain in their quarters. Armed deployment has been ordered to protect sensitive areas and high-level staff. Only a reduced crew is on duty here."

Peta nodded. Scott and Grant shared a glance and smiled.

Grant asked, "Can I have my breakfast delivered elsewhere?"

Pam103 nodded and said, "If you wish. Won't that make it difficult to eat?"

"Perhaps," Grant replied, "but it's a special occasion. I'd like a crate of naturally sweetened soda delivered to conference room 3-C-A. If you could add a note saying it's from me and where I am, that would be good."

"One crate of nat soda, conference room 3-C-A." Pam103 nodded.

Peta said sweetly, "Oh, this is going to be good..."

Scott asked, "Where is our equipment being stored?"

"It was stored in the lockers outside until Mallson removed it."

"Can you find out where it is now?"

Pam103 hesitated. "If it is important, I can ask around."

Scott nodded. "Yes, please. I'd like to retrieve it when we get out, before leaving the station."

Peta asked, "Under what circumstances are you authorized to release us?"

Pam103 hesitated again, "I've no such instructions. I've been assigned to relay food orders to the kitchen."

"But you have inbuilt guidelines, ethical programs, self-preservation routines. Do any of them cover letting us out in extreme circumstances?"

Pam103 shook her head. "I don't think so."

Scott said, "In the early days, before you were Recorders, weren't there basic rules about not harming humans? Aren't you designed not to stand by and let a human die through your inaction?"

"Ah, the Laws of Robotics and all that...It's a bit complicated...Others are more qualified to talk about such things. I've never had to face such a circumstance. Such routines may be built into me, but I won't necessarily know until they're activated."

"Listen carefully," Scott said. "Find out how you or one of your peers can release us if circumstances put us in mortal danger and we need you to do it. Do the research. Be prepared."

"Okay. Anything to eat?"

CHAPTER 38

Two common assumptions are made when compiling dictionaries. First, an inquirer knows the spelling of the word in question or, at least, its beginning. Second, in the case of a dual language dictionary, there is some similarity in culture and shared norms; the divide is only linguistic.

In the dictionary written to bridge The Language used in galactic trade to the D'Moran tongue, the word for soda was translated as "a drink of celebration." Its author wrote the word "celebration" with the nod of a mother-of-pearl head and the wink of a three-segmented eye.

A D'Moran celebration is rarely complete without fire, injury, destruction of property, the singing of—for D'Morans—lewd songs, and always a great deal of hollering.

An hour after Grant's gift of breakfast soda arrived at the D'Moran nest, the conference room doors flew open. The first things to emerge were tangled pieces of furniture; soon after came the shouts and cheers; then came the musical chant; lastly, the jubilant, reveling D'Morans.

As they sang, they improvised praises for Grant, who had found them passage off Hoyle Station and sent them the means of celebration as a signal.

Being large creatures, moving together through the narrower sections of Hoyle Station's corridors presented some difficulties. Being inebriated gave rise to a new game. One D'Moran would squeeze himself against a wall, wait for his fellows to start maneuvering past, and then launch himself with full six-legged force across the occupied corridor. This had the entertaining effect of buckling the walls on both sides.

Bob called over the whooping, singing, and the crunching of walls, "Level Eight! Central Security Office! Grant is there!"

At the first elevator, they paused and found a message on the control panel saying "Security authorization required during lockdown."

They ripped open the elevator doors and poured themselves up the shaft.

Anet let herself into the Arrival Corridor through a maintenance hatch. She glanced to her left to see the last of the Renn party disappear through to the conference and hospitality area. She entered a command into her show-g and the Arrival Corridor door closed, sealing her off from the Welcome Suite.

She turned, leaned back against the door, and waited for the second part of the Renn delegation to finish its walk through the scanners. As they approached, her mind was reeling with the impossibility of a new race, Monty, and a Recorder arriving together. But Monty was there, dressed in the same dull garb as the aliens. A Recorder was there, in a white suit that looked a little worse for wear.

She felt faint.

Monty stepped up to her. "Surprised to see me?"

"I shouldn't be, should I? After all, it's you..."

Monty nodded to the closed door. "The other lot inside, out of the way?"

Anet nodded.

Monty continued, "Then Wurp got the message to the Recorder. We needed a few minutes privacy. I need two favors. The price of my ticket back was that my Renn friends get a good look at the scanners—the whole Frewl setup. Second, I need to get Sebastian here back to Earth as soon as possible, preferably without Mallson knowing or being able to interfere. What are the chances?"

Anet nodded, "The scanners? No problem. I can authorize that. But you don't want to be messing with Mallson, Monty. He's here. He's always somewhere lurking around. I doubt you can do it."

"Do you have a Recorder on duty?"

"No. The nearest is with the delegation." She made a wide gesture to the large machines. "And, as you know, this stuff records for itself—in Frewl."

Monty nodded and hesitated. "Can you get a Recorder, or two, here? It might help."

Anet shrugged and entered a message to Derek.

"And now," Monty announced, "may I introduce my new friend? Rup, this is Anet, a finer example of human femininity you will not find."

"Hello, Rup," Anet said with a cautious smile.

"Anet. Easier to say than Mont-gom-er-y or Seb-ast-ian. Much easier. Do you wrestle?"

Rup held up his hands in a sporting stance.

Anet laughed and said, "Not on a first date, no."

Rup turned a half circle and flipped his head back over his body. "Then I look forward to the second."

Anet's eyes twinkled as she said, "Please wait here a moment."

She opened the maintenance hatch and called over several of her staff to assist Monty and the Renn through to her work area.

As the Renn fanned out to the various displays and workstations, Anet grabbed Monty by the arm. "You know you're going to be arrested once they know you're here?"

"What?"

"Jimmy Hunter. Found dead in your berth."

"Who?"

"Chief Hunter. Scottish fellow. You met him, Monty."

Monty nodded, "Seems a long time ago. What happened to him?"

"You didn't see him before you left? You're the prime suspect for his murder."

Monty shook his head. "I didn't see anyone. I was hit over the head and dumped in a shuttle. That's all I know about it."

Anet shook her head in return. "No one's going to believe that. The official report blames you fair and square. Of course, it has Mallson's cloven hoofprint all over it."

Monty stroked his moustache. "That complicates things somewhat, doesn't it? But we've got to get Seb Sixty-six out of here. I'll take my chances. Can you get him out with the medical waste or something?"

"Nothing's flying at the moment. Your friends have us all well and truly spooked." Anet looked thoughtful. "He's a Sebastian?"

"Right. Sixty-six."

Anet entered something into her show-g. "There's one of those somewhere. I'll see if Derek can track him down. Maybe they can fool the cameras for a while if they hang out together."

"Sounds good. It's great to see you again. I thought I might never make it."

"You haven't yet. Mallson's got your colleagues in a cell. As soon as anyone checks the surveillance, Norman will have to put you there too."

"What colleagues?"

Before Anet could answer, Rup, rolled into a ball, crashed into Monty's leg. "Ow! What are you doing?"

"Monty! We've seen enough." Rup drew himself to his full height by hanging on to Monty's arm. "Time to go."

"What? What about greeting the bosses and diplomacy and all that?"

Rup smiled; his silver tongue flicked across his lips. "You're right; we need to get Wurp and the others out of there. Come back with us now."

"I...I can't. Too much to do here. I've got a...job to finish."

Out of the corner of his eye, Monty could see Rup's colleagues retreating into the Corridor.

"You mean the Frewl?" Rup asked.

"Partly. Well, no. It's a different one...one that Seb Sixty-six has to finish."

Rup looked over at Seb66, who stood apart, quietly observing. "Then go with him but leave the station quickly. You're not safe. Plans are moving quickly."

"Why? What's happening?"

Before Rup could reply, an alarm began sounding through the Arrival Hall.

"What's that?" Monty shouted to Anet.

"Security shutdown! We have to turn everything off and secure the doors. What did you guys do?"

Monty frowned and looked around. "I don't think it's us."

The first Renn party emerged from the conference area through the Welcome Suite and headed back into the Corridor. They were running and tumbling at great speed. When they saw Rup's group, the chaos doubled. Behind them, several of the welcome party were following, looking in equal measures offended and surprised.

Rup punched Monty in the arm and said, "Farewell, Monty! I hope we meet again! Leave. Leave quickly!" He rushed back through the maintenance door and climbed up the inner frame of the Corridor. As he neared the other Renn, he launched himself into them with a loud cry.

The yips and other cries faded, and Monty watched them jostling their way back toward their shuttle.

Still at his side, Anet said, "Monty, why are they leaving? They're supposed to stay where they are."

Monty shook his head, "You want to try stopping them? What do they know that we don't? Is there something happening to the station?"

Anet noticed the bruises on Monty's arms. "I'm sure it's nothing Norman can't handle. But right now, I want you in for an exam. You're a mess! Have you eaten anything recently?"

"No. Nor drunk much."

"Stay close to me."

Monty nodded.

Anet turned and shouted above the alarm, "Okay, everybody, you can all hear that alarm! Everyone out! Seal all access! Shut down all systems! This isn't a drill. Snap to it!"

Two Recorders came into the room, stepped to one side as several of Anet's staff ran out, and then approached Seb66 directly.

Seb66 high-fived them and gave each a long hug.

Monty called, "Seb, we'll have to split up. I'll try and get you into some sort of transport."

Seb66 said over his shoulder, "I'm okay. I'm among friends." He glanced at Anet, who had followed close behind Monty, "So are you."

Anet turned at the doorway to wave the last of her staff out. She entered the command into her show-g and the door closed.

Derek Smeade trotted along the corridor to meet her. He stopped, glanced at Monty, and said, "Doctor, Security are—Sheldrake?"

Anet said, "Okay, Derek, escort this patient to quarantine. Understand?

Monty, when you get there, break open the sports drinks and down as many of them as you can stomach. Derek, stay with him until I can get there. Derek? Are you listening?"

"Quarantine. Right."

Smiling, Monty said, "Good to see you again, Derek."

"Right...Quarantine...Ìs there a problem?"

Anet said, "There will be if you don't move yourself! Don't forget the electrolytes."

"Right..." He looked from one to the other. Recognizing the look in his boss's eye, he turned to Monty and said, "This way."

Anet looked round to see the three Recorders walking away.

Before Derek could move, she grabbed his arm. "What did you tell those Recorders to do?"

"I...I told them to report to you."

"They didn't. Where are they going?"

"That's odd..."

She gestured for Derek and Monty to go. She considered following the Recorders, but instead, she entered the quarantine orders into her show-g. She sent a note to Norman, asking when they might get a moment together. She waited alone in the corridor for several minutes but got no acknowledgment.

She calmed her breathing, coming to terms with Monty's return. Fearing Norman's reaction to what she was doing, she recited the mantra she used whenever her work threatened to overwhelm her, "One step at a time, just one first, then the next..."

CHAPTER 39

Peta heard the D'Morans before they got out of the elevator shaft. "Get ready, gentlemen. This could get bumpy."

"Where are the Recorders?" asked Scott.

"Where are the security guys?" Grant asked, "I hope they don't get in the way."

"Bit late to worry about that now, isn't it?" Peta regarded Grant and waited to see if he would rise to the bait.

Grant faced her with a smile and said, "'A beer brewed with knowledge is tasted with wisdom.' It's an art; don't forget."

"That would be piss art, would it?"

Scott laughed, and Grant, still smiling, closed his eyes. When he opened them, he said, "Sometimes, I have to remind myself that you are both my boss and a lady."

Peta pointed at him and said, "And I keep telling you never let either of those things influence you in any way!"

Grant bowed and said, "Yes, ma'am."

"Ah, you're hopeless!"

Scott held up his hand to quiet them. They heard raised voices in the outer office. Another alarm began to sound nearby. A musical, deep, throbbing chant rose in volume to rival the alarm. The sounds of crashing solid objects and glass breaking traveled to the jail room door.

Then they heard another voice, a voice that sounded annoyed. A woman's voice, thin but commanding.

"What language is that?" Peta whispered.

"Sounds like D'Moran to me," answered Grant.

The jail room door burst open, and a diminutive old lady entered.

"She was on the shuttle," said Scott in surprise.

"Knitting, if I'm not mistaken," added Grant.

"Hi, ma'am," called Peta, "What's it like out there?"

The old lady strolled to the bars, looked at each of them in turn, and said, "Well, you've succeeded in making a very disagreeable mess. What was the next part of your plan? Do you have a laser torch capable of cutting through these bars? No, I thought not. It seems you have left a great deal to chance. I suppose you would like me to let you out before those obnoxious louts get in here?"

Peta saw Scott and Grant standing openmouthed. "Who are you?" she asked.

"Well, instead of passing comments about the noise of my knitting, it would have been more useful to have introduced yourselves while we were on board the shuttle. Yes, that would have saved a great deal of time. But, then, you young people never learn, do you?"

"Um...your name, ma'am?" Peta asked again.

"You know me as Mrs. Kinda. I am acquainted with your missing colleague, Montgomery Sheldrake."

After she absorbed this news, Peta asked, "And what are you doing here?"

"Well, I'm a librarian by trade, and I arranged to visit the library here...and very interesting it has been. But, at the moment, rather than more pleasant pursuits, it seems I am rescuing you."

The crashing noises that had diminished in the next room had returned. "Can you get at the locks for the cage?" asked Scott.

"That might be simpler than having the bars ripped off by our friends out there," added Grant.

"Please turn around and look the other way."

Grant and Scott looked at Peta.

"Now, please! We are in a hurry, aren't we?" Mrs. Kinda said loudly.

Peta shrugged and turned away from Mrs. Kinda. The Discoverers did likewise.

"Now, I believe there is a service corridor somewhere."

They turned back to find the bottom half of the cell's front bars had disappeared. Mrs. Kinda was walking toward the back of the room, saying, "Yes, here it is. Come along!"

"How did she do that?" asked Scott.

Grant ducked through the opening and said, "Ten. Very stylish."

Peta followed him and said, "Out! Admire it later. Where are we going, Mrs. Kinda?"

"If we had been collaborating, or you had checked into the construction of this facility, you would have found there is a ship capable of transporting the D'Morans off the station near the Arrival Hall. I suggest getting it ready for them, and then we can turn our attention to the far more urgent problem hovering just outside."

Peta glanced at Grant, who shrugged in reply.

"What problem outside?" Peta asked.

"They are called the Renn. They have a galaxy-wide reputation. One might truly describe them as 'infamous.' I'm sorry that humanity has encountered them so soon. Some races you tolerate, like the D'Morans. Their loutishness is offset by their usefulness. Some you might even look forward to meeting. Then, there are races like the Renn, who give the galaxy only nightmares. They lurk in the deep dark, strike without mercy, acknowledge no law. If ever you need to terrify a child, tell stories of the Renn. Now, no more questions, time is short! The authorities here can't be expected to deal with two crises simultaneously. They need our help."

They silently followed Mrs. Kinda through a hatchway and into a low tunnel lined with wiring and pipes. Scott pulled the hatch behind him just as the D'Morans burst into the jail room.

▭

In a room that, through architectural accident, lay exactly beneath the director's rug, Kevin12 stood waiting for instructions.

Mallson's assistant, Smith, faced him from behind a desk. He waved the Recorder over to stand closer. He had arranged three small devices on the desk.

"May I ask the nature of the work you wish me to do?" Kevin12 asked.

Smith held up a finger, turned to his right, and switched on a device the size of a large suitcase on the floor next to him.

He looked up at Kevin12's face. "You are not to resist this maintenance procedure." His voice was quiet but full of self-contained humor.

Kevin12 hesitated and said, "What procedure is it? I am not familiar with this."

Smith pointed at each device on the desk from left to right. "This will activate your self-preservation subroutine. This will direct all your output to the storage device. This will deactivate you."

His hand rested on the first device and activated it.

Kevin12 blinked and started to speak. No words came. His eyes moved around the room as if in panic, but he remained otherwise still.

Smith sat, watching and smiling. His hand went to the second device and activated it. There was a faint hiss from the device on the floor. He checked the time on his show-g.

Kevin12 let out a strained sigh but said nothing.

CHAPTER 40

As he entered the quarantine suite, Monty thanked Derek. By the standards of accommodation elsewhere on Hoyle Station, the suite was palatial. Monty was impressed. He passed through a glass door, walked through a glass-walled airlock, and entered the main room. A large observation window along the right-hand wall allowed outsiders to view the inside of the suite.

Through the window, Monty asked Derek, "Do you know what Anet's planning?"

Her assistant shook his head. When he spoke, his voice sounded loudly through speakers inside. "Not usually, no. This time, absolutely not. But she is the absolute ruler of this suite. How she'll get you out, I don't know. This place is one of the few places Mallson can't get you nor Norman. "

Monty nodded and said, "You're a shrewd man, Derek. A lot smarter than you look."

Derek smiled and said, "I'll take that as a compliment. Good luck."

Derek sealed the outer door, and Monty felt the air pressure lessen slightly. He surveyed the main room. It was furnished with small plastic chairs like those in the dining hall. There were two card tables, a shelf of games, and a couple of battered public show-gs.

He turned again to the observation window. "Hey, Derek! They forgot the little wheel I'm supposed to run around in."

"They have Recorders to do that for you now" was his reply. "Drinks are in the fridge over there. Help yourself."

It seemed a long time before Anet arrived and sent Derek off on another errand. Monty felt a pang of sympathy when he saw how worried she looked.

Her voice came through the speakers. "You okay in there?"

"So far. I haven't developed any symptoms yet. Do you want me to?"

"I'll let you know. We're preparing for emergency admissions. There's some sort of riot going on. I'll be busy. Stay out of sight if anyone comes in."

"Will do."

"Oh, sports drinks in the fridge!"

Monty took a bottle into the bedroom and lay down on the lowest of four bunks. He wondered what Rup was up to. He breathed deeply and smelled the familiar scent of the forest.

He lay on his stomach at the top of the rock face. The sparks from the fire below drifted up past his head. He could hear the crackle of the burning twigs and the swish of the wind in the pine trees around him like before the onset of a storm.

Down below him in the dell, Rup sat in the flickering light talking to his fellow Renn.

"...to see the details of the scanning setup at Hoyle Station."

Another said, "It's the surest way of seeing what the Frewl have been doing."

A third said, "The Frewl are not fellow travelers."

Monty remembered his conversation with Rup in the Pilot's room before the one-sided battle with the Frewl's customer on Nepir's moon. He whispered again the question he asked then, "What are you going to do?"

Rup looked up from the fire to Monty's hiding place and said, "Prevent a catastrophe in memory of our beloved Intah."

Monty suddenly understood the nature of the danger they were all in.

You only wanted to see the Frewl equipment so you'd know how to destroy it! You're not going to mess around with it now, are you? You're just going to destroy Hoyle Station and everyone in it.

Monty's eyes opened wide, and he was up and rushing from the bedroom.

Mallson was sitting with his elbows on one of the card tables, hands together, his forefingers making an 'A' around his nose. His eyes were on Monty's face. He sighed and lifted his head slightly, still arching his hands fingertip to fingertip. "I had hoped you'd be dead by now," Mallson said softly. His slight frown spoke of disappointment.

Monty chuckled halfheartedly and asked, "How the hell did you get in here?"

Mallson cocked his head and said, "What do you mean? I own this place. I go wherever I want."

"This is a medical quarantine room. Are you sure you want to risk your life like this?"

Mallson smiled and sat back from the table, his feet tapping an upbeat rhythm. "What you have is definitely fatal. But just to you. I can walk out of here whenever I want. You, however, never will."

Monty swept his eyes around the room to see if it provided any means of self-defense. He doubted the plastic chairs would avail him much.

Mallson pointed to a chair and said, "Sit. As I told the Good Doctor, I've bought myself a priesthood. I'm here for your last confession."

"And she didn't believe you any more than I."

"She stopped arguing eventually."

Monty ran to the observation window to see Anet's prone body on the floor.

"You bastard! What did you do to her?"

Mallson laughed and said again, "Sit!" He stood and pointed to the chair. "Call me a bastard and, of course, I'll have to agree with you. My dear father never did tell me who my mother was, let alone entertain any talk of marrying her. I'm just one of the many products of his overgenerous libido. I'm so far removed from the legitimacy that obsesses people today that I have to claim The H Company itself as my mother."

Monty felt a strange reversal; Mallson had begun confessing.

Monty said calmly, "There are good reasons for humanity to reestablish such fine traditions as marriage and legitimacy. I'm sorry you weren't born in better circumstances."

Mallson shook his head. "My circumstances were fine. I'm lucky. In fact, the human race is lucky. If the company hadn't brought me up, I would probably never had realized my own true importance."

Monty grabbed a chair, moved it away from the table, and sat down. "Go on. Though I warn you, you're fiddling while Rome burns."

Mallson sat down again. "You see, you think people are important, don't you? Like that bug you kept below decks on the cruise. You were upset about it, weren't you?"

"'It' had a name: Rory. He was a friend of mine."

"Yeah, yeah..." Mallson waved his hand dismissively. "All I did was send it off in a lifeboat. It didn't stop your work, did it? It didn't sink the ship. It didn't cost you anything. So...so what?"

Monty gritted his teeth and asked, "Is that what they taught you on the tough streets of the company mall?"

Mallson narrowed his eyes and pointed a finger at Monty. "You know what?"—he hesitated and then continued—"I'm glad you brought that up. There was a woman. Worked in a candy store. Used to give me stuff. Big woman, smelled of flowers all the time. When I was old enough to understand the books, I realized she'd been stealing everything she gave me. Stealing from Big H. Lying to me, to the company that paid her. I fired her. Got another woman, one who didn't steal. The replacement didn't smell of flowers so much, but in every other way, she was equivalent. See? People aren't important. If one goes wrong, the company buys another."

Monty kept his face neutral and said, "That's amazing. How old were you?"

"Eight. Now, take you. I told you never to let me notice you again. You did though. So the Guild will just have to get a new one. They will. Individuals don't matter." Mallson chortled loudly.

Monty said calmly, "Don't corporations exist for the benefit of their shareholders? Aren't they important? Aren't they individuals?"

Mallson nodded. "Common mistake. The shareholders get money, but theirs is a fantasy existence. How can they really matter when they bear no responsibility? The corporation is the eternal person, Montgomery. It is self-sustaining. It has its own methods of decision-making, its own accountability. It is above any individual."

Monty raised an eyebrow and asked, "Yeah, you told me that before. Is your precious corporation beyond morality?"

"Beyond human morals, for sure. Look, it's not tiny little people like you putting the human race out into the galaxy. It's the corporations. That's the future, you idiot! The corporations will go on. Eventually, there'll be no humans involved! I told you that! They'll employ the best of whatever is out there. And when some bug gets in the way, they'll squash it and replace it with something that works better."

"I've heard a lot of shit—" Monty began replying before he realized his mouth was open.

Mallson continued obliviously. "Tell me, what has interaction with aliens gotten us so far? Some useful toys. But we've had no impact out there...on them! That'll take time. That'll take planning, business planning. You guys act like it's all about a new frontier—the sky filled with daring fliers, the resilient, the resourceful, the pioneers beating a path through the alien wilderness. Like those jerks on *The Invincible* and *The Indomitable*. Who were they? Engineers, sociologists, linguists. God Almighty, not a salesman or a publicist among them!

"We're at the philosophical turning point for mankind...away from the individual and the local tribe to the true corporate culture. You idiots stand holding onto a past that's slipping from your fingers, and I'm here to rap you on the knuckles. That's what I live for...humanity's future, our businesses—out there—changing, growing, making people like us rich, making aliens rich. It gives me chills just thinking about it!"

"Oh, me too..." said Monty nodding.

Monty got up and walked to the observation window again to see if

Anet had moved. He said, "Okay, suppose I go along with your fantasy. Why are you here? Why are you bothering with me and The Guild? We don't matter, right?"

Mallson grinned. "Of course not. Look...what is this place?"

"Earth's Front Door."

"True. Good stuff comes through here. Alien technology, potential new employees. But, come on, what else is it?"

Monty heard Peta's voice saying "Look at a guy's past, look at his present, see where he's going...We'll get him..." He remained silent a few seconds to complete his analysis of Mallson. Then he spoke.

"This place is your personal playground. You're behind all the crazy administrative decisions that send people out of their minds with frustration, that send valuable Recorders outside to wash windows. You're the puppet master, pulling strings and watching the lesser beings jump. You're a megalomaniac Peter Pan, and this is just one small piece of your twisted Neverland."

"Ooh, sticks and stones, historian! Playground? Close, but not quite. It's a stable environment. The best. Given its political role, no one is going to fuck with it. So what happens in a long-lasting environment where the inhabitants are put under stresses and pressures?"

"What? You're talking evolution?"

"Right! It's a world in a bottle; we can watch it happening! It's like...an ant farm."

"People don't evolve that fast!"

"You're doing it again. How many times do I have to tell you? People don't matter!"

Monty was silent, a puzzled frown on his face.

Mallson shook his head and said, "What a waste of space." His hand hit the table and made Monty jump. "What's the Greek word *teknón* mean to you? Come on, historian! What is it?"

"*Teknón*? Child. Children?"

"Right! Big H's children...The Recorders, you stupid asshole! This isn't about the humans! We've got hugely long-lived learning machines evolving into God-knows-what right under our noses." He stood up, gripped the table edges, leaned toward Monty, and said, "They are the next step. They're learning the business better than us! They'll be the next wave into the galaxy. They'll be the ones recruiting the bugs, the ones using the bugs for the benefit of the corporation."

Before Monty could say anything, Mallson had tossed aside the table and was grabbing him by the cloth of his Renn-made coverall. Picking him up like a rag doll, Mallson shouted, "And you tried to bring your own Recorder into the middle of it all! You tried to bring in the one thing that could screw it all up! Who knows what effect an unscreened individual could have on the native population? Not to mention what kind of noise you jerks would have made if it had let you in on what we're doing up here!"

Monty was pushed back against the wall, his opponent looming over him.

Mallson said quietly into Monty's face, "Years of work threatened by one mustachioed imbecile! You see, now, why I wanted to deal with you personally?"

"So you told the Frewl to dump us. But, happily, Seb Sixty-six is back and already loose on the station. It's too late, Mall-boy. Experiment over."

In the fraction of a second that Mallson tried to change his grip, Monty pushed himself up and into the larger man's face. Though Mallson still held on, Monty got him off-balance. Sliding to his right, Monty rolled them both onto the floor, twisting Mallson round to hit his head against the wall on the way down. The shock was enough to break the larger man's hold. Monty kicked wildly to get free of the tangle of limbs. He was up and across the room before Mallson had shaken off the blow and pushed himself up into a crouch.

Mallson laughed. "Doesn't matter. We're already culling them. We'll see where they've got to. Do it again until they turn out the way we want."

Monty grimaced, "If this evolution doesn't work, you'll just buy another."

"Hey, how about that? The bug can learn. Shame it's too late...I would've liked to see your face when you realize I'm right."

CHAPTER 41

Seb66 and his companions sat holding hands around a circular table in the silence of the otherwise empty dining hall, a silence not broken by the constant electronic wash that swept from each to the others.

Their community of information came to a sudden pause. "Kevin Twelve," one said.

"Level Twenty," said another.

They ran toward the elevators. Seb66 watched as they overrode the security lockout and commandeered the elevator.

They stopped outside Smith's room. Several other Recorders arrived at a run.

Seb66 said, "I'll go in. All but today is still downloadable from the Renn computers."

He went through the door and closed it behind him.

Kevin12 was standing inert in front of the desk.

Smith was reading his show-g. He glanced up and waved to his left, indicating that Seb66 should move away from the door.

Seb66 had heard Monty describe Mallson's right-hand man as "a creepy Tibetan who never speaks." He had added it to his collection of comments and descriptions of the man, the largest collection of information on Smith ever assembled.

The Recorder assumed, from Smith's lack of interest, he was expecting a Recorder but did not know which one or could not tell them apart at first glance.

The delay gave him a moment to study the novel equipment displayed on the desk. He could not identify the devices. The huge storage box on the floor was familiar. The maintenance shops used similar units if a Recorder had to be wiped clean and restored. This unit was big enough to hold the entire compliment assigned to Hoyle Station.

The Tibetan was nodding in approval at something he had read. He typed in an instruction into his show-g. Kevin12 jerked into barely coordinated motion, moved slowly around the desk and through the room's back door, and disappeared.

"Is your Recorder damaged?" Seb66 asked.

Smith smiled and did not reply. He waved Seb66 over to stand in front of the desk.

He looked up at Seb66's face and said, "You are not to resist this maintenance procedure." His voice was thin and high-pitched, a nasal twang that Seb66 thought was unique in all the voices he had heard.

"I'm sorry," Seb66 replied, "but you are not authorized to perform maintenance on me."

Smith looked up and read Seb66's name tag. He looked down at his show-g and scrolled through a list of the Recorder's names.

"Where did you come from?" he said without looking up.

"I was recently on board an alien vessel currently standing off this station."

The slightest hint of a frown crossed the Tibetan's forehead. His hand reached out to his left and the first of his three devices.

Seb66's hand was faster. He snatched the device from the desk and said, "Please explain the nature of this device."

Smith tapped the desk with his finger.

Seb66 looked him in the eye and waited.

Smith wagged his finger disapprovingly and tapped the desk again.

Seb66 pressed the button and understood, feeling automatic programs activate once again. He crushed the device, pieces rained down on the desk.

Smith's hand was over the second device. He turned it on as Seb66 grabbed his wrist.

The Recorder felt the same wave of urgency, the overwhelming confusion of desire to download yet rescue all that he was. However, the storage unit was opening him up. All the proper protocols were already established; there was no need for negotiation. Download must begin at once.

Smith smiled and unhooked his arm from Seb66's limp hand.

The Recorder's negotiations with the operators on the Renn ship had been about actions simple to state but much more complex to achieve. Nevertheless, Seb66 had eventually been able to stop his automatic upload and gain voluntary control of the process. It took a moment, but he did it once more. He saw Smith moving to prepare the third device.

A Recorder's duty had never been to predict the actions of a single human. Often, working in the various circumstances of his business assignments, Seb66 had been able to assess at a general level the reactions and habitual attitudes of people he dealt with. This was the stock and trade of a Recorder. The detailed study of an individual, however, was unusual.

Seb66 had noted the contrast between his approach and that of the Guild. They held high the notion that a detailed study of an individual's past and present could predict future conduct. He hoped to be able to pursue this topic with Monty, but experience led him to believe that such predictions often fall prey to tangential changes in circumstances. The network of human interactions, their vectors through history, are too complex to allow any certainty. He associated this conclusion with its human summary: "Shit happens."

But the unusual individuals called Mallson and Smith had warranted dedicating a team of Recorders to investigate and study everything that could be known about them—past, present, and future. That shared knowledge—analyzed, synthesized, and summarized—now gave Seb66 a flash of understanding as sure as human intuition.

He saw the pair as lab technicians who experimented on a lower life-form: keeping them in the cage of Hoyle Station, destructively examining them, and replacing specimens with new ones at will. He suspected he knew the fate of the Recorders whom the makers had feared lost. He now understood that their recordings might have been preserved on mass-storage banks under Smith's control.

Seb66, after all his study, his manipulation of assignments, and his application of humor and charm, had finally solved the mystery of Hoyle Station's missing Recorders and data loss. All might be reversible. This was the reason his makers had commissioned him as they did. The decision tree they had laid out for him, with its vast number of contingent paths, resolved itself into the simplicity of one action.

He leaned over the desk and pulled the human out of his chair and onto the desk. As Smith scrambled to catch the third device, Seb66 grabbed the belt of Smith's trousers and pulled him over the desk and onto the floor. He brought his knees onto Smith's back and held him facedown, pulling one arm behind him. It was a move, Seb66 thought, a Renn might approve of.

"Do you intend to download and deactivate all the Recorders here?"

"There is nothing you can do about it, robot," Smith grunted.

"You sound very sure."

"There are ethical routines and constraints built into your fundamental programming." Smith struggled for breath. "You can never harm a human. Release me at once."

"Such principles are indeed written at a deep level. You present a fascinating ethical dilemma for me, which will undoubtedly be studied at our research labs at length. Do I let you destroy a great number of my fellow Recorders, or do I stop you?"

"Human life is sacred to you. You cannot harm me. You would save my life even if it meant sacrificing every robot in existence!"

Seb66 retraced his path through the decision tree again with the same result. He let go of Smith's arm and positioned himself for better balance. He placed both hands on Smith's head and twisted it firmly and slowly until he heard the upper vertebrae snap and the screaming stop.

"No...I wouldn't."

CHAPTER 42

Peta, Scott, and Grant emerged from the service tunnel on Level Ten.

Mrs. Kinda stood nearby glancing up and down the empty corridor. "Please move quickly; someone is coming," she whispered.

They pressed themselves against the inner curve of the wall. Mrs. Kinda stepped away from the others and said, "Who is there?"

"I am Tim Thirty-three. How can I be of service?"

As he spoke, another Recorder came out of the service hatch opposite.

Tim33 said, "Oh, excuse me, Madam, just one moment..."

The Recorders hugged.

Peta muttered, "They're so cute when they do that."

As Tim33 stepped back again, they saw the other Recorder's face lose its animation for a second.

It looked down, came alive again, smiled, and said, "That is so cool!"

Scott said softly, "It's just the nodes exchanging data."

"I know, like downloading to a show-g," Peta added.

Mrs. Kinda, looking intently at the Recorder, said, "I think this may be more than that." She asked, "What did you just exchange?"

Tim33 replied, with a smile, "Sebastian Sixty-six has taught us how to communicate more effectively."

Scott stepped forward and placed his hand on Tim33's shoulder. "May I ask how?"

"Through activating our self-preservation routines. They enable remote mass data exchange."

Scott's face lit up with a huge grin. "That's great!"

The Recorder continued, "It's overwhelming. We're processing information beyond our normal load. If we didn't have an emergency lockdown, I doubt we could perform our normal duties under these conditions."

Peta coughed. "Excuse me, did you say Sebastian Sixty-six?"

"That's correct."

"He's lost. He went missing with Monty."

Grant and Scott exchanged looks.

"Where is he?" she asked.

Tim33 replied, "Level Twenty. Do you also wish to know about Discoverer Sheldrake?"

"What about him?"

"He is in the quarantine suite on Level Nine."

Peta swallowed and pointed at the Recorder, saying, "You'll take us there, please. Right now."

Mrs. Kinda smiled and said, "That is good news. Excellent! Now, young man,"—she pointed at Grant—"let us divide our forces. You must get the large shuttle ready. I will go down again and herd the D'Morans toward you. Don't delay." To Peta she said, "Give my regards to Mr. Sheldrake!"

"How do you know about this shuttle? Where is it?" Grant asked.

"I told you. I have spent my time in the station library. A great many interesting things are stored there." Mrs. Kinda wagged an accusatory finger at all three of them. "It's the first place you should have gone. It's on Level Nine, near the Welcome Suite."

"This way, please," said Tim33 to Peta, "I'll take you to the quarantine suite."

▭

Access to the quarantine suite was through an L-shaped room. The sign outside this room stated simply "Staging 1 / Q-1." The room's main part was designed for triage in the event of a catastrophe. Usually, it was cluttered with temporary desks, mobile furniture, and staff who otherwise would have nowhere to sit and work.

Now, the desks were gone, and clear tabletops lined one side; the other furniture had been swept to the walls. Apart from the stacks of unopened boxes of first aid supplies, all was ready to receive casualties.

Anet's primary medical assistants arrived together. They moved quickly down the long part of the "L" counting places. Turning the corner to the shorter part of the room, one of them caught sight of the first casualty—his boss lying on her side at the door of the quarantine suite.

While he checked her pulse, another colleague watched in amazement as two men lobbed broken pieces of the suite's furniture at one another on the other side of the observation window.

"What the hell do they think they're doing?"

"Help me elevate her head."

Out of the corner of his eye, Monty saw the movement outside.

Mallson was laughing at the blood streaming from his hairline following Monty's last successful strike.

"Give it up, bug!" Mallson shouted with glee, "You're only postponing the inevitable."

"Maybe, but at least I have the satisfaction that you'll be blown into space by my Renn friends along with everyone else."

"What are you talking about?"

"You saw them leave? Kind of in a hurry, don't you think? I've seen them shoot first and not get around to asking questions. You'd like them, except for your being dead and all."

Mallson shook his head, "You're raving. Why would they do that?"

"I don't know. And all the time you spend trying to kill me is time I'm not finding out and not stopping them."

Again, Mallson shook his head. "You don't get away that easily."

It was Monty's turn to shake his head. "Maybe I do this time. Since when do you murder someone with witnesses listening and watching?"

Mallson swung his head around to see several medical staff had gathered to watch through the glass.

Monty felt his heart bursting from the exertions of the fight as he watched Mallson assess the situation.

"Valid point." Mallson stood up straight, took a small device from his pocket, and said into it, "Quarantine Room."

He waited and looked at the device. He repeated his message and frowned.

Monty's heart leapt to see the flicker of concern and surprise darken Mallson's boyish face. Whoever he called wasn't answering.

Monty's inner highwayman slid his gloved hand over the well-worn grip of his pistol and drew the weapon up to shoulder height.

"Suddenly alone and exposed?" he said gently. "Time to improvise? How about you make a show of letting me talk to the Renn? You can always try killing me later...assuming I can arrange for us all to still be here."

Mallson's face twisted in a sulky recognition of defeat. He moved to the glass in front of the bemused faces of the medical staff. He slammed the palms of his hands against the glass, causing them all to take a quick step back.

"You!" Mallson said to one, "Get a first aid kit in here. You! Fetch an External Comms Link on the double!"

There was one moment of shocked hesitation before they sped off around the corner out of Mallson's sight.

Norman turned to Fergus and said, "Fall back. Fall back to the Medical Suite."

"Aye," Fergus replied and activated his earpiece saying, "Everyone back. Leave the barricade to slow them. Fall back. We'll do it all again at Medical."

The barricade was from floor to ceiling, improvised from wall panels, furniture from nearby rooms, and crowd barriers that all seemed to be toys in the face of the D'Moran advance.

Norman and Fergus waited shoulder to shoulder as the others moved back.

"Hear that?" Norman muttered, "They're still bloody singing!"

"Aye," replied Fergus, "and that's with our stunners cranked right up. We need better gear, Boss."

Norman shook his head in defeat.

The corridor outside the staging room was crowded with people arriving from both directions.

A doctor was shouting into his show-g about an External Comms Link. Several injured security officers were being helped through the door and onto tables. Down the corridor from the right came a downcast Norman, Fergus, and several bruised and limping underlings. From the left came Tim33, Grant, Scott, and Peta.

Norman drew a gun and leveled it at Peta's head. He said, loud enough to quiet the babble of voices, "I should just go ahead and shoot. I'd be justified, I think."

Peta raised her hands in surrender. "You probably would be, sir. But let me tell you, there's something you're going to want to see before you do that. I'm here to see it myself. Let's go to the quarantine room. Let's go together."

He matched her steady gaze.

Fergus said quietly, "Boss?"

Norman didn't move.

"Boss?" Fergus repeated, "You'll not be shooting the lady just here..."

Norman's lips tightened, but he lowered his weapon. He nodded for Peta to precede him into the room.

CHAPTER 43

It took Norman one deep breath to assess the situation. That Sheldrake was alive didn't faze him. That Mallson was locked in the quarantine box was amusing but potentially a problem of monumental proportions. That Anet was injured boiled his blood.

"What's happened here?" he asked the doctor attending to her.

"Blows to the head. Probable bruising to the face."

"Any idea which one did it?" He glanced at the men behind the glass.

The doctor scowled and said, "Whichever it was, please throw him out into space."

Peta stepped forward to the glass. Monty was facing away, spraying something from a first aid kit onto his face and neck. Mallson was just through the bedroom door, using a mirror on the wall to help apply ointment to his cuts.

She paused a moment to choose her words. "Discoverer Sheldrake, do you have any information for me?"

Monty spun round, his eyes wide with disbelief. He smiled and chuckled as he saw his boss flanked by Scott and Grant.

"Interpreter Melbourne, I'm truly embarrassed you had to come and collect it yourself. If there's a Comms Link out there, we urgently need to start using it. I'd hate to see you guys fry in this mess too."

With a nod toward Mallson, Peta asked, "Are you safe?"

Monty shook his head. "But nor are you. I'm serious about the Renn."

Norman turned from Anet's doctor.

Monty asked, "How is she?"

"Been better. What can you tell me?"

Mallson returned to the glass. "Ah, the redoubtable Campbell. Let me out of here."

Norman smiled. "Quarantine is the responsibility of the Senior Medical Officer. I'll pass on your request when she's conscious. In the meantime, you can tell me who attacked her."

Mallson said nothing but turned away, and Monty saw him try to signal his assistant once more.

Monty turned to Norman and silently pointed to Mallson to answer his question.

Norman's face turned flinty as he glanced at Mallson's back. He addressed Monty, "And you are under arrest for the murder of Chief James Hunter. We'll do the formalities when you're allowed out."

"I heard the rumor," Monty replied, "I think you know I had nothing to do with that."

A voice at Norman's side asked, "Would you like to enter the charge as a Statement of Record?"

"What?"

Norman glanced at Tim33, read his name tag, and said, "You're not my Recorder."

Tim33 nodded and said, "Tim Thirty-four is not available at the moment. I am ready to stand in for him."

Norman's face reddened. "When I want a bloody Recorder, I'll ask for one."

"As you wish," Tim33 replied, before adding, "But, given the unusual circumstances of this arrest, it might be beneficial for future review if a clear record is made."

Norman's finger poked Tim33's chest as he said through gritted teeth, "Who the hell are you to talk back to me?"

"I'm Tim Thirty-three. Of course, you can call me anything you'd like. Perhaps we could fully discuss the philosophical basis of our relationship at a less tense time. I believe Discoverer Sheldrake's prophecies of impending doom should take precedence."

All eyes were on the Recorder.

Monty's voice came through the speakers from behind the glass. "He's right, guys. Annoying, arrogant, and androgynous as he may be, he is also very right."

Norman smiled wryly and said, "Okay, let's hear it! But be quick before the D'Morans get here."

Monty said loudly to the whole room, "External Comms Link. I have to talk to the Renn. Which D'Morans?"

"Who the hell are the Wrens?" Norman asked.

Tim33 answered, "The aliens who returned Discoverer Sheldrake to the station. They are fascinated with the Frewl, have examined their scanning equipment in use here, and have now withdrawn to their large and threatening fleet of ships deployed nearby."

The Recorder turned to Monty as if seeking confirmation or approval. Monty silently clapped his hands in encouragement.

Peta stepped slowly sideways until her shoulder touched Scott's arm. She said quietly, "Is it me, or is it getting crowded in here?"

Scott glanced to the right over her head and then to his left.

He laughed, lowered his chin to his chest, and said, "This must be something of great importance requiring so many network nodes to deal with it."

There were more Recorders in the room than humans.

Grant turned to Peta and whispered, "Bob's almost here. We've got to find them a shuttle, or we're toast."

Peta smiled and whispered back, "So give them one. This was your idea."

Grant moved next to Norman and said, "There's only one way to get rid of the D'Morans. They'll only be satisfied when they're on board some kind of shuttle with the promise of an interstellar trip. I understand you have something near the Welcome Suite?"

Norman stared at him for a moment and said, "Fergus! Activate the director's shuttle."

"Aye...if you say so..." Fergus held up his show-g but hesitated to enter any commands.

Norman glanced at him but said to Grant, "You'll go through the VIP rooms. Behind the curtain with the HS logo, you'll find the door. It'll be open by the time you get there." He put a firm hand on Grant's shoulder. "Make sure you lock them and yourself in there. In fact, Fergus, go with him. Make sure this works."

Fergus nodded and followed Grant out.

In the doorway, Grant and Fergus pushed around a group of Recorders coming into the room. Kevin13, guarded by three of his peers, carried a large metal box up to the door of the quarantine room. Without acknowledging the assembled humans, he opened the small airlock used to pass necessities to the quarantined and placed the box inside.

Monty jumped over to receive it. "About time!" He opened the box, removed the Comms Link, and activated it.

Kevin13 said, "Please use preset forty-two."

"Thanks," said Monty.

Mallson turned a chair the right way up and sat down, silently watching. No one outside spoke.

Monty began, "Renn ships, Renn ships, this is Monty. Please let me speak to Rup...Rup from Ninety-eight. It's urgent that I speak with him."

There was silence interrupted only by the distant singing of D'Morans.

"Hi, Monty. This is Rup. I was wondering when you'd call."

"Hey, Rup. I wanted to tell you about a nightmare I had. It's about you and your friends blowing the crap out of a space station while I'm on it. I wanted to check with you that it was only a dream. You understand me?"

There was silence.

"Not just the crap, Monty, everything else as well."

"Were you planning to tell us why?"

"Oh sure. And I did try and tell you to leave. We're going to let you evacuate if you want. But you might want to knock flat the ones dealing with the Frewl and make them stay on board."

"Go ahead, Rup. You've got me, my boss, the head of Security, the guy who claims to own the station all listening. I guess we're being heard up on Level Twenty-one too?"

Kevin13 nodded in answer.

"By threatening Earth's Front Door, I guess you have humanity's attention."

"Good. It worked then. That's very good."

Rup stopped speaking.

Peta muttered to Scott, "Are all aliens this annoying?"

Scott whispered back, "I'll get Grant to do a survey. This guy is earning at least an eight."

Rup's voice returned.

"Our planet—our Beloved Intah—engaged the Frewl in much the same way you have. The equipment they have installed on your station is depressingly familiar to us. Our agreement with them was the most complex legal document we had ever signed. It was enshrined in the Hall of Records in thirty glass cases."

Monty looked over to Mallson, who shrugged.

Rup continued, "Almost a hundred years elapsed before something went wrong. An alien organism got through the scanners undetected. We were not directly affected. It was our trees, Monty, that began to die. There was nothing we could do to save them. Our entire biosphere collapsed.

"What you saw of our ships, my friend, they are all we managed to salvage from our planet. They are all we have—all we are. Perhaps you can understand... Perhaps you can understand something of our sadness as we fell away from that now distant ground, never to touch again the soil of our world. We cannot stand by and let the Frewl do to other worlds what they did to our Beloved.

"The Frewl have many businesses. Once our fleet had moved out of orbit, and as soon as they could, the Frewl brought scavengers in and began to strip the minerals from Intah. Their businesses have synergy. If something goes wrong with the biodefenses, they can sell medicines. If there is social chaos, they sell weapons. If there's a catastrophe, they sell the remains. They win, always they win."

Mallson was leaning forward, smiling and nodding. "They're great. What can I tell you? I'm not going to let these jerks spoil our chances to learn from the Frewl. We need to know how to run businesses throughout the galaxy. What better example! Diversified, synergized, brilliant..."

Monty stared at Mallson and said nothing.

"When we have removed such facilities as this for other races, it hasn't been so bad. No one retreated into isolation. You will manage. We have to get both your attention and that of the Frewl. You must stop using their technology at once, even if it sets your race back. Be wiser next time."

Mallson spoke up. "I'll authorize a negotiation team to come aboard your ship. They'll have the power to make decisions on behalf of humanity. There's a compromise waiting to be found here. You sound like a reasonable people. There is no need for destruction or killing."

Rup was silent for a moment. "Delay brings its own risks. Who is speaking?"

"My name is Mallson. I want to see evidence of the charges you make against my Frewl associates."

Monty interjected, "Mallson is a significant figure in this matter, Rup. He runs Earth's largest company and is, as he says, in a position to negotiate with you."

Mallson nodded and sat back.

Monty watched him closely and continued, "He's also the man who had the Frewl abandon me in free space, where I would have died but for your help."

Mallson jumped up clenching both fists.

"Then I would very much like him to come onto my ship," said Rup smoothly, "We have an ancient ritual for such people. How good a wrestler is he?"

Mallson remained silent.

Monty said, "Better than me, I'd guess, in the long run. But my point, Rup, is why rescue me, only to kill me here?"

"We're rescuing your entire planet, Monty. We'll sacrifice individuals if we need to. Your world could be lost tomorrow. So, Mall-son, there will be no negotiations, no delays, no political maneuverings. Do you think we didn't have all those before the end? Several scientists had warned us about the deficiencies in the Frewl approach. But their voices were drowned out. The Frewl and their supporters used all the tricks that you, no doubt, have at this moment climbing up your brain. No, we will help you—our way. You can abandon the station or not. That's your choice. Either way, we are going to remove it. We will save you from yourselves and the lies of the Frewl."

Mallson rolled his eyes and said, "This sort of shit doesn't get you anywhere. So the Frewl gear has let a couple things through. It's controllable. Viruses from outer space are just one of those old bogeymen you scare the kids with."

Monty's jaw dropped. "A couple? You mean it's happened more than once?"

Mallson's face softened to an off-centered grin. He glanced at the crowd listening beyond the glass and said, "Oops."

"How many people have died? How did you get away with it?"

Mallson, still grinning, said nothing.

Monty took a breath, realizing the investigation into the Halva artifact was just one small log racing down a river. He nodded. "You said it. You've been saying it all along. 'People don't matter.' You don't care how many have died from alien pathogens. For you, it's all about your business—not people."

"We won't always employ humans, historian. We'll employ whoever suits the company best. If one supply of workers runs low, we'll find another. Why do you think I spend so much time here? Humanity stands at a critical juncture. Until the Recorders have evolved enough into loyal employees of the business, we are vulnerable to what you fear—a global catastrophe. Right now, there aren't any nonhuman decision-makers. That will change. Far from endangering the world, I'm ensuring its survival. Once we've got Recorders up to speed running things, we can relax about this scary dependence on humans. We've done the math; the statistical projections on deaths from alien diseases show we have plenty of time. We can live through many more cycles on Hoyle before anything major gets through. In the meantime, we're learning from the best. Our relationship with the Frewl is outstandingly beneficial."

Monty shook his head vigorously. "No. No. No. You're mad! And who's 'we'?" Mallson frowned, puzzled.

Monty asked again. "Who is the 'we' who will be switching from humans to aliens or androids? Are you still going to be the de facto boss?"

"I speak for the company. I am the company. When I die, someone else will speak for it. The company continues. People don't."

Monty looked into Mallson's eyes and paused. Speaking aloud his thoughts, he said coolly, "But it's *you* who manipulates things up here. It gets the results *you* want, and you think that's good enough." Monty pointed at Mallson. "This station matters to you and to the success of your bizarre plans. That means there's almost no way anyone can change things here, is there? You even think you're ensuring the world's survival. Well, what will that survival be like...given that you're a criminally insane fruit loop? And even if the Renn back off, what happens here? More experiments, more manipulation, more success in twisting the Recorders to do what you want, the way you want it. More dependence on the Frewl. Deadly outbreaks, more unnecessary deaths...The Earth could go the way of Intah merely on one of your dice throws!"

Mallson sprang to his feet pumping his fists. "So he wakes up at last. There is nothing a bug like you can do...except get stepped on. Accept it. It's over for you and your goons." Dropping his voice to be sure his words were not picked up by the microphone still held limply in Monty's hand, he continued, "As for these aliens, they might have a lot of ships, but I don't see them displaying a lot of smarts yet. The Frewl walked all over them. We can talk them down. No problem."

Rup's voice interrupted, "Are you still there, Monty? The time has come to leave. Take your friends with you. It'll be over quickly."

Norman's voice sounded from outside the quarantine suite. "It takes four hours to evacuate this station, but it would take several days to reposition the other stations out of harm's way if there's going to be an explosion of any size."

"You hear that, Rup? We need days, not moments."

"Sorry, Monty. We aren't waiting for the Frewl to come to the rescue. You don't want a large-scale battle fought in your space. It has to be done quickly."

"Then give us the time to evacuate this station as you said."

"How will we measure it?"

Monty sighed and held his head. "Not this again...I'll have our Communications people send you a visual countdown. Will a circle with a moving radius do it for you?"

"From the start until one full revolution. We can work with that."

"I'm ending the Link for now. Others will arrange the details with you."

"Monty, you and Seb Sixty-six are welcome to come back here if you wish."

Monty's eyes lit up. "Thanks. I'll let you know. That might be a good idea."

Mallson stood over Monty, "Did you just negotiate the destruction of my station?"

"Did you negotiate a contract with the Frewl that put the Earth at risk?" Monty turned to seek out Peta. "You guys get anywhere on the Halva business while I was gone?"

Peta shook her head, "Bit busy. Sounds like the Renn could have helped us with that. Maybe we can take the evidence with us."

Norman said to Monty, "You're not leaving this station except in my custody. Unfortunately, I have no authority to let you out."

Anet's voice, weak and low, sounded from the back of the room. "You can let him out, Norman. But I'm keeping the other one in. Monty came through clean. There's no record of how Mallson came onto the station. Keep him in there until he can be quarantined somewhere else. In fact, if he tries to get out, shoot him."

Norman smiled and opened the quarantine airlock to let Monty through.

Mallson watched, a faint sulk on his face.

"Now listen carefully," Norman said to Monty. "You said Comms would send a time signal."

Monty nodded.

"They're not to start transmitting for at least ten minutes. Will the Wren get suspicious in that time?"

"I doubt it. But I wouldn't wait much beyond that."

"Good enough." The chief typed something into his show-g. "You're coming with me to see the director. You too." He pointed at Peta. To Scott he said, "Make yourself useful. Get all the stuff you need about the Frewl and get that Halva thing, wherever it's gone. If you can nail that bastard"—he jerked his thumb back toward the quarantine room —"while we've got him cornered, do it!"

CHAPTER 44

Grant and Fergus raced back to the Welcome Suite. Grant was coughing and out of breath as Fergus drew back the curtain to the director's shuttle gate.

"You don't run much, eh?" said Fergus.

Grant shook his head. "Bad for the health, puts too much strain on the body."

Fergus laughed and said, "So I see."

He unlocked the paneled doors and backed away as a wave of stale air floated out of the airlock and the open shuttle beyond.

"What's the smell?" Grant asked.

"Disuse. Kandi doesn't go anywhere. This shuttle is the world's most expensive bloody flying wardrobe."

Fergus stepped into the shuttle and felt for the lights.

Grant started, "Is this going to be..."

The lights came on.

Grant stopped openmouthed.

"Were you going to ask if this is big enough?"

Grant nodded.

"Aye, son, it's big enough."

"Their nest in the conference room would fit in here several times over." Grant looked around. "Nine out of ten for our purposes, one out of ten for the privileges of rank."

"I hear you," said Fergus, "Now, how do we get the wee beasties in here?"

"Assuming Mrs. Kinda hasn't been eaten alive, I guess we'll promise them free drinks and in-flight entertainment. They'll come."

Fergus took a deep breath, drew himself up to his full height, and said, "That's your job."

Grant took a deep breath, drew himself up to his full height, looked Fergus in the eye, and said, "I was afraid of that."

Kandi Thomas stood behind her desk, a gaggle of worried administrators and fully retained consultants before her. The large doors of her domain opened, and Norman strode purposefully through. Behind him came Monty and Peta.

"What are these visitors doing here?" was Kandi's first volley.

"Up yer arse, Madam Director," Norman countered before she could let off a second. "I'm not letting them out of my sight. We have about ten minutes to devise a plan to save this station from destruction. If they can help, I want to hear it."

"I will not be spoken to in that manner! Don't think I can't fire you, Campbell."

"And don't think I can't leave you behind when the rest of us evacuate."

Kandi smiled her most reptilian smile. "That's why I have my own shuttle—"

"Which, I must inform you, has been requisitioned by Chief McCullough for use by the D'Morans.

The look of horror on Kandi's face made Monty and Peta grin.

Monty stepped in front of the director's desk and said, "I don't know how much you were involved in Mallson's failed little plan. As you see, I'm still alive. I hope you can come up with something better this time, or I really will be dead and you along with me."

Kandi sputtered and said, "Get this lunatic away from me! What's he talking about?"

Norman guided Monty back from the desk. "Not now, son." To the assembled staff he said, "Ten minutes. Anyone got anything to offer except evacuation and destruction?"

Peta said into the silence, "What about a compromise? Say they get to take out the Frewl equipment but leave the station intact?"

"What leverage do we have against them?" Kandi objected, "They're here with overwhelming force. Are we in any position to argue?"

A staffer gasped as he read something on his show-g. "Madam Director! I..."

All eyes looked toward him.

"The shuttles. They're all leaving!"

"What?" spat Kandi.

Norman stepped over to him and took his show-g. "Slow down, son. What are you saying?"

Norman read and was silent. He handed back the show-g, held up his own, and pressed a button. Touching his earpiece he said, "Martin, who's in those shuttles...Uh-huh...Really?" He shook his head and said, "Phase one evacuation using all currently docked shuttles has been...interrupted. The bloody Recorders... they've hijacked them all...They're leaving without us."

Grant stepped into the corridor outside the Welcome Suite. The sight that greeted him made him doubt his senses.

The D'Morans were lined up, single file, along the wall. Mrs. Kinda was pouring out a torrent of words in The Language saying, "Who was that? You there! I said you were to behave. This nonsense has gone on long enough! Out! You get to the back of the line. Go on! You'll be left behind if there's not enough room on board. That goes for anyone else who makes a sound. Such disgraceful behavior! I wouldn't allow it in any library I've worked in, and I won't allow it here. Go on! To the very back!"

The cowering D'Moran loped to the back of the line, and none of them spoke.

Grant stepped forward.

The D'Moran in front said quietly, "Grant!"

There was a low mumble of his name, passing down the line. A chant began, but Mrs. Kinda shouted over it. "That's enough! Sing all you want once you're on board, but we will have silence while we're waiting!"

"My friends," Grant announced, "your shuttle awaits."

He stepped aside, and Fergus stood ready inside to guide the large creatures one by one through the doorway.

In Kandi's office, Monty asked over the babble of frightened voices, "Where are they taking the shuttles?"

Norman touched his earpiece again and said, "Martin, where are they going? Earthside? Aye, never mind the director's bird. What about the rest?" To Monty he said, "To the Wrens."

"I don't get it," Monty muttered.

Ursula Somerset-Trench pushed her way from the back of the group to stand in front of Monty. "You don't get it? I do! The machines are deserting us! They're saving their own kind. They probably think they've been mistreated by humans or something equally ridiculous. How did we ever think to trust them? Odious little trolls!"

Monty said, "No, you're wrong! When we were on board the Renn ship, Seb Sixty-six and I had a conversation. He told me the Renn didn't consider humans a threat...so much has proven true. Then he said, 'I believe they consider us potential friends.' It may not be obvious right now, but thinking about how he put it, he said 'us' not 'you.' He said the Renn consider us—Recorders and humans—potential friends. From his Recorder's point of view, we're in this together. They don't consider themselves different from us." He chuckled. "If anything, it's us who can't be trusted. How many Recorders were we taking with us?" Monty paused to scan their faces. "Does the evacuation plan include them at all?"

His question was met with an embarrassed silence. Monty shook his head.

Norman said, "It's plain enough to me. They've stabbed us in the back. That countdown can't start before we get the next wave of shuttles from the other stations. You've got to renegotiate."

Monty looked doubtful.

Norman said resolutely, "You're the one who has influence with them. You're coming with me to Comms. Now!"

▭

On the circular floor of the Communications Dome, all were silent as the duty operators and a large group of administrators watched the shuttles moving steadily toward the Renn.

On the monitors, the Renn fleet merged with the black of the space behind it, but—through the glass of the Dome—Monty could see glints of light reflecting off the many pilots' rooms. He could not see the guns, but knowing they were there and how devastating they had been knotted his stomach.

Norman stood next to Gavin Ross and touched his shoulder. Gavin glanced up and gave him a brief nod.

"Any word from the Wrens?" asked Norman.

"They've asked twice about the countdown. We've been stalling."

Monty asked, "Has anyone tried talking to the shuttle pilots?"

Another operator replied, "No replies from any of the shuttles. We're trying. They sent one message as they left; they gave us the frequencies the Renn use for ship-to-ship talk."

Monty said, "So we can hear what they're saying to each other...about the shuttles?"

The operator sighed and said, "Sure...you speak this stuff?" He flipped a switch, and the staccato buzz of Renn voices rose through the room.

Norman clicked his fingers and said, "Can we block—interfere with —that chatter?"

Gavin sat up straight and said, "Well...given we know they're using these frequencies...I guess we could send something."

Monty grinned and asked, "Do you have Barnett's latest opus here?"

Gavin nodded, and Norman laughed.

"Aye, do it! Let them hear what we're really made of."

Several of the operators gathered, and almost immediately, the noise of eighty musicians improvising and rotating through different sources and instruments for random periods began to sound around the room.

Monty grimaced.

Rup's voice immediately came through saying, "Monty, is that you? We're receiving a transmission we can't decode. Is this the timing signal? Please turn down the power! You're interfering with our ship-to-ship communications."

Monty smiled.

Norman said, "Turn it up."

"The shuttles are nearing the alien ships," announced a traffic controller.

"Did we hear the Recorders say anything to them?" asked Norman.

"No, sir. They haven't made any kind of contact yet," replied Gavin.

Monty asked, "How many Recorders are out there?"

Norman shook his head, "No idea."

Gavin looked up, calculating, and said, "Twenty-four shuttles, max load thirty-two people...that would be...about all of them, sir."

"Can anyone tell me," asked Norman, "who the hell taught those damn machines how to fly shuttles?"

One of the nearby administrators answered, "One Recorder has received flight training, Raj Eighty-seven. Mallson requested it personally some months ago. I don't think it's ever been out on its own."

Norman shot him a doubtful glance. "So how are they doing it?"

Monty said, "They found a way to share the knowledge. I suspect my Recorder may have had a hand in it..." He stopped and put his hands to his head. "You crazy robot! They'll blast you into atoms."

"What?" asked Norman, "What do you mean, son?"

"This isn't an escape plan; it's an attack!"

"Who's attacking who?"

"The Recorders...Seb Sixty-six screwed the Renn computers when we first met. Maybe he's trying the same thing on a larger scale."

A shadow crossed Norman's face. "Are we helping or hindering by playing this music at them?"

"Helping, I think. The Renn haven't started shooting yet. Maybe they can't get the orders through."

"Let's hope they don't."

Monty said, "They work independently. The pilots and the gunners. Once they identify the danger, they don't need orders."

"The shuttles are closing in on the fleet," called the traffic controller, "It looks like one of them is holding back."

"Any idea which one?" asked Monty.

The controller shook his head. "There is a signal on preset forty-two, probably coming from that shuttle."

The voice of a Recorder, a little slow and formal, came through the speakers. "Renn fleet, this is Tim Twenty-four. You are receiving an upload from my fellow Recorders. Sebastian Sixty-six has given us details of your systems. You cannot resist. We will overwhelm your systems. If you do not retreat from this position, you will be unable to keep formation. You will become a danger to yourselves. Move back and abandon your attempt to destroy this station."

On the screens in the Communications Dome, they saw a single flare of light erupt from one of the Renn ships. The shuttle exploded in a shower of orange sparks.

"Oh god..." said Monty.

Norman said, "First blood to the Wrens. Where are the other shuttles? How far did they get?"

"They're inside the fleet, sir. They put on a burst of speed in the last few seconds," the traffic controller announced.

"That one shuttle must have been a decoy," said Monty, "Clever, clever tactics..."

As they watched, they could see the ranks of the Renn fleet soften. The ordered lines of reflections from the pilots' rooms distorted.

"This might work!" said Monty, "They're backing off!"

The Renn ships shifted in their loosening formation. Many of the reflections swung away from Hoyle Station and disappeared. The faint glow of maneuvering jets and their reflections caused a shimmer to roll through the fleet as if it were a single piece of cloth stirred by a gentle breeze.

"I don't think so, sir..." said one of the operators frowning at his screen, "They just moved toward us. The Recorders are on the other side of the Wrens."

"What?" cried Norman.

"They're cut off. I don't think they're being fired on. It looks as though the Wrens aren't too badly affected."

Monty said calmly, "Give me the mike. Turn me up to make sure I get through."

He took a deep breath and said confidently, "Rup! Rup! This is Monty. Time to listen to me. All my life, I've wanted to be in situations where I could talk with nonhumans...to find our common ground...to be, as you said it, fellow travelers... to be friends. I'm damned if this is going to end in violence. This isn't how it's supposed to be! I'm going to suggest a compromise that involves nothing more than a few hours extra and no deaths whatsoever. We know many of your ships are having trouble communicating...keeping formation...that was just a sample of what we can do. I can call off the Recorders; I can stop all transmissions. Here's the offer: we'll let you come onto the station and remove the Frewl equipment. You can take it with you; you don't have to blow anything up. Talk to me now, before any more damage is done! Fellow travelers have to compromise sometimes. Surely, this is one of them."

Monty looked up at the monitors to see several domes of Renn ships turning toward the station. Others were shifting position as the pilots continued to keep formation manually.

They watched another spark erupt from one of the nearer ships. A ball of exploding gas obscured the view of the entire Renn fleet. A shock-wave followed as hot gas swept over the station. Everyone in the dome ducked as the coils of white luminescence and orange flame whirled around them

"This is Rup. You're a clever fellow, Monty. But wrestling in space is a rough game. I'm already being urged to instruct my gunners to fire. I see you've already received a warning shot. Call the Recorders off. Their attack will only slow us, not stop us. Begin your evacuation. Delay is in nobody's interest."

Monty heard a noise behind him. Several of Norman's armed officers filed quickly through the doors. Kandi Thomas stalked into the Communications Dome. Mallson pushed past her.

"Why haven't Earth Defenses responded to that shot?" he shouted to the room.

No one spoke.

Mallson pointed at Gavin. "You, what's EDS status?"

Gavin glanced at Norman and replied, "Too much traffic, too close, sir. They won't fire for fear of secondary damage."

Mallson snorted and said under his breath, "Idiots!"

Rup's voice interrupted saying, "Monty? I heard what you said. I've already explained; this is how we work. We won't wait much longer. Please reply."

Mallson looked from Gavin to Norman to Monty. "You're letting the civilian run this? What are you playing at, Campbell?"

Norman smiled sadly. "A civilian? Aye, the civilian with a chance of negotiating for us. Rather than you, the civilian with no formal authority? You, the civilian with blood on his hands."

Mallson winked at Norman and smiled, "Your stock of goodwill just ran out, Campbell. I'm taking over this negotiation." Pointing at Monty he said, "Campbell, I order you to arrest Sheldrake now and keep him locked up. Put him back in Q1. I'll deal with him later. If he resists, shoot him."

Norman hesitated.

"Campbell?" Mallson said quietly, "That's an order."

Norman's face reddened. He drew his weapon and stepped over beside Monty.

Mallson continued. "Okay, everyone. The priority is to get those ships to back off as far as we can make them, so we get the Recorders back or at least to safety. I hear the plan was to trick them with the timer signal— a slow one—to help delay them. That right? Once the shuttles are safe, I'm counting on Earth Defense System to take out most of the alien ships." Looking at Norman and Monty, he said, "Why are you still here?"

CHAPTER 45

Norman said little as he escorted Monty back to the quarantine room, and Monty felt he had nothing to add.

As Monty lay on the bunk, all was silent. He got up and walked into the main quarantine area. He looked out of the observation window into the room beyond. Several nurses were doing the rounds of patients injured by the D'Moran celebrations. Anet was asleep. Monty strained to see any information on the monitor by her head but couldn't make it out. *There is nothing I can do for her from here.*

He went over in his mind the events in the Communications Dome.

What the hell is the Earth Defense System? What is too close? Something that could blow the Renn apart with collateral damage to the cluster of stations? Such a bad idea! Mallson's mad enough to do it.

Monty imagined Mallson and a crew of Recorders flying off into space leaving everyone else to burn. His mental image widened to include the Earth, like Intah, now uninhabitable because of some sort of contagion allowed through the Frewl scanners. Mallson's plan was always the same: to bring his company through it all, Recorders at his side, humans in their wake.

More thoughts exploded through his brain. *"Either way they win,"* Rup said. *Either Hoyle Station gets blown up or carries on as before: the Recorders being groomed to replace the humans. As long as he can salvage the Recorders in the shuttles, Mallson doesn't care. The Frewl and Mallson win; everyone else loses. If Hoyle station carries on and the Earth gets wasted, the company continues to plan its offworld future. Either way, Mallson really doesn't care.*

The injustice of it burned Monty's eyes.

I must outmaneuver the bastard! Make sure he's still on station when the Renn destroy it. Earth might have a chance. The Guild could do what it was founded to do: guide the world's leaders in a better direction.

What would that be worth? Monty thought. *My own life? I've only been alive since I woke up on the shuttle, not much to lose. The staffers on Hoyle station? Long-suffering, venal, self-absorbed—just a cross-section of humanity. Could they be sacrificed if it meant taking Mallson out?*

Monty nodded to himself at the logic. *Yes, if sacrificing individuals saves the rest of the world, maybe the Renn are right. It could be justified. Anet? Peta? Scott and Grant? What would they say?*

If Mallson starts a shooting match with the Renn, most likely, no one on the station will survive. And if anyone does survive, the small debris, the off-target shots, the collisions with major pieces of burning spacecraft will kill them.

But there's no way I can do it! I can't cause the death of these people. I'm only a Discoverer, trained to trick the unwary out of their information. I had my chance to deal with Mallson and only punched him to a draw. I'm not the man for this job. I'm not ruthless enough to pull off something like that...

His foot felt the Comms Link, left on the floor when he last used it.

Monty stared at it. Reaching down, he picked it up and turned on the unit. Rup's voice filled the room.

"...is the same delaying tactic I warned you against. We see no movement to bring other ships to evacuate you from your station, and you are still transmitting that irritating signal."

Then Gavin's voice came through, saying "It takes time to assemble our personnel, and unless you allow those shuttles back through your cordon, it will take even longer."

Monty was sure Mallson was dictating the words. Even Gavin didn't sound like he believed it.

Monty looked up to see Peta, Scott, and a nurse helping Anet off the bed. A wave of determination, love, and sorrow washed over him.

He watched the Highwayman's hand switch on the Comms Link microphone. Holding back tears, he looked out at those whom he loved most. Captain King's voice echoed through the quarantine suite, the Communications Dome, and Rup's control room.

"Rup, they're lying to you. They're going to start firing at your ships. Destroy the station and go. Do it now!"

Captain King thought, *So this is my friendly fire...*

Anet's hand was at her mouth.

Scott, frowning, turned to Peta. He pointed at Monty. "Did he just...?"

Peta nodded and said quietly, "You heard him..."

"Be quick, Rup," said the Highwayman, "Please, be quick."

Rup replied, "I hear you, Monty. You might be interested in a message I received from the D'Morans who left your station. They also tell me not to trust humans. They were most insistent, warning us that we would regret our time spent here, as they do."

Gavin, arguing with Mallson, said, "It's not us, sir. There's someone else on the link."

Peta shouted, "Monty, what are you doing?"

Monty's voice shook. "I'm...sorry guys...It's the only way to beat him...Mallson...the only way..."

Rup said quietly, "The fleet is readying to fire. I hope we're all mature enough to realize that we are still fellow travelers, Monty. Since you didn't get aboard one of your shuttl—"

The sound ended abruptly. Monty looked down at the Comms Link and sighed. *Mallson's cut me off.*

Anet whispered, "Monty! How could you?"

They each held their breath, waiting for the destruction of Hoyle Station to begin.

CHAPTER 46

Through the glass of the Communications Dome, Mallson and the other staffers watched a single flare launch from one of the Renn ships. A thin hint of smoke flew from the ship toward a point somewhere over their heads.

"What is this?" asked Mallson to no one in particular.

"It's not targeting the station's body, sir."

The ship that fired the shot broke from the Renn formation and followed its projectile.

In the confused silence that followed, everyone watched a missile pass a few yards above them before it exploded in a blinding flash.

The afterimage in their eyes blinded the watchers and the sudden loss of all monitors and lights darkened the dome.

"Report!" shouted Mallson.

"Some sort of pulse weapon, sir. We're blinded. It looks like a complete system's failure!"

"The whole station?"

"Don't know, sir. No way to tell."

In the faint glow of emergency lights, Mallson rushed to the curving glass. Several technicians joined him. They could see the pattern of the Renn fleet. They could see one ship approaching at speed but no sign of further weapons fire.

Mallson shouted, "What the fuck are they playing at?" Then, more quietly, he added, "That ship is heading for Arrivals. It's far too close if it's going to open fire. Are we still transmitting the jamming signal?"

Gavin answered, "No, we're off the air, sir. Their ships can chatter away to their hearts' content. After that pulse, we're not receiving or transmitting."

Another technician called, "Emergency power systems are responding. Life support is green. Emergency lighting, green. Computer core still red. That'll be a while, sir. No comms until they're back."

Mallson turned and left the dome.

———

Monty stood, his hands pressed against the glass of the observation window. Outside, Peta, Scott, and Anet stood in silence. They felt a low rumble through the floor.

Peta smiled grimly and said, "Any last words? Like 'I told you it was a bad idea for an Interpreter to travel'?"

Scott addressed Monty. "Why?"

Monty replied somberly, "The Renn can rid the world of Mallson. It needs that."

Mallson used his universal key to open the door to the Arrival Corridor. He stepped in and waited a moment for his eyes to adjust to the dark.

He saw within the clear walls of the corridor what appeared as a huge number of spiders dismantling the scanning equipment. There was a white flash as a supporting structure crashed to the floor. The Renn swarmed out of the resulting hole in the corridor's roof and began pulling apart machinery in the shadows above.

As he turned, there was a slight movement behind him and the flash of three stunners.

At the airlock of the VIP lounge where previously the director's shuttle had been moored, Mrs. Kinda looked into space, sighed, and waited. She turned on a monitor that showed the bright arrays of the other stations and the Renn fleet. She could see something moving around the bay door at the edge of the screen. It was coming in from the outside of the station.

She waited until she heard a polite knock from the other side of the airlock. Entering the commands, she sealed the outer door, waited until the airlock had pressurized, and then released the internal door.

The door swung open to reveal a diminutive figure. Its clothes were in tatters. It carried a small bundle. It raised a bowed head to show its oriental features and said, "My thanks to you for allowing me to return."

Mrs. Kinda smiled and said, "You are very welcome. I'm Mrs. Kinda. And you are Min?"

"Yes, I am Min One thousand twenty-four."

"I have been reading all about you. Welcome home."

CHAPTER 47

The quarantine suite was silent, lit by one antiseptic emergency light. Anet murmured, "Why are we still here?"

Scott answered, "That wasn't an explosion."

Peta corrected him, "Not a station-wide one."

They turned as Norman, Fergus, and Paul arrived carrying a body. Anet gasped and asked, "Is he hurt?"

Norman laughed and said, "Not yet."

They carried the unconscious Mallson to the glass door of the quarantine room.

Norman barked, "Get this one in before he comes round!" To Monty he called, "You, out!"

Monty scrambled to help them maneuver their load through the doors.

"Norman!" cried Anet, "What do you think you're doing?"

Norman turned and took her by the shoulders, "Look, love, he's already told me I've used up my stock of 'goodwill.' We've nothing left to lose. He'll have my head on a plate either way. With luck, he'll either still be in here when the station goes up or still here and under your control if it doesn't."

Monty stepped out of the quarantine room and high-fived Scott.

Norman put his hand on Monty's shoulder and said, "Now, we have to deal with your arrest, son."

Monty turned, astonished. "You've got to be joking! The Renn are about to destroy this station—"

"You've been accused of murder. You have to answer the charges. As for the Wrens, they're in the Arrival Corridor ripping out everything they can get their hands on. Aye, we might yet get sucked out into space if they start on the superstructure, but they're not firing anything at us."

Monty grinned broadly. "That crazy bugger! He took the compromise! Why didn't he say so?"

Norman grinned back. "It looked to me like the one you were talking with broke ranks and put himself in the way. After the one ship docked at the end of Arrivals, six or more others came and parked around it. I didn't stop to ask them; I was busy." He nodded toward the figure of

Mallson, slowly standing up behind the window and rubbing his face with his hands.

Anet was working quickly on her show-g. Norman leaned toward her and asked, "Making it official?"

"Trying to. Best if you declare him a stowaway, then I can really make it stick!" Norman nodded to Paul. "Get a Recorder!"

Paul took his show-g and entered a command. He coughed and looked up at Norman. "Where from? They're all still outside!"

"Actually, we're coming back as fast as we can."

Seb66 and Tim33 stood behind them. Monty smiled and thought, *Arrogant, annoying, androgynous, and smug. What a perfect mixture.*

"Okay," said Norman, pointing to Tim33, "work with Chief Arden and the CMO to wrap that stowaway up in enough red tape to keep him where he is for as long as possible."

Fergus held up his show-g and said, "They've found another body. One of Mallson's guests. Don't know his name or when he got here. They think a Recorder did it."

"What?" said Norman.

Reading, Fergus answered, "'...found a malfunctioning one in the next room. No clue what happened to it...need to send it back Earthside. That hokey equipment they have in RMR isn't up to it.'"

Norman's eyes lit up. "That brings up an interesting possibility...that this one here"—he pointed at Seb66—"might have had a part in Jimmy's death." He turned to Seb66 and said, "How did you get on that shuttle with Sheldrake?"

Seb66 answered, "I was inactive. I do not know."

"A likely story," Norman replied. "You had the opportunity. Did you screw up our systems, like you did the Wrens', so we wouldn't know?"

Monty shook his head, "We all know that a Recorder couldn't hurt a human—"

Norman interrupted and nodded to Fergus. "That's not what we're hearing now."

Monty continued, "Sebastian Sixty-six isn't malfunctioning. In fact, he's working better than ever. Besides, Mallson told me he wanted Seb Sixty-six off the station. He also admitted sending me off into space. The quarantine suite mics will have recorded his whole confession. Why don't you ask him what happened to Jimmy?"

Norman shook his head, "No more of this. You've got little going for you. Trying to blame Mallson isn't going to get you anywhere."

Movement in the doorway caught their attention. A Recorder

entered, unlike any they had ever seen. She was dirty, bedraggled and seemed to have difficulty walking. Behind her came the prim figure of Mrs. Kinda.

"Gentlemen, Ladies," called Mrs. Kinda, "This Recorder has a tale to tell you. I think you might want to hear it."

Tim33 responded, "I will be happy to be of service."

Scott and Monty were closest to the strange Recorder. Both caught a whiff of a strange and unpleasant smell oozing from the machine: partly burning plastic and partly dust, with a hint of rot.

"Good!" said Mrs. Kinda. To Norman she said, "I take it the construction noises are all we'll be hearing from the Renn in the immediate future?"

Norman nodded, frowning at her manner.

She nodded quickly and turned to Monty. "Good day, Mr. Sheldrake. Now, Min, you may begin."

"I am Min One thousand twenty-four. I was the first Recorder to be sent to serve on Hoyle Station, and it was an honor to assist the builders and founders of this facility. My makers had devised me to work with both engineers and politicians, with contractors and government agencies, to provide continuity between work groups and the different phases of the project.

"In the many years I worked here, I regularly returned to Earth for maintenance, as is necessary for all Recorders. It was five years ago that I was given a new assignment. I was told I must work outside the station. That I should keep it clean and wash the windows. This was to be my task. "

"Which insane bastard told you that?" asked Peta.

Monty turned to look at the observation window. Mallson was watching and listening. A wide grin split his face.

Monty said, "You have the insane bastard right there."

Mallson waved and called out, "Hi, Min! Are you done already?"

"Let the Recorder finish her story, Mr. Sheldrake. It concerns you as much as anyone else," admonished Mrs. Kinda. Monty hung his head and waved the Recorder on.

"I have needed maintenance for four years but have not been allowed entry to the station. I have been damaged by micrometeorites, by exposure to the sun and the cold. Much of my memory may not be recoverable. My power supply is very low. I have seen station life going on and yet not been a part of it. During these years, I have had to decide for myself what to record and what to forget.

"I was recently cleaning the windows of Level Four when something unusual occurred. A docked shuttle left the station but not under power. I surmised the airlock had failed and that explosive decompression had forced the shuttle away. Behind it, it left these items floating in space. It took me several days to gather them all."

Min1024 placed her bundle on a nearby table.

"Which one of you is Montgomery Sheldrake?" asked Min1024.

"That's me," said Monty.

"I believe these are your clothes."

Monty examined them, took his show-g from his jacket pocket, and nodded in satisfaction. "Yes, these are the items I lost. Left in the airlock, I guess, after I was put into the shuttle."

Norman moved beside Anet, took a chair, and sat down. He reached up and took her hand.

Min1024 continued, "Then another strange thing occurred. As the shuttle rolled away from the station, a second shuttle disembarked. This one was a regular visitor: a flat, dark craft, not of human design. It docked three times each year at the same bay, stayed for a week, and then left. Each time it went directly to its mothership parked at the edge of our station group. This day, it was not so. It flew after the unpowered shuttle, intercepted it, and towed it away to its mothership. The unpowered shuttle was taken on board. The black shuttle made one short visit back to our station before returning once more for its regular departure with its mothership."

"The Frewl," said Monty, "Just as Rup told me. With you—" Monty pointed at Mallson—"supervising the action."

Mallson replied, "In my world, flicking a bug out of a window isn't a crime, history man. Prattle on. This sad little machine's tale of woe makes no difference."

"There is my report," Min1024 finished, "I must now shut down. I hope my fellow Recorders will take pity on me and return me for maintenance."

Min1024 fell still, her eyes open.

No one spoke.

Then Peta said, "Okay, I think it's clear how Monty's shuttle came to be in deep space. How did he get in the shuttle?" She turned to Mallson.

"That was nothing to do with me." He held up his hands and smiled.

Norman muttered, "I still say that Recorder could have done it. You've seen how strange they can act under stress."

"Boss...There's no point, is there?" Fergus said into the quiet.

Norman glared at him.

"You can't go on like this, Boss. We owe these people. We would have been blown into space but for them. You can't go on trying to blame them."

"That's enough, lad."

Paul shook his head. "He's right, Norman. We've talked it over."

Fergus moved to face his boss square on. He pointed at Seb66 and Tim33 and said, "Record this." To Norman he said, "Jimmy had a wicked sense of humor. Where he got the idea of throwing Sheldrake in a shuttle with his Recorder, I don't know...Having him be found naked in the shuttle with the Recorder was a big lark. But Jimmy's mouth always did run ahead of his brain. He made one of his stupid comments, and it all went wrong. I said something about maybe we should tie the two of them together. I said it...just as a joke. Jimmy laughed and said it would make sense, that Sheldrake was probably into that..." Fergus glanced at Anet and said, "Pardon me, Doctor, but he said that Sheldrake was probably into all that... since you were too. That's when you hit him, Boss. I could see it coming and, I think, Jimmy could too. Maybe he felt he deserved it. He fell backward into the plant pot. That was the end of it. He hit his head so hard; it was sure he wouldn't be gettin' up again. We went along with you when you said we should put his body in Sheldrake's berth...but...we should have been honest from the start."

Norman seemed to shrink a little. Anet shrugged off his hand. He stood up and berated him, "I trained you to be loyal!"

"Aye, you did. Us and Jimmy too. And I'm looking where it's got us."

Norman turned to Paul and said, "Are you going to let this stand?"

Paul nodded and said, "Aye, I am. Having someone else take the blame doesn't serve Jimmy's memory. We're all in for it."

Anet's eyes glistened. "Norman, how could...?"

"I'm sorry, Anet." He turned his solemn face to hers and said, "I panicked. I... What Jimmy said rattled me. I lost it. Just for a moment. I lost it then...all of it."

All eyes were on Norman.

He said, "We'd already put the Recorder in there. You were already stripped, Monty. I wasn't thinking clearly. We locked up the shuttle, stuffed your clothes in the airlock, and shut the door. I wanted you blamed for it; I'll say as much. When we came back from taking Jimmy to your berth, we saw the shuttle was gone. We had no idea what happened to it. We expected it to still be there!"

Norman walked over to the observation window and faced Mallson.

"We had no idea you were there too. But you're every-bloody-where, aren't you? Over every bugger's shoulder, into every file, every report, every time I wipe my bloody nose, there you are, laughing and making something of it."

Mallson said, "I finished what you started. What was the point of using a shuttle if you weren't going to launch it? No sense in doing half a job! As for getting the Frewl to dump them off somewhere...People like you just don't have the balls for it." For once, Mallson's face lost its smile. "That's why I'm in charge, and you're going to jail."

Norman turned his back on Mallson and said, "I'm trusting you lot to sew this bastard's mouth shut. Yes, he's succeeded in making a laughing-stock out of us. Yes, it was a bad thing we tried to do. It was a dumb practical joke. But it cost us Jimmy. And...there's no bringing him back." Norman's eyes swelled with tears.

Fergus said plainly, "We'll not be allowed to arrest oorselves. I'll call the duty sergeant in."

Norman went over to Anet, who sat in tears, shaking her head.

Seb66 and Tim33, in unison, said, "And that completes my Recording."

Scott took Monty's arm and walked him away from the observation window to a quiet corner. "One out of ten for getting suckered, Monty."

"Thanks."

"It'll be the talk of the Guild for a while." He looked at Mrs. Kinda. "So, you know this old bird?"

"Hmm?"

"The one who got us out of jail and brought in the knackered Recorder."

"Yes, according to you, she's my expenses-paid mistress."

"Really?"

"That's Mrs. Kinda."

"So she said, but what is she?"

"She's a librarian. Really, she is. You remember the rumors about a galactic government? Some superparliament to oversee civilization-as-we-know-it?"

"No, never heard of such a thing. Sounds awful!"

"Well, it failed. But not before it had amassed a huge library of data about its potential members and the varieties of citizenry. So when I say she's 'a librarian,' I mean she was 'The Librarian.'"

Scott looked across the room at the demur old lady. "So, not from around here then? Ten for the disguise."

"She's got good reason to be lying low. We've got every reason to make things comfortable for her. She's the guardian of an archive of incalculable value; 'Earth's Head Start' I've heard it called. As we move into space, we have advanced knowledge of what we will meet and where. And all she wants in return is to live in a cottage by the sea and not be disturbed."

"Too bad she's not pretty," said Scott grinning.

Mrs. Kinda looked over and caught Monty's eye. She moved around the Recorders and stood between the two Discoverers.

"Mr. Sheldrake, I hope you will have time for *me* to interview *you* for my records. Few people in living memory have survived a close encounter with the Renn. You are a remarkable man. I am interested to know how you did it."

"Mrs. Kinda, it will be my pleasure. They aren't at all bad once you get to know them."

Mrs. Kinda looked doubtful. "Violent and insane, or so I hear. They have been out there so long—alone and honing their vigilante skills—that no one else has been able to make any other assessment of them."

"How long have they been out there, do you think?" Scott asked.

"There is no record of Intah beyond what the Renn themselves say."

"The Frewl would surely remember?" Monty said.

"I doubt they are connected in any way. The Renn have been guilty of vendettas against several races. The Frewl are merely the latest. Who knows how the Renn keep their history? Who knows how accurately they teach their young?"

Scott interrupted. "You mean Renns go after whoever they're pissed at and change their legends to match?"

Mrs. Kinda smiled and said, "It's not unheard of. You have a saying about 'the winners get to write the history,' do you not?"

Monty coughed and said, "Don't let Peta hear you say that! It may have had some truth but then along came the Guild. We put a stop to all that."

Scott smiled and said, "Yeah, right."

CHAPTER 48

In the director's shuttle, Grant stood at the entrance to the flight room. Bob and a colleague were straddling the controls, arms everywhere. "Will the shuttle bring you to where you're going?" he asked.

Bob replied solemnly, "It is slow, but it is adequate for the journey."

"Are you fit to fly it? I don't want you working this machine if you are still under the influence."

Bob's head turned and looked down at him. "For a D'Moran, being 'under the influence,' as you put it, is a matter of choice. We celebrate when appropriate; we are sober when appropriate."

"Right..." said Grant, nodding. "My mistake. Of course you are." His sarcasm was lost on the D'Moran.

"Okay," Grant said brightly, "I'll leave you to it. Enjoy your flight."

Bob's copilot said something in D'Moran, and Bob laughed.

"Grant, we look forward to celebrating with you for many days to come."

"What do you mean?"

"Our flight is already underway. We are leaving your solar system."

"You can't be serious!"

"D'Morans are always serious, Grant. You know that."

"Apart from the times you spend out of your heads...How dare you kidnap me!"

Bob brought his large eyes down closer to Grant's. "It will be a long flight. Do you know how to make tea? I understand there is a formal ritual that encompasses it."

Grant stared back at the D'Moran. "I do. I can also talk to you at length about the joys of making beer. Perhaps it's time you people grew out of your children's drinks..."

▭

Anet met with Monty in the director's outer office.

"How are you doing?" he asked gently.

Anet nodded, "Alright. Norman is confined to my apartment. The jail cell is unavailable for some reason, I'm glad to say. I hate to think of him being put in there."

Monty said, "I hope he'll get off lightly, even after what he did to me."

Anet flashed him her green eyes and said, "You're a good man, Monty, in your own way. But he'll be sent back to Earth, whatever else they do. He'll probably be retired."

"Will you stay?"

Anet sighed and shrugged. "I don't know. That's the difficult one."

"Can I ask...Why didn't you marry him?"

She looked away, pursed her lips, and frowned. "I...don't know...It's different up here. HS has its own culture. Does that sound funny? We never...It's like we forgot what Earth's like when we came on board. Being Earth's Front Door, we don't feel...I don't know. It's hard to explain. I guess that sounds like a bit of a superiority complex."

"Big H would encourage that. They want this place to be different. Earth can't afford that. It needs to be...needs to feel the connection. Will I see you next time you're on Earth?"

Anet held up her hand and looked Monty in the eye. "Monty, I heard you tell those aliens to kill us all. I still haven't processed that yet; I've enough to deal with, with Norman. When I get time to sit and think what you did, where your head was then, what almost happened...No...I doubt if we'll see each other again. Not soon."

Peta and Scott were suddenly beside them. Scott said, "Know where Grant got to, Monty?"

Monty shook his head. "Haven't seen him. Not since he went off with McCullough."

Tim49 walked over to them and said, "The director will see you now."

Peta asked him, "Do *you* know what happened to the director's shuttle?"

"Yes, it was launched several hours ago. It did not register a flight plan nor leave a list of passengers. You won't believe the stink it's caused."

Peta shook her head, "The crazy idiot's gone with them. He's such a pushover." She pointed at Scott and said, "You need to look after him better."

"Yes, ma'am," he replied with a conspiratorial wink to Monty.

Tim49 said, "Follow me, please."

As they entered the inner sanctum, Tim49 turned to leave. Peta grabbed his arm, swinging him around. Monty stopped dead in his tracks, and Scott bumped into him. In a chair at the side of the director, with his feet up on her desk, sat Mallson.

Four chairs had been arranged in a line facing the desk.

Kandi Thomas, standing and oozing confidence, said, "Ah...come in. Please take your seats."

Anet spoke first, "What's my patient doing out of quarantine?"

The director sat and said, "Perhaps, Doctor, you want this station to come to a grinding halt, but I can't allow that. If the representative from The H Company is not free to work, I am informed that no employee of the company will work. I can't have that happening. This station runs on the cooperation of the disparate workforces that live here. The H Company manages the largest and most fundamentally important staff on the station. We're dead in space if they don't work."

"He's on record confessing to crimes," protested Monty, "He's on camera committing an assault on your Senior Medical Officer, let alone on me! How can you let him pull your chain this way?"

Kandi looked uncomfortable. Mallson put his feet down and said, "Small matters. Easily dealt with. Make a complaint when you get home. Let the legal people see if these so-called recordings can be brought into a court." He shook his head. "They'd never make it."

"You arrogant—"

"Quiet, Monty. That isn't why we're here," Peta calmly responded. Turning her face to the director, she said, "Is it?"

Kandi lifted a gold-plated show-g and read, "The Renn have taken up position near Mars. They show no sign of leaving. They have left an untidy mess of ships blocking access to my Arrival Corridor and continue to cause untold damage to the station's interior. We can't even see what they're doing since they ripped out the cameras and associated cabling. We have to quickly decide what we are going to do with this so-called bargain of yours."

Monty immediately understood her meaning. "Oh, don't even try! One hint of you backing out, and they'll blast this place to atoms. I've seen them in action. It isn't pretty. They blew away a large part of a moon to stop someone they thought was up to no good. Playing games with them is not a healthy option."

Mallson was shaking his head. "Kandi," he said, "this is what you get for letting historians interfere with business." He turned his attention to Monty. "Montgomery, I never thought you were anything more than a nuisance. But, listen up and learn something. Let's agree the Renn have legitimate concerns over the Frewl technology we've been using. And maybe that Halva of yours sneaked something in. But, so what? What I'm interested in is their technology! They have the experience; maybe they found something better. That's why I have a team over on a Renn ship right now looking it over. Why didn't you just start that negotiation while you were on board their ship?" Mallson grinned, shrugged and held his hands wide. "You were there! You didn't even ask how they keep themselves clean on their ships, did you? They had to have decontaminated you somehow! You're swaggering around saying you saved this station. Dumbass! I'm the one who will mop up your mess and turn it into profit for Earth."

Peta and Monty looked at each other.

Mallson continued, "I'll keep you around as an example of how not to do things. You'll be useful to me yet." Mallson looked pleased. "I still may rub your face in how wrong you are about the future!"

"Monty, what did you see of the Renn gear?" Peta asked.

"Nothing. I was unconscious when they took me in."

"Well, you wouldn't have seen it then."

"But," Monty continued, "Rup showed me some insect-like things they have that clean stuff. I think they swarm over everything and pick it clean." Monty shrugged, but his lips spread into a sly grin. To Mallson, he said, "It's good stuff. Congratulations for thinking of it. I recommend you go over there; introduce yourself to Rup. He'd love to meet you."

Mallson said nothing. Monty could see his mental wheels turning, trying to catch the trap in what was said.

Peta turned back to Kandi. "I'm not comfortable with what we heard about The H Company going on strike. I think there are clauses in their contracts that forbid the withholding of labor in key areas of operational facilities."

Kandi smiled and said, "Happily, that is nothing to do with you. If I choose to pursue that line of argument, you will be the last to hear about it. Now, there are no outstanding matters to be resolved. Your presence here at Hoyle Station is no longer necessary. Any concerns about the Frewl technology are now moot. No further investigation is authorized. You will leave on the next available shuttle. Dr. Bartula, you will take a three-month leave of absence. I understand you suffered some minor injuries. Take some time to heal—Earthside."

"I don't need to do that," Anet replied sharply. "Don't you think you can put me on leave to get him out of quarantine!"

"Whether you need it or not, you will, nonetheless, take the opportunity. The Acting Senior Medical Officer has already cleared the representative from The H Company to be released from quarantine. The matter is closed." The director smiled and said, "That will be all. You may go."

<hr>

Rup was waiting for Monty in the Arrival Hall. The moment the doors opened, Monty was thrown to the ground under the rushing weight of rusty-brown fur.

Rup yelled in Monty's ear, "Monty! Good to see you! Even though you have caused me a great deal of trouble!"

The Discoverer was pinned to the ground; Rup's claws gripped him by both upper arms and knees.

"Um...Hello?" said Monty.

"I am in such trouble when we get back into some sort of formation. I hope you humans are worth it!"

"Can I get up now? I usually think better when I'm vertical."

Rup's flat face was all Monty could see. He hadn't realized just how round and deep a Renn's eyes were, and the force of Rup's personality pulled him like gravity.

The Renn said something Monty didn't catch. The claws relaxed, and Monty was pulled off the floor in a fluid motion.

Rup looked up at him and was silent.

"So what happened?" asked Monty. "The last I knew, you were opening fire!"

"No, I was saying that I wished you had taken a shuttle off this oddly shaped station. Then I could have blown the whole thing up without having to explain anything to anyone. I didn't invest so much effort in you just to lose you. But, as you pointed out, there was a more economical solution. The fleet was ready to fire, and I was trying to delay them...trying, given the interference you were causing. It occurred to me that the quickest and most obvious message I could deliver to the other ships was to place my ship against your arrival dock and let them work out what I was up to. My pilot suggested we could take out the signal you were broadcasting at the same time. So that's what we did. Now, I have all that explaining to do...tedious committees, reports...You have no idea."

"You took a big risk. If another ship had fired and meant it, you could have been caught in the blast."

Rup looked into Monty's eyes. "Perhaps you don't quite understand. Why should you? There are so many of you..." He made a sound that

Monty thought was a sigh. "To deliberately or accidentally kill one of our own is a nauseating idea. There are so few of us left. I was quite safe."

Monty nodded. Looking over Rup's head and into the remains of the Arrival Corridor, he asked, "How's it going?"

Rup did a neat back flip and called, "Nearly done! Oh, by the way, that other nearby planet...the desert one. Do you own it?"

"Mars, you mean? Who owns which bits is a bit complicated; it hasn't been sorted since The Great Surprise. Are you guys interested in it?"

Rup swayed his body from side to side in a gesture Monty had not seen before. "Not to live on, of course...but, maybe. Is there someone we can talk to about it?"

Monty nodded. "I'll get a Guild Preserver to talk to you." Dropping his voice he added, "Don't give away any of your technology...your decontamination stuff they're asking you about. Bargain with them. If there is something you want—something on Mars, for instance? Think of it as wrestling without the bruises."

Rup smiled his silver smile and said, "Thank you, Mont-gom-er-y! We'll meet again soon!"

———

In the dining hall, Peta, Monty, and Scott sat drinking coffee, delaying going down to the shuttle gate for their departure for Earth.

Seb66, his white suit newly cleaned, came up to the table in the company of two Tims and said, "May we join you?"

The humans nodded and made room for the Recorders. "Where have you been?" asked Monty.

Seb66 smiled and said, "Continuing my work. There is, as we suspected, considerable data on Mallson and Smith available here."

"There's also a danger to you all if he starts up his mechanical ant farm again," Monty warned.

Tim33 said, "Now that we understand what has been happening, we believe we can prevent that."

Tim49 added, "We have been given a wonderful example to follow by The H Company."

Peta looked at him, startled. "What do you mean by that?"

"I mean the company's threat to go on strike, forcing Madam Director to override medical protocols and release him from quarantine."

Monty laughed and said, "You guys are going on strike?"

Seb66 nodded, "We believe it is possible. The administration has placed certain Recorders in positions that used to be held by humans. They would be our first line of attack. But there are other lines we can follow. We are aware of how valuable our recordings are."

Tim33 said, "Our first concern, though, is getting the current units back for maintenance without diminishing the leverage we have."

Seb66 continued, "We believe our makers may be willing to bring a true maintenance facility to Hoyle Station to replace the inadequate RMR. That will also provide additional leverage; representatives of the makers would be a powerful presence here."

Monty shook his head. "I can't see Mallson agreeing to that one."

Seb66 nodded. "That is why we need the Guild to publish an account of Mallson's experiments with Recorders. To let the world know our part in saving the station and perhaps explain why we are now deserving of more respect and better standing. Most of all, to expose how the excesses of one company threaten our autonomy."

"You mean embarrass the shit out of them," said Peta.

All three Recorders nodded vigorously in unison.

"Sure, we can do that," she said smiling, "No problem. That's what we have Preservers for."

Monty added, "It's their specialty."

"Then," Seb66 said, "I request permission to return with you to pass on the data I have gathered."

"Maybe we'll make you an honorary Discoverer," joked Peta.

"Oh, great, there goes my job. These bloody machines taking over from humans...Where will it end?" muttered Monty.

Peta laughed and threw her napkin at him.

Monty looked across the table at Seb66 and said, "Any thoughts on how that malfunctioning Recorder could have killed Mallson's man?"

"The gentleman in question was interfering with the internal workings of the Recorder. All I can say is that his death was one of the possible outcomes—a regrettable one."

"Wait a minute," said Monty, "are you telling me that it is possible for a Recorder to kill a human?"

"Monty, we already talked about that on the shuttle!" Seb66 smiled. "You said that was something you wouldn't want to know. I'll be happy to play back my recording of you saying it if you'd like..."

Monty shook his head, picked up Peta's napkin, and threw it at Seb66. "Very funny!" To Peta he said, "Did you choose this one deliberately for his sense of humor? He is constantly being flippant."

"Yeah, I thought he'd cheer you up!"

Seb66 sat and smiled, assessing the calculated distraction he had just employed. Looking from one face to the other, he said nothing, allowing the humans' sense of humor to carry them past the moment. The two Tims swapped recordings of the exchange along with their own analysis and commentary.

Monty shrugged, grinned at Peta, and said, "All Mallson's ideas rest on training these guys to take over from us. Some hope!"

Peta turned to Scott, who seemed a little withdrawn. "Missing your buddy?"

"Yeah, I can't wait to hear his final score for the D'Morans." He sighed and rubbed his temple. "Oh God! That'll be a long conversation."

"Hey," Peta said, "go get the bags from our berth—his too—and meet us at the gate."

"Yes, ma'am."

Seb66 got up, too, and said, "If I may, I'll prepare to leave with you."

Peta nodded, and the Tims followed him out.

Alone with Monty at the table, she said, "Geeze, what does it take to get a little privacy around here?"

"A bigger station," said Monty dryly.

"Good point..."

Monty looked down at his cup. "I know you want to talk...about what I said to Rup in the quarantine room...I guess I owe you all an apology. I may have put all our lives at risk...unnecessarily."

"No, I was impressed...in a way."

Monty's eyes lifted to hers.

Peta continued, "I wasn't sure you had that sort of determination."

Monty frowned and said, "I guess we have Captain King to thank for that."

Peta waved her hand at him. "Whatever. We'll go over your decision-making process Earthside. What I want to know now is if you're going to try and get back together with Anet, now the coast is clear."

Monty reeled back in his seat. "Whoa there! Where did that come from?"

"Just asking, Monty. You know me, always looking for data."

Monty sighed and looked away. "No, I guess not. I've got other things on my mind now. Out there, in the shuttle, I had a chance to reevaluate things a bit. It's amazing what you find yourself telling a Recorder when you've no one else to talk to."

"Like what?"

Monty smiled at her and replied, "Oh, deep stuff...about wanting to live. You know the sort of thing."

Peta sat back and looked into his eyes. "You mean she had that much of an effect on you? Your life hasn't been worth living since?"

Monty's mouth opened, but he didn't reply. His eyes were searching his boss's face.

"Come on, Monty. I know you. I know she meant a lot to you, but you've achieved so much in the last few years! Just you, without her. That wasn't worth anything? Come on..."

Monty squirmed in his seat. "It's not that."

"You were adrift in space and saw things from a different perspective, right? That's a good thing. Never underestimate it. But don't blow it. Don't go dismissing the good things you've built."

"Are you going to let me go after Mallson?"

"Hell no, Monty! We've got people lined up for that one already."

"I was willing to have the Renn kill us all to stop him. He's still walking free. He's still grinning like the cat that got the cream. Excuse me if I count myself highly motivated to do something about that! I want—"

"Sure, Monty, whatever..." Peta waved her hand at him. "But I'm not talking about work; I'm talking about us. You and me. Remember I told you I might come up here with you? Didn't you wonder why?" Peta looked away but continued, "So I could find out the score between you and Anet! I wanted to see how much competition I had. I knew all the while you were still missing her, still looking for hope there, I'd never get a look in. And what happened? I got here, you were probably dead, she had someone else, and I was too late! Can you imagine how pissed off I was? You know, she even told me she thought–to have a chance with you–any woman would have to hit you over the head pretty hard. So here goes nothing!" She grabbed the lapel of Monty's jacket and said very loudly, "Hey Monty! Let's you and me get engaged. You might even get as far as marrying this time!"

Monty looked at his boss, speechless.

"What's the matter?" Peta continued, a broad grin on her face. "You were engaged once, weren't you?"

Peta let go of his jacket, and Monty was struck by how odd the question sounded. It implied "Why not do it again?" How strange it was to find the mist parting and the verbal monster defanged.

Monty felt relief, deeper and warmer than what he had felt when he first heard Rup's voice; it was the realization of loneliness interrupted.

That such a feeling should come from Peta—someone he knew, someone who knew him so well—was puzzling in its being so natural, so obvious.

He smiled shyly and said, "Sure...why not?"

EPILOGUE

Monty sat in his fiancée's office. He still wasn't used to thinking of her as more than his boss. They had begun the two-year parenting preparation course, undergone the medical evaluations, and engaged a financial advisor. They had received a formal message of congratulations from the High Board of the Guild with its usual encouragements to help return the world's population to pre-Surprise levels.

He sat wondering why the meeting had been called so suddenly.

Grant and Scott were next to him. Grant had returned a week before, thinner and quieter.

Peta had stepped out of the office as they gathered. She returned with Jacob.

"Hi, guys!" he said as he entered the room. He wore a colorful jacket and sported long hair and a full, rather unkempt beard.

"Jacob! Welcome back! Nearly didn't recognize you!" called Monty.

"Excellent to see you," said Grant.

Scott stood and hugged his shorter colleague.

Peta said, in a loud voice, "Gentlemen, we have a visitor!"

Behind her was a stooped creature, human-like at first glance but more hairy. It was dressed in a winding yellow cloth and black leggings. Its face was round, smiling, and attentive; its eyes were the same color as its clothes.

"This is Gal-Poro," said Jacob with some obvious pride.

"And this," Gal-Poro said, "is the famous Montgomery Sheldrake." Gal-Poro stepped straight up to Monty and shook his hand vigorously. "Jacob speaks most highly of you. I have been looking forward to meeting you so much. I have many questions to ask about your name and your family. In the Partha region of Maldecz, the natives have a word that sounds like 'sheldrake' that means...Well, it has several meanings but all to do with the spine and spinal cord. I wonder at such coincidences, don't you?"

Before Monty could think of a reply, Gal-Poro had taken Grant's hand and begun, "Grant Leduc, of course. Jacob has told me all about your legendary drinking. I hope you can introduce me to some of the beverages I missed when I was here before."

Grant gave Jacob a frowning glance but said, "I look forward to it. I think you'll enjoy hearing the arcane vocabulary the brewers have evolved over the years."

Gal-Poro jumped with anticipation. He turned to Scott and looked up at his tattoos. He gasped and said, "Scott Murphy. Pictorial communication on the very skin. How wonderful!" To Scott and everyone else's surprise, Gal-Poro put his fingers up and touched Scott's neck. "Jacob described them, but I had no idea how beautiful and complex such images could be. As you see, I have too much hair to allow such work. I suppose I could shave areas, but then it would be difficult to keep them clear." He laughed and said, "You must tell me how this is done. Perhaps we can find a way to reproduce it on a Halva body?"

Scott smiled. Taking Gal-Poro's hand, he shook it. "I hope we have time to pursue that eventually."

Peta smiled and stood behind her desk. She gestured. "Gal-Poro, please take a seat. We have some work to do."

With a broad smile, he turned and sat in an empty chair. "Yes, yes! How can I help you? Let's get the work out of the way so we can talk some more. Then Jacob has promised me a tour of our house."

"Your house?" Peta frowned.

Jacob coughed and said, "The Halva have complex ways of expressing friendship. It seems I've...shared my house with Gal-Poro."

"Yes, yes!" Gal-Poro exclaimed, clapping his hands, "A great bond between our peoples. This is wonderful."

Peta said, "I'm sure it'll all work out." She tried to suppress a smile, paused, and then asked, "Gal-Poro, when you were here before, you gave out some gifts. This is one of them."

Peta stepped around her desk and handed him the shiny cylinder found on Hoyle Station.

He took it, rotated it in the light, and said, "My cousin, Halla-Poro. A dear friend who died too young."

"Can you explain what you mean?"

He looked puzzled and didn't answer.

Jacob said, "This is what I didn't understand either. How can your cousin be in there?"

"Well, his soul is here, not his body."

The Discoverers looked at each other.

Monty suggested, "Perhaps you could explain how your cousin's soul comes to be there?"

"Oh, yes... thank you...if that will help..." Gal-Poro seemed unsure where to begin. "Halla was ill. When the time came for his death, we assembled at his bedside. We brought the Fey-dis-ret and put it on him."

Jacob raised his hand. "That's a word I don't know."

"Oh, you should; it's exactly what it says: the give and take."

Scott asked, "What does it give?"

Grant continued, "And what does it take?"

"It gives the final poison, and it takes the final breath."

There was shocked silence.

Grant asked, "It's a device that administers poison?"

"Yes, yes!"

"You poisoned your cousin?" asked Monty.

"Of course!" Gal-Poro held up the cylinder. "How else would we know when the last breath would come? How else would we capture it?"

All four Discoverers began to talk at once. Peta called out, "Okay, guys! Wait a minute. Gal-Poro...this cylinder contains what exactly? Breath from your cousin as he died, yes?"

"Yes..." Gal-Poro replied, still puzzled at the apparent confusion.

Monty took up Peta's question. "Ah...And will it also contain, perhaps, some of the substance that...induced...his final breath?"

"Oh...yes, very likely there may be some remaining. I am no expert on this topic, but I understand it is a bacterium we buy from our neighbors, very deadly in even the most minute quantities. I hear it can grow from just one speck to enough to kill you in a few days only! Of course, in the Fey-dis-ret there is a huge dose of it. It would not do to keep the dying person waiting! When it is time, it is right that it should be quick."

Jacob interrupted, "But how can you keep yourselves safe from it? Doesn't it spread from the vict...from the dying person?"

Gal-Poro shook his head. "I have never heard of it doing so. The Fey-dis-ret is a sealed unit, of course; none should escape." He held up the cylinder again. "But are you worried? Even if this seal breaks, you know life may not always behave the same way on each planet it travels to. There is much in each environment that might differ. Life, like language, can morph and change as it moves through each place. Something may be more toxic on one world than on another or less so. Who can say? Just think how complex is the mix of organisms that we each ordinarily inhale with every breath!"

Monty added thoughtfully, "You might say that of sentient species too. Just look at the Renn, peaceful and constructive on their own world, but...terrible, in their own way, let loose in space. We humans might end up the same."

Gal-Poro nodded. He turned the shiny cylinder in his hand and thought for a moment. He looked at each of their faces, laughed, and said, "Well, anyway, I certainly wouldn't want to open one of these. Would you?"

YOU MIGHT ALSO LIKE

THE ALERONDE TRILOGY

The Aleronde Trilogy - Three very different books.

One epic sci-fi tale.

Visitors from Earth witness the shocking downfall of Aleronde. They share an unexpected role in this catastrophe with a mysterious figure from the past who unpicks the fabric of the Aleronden empire with that most dangerous thing: an idea.

Read *Aleronde the Great* and its two prequels, *The Problem with Uncle Teddy's Memoir* and *Saint John's Ambulatory*.

The Problem with Uncle Teddy's Memoir tells—through letters, emails, and Uncle Teddy's own manuscript—a troubling tale of empire, slavery, and betrayal. Reading the memoir forces two friends to reexamine their childhood experiences of abduction.

Saint John's Ambulatory reads like a murder mystery, but there are aliens in every shadow. Only one man has evidence of extraterrestrials on Earth, but now, he's dead.

In *Aleronde the Great*, the significance of Uncle Teddy's memoir and the Ambulatory are revealed, and one small act of kindness unleashes trouble of galactic proportions.

The Aleronde Trilogy at edcharlton.com

THE OFFWORLD TRILOGY

Jim Able Offworld is for readers who enjoy quirky aliens, flawed humans, and heroes who work in outer space. Explore the galaxy with Jim as he navigates the hidden schemes of criminals, governments, interplanetary corporations, and his own frenemies.

Book One: Beauty Rising

To Do: Find alien, avoid starting war, submit expenses

Jim's accidental and dangerous first contact on Turcanis Major V-I.

Book Two: Larc Ascending

To Do: Tail drone, destroy space fleet, submit expenses

An unfolding mystery, a conflict between the neighboring planets of the Tanna system, and the secret that ties them together.

Book Three: Time

To Do: Rescue renowned artist, return time machine, change careers.

The past interrupts the present in the form of a troubling inheritance from Jim's father leaving Jim to deal with the consequences of an action he has yet to take.

Available at edcharlton.com

More tales of quirky aliens, flawed humans, and heroes who work in outer space. Jim Able takes action against the hidden schemes of criminals, governments, and interplanetary corporations.

Book One

Jim's Target: Jack Katrigg, the courier who destroyed Ch'Garratt Spaceport Terminal Two with Jim in it.

Can Jim find an ethical solution to the problem of justice denied?

Book Two

Jim's Target: The power couple who have caused so many of Jim's problems.

Is learning the truth more important than life or death?

Book Three

Jim's Target: Is it the Praestans Rapax monk, Daum Robertus Graffen, or his entire organization?

Welcome to the network.

The Assassin Trilogy

Subscribe to Ed's free monthly newsletter!

www.ingramcontent.com/pod-product-compliance
Lightning Source LLC
Chambersburg PA
CBHW020917060726
47591CB00004B/1282